THE STAN TURNER MYSTERIES

by William Manchee

Undaunted (199...)
Brash Endeavor (1...)
Second Chair (200...)
Cash Call (2002)
Deadly Distractions (2004)
Black Monday (2005)

"...appealing characters and lively dialogue, especially in the courtroom . . . " (*Publisher's Weekly*)

"...plenty of action and adventure . . . " (*Library Journal*)

"...each plot line, in and of itself, can be riveting . . . " (*Foreword Magazine*)

"...a courtroom climax that would make the venerable Perry Mason stand and applaud . . . " (Crescent Blue)

"...Richly textured with wonderful atmosphere, the novel shows Manchee as a smooth, polished master of the mystery form . . . " (*The Book Reader*)

"...Manchee's stories are suspenseful and most involve lawyers. And he's as proficient as Grisham . . . (*Dallas Observer*)

"...fabulous-a real page turner-I didn't want it to end!" (Allison Robson, CBS Affiliate, *KLBK TV, Ch 13*)

Also From
William Manchee

Twice Tempted (1996)

Death Pact (1999)

Plastic Gods (2003)

Yes, We're Open (2004)

For more information visit:

http://williammanchee.com

http://toppub.com

http://mancheelawfirm.com

CACTUS ISLAND

To my wonderful daughter-in-law,

Danell Manchee.

We are blessed to have you as part of the family.

Cactus Island
A Stan Turner Mystery

Book 7

by

WILLIAM MANCHEE

Top Publications, Ltd.
Dallas, Texas

Cactus Island

©) COPYRIGHT
William Manchee
2006

Cover Design by William Manchee

Top Publications, Ltd.
3100 Independence Parkway, Suite 311-349
Plano, Texas 75075

ISBN #1-929976-36-4
Library of Congress #2006902487

Prelude

March 8, 1991

Complete honesty in marriage will likely lead to an early divorce. At least that's my experience. In the beginning I told Rebekah everything but it soon became apparent she couldn't handle many of the perils and predicaments I often found myself in. She was a worrier and panicked easily. If I had told her everything she'd have gone crazy with worry and driven me nuts in the process. Our marriage wouldn't have survived. So over the years when I came home at night I talked less and less about work and if there was a problem I wouldn't tell Rebekah about it until it had been solved. This had worked well and helped us make it to our twentieth anniversary, but the secret that I shouldered alone this day could well destroy us.

It was a cold drizzly day in March when family and friends had gathered at St. Ann's Catholic Church for a funeral mass. It was my son Peter who was supposed to be in the coffin that lay on the table in front of the onlookers who had gathered to pay their last respects. I say *supposed to be in the coffin* because this coffin was empty. The official story was that Peter had drowned in a flash flood. He was driving Rebekah's car, got into some high water, and was swept away into a storm drain. When the car was found, Peter wasn't in it. Speculation was that he left the vehicle and tried to swim to safety but drowned in the process. His body was never found.

Peter was our third child and our youngest son. He had two older brothers, Reggie and Mark, and a younger sister, Marcia. At sixteen Peter had developed into a handsome boy with a slender build, dark hair, and olive skin. He looked more like Rebekah than me, but he had my easygoing personality and independent spirit. God had also blessed him with a natural charisma and a near genius IQ. He had everything going for him in this, his sophomore year of high school—an accomplished debater on the school's championship debate team, a varsity swimmer, and a member of the student council. But now he was missing and presumed dead. Tears welled in my eyes as I struggled to keep my composure. This was all too much for any parent to bear. Rebekah looked over at me with bloodshot eyes. I tried to force a smile, but couldn't manage it. Her empty gaze went back to the coffin.

Over my shoulder I saw my law partner, Paula Waters. She looked at me sorrowfully. She knew better than anyone what I was going through. She loved me and I loved her. But our love was like a rose that lacked an essential mineral and would never blossom. It was not our fate to be man and wife, yet our bond was too strong to allow us to drift apart. For me it wasn't so bad because I had Rebekah and the kids, but Paula didn't have anyone she truly loved before she met me. She'd married Bart, and they were good together, but it was a marriage more of convenience than passion.

I looked back at Peter's casket as the funeral mass began. Father Michael, who had known Peter well over the years, gave the mass. In his homily he spoke of spending time with Peter at summer camp and youth retreats he had attended. I thought back to one of those retreats that I had been a chaperone. We had gone to Lake Murray in Oklahoma and everyone was taking a swim. Peter saw the water mocassin first and pointed excitedly to its head sticking out of the water. I almost laughed out loud as I recalled how quickly everyone frantically evacuated the swimming hole. Peter and I hadn't moved. We knew the snake wouldn't bother us if we left it alone. Everyone was amazed at our nerve, particularly Peter's friends who thought him somewhat of a hero over the incident. Rebekah looked at me, probably wondering how I could be smiling at a time like this.

When the moment came to hear from those who wanted to say a few words about Peter, a long line formed at the lectern. Reggie was the first to speak. He said, "What was most remarkable about Peter was his respect for everyone he encountered. He loved to talk with anyone who would listen. Whether it was the school principal or the janitor, it didn't matter. Peter treated everyone with respect and admiration. He was never judgmental or condescending.

He loved everyone and everyone loved him. I will miss him."

Reggie smiled and then nodded to Marcia who was next in line. She was fourteen but with three older brothers she had matured early. Her face was solemn as she began to speak. "Peter was not only my brother but he was my best friend. We spent a lot of time together and would talk endlessly about everything. He always had time for me no matter how busy he was. I couldn't have asked for a better brother."

Marcia broke into tears and someone handed her a handkerchief. She left the lectern and took a seat next to Rebekah. Mark was next. He got up, swallowed hard and said, "What I remember most about my brother Peter was his imagination. He loved to write and tell stories, particularly science fiction and fantasy. We played a lot of games together, talked about exploring space, and planned trips to far away places that we wanted to visit some day. He often said he'd like to be a lawyer like Dad or maybe even a writer. I think he could have done either one. I think he could have done anything he wanted. Goodbye, Peter. I'll miss you."

When the mass was over, there was a reception and then we went back to the house. It was very late that night before everyone left and we were alone. After saying goodbye to the last of the relatives and friends, I went into the living room where Rebekah was lying on the sofa staring up at the ceiling. I loved her with all my heart and soul and it killed me to see her suffering the way she was. I wanted so much to tell her the truth—to reveal to her the secret that was weighing so heavily on my mind, body and soul. But that was unthinkable. For anyone who discovered the truth would suffer the same fate as Peter.

Chapter 1

Windsor V. Windsor
6 Months Earlier

Since the first day out of law school I'd pretty much been a workaholic. It comes with the territory when you're a young attorney trying to get established. I went directly to the DA's office out of law school and as an assistant DA was expected to work eighty hours a week. Nothing changed when I came to work for Stan Turner and we formed the law firm of Turner and Waters, P.C. I suppose I could have cut my hours a bit and started living a more normal life, but now I was a partner and things were different. Stan didn't have the time or inclination to hover over me to make sure I was doing my job. He expected me to do it and never questioned how I went about it. I appreciated his attitude but also felt the weight of responsibility thrust upon me.

When we first formed the partnership, I was in love with Stan and hoped he'd fall in love with me. Unfortunately that hadn't happened and I was forced to face reality and move on. Not that I had gotten entirely over Stan, for I hadn't, but I finally realized that our relationship could only be professional and decided that was better than nothing. Things had certainly changed now that I was married to Bart Williams. He was a strong, patient, thoughtful man who would do anything for me. I certainly didn't deserve him, but I was glad he had stuck by me. Now it was hard to get up early each morning and when afternoon came, I started thinking of getting home and being with him. It was amazing. I actually had a life! Unfortunately, we were as busy as ever and as much as I wanted to go home early, I found myself hard at work until seven or eight every night. Fortunately, Bart had the same problem working at the Collin County DA's office in McKinney thirty miles north of Dallas, so we learned to appreciate what little time we did have together.

As I sat at my desk early one morning I gazed at my calendar to see what was on tap for the day and noted that I had an appointment at 11:30 a.m. with Cheryl Windsor about a possible divorce. I didn't usually do divorces, but Jodie, our legal assistant, informed me Ms. Windsor had been indirectly referred by Stan's wife, Rebekah. She said the least I could do would be to talk to her. The funny thing is, once you talk to a prospective client, it's hard to turn down their case, even if you know you should.

It was late August and there was no sign of an end to the summer's heat, so I wasn't surprised to see Cheryl was wearing a tank top with a short jean skirt. She was gorgeous. I wondered how she managed to look so good since I knew from our phone conversation that she had three children. I hoped I would be so lucky, that is, if Bart and I ever decided to have kids. As soon as she sat down and crossed her long tanned legs, she began telling me what had gone wrong with her marriage.

"My husband is having an affair."

"Really? How do you know?"

"He's been working long hours lately and seems to use any excuse to be out of the house. We haven't had sex in months. I didn't want to accuse him of anything until I knew for sure he was being unfaithful, so I followed him after work one night."

I raised my eyebrows and replied, "That's quite gutsy of you. Most women would have hired a private detective."

"Hey, I'm not most women," Cheryl said, "I'm not going to let that son of a bitch humiliate me. If he's screwing around, he's gonna pay."

"And he should, but there's no reason to take chances. We live in a dangerous world and you shouldn't take risks like that."

Cheryl shook her head. "Don't worry about me. My father was an ex-Marine, so he taught me how to defend myself."

"Even so—"

"Besides, I grew up with three older brothers, so I learned how to handle men early on."

I nodded. "So where did your husband end up?"

"At the Fairmount Hotel, room 1612. I got the number from the desk clerk. I told him I'd forgotten what room my husband and I were in. You know. They all look alike. He made me show him my

ID but that wasn't a problem. I watched the elevator and thirty-five minutes later a woman took the elevator to the 16th floor."

"So, that doesn't necessarily mean—"

"I know exactly what it means. The woman was my best friend—my maid of honor at our wedding for godsakes. It couldn't have been a coincidence. They're having an affair and I'm going to kill both of them!"

"Wait a minute. Calm down. You're not going to kill anybody."

"He's had a thing for her from the first day they met," she said tearfully. "I could tell by the way he always looked at her, but I never expected Alice to give in to him. She and I have been best friends since we were fifteen."

I handed Cheryl a tissue and replied, "I know it's hard when you've been betrayed by the two people in the world that you love the most, but in today's world it's not that unusual. Loyalty is a scarce commodity."

Cheryl folded her arms and looked away. I opened a file and pulled out a divorce questionnaire. It was yellow from age. I didn't like divorces much and avoided them whenever possible, but I kinda liked Cheryl's feisty personality. "From now on you let me handle this. I don't want you talking to your husband, or Alice for that matter. It will just rekindle your anger. I'll get a temporary restraining order so you can stay in the house and he can't abscond with any of your community property."

"I don't want the house—too many bad memories. I'll move out. Just make sure I get a nice fat alimony check."

"They don't have alimony in Texas, but I can get you temporary support until the divorce is final and, of course, child support."

"Good. How much?"

"I don't know. It depends on his income and other factors."

"He makes a lot of money—more than two hundred grand a year."

"Then you'll probably get 25 to 40 percent of his after tax income since it's community property. . . . What's your husband's name?"

"Martin Roger Windsor."

"What does he do for a living?"

"He's a pharmacist by trade, but more of a businessman nowadays."

"Where is he employed?"

"Village Drugs in Richardson is where he hangs his license. He owns the place along with twelve stores just like it in North Texas, but he doesn't spend much time filling prescriptions."

Cheryl said that Martin was thirty-nine years old, a graduate of Central European University in Hungary, and since he had immigrated to the United States, had become an avid golfer.

"Windsor isn't a Hungarian name, is it?"

"No. His real name was Martin Kutrovatzlik. Nobody could pronounce it so he had it changed. He said it was a distraction he didn't need when he was doing business. He thought it was better to be perceived as British or American anyway."

She said he would often take off for weeks at a time to play in amateur golf tournaments across the country and around the world. He had a bad temper, she said, and would be very upset when he found out she was filing for divorce. I assured her the TRO would protect her, as Martin would not want to prejudice the judge against him. That would be suicide if he had a lot of assets to protect.

"Speaking of assets, what all do you own?" I asked.

She shrugged. "This may surprise you, but I really don't know. Martin is very secretive about our financial affairs. I know he owns the drugstores, of course, and there's lots of cash. Our home is worth about $550,000 according to the tax bill I got in the mail the other day. There's a shopping center where one of the stores is located. I heard him tell someone it was appraised at 1.2 million. There are a few stocks, bonds, and a $10,000 CD."

"So, do you have many debts?"

"No. None at all. My husband doesn't believe in credit. He always said if you didn't have the cash to pay for it, you didn't need it."

"Hmm. Interesting. So that adds up to about two million without the drugstores."

"That I know about. I'm sure there's more."

"Well, we can do some discovery to find out exactly what he has, and if he is less than forthright with his responses, I know a private investigator who can help us locate everything."

"I doubt your PI will find anything. My husband is very good at hiding money and covering his tracks. His first wife and I are friends, and we compare notes from time to time. She told me when they were going through their divorce she hired the best divorce attorney in town, but he couldn't find squat. Fortunately, Martin didn't like the attorney probing into his affairs so he offered a huge amount of child support if she'd make him back off."

"Well, if you have any other ideas, I'm listening."

"I do, but I need to verify a few suspicions before I can share them with you."

"Okay, Let me know when you're ready to fill me in."

I escorted her out into the reception area and met Stan coming in the door. His eyes lit up when he saw Cheryl. He nodded at me without taking his eyes off of her. A few moments later, when I was back in my office, Stan walked in and asked, "So, who's the new client?"

"A new divorce client, Cheryl Windsor."

"Hmm. She's a knockout. Is she a model?"

"No, she's a housewife," I replied.

Stan shook his head. "And some bastard's divorcing her?"

"She's divorcing him—couldn't keep his dick in his pants."

"Not a smart guy. . . . Do you need any help on her case?"

Stan looked at me expectantly. I couldn't believe the gleam in his eye. I felt like strangling him. Cheryl had turned him on like a light switch. "Stan. Must I remind you you're a married man?"

"What, now that you're married, you've become Rebekah's best friend and guardian?"

"What?" I gasped. It *was* ironic. From the first day I joined the firm I had tried to subvert Stan's marriage and win his affections. It hadn't worked. I thought I had my feelings for Stan under control, but his overt flirtations with Cheryl had irritated me—rekindled a jealous obsession that I'd thought was buried. If I couldn't lure him away from his wife, I certainly wasn't going to let some other bitch do it!

"Something like that. . . . Anyway I should warn you Cheryl was referred to us by one of Rebekah's friends, so I'd play it cool."

"Okay. Relax. I'm just admiring a pretty woman like any red blooded male would do under the same circumstances. I have no intention—"

"Yeah, well, we both know you're not invincible."

Stan gave me a hard look. "I guess you've proven that, huh?" he mumbled as he left my office.

That incident occurred the night before my wedding. Even though I'd officially given up on him and was about to marry Bart, I found myself trying one last time to seduce him. By then it was kind of a game for me—a challenge I couldn't resist. Much to my shock he gave in and kissed me passionately. I could have had him then and there, minutes before my wedding, but then it finally hit me like an avalanche. I couldn't do it. I couldn't destroy Stan, the man I truly loved, and that's what would have happened had I took Stan away from his wife and family. So, I married Bart and I have no regrets. Now I have both the men I love in my life. At least that's what I keep telling myself.

After stewing over this for several minutes I got back to work. I had a divorce to prosecute, a client to protect from a wayward husband, and assets to find. I didn't have time to brood over my shattered heart.

Chapter 2

The Accident

My cell phone rang as I was pulling into my garage. I hated after-hours calls as they usually meant my evening would be ruined. After a ten-hour workday all I wanted to do was grab a beer and watch Monday Night Football. The call turned out to be from my youngest son Peter. Peter was on a boy scout camping trip to Camp Comfort at Possum Kingdom Lake in West Texas. It was named Camp Comfort because it had every amenity you could ever want—cabins, flush toilets, a mess hall, rowboats, canoes, swimming area, gun and archery ranges, a baseball field, and even a campfire area with bench seating.

The connection was very poor and I could barely hear Peter's voice through the static. He was talking rapidly and I could tell he was upset.

"Peter? What's wrong?"

"There's been an accident with the camp Jeep."

"Were you involved? Are you okay?"

"No. No. It was Jimmy and Steven. They ran off a cliff."

"Oh, Jesus. Are they okay?"

Static came out of the receiver on my cell phone. "Peter. You're breaking up. Can you hear me?" There was more static and then the line went dead. I flipped through the cell phone's address book, found Peter's number, and pushed send. He answered but just a second later the signal failed again and I lost him. I decided to wait a few minutes and try again. My stomach tightened as I contemplated Jimmy and Steven's fate and thanked God it hadn't been Peter. The last garbled words from the cell phone, before I lost the connection, were something about Steven being arrested and his needing a lawyer. Figuring there was no time to lose, I scrambled into the house to tell Rebekah what had happened.

"They went off a cliff? Oh, my God. How could that have

happened?" Rebekah asked incredulously. "What about Steven? Was he hurt too?"

I shook my head. "I don't know. Peter didn't mention him being hurt."

"Does Jenny know? Oh, my God. I should go to her."

Jenny Caldwell was Steven's mother. She was a single mom working as a legal assistant. She and Rebekah were good friends having crossed paths at school and in cub scouts.

"You give her a call. I need to get going. It's a two-hour drive to Possum Kingdom Lake."

"No. Wait. I want to come with you," Rebekah said. "Jenny will want to come too if Steven is in trouble. There's no use taking two cars."

"Okay, that's fine, but just hurry."

"Oh, Jesus. Are you sure he was arrested?"

"Well, the connection wasn't very good, but I think that's what Peter said."

"Oh God, Stan. This is horrible. I hope Jimmy's okay. I should call his mother."

"We better not," I said. "We don't know what happened yet. We should wait until we know more."

"I don't know. If it were I, I'd want to know."

"What will you tell her?"

"Just that we heard there was an accident."

"Go ahead, but make it fast."

I had never met Jimmy's mother but Rebekah had known her from cub scouts. Peter and Jimmy were in the same den and Barbara Falk was the den mother. I asked Rebekah about Jimmy's father. She told me that Barbara and her husband were divorced. She didn't remember his name, but apparently he had fallen in love with another woman and just up and left.

While Rebekah called Jimmy's mother, I called Mark down from upstairs to fill him in on the situation and inform him he was in charge for the evening. Mark was nearly eighteen now, an excellent student, and reasonably mature for his age. We had no reservations about leaving him in charge of his sister Marcia and Jenny's daughter Mel. Mel and Marcia were almost the same age so they would share Marcia's bedroom that night while we were gone. It wasn't likely we'd be back before dawn. With the logistics of our journey in place, all we had to do now was break the bad news to Jenny and bring Mel over to the house.

Rebekah got off the phone long enough to report that Barbara had already been called by the Scoutmaster and was on her way to the hospital in Mineral Wells. Then she called Jenny. After Rebekah explained the situation, Jenny accepted our offer of a ride to the hospital. Rebekah left immediately to go to her place to pick up Jenny and bring Mel back to the house. While I waited for them to return, I called the Palo Pinto County Sheriff's office.

The dispatcher advised me that the victims had been transported to Palo Pinto Hospital in Mineral Wells. I asked her if she knew about Steven Caldwell.

"He's being booked right now," she said.

"What are the charges?" I asked.

"Negligent homicide."

"Jimmy's dead?"

"I'm afraid so."

Feeling a little shaky, I walked over to a chair and sat down. The thought that Jimmy might die hadn't crossed my mind.

"Jesus. . . . Has bond been set?"

"Hang on." There was a pause. "No, they're waiting to get the results of the blood test."

"How will that effect his bond?"

"If Mr. Caldwell was drunk, then the charges will be bumped up to manslaughter."

"Manslaughter? Come on. That's ridiculous," I said incredulously.

She sighed. "Hey, I'm just passing on what I've overheard. You can call the detective on the case to get more information if you need it."

By the time I got off the phone, Rebekah and Jenny were scurrying around getting the kids settled. I was sick inside. I couldn't believe Steven Caldwell was in such serious trouble. He was one of the most responsible teenagers I'd ever known. How was I going to break the news to Jenny that Jimmy had died and Steven would soon be charged with criminally negligent homicide or even manslaughter? Criminally negligent homicide had a sentencing range of sixty days to two years. That was bad enough, but if Steven was convicted of manslaughter it would be two to twenty years. I decided to wait until we were on the road to give Jenny the bad news—no need to worry Mel.

We took Highway 121 to Ft. Worth and just past the airport hit a string of thunderstorms. Lightning lit up the sky and deafening thunder rocked our station wagon. At times the rain became intense and visibility got so poor we had to slow down to a crawl. By the time we reached Weatherford the rain had stopped. It seemed like the right time to tell Jenny what her son was up against.

"It can't be true," she sobbed. "He'd never drive recklessly. He loved those kids. There must be some mistake."

"You're right. It doesn't sound like Steven. There must be some other explanation."

She leaned forward and gripped the back of my seat. "This can't be happening. Steven was doing so well in school. Please, Stan. You've got to do something. Steven can't go to jail." I turned and saw her wiping the tears from her eyes. Rebekah handed her a tissue and sighed. I could see she was nearly as upset as Jenny.

I took a deep breath and stared at the open road ahead. "I know. Don't worry. We'll figure this out. I'm sure Steven will have an explanation for all of this. Just sit back and try to relax."

It was really stupid asking Jenny to relax, but I didn't know what else to say. Usually, a person wouldn't be held for possible DWI unless they had failed a field sobriety test. The subsequent blood test would be the deciding factor. If the test showed a blood alcohol level above 1.0, he'd be presumed to be intoxicated and most likely charged.

It was after nine when we arrived at the hospital. The parking lot was deserted except for a few cars parked around the entrance of the emergency room. In the reception area a nurse stood hovering over an open chart.

"Hi. We're here looking for the scouts who were in that Jeep accident at Possum Kingdom Lake."

The nurse looked up and squinted. "That group is all down

in the waiting room." She pointed toward a double door. "Through that door and to your left—second door on the right."

In the emergency waiting room I recognized the Scoutmaster Roger Dickens in the corner talking to one of the parents.

"Dad. Mom!" Peter said as he came running over.

Rebekah and Peter embraced. "Oh, Peter," Rebekah moaned. "I've been so worried about you. Were you hurt?"

Peter shook his head. "No. I wasn't in the Jeep. I stayed back at the camp to fish."

"Thank God," Rebekah replied.

Roger Dickens came over and put his arm around Jenny. "I'm so sorry. I can't believe this happened. Steven is okay, though. He wasn't hurt."

"Can you tell us what happened?" I asked.

"It was a horrible accident. You know the curvy part of the road just before you get to the camp entrance?"

"Right."

"Well, I guess Steven took it too fast and lost control of the Jeep. They went off the cliff and the Jeep landed in the lake. Somehow Steven managed to jump out, but Jimmy was found still strapped in his seatbelt. The sheriff isn't sure if he died from the crash or the fire that broke out afterwards."

"Were there any witnesses?"

"I don't think so. Steven had gone to town to get some supplies for breakfast. Jimmy volunteered to go with him. Steven's a good driver so I never suspected—" Dickens took a deep breath trying to maintain his composure. "I never dreamed something like this would happen."

"It's not your fault, Roger. But what I don't understand, though, is why Steven was arrested. If it was an accident—"

"He was talking crazy, like he was drunk or on drugs or something. I don't know if he hit his head on the windshield or what, but he claimed a spaceship ran him off the road."

"A spaceship?"

"That's what they say he said. I didn't hear it myself. I know it sounds crazy. I don't know what to think. It's not like Steven to make up stories like that. Particularly since Jimmy was killed in the accident. I figure he must have seen a helicopter or a hot air balloon and was distracted. You know how a boy could be distracted by something like that."

"Is Steven a science fiction fanatic?"

Roger shook his head. "No. He plays Dungeons and Dragons and reads a lot of comic books, but that's pretty typical of kids his age."

"Where's Jimmy's mother?"

"They took her to the chapel. There's a minister with her right now."

I shook my head. "Oh, Jesus. What a horrible thing to have to face. I'll leave Rebekah here for a while in case you all need any help with Barbara."

"That would be good. Thanks, Stan."

"I'm going to take Jenny over to the sheriff's office and see if we can get Steven released."

Dickens nodded. "Good luck."

Jenny was quiet on the way to the sheriff's office. I could only imagine what was going through her mind. A spaceship? Where had that come from? Was Steven suffering from a head injury like Roger suggested, or had he taken some kind of hallucinogenic? I was anxious to talk to Steven and get his side of the story.

We headed for the Palo Pinto Sheriff's office which was in the Courthouse just off Highway 180, twenty miles west of Mineral Wells. It took us about thirty minutes to get there. They said we couldn't miss it and they were right. Two miles east of Palo Pinto we saw the big courthouse protruding high above the tree line, a strange sight for a town whose downtown was scarcely two blocks long. The parking lot was empty with the exception of a single patrol car and an old Chevy pickup. We parked on the curb in front of the building and entered through the main entrance. A young female deputy was on duty at the front desk. We introduced ourselves.

"Has there been a bond set yet?" I asked.

"Judge Applegate won't set his bond until morning, so he'll have to stay in jail tonight."

"Can't we call him and get him to set it now?"

"I wouldn't recommend disturbing him. He's got a nasty

temper and you wouldn't want to get on his bad side."

She was right. Some of the small town judges were very temperamental and could turn on you in a hurry. It was particularly dangerous for out-of-county counsel who often didn't know how far they could push the local judge. I figured Steven would survive one night in jail, particularly since he would probably be the only inmate in residence that night.

"Well, can we at least see Steven?"

"Yes, one at a time."

"Okay, Jenny. You go first. I'll wait."

She nodded and the deputy led her down a hallway. When the deputy returned, I asked her if she knew anything about what had happened.

"Just hearsay. Your client was talking really crazy like he'd been on LSD or something. Claims a UFO caused the accident."

"So I heard. Did anyone interrogate him?"

"A couple detectives did."

"What were their names?"

"Ben Hayden and Bert Hollingsworth."

I took a business card out of my wallet and jotted the names on the back. In my haste to leave I'd forgotten a legal pad. I wasn't a big note taker anyway, so it was no big deal. I found if you listened carefully to people you'd remember the important stuff. "Was Steven hurt at all?" I asked.

"They took him to the hospital first, just to check him out, but I guess there wasn't anything seriously wrong with him since they brought him here and put him in a cell."

"How was he acting when he got here?"

"Quite normal, but they may have sedated him at the hospital."

"Have there been any reports of UFO sightings in this area?"

She laughed. "You're not buying into that boy's story, are you?"

I smiled. "No. Just covering all the bases."

She shook her head. "Well, we do get calls from time to time about strange things flying around, but they usually turn out to be military aircraft, small planes, or weather balloons."

"Any reports tonight?"

She shook her head and replied, "No. Sorry."

Jenny came back to the waiting room and sat down. She was obviously in shock. I went over to her and put my hand on her shoulder. She didn't look up. I was escorted back to a small detention room where Steven was pacing back and forth. He was tall, clean cut, and blessed with a handsome face. I knew him to be laid back and a little shy. It was no doubt he'd make a good impression on a jury.

"Hi, Mr. Turner."

"Hi, Steven. Sorry about what happened tonight."

He shrugged. "I'm just sorry about Jimmy. I can't believe he's dead."

"It was an accident—just a tragic accident," I said.

"No. It was all my fault. I just panicked. I've never seen anything like that before. For a moment I was just mesmerized. You know. It was like my body was frozen."

"Why don't you start from the beginning," I said. "I don't quite understand what happened."

He took a deep breath. "Okay. Well, I was in charge of the mess hall at the camp and we were out of eggs, sausage, and a few other things. Jimmy was on KP duty and looking for a way to escape his assignment. Nobody likes KP duty, right?"

"Right," I said, forcing a smile.

"Anyway. I told Roger I'd take the Jeep into town to get what we needed. I liked to drive it, so I often volunteered to run errands. You know what I mean?"

"Sure, I understand. Who owns the Jeep?"

"It belongs to the Triangle Council. They own the camp and they keep it here to use for maintenance and to run errands."

"Uh huh."

"I felt sorry for Jimmy so I told Roger I could use his help. He agreed so he and I left about four o'clock. It's about twenty minutes to town and half way there it started to rain hard. We stopped and put the top up and then continued on to town. It took us about a half hour or so to get what we needed and gas up the Jeep. Before we left, we played a couple video games, so it was about 5:15

p.m. or so when we started back to the camp. Jimmy was excited about riding in the Jeep and I guess I was showing off a bit. The rain had stopped so I opened her up."

"How fast were you going?"

"Oh, maybe 60-70 mph which really isn't that fast. It handles great on mountain roads."

"So what happened?"

"When I got to that the last curve, you know, before you get to the main gate, I heard a loud noise and noticed a huge spaceship flying overhead. It was so weird I couldn't believe it."

"A spaceship?"

"Right. Yeah, it was kind of rectangular, but with blunt corners—oblong, I guess would be more accurate. It was moving pretty fast but not as fast as a jet—kind of gliding across the sky."

"How high was it?"

"I don't know. It sounded really low. That's why it got my attention. You don't usually hear jets or airplanes unless they're pretty low. I thought it might be landing."

"How big do you think it was?"

"Maybe the size of a football field."

"That big? Wow!"

"Yeah, it was incredible. I just couldn't take my eyes of it. By the time I looked back at the road we were heading straight off the cliff. When I tried to veer back onto the highway, I lost control of the Jeep and we started to roll. I don't remember much after that. I must have blacked out."

"Did they give you a thorough examination at the hospital?"

"I guess. I spent about an hour there until they brought me here."

I shook my head. "It's a miracle you didn't die."

Steven nodded. "I know."

"So, Steven. You know this all sounds quite bizarre—the spaceship, I mean."

He looked away. "I know, but that's what happened."

"The sheriff thinks you were drunk or on drugs."

"I wasn't. I don't drink at camp and I don't do drugs *ever*."

"But you told them you saw a spaceship?"

"That's what it looked like. They asked me what happened so that's what I told them. I know it sounds crazy now, but what I saw had to be from outer space. It was the most incredible sight I've ever seen. I wish you could have seen it. It was totally awesome."

"Listen, I don't know what you saw and I'm not going to try to convince you that you didn't see it. But let's not mention the word spaceship from now on, okay?"

"Okay, I understand. What should I say?"

"Just say you were distracted by something, you're not sure what it was—a large bird, a plane, whatever—and you just lost control of the car. It was simply an accident—end of story. I don't want you to spend the rest of your life in a mental institution."

Steven looked down and took a deep breath. "Okay, Mr. Turner, whatever you say."

"Good. Then I'll be back first thing in the morning to get you out of here, okay?"

Steven looked up and his mouth fell open. "You can't get me out now?"

"No. I'm afraid not. The judge won't set bail until morning."

Steven's stood up and began to pace frantically. There was a look of utter disappointment on his face but nothing I could do or say was going to make him feel better, so I left. Once outside the room I half chuckled at the thought of having to blame the accident on an alien spacecraft. Wouldn't that be a hoot? But Steven seemed quite sincere in his belief that a spaceship of some sort had distracted him and caused this horrible accident. I wondered if we'd ever know what really happened, and if it was even remotely possible that Steven Caldwell was telling the truth.

Chapter 3

Spy Shop

Tracking down assets of a high rolling husband wasn't my idea of fun. It involved a lot of leg work—reviewing tax rolls, pouring through deed records, endless hours on the telephone talking to contacts with the phone company, the secretary of state's office, and the state comptroller. Then there was the surreptitious contact with ex-employees, ex-girlfriends, and business rivals who might have inside information on hidden assets. Not having the stomach for that sort of thing, I called Paul Thayer, our PI, and gave him that lovely job. He took the assignment without comment and said he'd get back to me in a couple days.

I could have waited until the case was filed and then sent out discovery to get this information, but that would have given Martin Windsor time to cover his tracks. The element of surprise was key to finding the full extent of his assets. In fact, I wasn't planning to serve citation on Windsor until I had Paul's report in hand. My strategy was to ask the court for a TRO prohibiting the sale, disposal, or dissipation of any assets that he owned. The more assets I could specifically list in the application for the TRO the better. The TRO would be granted routinely, but ten days later there would be a temporary injunction hearing, where I'd have to prove the need for extraordinary relief.

As I was considering all of this, I heard Stan talking to Jodie. Stan had been gone all day so I was anxious to hear what he'd been up to. I walked out of my office and into the reception area where he and Jodie were talking. He looked over at me.

I smiled. "Hey. You're back."

Stan sighed. "Yeah, thank God. What a day."

"Tell me all about it. Where have you been?"

"Mineral Wells."

"Mineral Wells? Why did you go all the way out there?"

"Peter's scout troop was camping up at Possum Kingdom, and the junior assistant scoutmaster and one of Peter's friends were in a Jeep accident."

"Oh, no. Are they okay?"

"Steven Caldwell, the junior assistant scoutmaster, is fine, but Peter's friend Jimmy died."

"Oh, Jesus. What happened?"

Stan filled me in on the details of the accident, their trip to the hospital, and Steven's bizarre story of being mesmerized by an alien spacecraft. They had stayed overnight and posted Steven's bond early in the morning after the district judge had gotten around to setting it. Steven's explanation of what caused the accident was so crazy I couldn't help but laugh. Stan didn't seem to be amused, however. For a minute I thought maybe he believed the story.

"So, you're not going to try to sell that scenario are you?" I asked.

"No, obviously it wouldn't play well, but what if that's the only defense we have? And since our client believes the story, don't we have an obligation to assert it?"

"Stan, don't even think about it. If you try to blame the accident on an alien spacecraft, not only will you lose the case but you'll never be taken seriously as an attorney again."

"How do you expect me to defend him then?"

"Make something up—a dog ran across the road. How could anybody prove otherwise?"

"I can't tell him to lie."

"Don't tell him to lie, just tell him to think very hard about the accident and come up with a better story."

I laughed. "Right. You want me to encourage him to lie."

"Well, we know there aren't alien spacecraft flying around, so I think you're encouraging him to *get real*."

"What if he's telling the truth?" Stan said with a straight face. "I was reading in a magazine that fifteen million Americans claim to have seen some kind of alien aircraft or UFO."

I shook my head. "Stan, you're scaring me. We've worked hard and gone through hell to build up a reputation as the best criminal defense firm in Dallas. If you even mention alien spacecraft, we'll be the laughingstocks of the southwest."

"Don't worry. I told Steven not to mention it again. We'll come up with something more credible. I don't know yet what it will be, but we'll think of something."

Just then Jodie walked in, a baffled look on her face and a notepad in her hand.

"What's wrong?" I said.

"I just got a call from the *Globe Inquirer*. They want to confirm a story they're printing for tomorrow's edition."

"What story?" I asked.

She looked down at her notes and said, "Well the headline is going to be, **'ALIEN SPACECRAFT CAUSES DEATH OF BOY SCOUT IN WEST TEXAS, Scoutmaster claims tragic accident caused by shock of seeing a huge spaceship.'**"

Stan laughed, "So much for keeping this under wraps."

"This isn't funny," I said. "We'll never live this down."

"Come on, Paula. You're overreacting. This will give us a lot of great exposure. Think of the press coverage this trial could attract."

"That's what I'm worried about. This is going to be a circus and we're going to look like a couple of clowns."

"What should I tell them?" Jodie asked.

"Tell them *no comment*," I said.

Jodie nodded and left. Stan walked off still wearing a big smile on his face. I couldn't believe he'd gotten us into this mess. Alien spacecraft? Give me a break. Nobody would believe such a ridiculous story.

The next day Paul sent me his report. After I read it, I called Cheryl Windsor to schedule an appointment to prepare for the temporary injunction hearing. She told me she had acquired a good deal of information as well. She wouldn't elaborate but said I would be quite proud of her. That boast made me very curious.

When Jodie showed her in that afternoon, she was carrying a cardboard storage box. She set it down next to a side chair and took a seat. She was dressed to kill—a black halter-styled crochet dress with a see-through waistband."

"I like that dress," I said, wondering why she was so dressed up. "Where did you get it?"

"Neiman's. I've been doing a lot of shopping since we split up. It helps fight depression."

"I bet."

Seeing her dressed that way made me nervous. She wasn't dressed for work and certainly not for an appointment with her lawyer. It was obvious she was meeting a man. Since she and Martin had already split up it was probably no big deal, but I wondered how long she'd been dating. If she'd been unfaithful during the marriage, I needed to know about it.

"So, tell me. Have you been seeing anyone since you broke up?"

She stiffened. "What?"

"Well, you're not dressed for church."

She looked down at her outfit and then back up at me. "Oh. Well, actually I am meeting someone for happy hour. Everyone says I should move on and not look back. Unfortunately, I have the children so that complicates matters a bit, but yes, I've been dating a little since the breakup—nobody special, though. I'm meeting him later this afternoon, as a matter of fact."

We talked awhile about Cheryl's three children—two boys and a girl ages three, five, and seven. She said Martin had threatened a custody battle if she caused him too much grief. She wouldn't let him have custody under any circumstances, she said. We chatted awhile longer and then I handed Cheryl Paul's report. It detailed much of the property that we already knew about but there were several surprises. Martin Windsor owned a limited partnership called Cimarron West, Ltd. It didn't do business itself, but was the major stakeholder in several resort hotels in Mexico and the Carribean. It also had a number of offshore bank accounts and other business interests, the nature of which Paul had been unable to ascertain.

When I was done, I asked, "So, what did *you* dig up?"

"Oh. . . . Well. . . . I installed several cameras and microphones around the house before I moved out."

"What?" I replied. "Are you nuts?"

"What? A girl's got to protect herself, don't you think?"

"Sure, but you must have a death wish. Aren't you worried he'll discover one of the bugs?"

"So, what if he does. He won't know who planted them. He's got lots of enemies."

"Where did you learn how to plant a bug, anyway?"

"The Spy Shop."

"The Spy Shop?"

"Uh huh. They have several stores around town. They sell all kinds of electronic surveillance gear—telephone taps, video cameras, tracking devices—and they have classes every Saturday to teach their customers how to use them."

I laughed. "You've got to be kidding."

"Nope. It was a lot of fun, actually."

I shook my head. "Well, what did you find out? Did you catch him partying with his girlfriend?"

She smiled. "Oh, yes and much, much more. I hope you have a VCR."

I escorted her to the conference room, stuck the video tape in the VCR, and pushed play. The screen flickered and then the living room of the Windsor's house appeared.

"I've got hours of this stuff—four or five tapes," she said. "Most of it's pretty boring, but here in about thirty seconds you'll see something very interesting."

I nodded and kept my focus on the TV screen. After a few seconds a dark, trim, muscular man appeared wearing only a pair of boxer shorts.

"That's Martin," Cheryl said. "In a minute you'll see Alice."

"Okay," I said, understanding now why Cheryl had been attracted to him. He looked like he could be a movie star.

"We're looking at the living room from a camera above the door to the kitchen," Cheryl said. "The door on the far side of the room leads to the master bedroom. The front door and the dining room are to the right."

There was a woman's voice coming from the master bedroom. Martin turned and yelled something to her. A minute later an attractive brunette appeared clad only in a pair of pink bikini panties.

"That's Alice, huh?" I asked.

"Right. What a slut, huh? I knew she had questionable morals, but I never suspected she'd betray me."

Alice had a small transparent baggie in her hand filled with a white substance that looked like cocaine. She sat on the floor and carefully poured a small amount of the powder on the glass coffee table. Martin joined her at the table with a couple of drinks. He watched her intently as she inhaled the substance. When she was done, she threw her head back and took a deep breath. Finally she got up and went to Martin. They kissed, tenderly at first but soon were making passionate love. Cheryl abruptly shut off the tape.

"I'd like to kill that bitch!" Cheryl screamed. "How could your best friend betray you like that?"

"I don't know, but it will definitely help prove our allegation of adultery and preclude him from getting custody of your kids," I said, "if we can get the video tape into evidence."

"Why couldn't we?" she asked.

"When were these tapes made?"

"I set up the cameras Saturday morning in several locations—the living room, bedroom, and the kitchen. They were shot Saturday afternoon and evening. I only had eight hour tapes. I retrieved them . . . well, I'm not sure exactly when."

"Getting surreptitious surveillance tapes into evidence is a complicated issue. You didn't have permission of either of the parties to film them. It could be an invasion of their privacy. The best argument we have is that it was your house so you had a right to install the cameras. Your husband would, of course, argue that you had moved out and were not in possession of the house any longer. It's a crap shoot whether a judge would let the evidence in."

"It doesn't matter. I doubt Martin will deny the affair. What I caught on this second video tape is more interesting."

"Really? Let's see it."

Cheryl removed the first video and placed the second one on in the machine. After a minute the same room appeared but this time there were three men seated watching a football game. Martin was in a stuffed chair and two other men were seated on the sofa. Everyone had a beer and there were chips and salsa on the coffee table. After a few minutes there was a knock at the door and Martin got up to answer it.

Martin escorted two men into the living room. One was thin and bald and the other one must have weighed 300 lbs. The bald man had a black briefcase which he put down next to the salsa on the coffee table. They were laughing and fooling around until the bald man said, "Okay, let's get this show on the road. I've got to get to the airport."

With that someone shut off the TV and the room became quiet. The bald man then leaned down and opened the briefcase. It was full of cash in neat stacks. It was impossible to tell exactly what denomination they were, but I suspected they were hundreds. That was the most common bill used by criminal elements. After one of the men examined the cash, he nodded to Martin and the bald man closed the briefcase. At that point someone turned the TV back on and the two men left, leaving the briefcase on the coffee table. When the football game was over, everyone left and Martin took the briefcase into the bedroom.

"I guess your husband has some illegal business going on."

Cheryl shook her head. "I thought I knew Martin, but this is a different man. I can't believe I'm married to a drug dealer."

"It was only one packet. It doesn't prove he's dealing."

"What about the money?"

"It could be for anything. But he's not very smart screwing your best friend and watching her use drugs. Did you ever see him use drugs himself while you two were together?"

"No. When I've indulged myself in the past, he's always declined. He does like to watch though."

"Where did you get your stuff?"

"Martin always found it for me. He said getting it was easy. I asked him a few times where he got it, but he just ignored the question."

"So, what do you want to do?" I asked.

"I don't know. Maybe we should tell him if he doesn't agree to a generous property settlement, we'll go to the police with these tapes."

"That would be extortion. We could both go to jail for that."

"Really, why?"

"I don't know. I guess because you shouldn't be able to buy your way out of jail. We can use this information to our advantage though, but we have to be very careful how we do it."

"What do you mean?"

"Well, we can let it slip that we know what your husband is up to, but we can't threaten him. We don't need to threaten him anyway. He'll understand pretty quickly that he'd better give you what you want, or suffer the consequences."

"How will you let it slip?"

"Once the case is filed and he hires an attorney, I'll have a heart-to-heart talk with his counsel. I'll convey to him the wisdom in quickly settling the case to avoid the risk of secrets being inadvertently revealed. It shouldn't be too hard getting the message across."

"Good. Do you need any more evidence? I removed all the cameras and bugs, but I can put them back if it would help."

"No, that won't be necessary. How did you manage to retrieve them without Martin finding out?"

"I don't remember exactly. It's kind of weird but when I got into my car this morning I found all of the equipment in my trunk. I can't remember removing it, but obviously I did."

"Wait a minute. You have no memory of retrieving it?"

Cheryl grimaced. "No, I really don't. I've racked my brains, but can't remember a thing."

"Could someone else have removed it and put it back in your trunk?"

"I don't see how. Nobody knew it was there except me."

"What if Martin found it? He might have stuck it back in your car to shake you up."

"No way. He doesn't have keys to my car and I always keep it locked. Besides, if he had found it he would have destroyed the tapes."

"Right. That would make sense. You must have removed it. It's just so weird that you can't remember anything."

I pondered this for a moment. As sincere as Cheryl seemed, how could she forget something as traumatic as retrieving illegal surveillance equipment? You don't do something like that every day. Something wasn't right. Either Cheryl was playing games with me or she'd suffered a short term memory loss. I supposed that was possible, but it didn't seem likely. I had been working with her for several weeks and hadn't seen any evidence of it. In fact, my impression was that she was highly intelligent, capable, and very much focused on her objectives in life. So, if she couldn't remember what had happened the night before, I suspected it was because she had been drunk or someone had drugged her. Either way I needed to know what had happened. I couldn't represent her effectively if I wasn't fully aware of what was going on in her life.

Chapter 4

The Circus is in Town

Paula was right about one thing, the circus was in town. From the time the *Globe Inquirer* story hit the streets on Wednesday the phones hadn't stopped ringing, and a crowd of reporters and science fiction fanatics had congregated in the lobby outside our office suite. After getting numerous complaints from our neighbors, building security escorted the intruders out of the building, and suggested they not come back. Most of them ignored this suggestion and continued to wait at the bottom of the steps just outside the building.

We also learned that Steven Caldwell had been forced to leave school because of the inordinate attention he was drawing both from students and the press. The full *Globe Inquirer* story claimed that there had been other sightings of alien spacecraft near Possum Kingdom Lake in years past, but failed to give any details. Then the story went into the usual history of UFO sightings and speculation as to why the spacecraft had paid a visit to our planet. As weak a story as it was, it still managed to raise the hopes of many a frustrated science fiction addict around the country and put the Steven Caldwell trial in the public spotlight.

Jimmy's funeral was held on Thursday at Restland Funeral Home. It had been reported in the newspaper that the body had been burned beyond recognition and that a positive ID wasn't possible, but nobody was disputing that it was Jimmy Falk's body that had been found in the Jeep. Paula, Rebekah, Peter and I attended the funeral along with other friends and family to pay tribute to a fine young man whose life had been truncated in a most tragic manner. Steven Caldwell had wanted to attend but due to the media attention and protests from several family members, we decided it would be best for him to stay at home. As we were standing outside waiting for the hearse to arrive, I noticed two men and a very thin woman standing well apart from the crowd of mourners. They looked out of place. "I wonder who they are?" I said to Paula, nodding in their direction.

Paula looked over at them. "I'd bet they're the two detectives and the assistant DA assigned to prosecute this case."

"Really? I can't believe they'd come to Jimmy's funeral."

"Well, all this press coverage has probably got them a bit nervous. They're not used to being under such close scrutiny."

"Hmm. Maybe we should introduce ourselves. It wouldn't hurt to say hello, and the sooner we know what they're planning, the better."

"Makes sense. Let's go."

We excused ourselves and walked over to the threesome. I smiled and extended my hand. "Hi," I said. "I'm Stan Turner and this is Paula Waters. Are you friends of Jimmy's family?"

The thin woman gave me a hard look. "No, I'm Carla Simms from the Palo Pinto County District Attorney's Office and these are Detectives Ben Hayden and Burt Hollingsworth."

We all shook hands, "We thought that's who you might be, so we thought we'd say hello."

"Yes," Simms said. "We were going to introduce ourselves before we left. We just came to meet the family, express our condolences, and let them know that we were very upset and concerned about their son's tragic death."

I nodded. "Right, that's certainly understandable."

Simms continued, "We wanted to assure them we wouldn't let all this media attention or the retention of such distinguished counsel as you deter us from vigorously prosecuting this case."

"Oh, yes," I said. "It is unfortunate about the media attention. I wonder how the *Globe Inquirer* got the story."

"Don't play coy with me, Mr. Turner," Simms spat. "You and your partner love media attention. I'm quite sure you know exactly how the story got to that disgusting tabloid."

Paula glared at Simms. "We didn't leak this story to anyone, and I'd be careful about making unfounded accusations."

Simms turned to Paula. "Don't worry, any accusations we make will be backed by rock-solid evidence," Simms said coldly.

"Your client's going to pay for killing that poor kid. In fact, I wanted to personally tell you and your partner that our investigation has determined that this was more than a case of negligent homicide or even manslaughter."

"What do you mean?" I asked.

"Based on the facts we know now, we've asked the grand jury for an indictment for murder."

"Murder! What the—"

"Yes, murder. It seems your client was dumped by his girlfriend Susan Weber last week, and guess who caused the breakup?"

"No," I said. "That's not possible."

"I'm afraid it is. Jimmy Falk was murdered by your client because he was outraged when he found out Jimmy was responsible for Susan breaking up with him."

"But he went off the cliff with Jimmy. He could have been killed himself."

"That's what he says. My guess is he jumped out of the Jeep before it went off the cliff. How else could he have survived the accident?"

Simms and the two detectives excused themselves, leaving Paula and I stunned. After a few minutes we went into the chapel for the service. It was a nice service but I couldn't concentrate on it. My mind whirled in disbelief at this latest development. How had this simple accident turned to murder? Those things that Simms had said just couldn't be true. I knew Steven Caldwell almost like a son. I could see him killing Jimmy in a passionate rage, perhaps, but it would take careful planning and cunning to kill someone the way Simms claimed it had been done. Steven couldn't have done that. Steven wasn't a cold-blooded murderer. That I knew.

When I got home, I went to see Steven. I had to ask him about Susan Weber. His mother answered the door and let me in. I told her I had to talk with Steven privately to protect attorney-client privilege. She reluctantly left us alone in the den. Steven sat across from me but wouldn't make eye contact. I suspected he knew why I was there.

"So, Jimmy's funeral was nice," I said.

"Was it?" Steven said, finally looking me in the eye. "I wish I could have gone."

"I know. He was a good friend, huh?"

Steven shrugged and looked away. "Well, not a close friend. We knew each other from being in the same troop, but he was a couple years behind me in school, so we didn't hang out or anything."

"You were friends with his brother though?"

"Right. Sam used to be in Scouts and he was in my grade so we were good friends."

"What about Susan Weber?"

Steven's mouth dropped and he turned a little pale. "How did you hear about her?"

"That's not important. What's important is that you withheld critical information from me. Why didn't you tell me Jimmy stole your girlfriend?"

Steven stiffened, looked away, and then took a deep breath. "I don't know. It just didn't come up. Why does it matter?"

"It matters because it gave you a reason to want Jimmy dead and now that's happened. The DA thinks you murdered him."

"No, I didn't want him to die. It was an accident."

"I know, that's what you keep saying, but the DA asked one question that's been bothering me. Maybe you can shed some light on it."

Steven shrugged. "What?"

"How is it that Jimmy died and you weren't injured at all?"

Steven didn't flinch. "I've wondered about that too. Why am I still alive after falling fifty feet down the side of a cliff? The only thing I can think of is that the aliens in the spacecraft beamed me up before I left the road. After the Jeep left the highway, everything went blank and the next thing I remember is waking up on the side of the highway."

"Oh, give me a break, Steven! Come on. Do I look that stupid? This is serious business. Your life is at stake. Nobody's going to believe your spaceship nonsense."

"I'm telling the truth. I woke up on the side of the road and when I looked down at the lake I saw the back end of the Jeep sticking out of the water."

I bit my tongue trying to keep my cool. "So what happened next?"

"A car came along, so I flagged it down and told the woman driving there'd been an accident."

"You didn't go down the cliff to check on Jimmy?"

"No, I wanted to, but the lady in the car said we should go call the sheriff. She said I wasn't in any condition to be climbing down there. It was probably too late anyway. No telling how long I'd been unconscious."

"So you don't have any recollection of how you got on the side of the road?"

Steven took a deep breath and mumbled, "No, sir."

We talked for sometime after that and Steven told me all about his relationship with Susan Weber. They had gone steady for over a year and had talked about eventually getting married. But problems arose when Steven graduated from high school and went to Collin County Community College. Besides being on different campuses, College turned out to be very demanding for Steven leaving precious little time for a meaningful relationship. Although Steven didn't want to admit it, they'd obviously drifted apart.

Apparently Steven and Susan ran into Jimmy one night and Steven introduced them, never imagining that the meeting would kindle a relationship between Susan and Jimmy. Steven admitted being upset when he found out Jimmy and Susan were dating, but denied being upset when Susan told him it was over between them. Somehow I didn't believe that part of his story. I warned him again not to talk to anyone about the case, and particularly not to the press. I suggested we might want to try hypnosis to help him remember what had happened after the Jeep left the road. He agreed that might be helpful.

When I left, I wasn't feeling any better about the case. Pretty much everything Simms had told us had been confirmed, and Steven's lack of memory wasn't helping. This was turning out to be a very difficult case, and somehow I knew it wasn't going to get better anytime soon.

The grand jury handed down the murder indictment against

Steven Caldwell the following week. Steven had been invited to testify before the grand jury, but I advised him against it due to his lack of memory and the extensive press coverage his alien spacecraft defense was attracting. Even though I was banned from the proceeding, I went to Palo Pinto anyway just to find out who the prosecution would call to testify. It was my right to talk to them as well. The first one I interviewed was Sylvia Bassett, the lady who had driven up after the accident. She worked in a local diner so I drove out there to meet her. She was a middle-aged woman who lived with her husband in a cabin near the scout camp. Her husband was a boat mechanic at a resort marina on the lake. We both got a cup of coffee and sat down in a booth. I asked her what she had seen that night.

"On the day of the accident I was coming home from work after my shift was over at five. It had been storming all day long but luckily had stopped by the time I left the diner. It's about a ten-minute drive home. As I was approaching the last curve near the entrance to Camp Comfort, I noticed a boy standing on the edge of the highway looking down. When he heard me approaching, he turned around."

"How did he appear to you when you saw him?"

"He looked dazed and confused. For a moment I thought he was going to stumble off the cliff. I rushed out and grabbed his arm."

"What did he say to you?"

"He mumbled something about an accident and a spaceship. I thought he was hallucinating. Then he started for the cliff mumbling that Jimmy was down there. He nearly took me off it with him. That's when I saw the Jeep sticking out of the water."

"What happened next?"

"I made him lie down in the backseat of my car and we drove back to the diner to call for help."

Sylvia seemed very confident and self assured. Not many women would have had the presence of mind to take charge of an accident victim the way she had. I figured her motherly instincts had kicked in or she'd had some kind of medical training.

"Did he have anything else to say while you were driving him?"

"He kept telling me that Jimmy was down there and that we needed to go help him. I told him we'd get help for Jimmy but in the meantime he needed to lie still."

"Did he mention the spaceship anymore?"

"No, but from the time I first laid eyes on him, he kept searching the sky like he was looking for something up there. Even when I was pulling him away from the cliff and into my car he was scanning the sky like a kid who'd just lost his helium balloon. I figured he must be in shock."

"What was Steven's appearance when you first got to him? Was he dirty? Were his clothes torn?"

"No, he wasn't dirty and his clothes looked okay, but he was sweating profusely. His T-shirt was soaked. It could have been from the rain, I guess, but I think the rain had stopped by then."

"What happened at the diner?"

"One of the girls called the sheriff and then we waited."

"You didn't go back to the accident scene?"

"No, the sheriff told me to keep Steven at the diner. About ten minutes later a sheriff's deputy and an ambulance came. They took Jimmy away and I told them what I knew. He said a rescue team was already at the scene of the accident."

"You mentioned that you've lived around here for quite some time."

"Since '69. My dad moved us here from Ft. Worth when he got a job with Southwestern Bell."

"Right. So, during the time you've lived here have you seen or heard about any UFO sightings?"

She smiled. "Well, there are folks who claim that spaceships often land on Cactus Island, but I've never seen one myself. I seriously doubt it's true, but it's good for tourism. I play along with it like everyone else in these parts."

"Really. Cactus Island?"

"Yes, it's an island in the middle of the lake. You can only get to it by boat. It's a favorite place for boaters to dock, and tourists go there to explore."

"Have you ever been there?"

"Sure, everyone who lives around here has been to Cactus

Island at least once. Exploring the island is a regular activity of the scouts who come to Camp Comfort. The kids from the YMCA and many of the church camps around the lake go out there as well. There's a big log raft with an outboard motor that the scouts use to transport themselves out there. I can see them leaving from my front porch."

"So, who is the resident alien expert around here?"

"Oh, that would be Doc Verner. He's an old World War II vet who has been obsessed with Cactus Island for more than thirty years."

Mrs. Bassett gave me Doc Verner's address and also directions to a marina where I could rent a boat to go out to Cactus Island. It's not that I believed that Steven had seen a spacecraft, but if he believed there were spaceships landing on Cactus Island, he might have seen something that he mistook for an alien ship. If Steven was fascinated by the idea of alien landings, that might explain why he took his eyes off the road for that split second that it took to lose control of the Jeep. At least it was a theory that was worth exploring.

I couldn't wait to explore the island, but then I decided it would be best to do my homework first, so I'd know what I was looking for when I got out there. That meant I needed to pay a visit to Doc Verner. According to Mrs. Bassett's map, Verner lived on the west side of the lake near the state park. I followed her directions but still managed to get lost, so I stopped at a gas station, showed them the directions, and asked them where I had gone wrong. They set me straight and ten minutes later I was driving up to an old ranch house, a dilapidated Cadillac Eldorado parked out front. Two ugly dogs immediately came running out, barking wildly. I hesitated getting out of the car, but finally decided if I didn't show fear, they'd leave me alone. I was wrong.

The smaller dog came straight at me barking and growling fiercely, so I quickly retreated back into the car. While I was contemplating my next move, I heard a voice chastising the dogs and telling them to get lost. Seeing a thin old man with wire rim glasses approaching, I got out of the car. The man reminded me of my father who had died years earlier. I smiled and said, "Doc Verner?"

"Yes," the man replied.

"Hello. I'm Stan Turner."

He smiled. "Thought them dogs were gonna eat you up, huh?"

I chuckled. "Well, you never know with dogs—they can be your best friend or your worst nightmare."

"Ah, my dogs wouldn't hurt a crippled flea. They just gotta get ta know ya."

"That's good to know."

"So, what can I do for ya?"

"Well, I've been told you're the local expert around here on UFO sightings."

Doc squinted and then a faint smile crept across his face. Finally he replied, "Ah, you must be that big Dallas lawyer I've been hearing about. Need an expert witness on UFOs, do ya?"

"Well, I don't know about that. Right now I'd just like to know about Cactus Island and the UFO sightings there."

"Well, what 'ave ya heard?"

"That people claim that some sort of alien beings use the island for a landing strip."

"Aye. That's a fact. I've seen 'em land there myself."

"Really?"

"Yes, twice. Once as a boy fishin' from the shore. The ship came from the west, gliding like a ghost over the lake, and then hovered over Cactus Island. I watched it in wonder as it slowly descended and disappeared into the island."

"It glided, huh? You sure it wasn't just a cloud shaped like a ship. Clouds can look mighty strange and their appearance can change dramatically as the light changes."

"Nah. I know what I saw. It wasn't any damn cloud."

"So, it disappeared into the island?"

He nodded, his eyes now glazed over like he was a million miles away. He said, "Aye, and on that day I vowed to find out what kind of creature had paid us a visit and where they'd come from."

"I see. What about the second time?"

He blinked and shook his head. "That was after the war. I was out of a job and just gettin' along by doin' a little guidin' for fishermen from Dallas and Ft. Worth. One night when I was bringing a couple of insurance agents back to the marina the wind suddenly picked up and the waves got so big they nearly capsized us. The strange thing about it was there were no storms in the area. We ended up anchoring in a little cove to wait for the wind to calm. That's when we saw a bright blue light and heard a high-pitched sound coming from above. We looked up and saw an enormous spaceship drift over Cactus Island and land on the island."

The larger dog came over to me and sniffed by shoes and pant legs. Then he looked up at me expectantly. I lowered my hand carefully and began petting him. He liked that and sat down directly in front of me so I could easily reach his mangy coat.

"What did the fishermen have to say about seeing this spaceship?"

"They were so spooked they could hardly speak. I tried to reassure them that they were in no danger, but they just insisted we get back to the marina immediately. I tried to talk to them about what we'd seen, but they ignored me and just drove off. I've never heard from them since."

"Hmm. So, I guess you read the *Globe Inquirer* story?"

"Aye, good stuff. I want to thank your client for that. I've been trying for years to get people interested in our alien visitors here at Possum Kingdom without a lick of luck."

"So, do you believe Steven Caldwell may have seen the same thing the other night that you saw years ago?"

"I'd stake my life on it. There's no mistake about it. I could tell by the way he described it that he'd been there and seen it for himself."

Before I left Doc's place, I asked him for the name of the two fishermen he had guided the second time he saw the spacecraft. I didn't figure he'd have their names, let alone their addresses or telephone numbers, but he surprised me by giving me two index cards with complete information on both of the men. Apparently he figured some day he'd need them as witnesses. The cards were old, yellowed, and bore the date of August 13, 1958, so I was quite sure the information was out of date. But at least I had a starting place in case I needed these witnesses to try to prove Steven Caldwell indeed saw a spacecraft on the night Jimmy was killed.

By the time I was ready to leave, the two ugly dogs had become my best friends. As I was walking back to my car, the dogs took off barking. I looked up and noticed two cars and a TV van pulling up. My heart sank as I recognized a reporter Amy Tan from the local ABC affiliate in Ft. Worth. She and her crew got out and approached us.

"Mr. Turner, we got a tip you were here," she said, pushing a microphone in my face. Are you investigating your client's story about seeing an alien spacecraft?"

A cameraman rushed up behind Tan and started filming the interview. I didn't know what to do. If I refused to talk to her, I could alienate her, but if I said the wrong thing I could prejudice my client's case. I decided to field a few questions and see how it went.

I forced a smile. "Yeah, well, you know we have to interview all the witnesses, and Doc Verner here claims to have seen something similar to what my client saw last Monday night."

"So you believe your client's story?" Tan asked.

"Well, you always have to assume your client is telling the truth no matter how strange and bizarre the story may seem. I don't frankly know what he saw, but I have a duty and obligation to thoroughly investigate the matter."

"Have you consulted other UFO experts, Mr. Turner?"

"No, and I don't know if Mr. Verner is an expert or not. This is the first time I've ever talked to him. At this point, I'm talking to everyone and gathering all the information I can. It will be some time before we decide on trial strategy."

"What about the accusation that your client killed Jimmy Falk over a stolen girlfriend?"

"Well, I've heard that accusation and, of course, my client denies it."

Before Tan could ask another question, I raised my hand. "Thank you all for your interest, but that's all I have to say right now. Perhaps later on after our investigation is further along, I'll talk to you again."

As I made my way to my car I noticed more cars and TV vans coming down the road. I looked back at Doc Verner in my rearview mirror as I drove off. He looked like he was in heaven being interviewed by Amy Tan. This was the day he'd been waiting so long to come. It was his fifteen minutes of fame. I couldn't wait to get home to see it all on the 10 o'clock news.

Chapter 5

The Interrogation

On Wednesday morning I had a couple of hearings in Criminal Court #two and then went to the clerk's office to file Cheryl's divorce petition and application for a temporary injunction. The judge signed the TRO and set a hearing on the application for an injunction for the following Tuesday. I figured by then I'd have enough evidence to get a favorable ruling. When I got back to the office, Jodie advised me I had a call from Detective Besch at the Dallas Police Department. Besch was a friend of Stan's. Why would he be calling me? I picked up the telephone.

"Paula, I'm so glad I caught you."

"Oh. What's up?"

"Listen, this is unofficial. You didn't hear this from me, okay?"

"Sure. What is it?"

"There's a lady down here who's being questioned about the disappearance of her husband and she's been throwing your name around."

"Me. Why?"

"She says you're her divorce lawyer."

A chill darted down my spine. I only had one divorce client. "You've got Cheryl Windsor down there?"

"Yes. I'm afraid so."

"What did she do?"

"Her husband has disappeared. Detective Perkins is trying to find out if she knows anything about what happened to him."

"Disappeared? How long has he been gone?"

"Since Monday. He's just suddenly vanished off the face of the Earth."

"Does Perkins suspect foul play?"

"Yeah. That's what he's thinking. Apparently she had a pretty big insurance policy on him."

"So, they're married. That's not unusual."

"Maybe, maybe not. If she's your client, I'd get down here. You know what a prick Perkins can be."

"Right. I'm on my way. Thanks for the heads up."

"If they ask you how you found out your client had been brought in for questioning, just tell them the maid told you. She was there when Perkins grabbed her."

"Got it. Thanks again. I owe you one."

Detective Besch had really gone out on a limb by calling me. Perkins would have his badge if he ever found out. I knew Stan and Besch had become good friends, but this was totally unexpected. I quickly packed up my briefcase and headed for the police station. Perkins wasn't happy when I advised him I wanted to see my client.

"She's not under arrest," he said. "We're just asking her a few questions."

"Fine. I need to talk to her for a few minutes before you continue."

"Why?" Perkins barked.

"Because I do. That's why. And if I let you question her further, I want to be there when you do it."

Perkins gave me a dirty look and then shook his head. He pointed to an open door. "She's in there. Make it fast."

I nodded. As I walked in, I saw Cheryl seated in a chair in front of a big metal desk. The room was cluttered with dusty books, files, stacks of paper, and a week's worth of dirty coffee cups. Cheryl stood up when she saw me. "Paula. Oh, thank God! How did you find out I was here?"

"Luckily we have a few friends around who keep us informed. So, what's going on?"

She sighed and gave me a grim look. "I don't know exactly. Like I told you yesterday, I took the kids over to the house on Friday to be with Martin for the weekend. He brought them over to my place on Sunday night. That's the last time I remember seeing him, but like I told you, I must have gone back on Monday because I found all the surveillance equipment in the trunk of my car Tuesday morning."

"You still can't remember anything that happened on Monday?"

"I remember getting up, fixing breakfast for the kids, and taking them to school. Then I went to the beauty salon to get my hair done. It was lunch time when I left. I remember worrying about how I was going to retrieve the cameras and bugs. I guess I must have gone over there but I don't remember a thing after leaving the salon."

"Do you have any idea what happened to your husband?"

"No. I swear to God. I have no clue."

"What have you told Perkins?"

"Just what I told you. I haven't seen Martin since Sunday night when he returned the kids after their weekend visitation."

"What about his office? Did you try calling him there?"

"Yes, but nobody there has seen him since Monday morning either."

"So, I heard you have a big insurance policy on Martin's life."

She shrugged. "Yeah. Martin wanted to be sure the kids were taken care of if something happened to him. His agent recommended a million-dollar policy, so Martin bought it."

Cheryl's explanation seemed a little self-serving. I doubted it was Martin who insisted on the big policy. If I'd learned anything about Martin, it was that he was selfish and inconsiderate. It would have been out of character for him to buy a big insurance policy. Guys like him figured they'd never die. Despite what Cheryl said, I was quite sure she had insisted on the policy. That didn't mean she killed her husband, but it did mean she was lying to me.

"Has Martin ever disappeared like this before?"

"No. He always tells me when he's going to be away."

"So, you have no idea where he might be?"

"No, swear to God."

"Because if you had anything to do with Martin's disappearance, I couldn't let Perkins question you."

"I didn't. Frankly I'm worried about him. I know we're getting a divorce, but I still have feelings for him. I don't want my children to grow up without a father."

Cheryl seemed sincere, but I wasn't a 100 percent convinced she knew nothing about his disappearance. I was tempted to tell Perkins she had nothing to say to him, but I figured that would just intensify his interest in Cheryl as a suspect. I found Perkins and told him Cheryl was ready to chat. He showed us to an interrogation room where Cheryl and I sat across from him.

"Has your husband mentioned having any business problems?" Perkins asked.

"No. He never discusses his business with me."

"You must know something about his business?" Perkins pressed.

"I know he invests in various ventures—resort properties mainly. I don't know the specifics."

"Are there employees or business associates we could talk to?"

Cheryl nodded. "Bernard Lansdale is his administrative assistant. He used to come over to the house a lot. I've heard him mention Marvin Greenberg from time to time too. I think he's a lawyer."

"Anybody else?"

"He has a secretary—Gloria Fellows. She answers the telephone when I call his office. That's about it."

"Do you know of anyone who might want to harm your husband?"

"No. But Martin was a very aggressive businessman. He has no qualms about taking advantage of someone if they let him. I'm sure he has a long list of enemies."

"Do you have any names?"

"No. Like I said, Martin doesn't talk business with me. He's always been very secretive about what he was doing. If he did tell me about anything it was always in generalities and he never mentioned actual names or places."

"You and your husband are separated?" Perkins asked.

"Yes. We're in the process of getting a divorce."

"How's that going?"

"Well, okay, I guess. We're working things out."

"Are you sure about that?"

"I beg your pardon," Cheryl said indignantly.

"Well, you just filed an application for a TRO, didn't you?"

"That's just standard practice," I interjected.

Perkins looked over at me. "Is it standard practice to allege infidelity and mental cruelty?"

"Well, not always," I replied. "But in this case it was appropriate."

Perkins leaned forward. "Isn't it true you and your husband were in a bitter divorce and that he was threatening a custody battle if you messed with any of his business interests?"

Cheryl shook her head."It wasn't all that bitter. Obviously he wasn't anxious to give me everything I wanted, but I fully expected him to eventually agree to a reasonable settlement."

"You know, if he was cheating on you, I could understand if you got pissed off and decided you'd had enough."

"Okay," I said. "Now you're talking like she's a suspect. If you have any more questions that will help you find Martin, that's fine. Otherwise, we're out of here."

Perkins sat back in his chair. "Okay. I guess I'm done for now. But don't leave town, Mrs. Windsor. We may have more questions for you as the investigation progresses."

As we left the police station, I suggested we get a cup of coffee at a diner across the street. She agreed and I spent the next hour with her delving deeply into her relationship with Martin Windsor. Since Martin had disappeared, I needed to learn more about him in order to help find him, or defend Cheryl should he turn up dead. She told me they had met on a flight from Dallas to New York. He was going there on business and she was making her annual visit to her sister who lived in New Jersey. They hit it off and he asked her if he could take her to dinner one night. That was the beginning of their relationship. They almost broke it off when she found out Martin was married, but he insisted that marriage was over. After his divorce, they got married and lived happily for several years. Eventually, however, Martin got caught up in his business affairs and spent little time with Cheryl. He did manage to get her pregnant, however, and when she told him he was going to be a father again his attitude drastically changed. Suddenly he had to be with her every minute to be sure she was happy and safe.

Martin's sudden concern for Cheryl once she became pregnant, intrigued me. Did Martin really love his children that much? It seemed out of character from what Cheryl had told me. I decided to explore that angle to see where it led. I started by asking about her pregnancy and delivery.

"Martin insisted I go to a private facility for prenatal care and the delivery. He said he didn't trust the doctors and staff at the other hospitals around town."

"What was the name of the facility?" I asked.

"The Ujhazi Institute. It's on Loop 12 west of Preston Road."

"Hmm. I'm not familiar with it."

"It's run by another Hungarian, Dr. Laslo Ujhazi."

"Really? Did they take good care of you?"

She nodded. "Well, there were complications. I had to have a C-section. I was in a lot of pain, so they kept me pretty doped up most of the time. I really don't remember much about either of my deliveries."

It seemed incredible to me that Cheryl couldn't remember anything about the delivery of her children, but maybe she was right and they had doped her up so much it clouded her memory.

"Hmm. Well, I guess you were lucky. Childbirth can be an extremely traumatic experience, I've been told."

"Yes, I was expecting the worst but it turned out not to be so bad. I'd definitely recommend the place."

"Is there somewhere your husband would go if he wanted to get away for a while? Did he have a favorite getaway?"

"He loved big cities—New York, Boston, San Francisco. His business ventures often required him to travel to these places. But when we traveled for pleasure, he always wanted to go to Las Vegas."

"Really? Did he like to gamble?"

"Yes, and he was very good at it. In fact, on several occasions he was winning so much we were asked to leave the casinos. One of them accused him of card counting."

"Was he a card counter?"

"I don't know. He wouldn't talk about it. He is a very smart man—great with numbers. I guess it's possible. But it wasn't just the gambling that he liked. He was fascinated by the bright lights and the nonstop action. We'd go to all the shows and play all the casinos.

We rarely slept and I'd be so exhausted when we returned that I'd have to take a couple days off just to recuperate."

"Sounds like you two had a lot of fun."

Cheryl sighed. "We did. I miss those days."

After our talk at the diner, I went back to the office. When I walked in, Jodie advised me that I'd received an urgent call from Detective Perkins. It bothered me that Perkins had already called. That could only mean he'd found something incriminating against Cheryl. At my desk, I dialed his number, and held my breath. He answered on the first ring.

"Perkins."

"Detective. This is Paula Waters."

"Oh, yes. Thanks for returning my call. I just thought you should know that your client hasn't been entirely honest with us."

"Why do you say that?"

"She told us she hadn't been at Mr. Windsor's place since Friday, but we just interviewed a neighbor who saw her there Monday afternoon."

"Really? Well, technically speaking she said she hadn't seen Martin on Monday. She didn't say she didn't go to the house. She might have said she didn't remember going by the house, but—"

"Oh, I think she remembers it quite well. In fact, she must have spent hours cleaning the place. The lab boys say it's the cleanest crime scene they've ever seen. They didn't find a single fingerprint, not one fiber, and no hair even on the hair brush. She must have boiled the toothbrushes because there wasn't a single trace of saliva on any of them. Even the sheets were clean like they were just out of the package."

"Well, Martin or anyone could have cleaned up the place."

"Nobody else was seen there."

"So you say, but I bet your witnesses weren't watching the house every minute. You really have nothing. There's no body and you have no evidence that incriminates my client."

"That's true. Your client is clever. I'll admit that, but I just wanted to let you know we're going to nail her anyway. She's not going to get away with cold-blooded murder. I don't care how good she is at cleaning up a crime scene—I won't rest until she's behind bars. You understand?"

Perkins' dramatic attempt to intimidate me would have almost been comical had the stakes not been so high. Perkins was a tenacious asshole and his promise to put Cheryl behind bars was no idle threat. He'd probably devote every waking hour to find the evidence he needed to put Cheryl away for twenty years to life, and he'd have an entire detective staff at his disposal to get the job done. I had my work cut out for me.

Chapter 6

The Evening News

As I was leaving Possum Kingdom Lake, I stopped and looked out at Cactus Island. Was it possible that aliens might have actually landed there? The idea seemed so ridiculous, yet at least four people claimed to have been witnesses to it. I was anxious to see if I could locate the two fishermen who had gone out with Doc Verner. Even if I found them, it was quite likely they wouldn't admit to what they had seen for fear of what people would think. If I were in their shoes, I'd probably do the same thing. After ten minutes of watching the tranquil island and scanning the sky for anything unusual, I laughed at myself for even thinking it might be true, and headed back to Dallas.

When I drove into my garage the door to the house opened and Peter ran out. "Dad! Dad! Hurry up. You're on the news."

"Oh, God. Already," I muttered under my breath and quickly went inside.

Everyone was gathered in the living room intently watching the report when I walked in. Rebekah looked up. "Hurry. They're about to start."

I sat next to Rebekah as the news story began with Ramona Mitchell, "Next. Have alien spacecraft been using Cactus Island at Possum Kingdom Lake as a landing site? Well, one Dallas attorney apparently thinks so. We're going live to Possum Kingdom Lake in West Texas where Amy Tan has an interview with attorney Stan Turner who's been out tonight consulting with UFO expert, Doc Verner."

Mark and Peter looked over at me like I was a lunatic. Rebekah was having trouble controlling her laughter. Marcia seemed confused. I sank down in my chair and focused on the TV.

"Thank you, Ramona. Earlier tonight we caught Dallas

attorney Stan Turner out at Possum Kingdom Lake at the home of Doc Verner, a local UFO expert. Apparently, Mr. Turner is taking his client's claim of being distracted by a UFO quite seriously."

They ran my brief interview and I immediately regretted having given it. What was I thinking? I could imagine what Paula would say about it the next day. The thought occurred to me that maybe I should call in sick.

Amy Tan continued, "Doc Verner claims that he too has seen the same or a similar spacecraft that accused murderer Steven Caldwell claims distracted him and caused the accident that took the life of a fifteen-year-old boy scout, Jimmy Falk. According to Verner, Cactus Island is a favorite landing site for spaceships because of its hard flat surface and isolation from the general populace.

"Verner doesn't know where these space visitors come from nor their purpose in visiting Texas, but he believes they mean us no harm. He says he's been trying to get the U.S. government to investigate Cactus Island for years but all his pleas have fallen on deaf ears."

Ramona cut in. "What's the mood of the community out there? Are they worried about these visitors from outer space?"

"No," Amy replied. "Most are just amused by the whole thing. They don't believe spaceships are really using the island as a landing strip, but they like the publicity they've been getting lately. They say tourism has tripled in the last week and the local state park and all motel rooms within fifty miles are 100 percent booked."

Amy Tan signed off and all eyes focused on me. "That was cool, Dad," Peter said. "Do you really think Steven saw a spaceship?"

I shrugged. "I don't know what he saw, but it's interesting that others saw the same thing."

"Stan, you've got to come up with another defense," Rebekah said. "This spaceship nonsense is a joke. People are going to think you and Steven are crazy."

"I know. I didn't plan to consider it, but then the media got hold of it. I can't just ignore it now."

"I believe it," Peter said with conviction.

"Why?" I asked.

"Because I've been to Cactus Island and it looks like a giant ship landed there. It's big and flat like a football field."

"That's what I've heard," I said, "and I've checked with the Corps of Engineers and they claim they've never touched the island. So, how do you explain this 135,000 square feet footprint in the middle of the island?"

Rebekah shrugged, "I don't know, but no jury is going to buy it."

"Probably not, but I still need to investigate it. In fact, I want to go back there this weekend and go out to the island. I thought maybe I'd bring Peter along since he's been there before."

"I want to come," Mark said.

"Me too," Marcia added.

"We should all go," Rebekah said. "It will be a nice outing. Possum Kingdom Lake is such a beautiful place. Anyway, if I'm going to hear about Cactus Island for the next six months, I'd like to know what everyone is talking about."

"Good," I said. "How about you, Reggie? Are you going to come?"

Reggie was a sophomore at Southern Methodist University. He was still at home a lot since school was so close, but his official residence was a dorm on campus. His enthusiasm for family outings had naturally waned as he got older and the expression on his face showed outright disdain for this particular outing.

He rolled his eyes. "No, I think I'll pass."

I smiled. "Suit yourself."

After dinner Rebekah and I sat down to relax and watch TV. Just as I got comfortable, Paula called. As expected she was very distraught about the news report and said we were going to be the laughingstocks of the legal community. I apologized for embarrassing her but suggested this wouldn't be a fatal blow to Turner and Waters, P.C. When I told her about our planned trek to Possum Kingdom Lake to view Cactus Island, she had a fit.

"Stan! You can't go out there again! The press will be watching you. You'll just draw more attention to this ridiculous defense. You need to let this spaceship thing die down and come up with something more plausible."

Paula was so paranoid sometimes it got to be very annoying. If she started worrying about something it was next to impossible to allay her fears. She was stubborn and tenacious, but I guess that was one of the reasons she was so good at her job. Once she set out to prove someone innocent, she didn't sleep until it was done.

"I just want to see it," I said. "We'll get there early in the morning and just stay a few minutes. Why don't you and Bart come along? It'll be fun."

"Oh, Stan. Come on. Don't do this. We've come so far. Don't throw away everything we've worked for."

"It's just a little excursion. We owe it to our client. Besides, there's no such thing as bad publicity for a law firm. Any kind of publicity is good."

Paula sighed. "Okay. We'll come. But I think it's a big mistake."

"Good. It will be fun. You'll see."

"Hmm. . . .Oh, by the way, I may have a new murder case myself."

"Really? Who was murdered? I didn't hear about it on the news."

Paula told me about the call from Detective Bingo Besch and her client being interrogated about the disappearance of her estranged husband. It was a bizarre story but I told Paula it was probably premature to conclude Martin Windsor was dead. I told her about another divorce case where three days before the trial date my client, the husband, disappeared. We went to the police but they refused to do anything because of the divorce situation. They assumed the husband just got fed up and left town. The trial went forward without my client and he lost everything. Six months later he called me, upset that his wife had been awarded custody of the children and all the community property. I asked him what he thought would happen if he didn't show up for trial. He said he thought they'd postpone everything until he returned.

After Paula hung up I took a deep breath and prayed I was right about the impact of the Steven Caldwell case on our booming law practice. I liked practicing law and couldn't imagine doing anything else. What if Paula were right and everyone thought I was an idiot for believing Steven's outlandish story? What if the telephone stopped ringing? I couldn't imagine selling life insurance again. Suddenly I felt sick.

Chapter 7

The Disappearing Man

As I drove to work the next morning, I found myself thinking about Stan being on the news. I was still mortified. I couldn't believe he was still considering the spaceship defense after I thought we had agreed to drop it. Stan seemed to be enjoying all the media attention and was starting to act like he believed there *were* aliens visiting Possum Kingdom Lake. And now he'd somehow talked me into going to see Cactus Island. Although I didn't expect to see anything extraordinary there, I had to admit I was kind of curious about the place. But really I hoped it would end up being a waste of time and Stan would come to his senses.

Later that morning Martin Windsor's divorce lawyer called me and said he'd agree to the temporary injunction as long as it was mutual. With Martin's disappearance, he was worried about Cheryl dissipating the community property in his absence. The judge would make it mutual anyway, whether I liked it or not, so I agreed. Once we had hammered out the language of the injunction, I ran it down to the judge and got it signed. Having the injunction in place made me feel a little better but not much. It occurred to me that Martin may have orchestrated his own disappearance and was trying to frame Cheryl for murder. If that were the case, he wouldn't pay much attention to a court injunction.

I had to figure out what had happened between Cheryl and him. According to Detective Perkins someone had seen Cheryl at Martin's house on Monday about the time he disappeared. Since Cheryl had no memory of Monday afternoon or evening, I had to assume the witness was correct. Had she really suffered a memory loss or was she hiding something? I had to assume for now that she was telling the truth. So, what caused her memory loss? Had Martin or someone drugged her or was she suffering some kind of traumatic amnesia as the result of an encounter with Martin? Both of those possibilities needed to be explored. I decided I might get some answers from Martin's secretary, Gloria Fellows, and his administrative assistant, Bernard Lansdale.

Village Drugstores, Martin's company, had its corporate office in the Park Central II Building in North Dallas. I checked the directory in the lobby and found out they were in suite 711. A bald man got in the elevator with me on the ground floor. I pushed seven on the elevator keypad and stepped back. The man looked at me but didn't smile. He looked familiar, but I couldn't place him. I felt uneasy as his eyes continued to check me out, so I looked over at him and frowned. He finally looked away. When he didn't push a button for another floor, I figured he must be going to the seventh floor as well. As the door opened on the seventh floor, I caught him staring at me again. I shook my head and stepped out. *What a pervert.* The door closed. I stopped a minute to get my lipstick out of my purse. I was expecting to hear the elevator moving again to its next destination. I waited a second but nothing happened. Curiosity overcame me, so I looked back. Was the man just standing there in the closed elevator? I walked back to the elevator door and pushed the down button. The elevator opened slowly. Expecting to see the man there, I wrestled for a quick explanation as to why I'd opened the elevator after just getting off, but when the door was fully opened there was nobody there. My heart skipped a beat and I nearly fainted.

It took me several seconds to compose myself. What was going on? How had this man suddenly vanished into thin air? Could the elevator have gone up a floor silently and let the man off that quickly? The elevator door closed and within a split second I heard a distinct hum from the elevator motor and the faint sound of the elevator cables straining under the weight of the elevator cab. I took a deep breath, tried to shake off my confusion, and looked around for suite 711.

On the wall I saw a sign that indicated suites 701-712 were to my left. As I turned to walk in that direction, I felt a hand on my shoulder.

"Ahhhh!" I screamed and twirled around. It was the same man who'd been in the elevator.

He said, "Are you all right, ma'am?"

I lurched back out of his grip and scrambled away. "Yes, I'm fine," I said breathlessly. I turned and walked quickly down the hall to suite 711 and stumbled in. The receptionist gave me an inquisitive look. I stood up straight and took a few deep breaths to stop my trembling. After my pulse had lowered to near normal, I made my way up to the receptionist and advised her I was there to see Gloria Fellows.

"Oh, yes," she said standing up immediately. "She's expecting you. Come this way."

She led me down a long corridor and showed me into a conference room. I sat down in one of the twelve maroon leather chairs that surrounded a large glass conference table. The room was cold and clinical with its white walls and pastel paintings. It seemed fitting for a pharmacist's office. A moment later a thin woman dressed in a smart pin-striped suit walked in. Her face was somber. She introduced herself as Gloria Fellows and sat down across the table from me. I told her that I represented Cheryl Windsor.

"Thank you for meeting with me," I said. "I guess you know Martin Windsor is missing?"

She nodded, "Yes, we're very concerned. It's so unlike Martin to just disappear like this. What does your client have to say about Martin's disappearance?"

"Like you, she is very distraught."

Fellows crossed her black-stockinged legs, folded her arms, and frowned. I felt a distinct chill. "You think Cheryl had something to do with Martin's disappearance?"

"Well, I heard she was at his home on Monday and nobody has heard from him since. And I know Cheryl despised Martin."

"Despised? That's pretty strong. Why would you put it that way?"

"Cheryl was a very jealous woman and she couldn't stand the fact that Martin had responsibilities far more important than catering to her every whim."

"Really? What responsibilities?"

Fellows rolled her eyes. "Running a business, of course. Martin was responsible for operations at all the Village Drug Stores plus keeping track of all the company's business interests."

"I see. So, Martin worked long hours and didn't have a lot of time to spend at home?"

"Yes, and that was unfortunate, but a wife must learn to accept the price of her opulent lifestyle."

Opulent lifestyle? This lady didn't talk like a secretary. I wondered if there was more to her relationship with Martin Windsor than taking dictation. She had an obvious contempt for Cheryl which suggested jealousy. I thought it wise to shift the discussion in a different direction before Fellows got so uptight that she'd clam up on me. "Well, let's assume that Cheryl doesn't know what happened to her husband. With that presumption, did Mr. Windsor have any projects going that might require his leaving town?"

"Yes, we have resort interests all over the Carribean. He often visits them to play golf. At least that's what he tells the managers when he shows up unexpectedly. Actually he goes there to make sure they are being managed properly."

"So, he does travel a lot?"

"Yes. But I've been all through that with Detective Perkins. I really don't have time to—"

"I know. I appreciate that you are very busy, particularly with Martin missing, but please bear with me. I might be able to help find him. Were there any properties that Martin may have been worried about and had contemplated visiting?"

She thought a moment and then nodded. "We have a 30 percent stake in a resort in Tobago. The manager apparently quit a few weeks ago and we've been concerned with the delay in replacing him. Martin mentioned going down there but hadn't made any plans yet."

"Do you book his travel arrangements?"

"Yes, that's why I know he didn't go. He didn't ask me to make those arrangements."

"Has he ever taken a trip and made his own arrangements?"

"No. Never."

"Have you checked your company credit cards for activity

since Monday?"

"Detective Perkins did. There hasn't been any."

For the next hour I continued to press Gloria Fellows for information that might be helpful in locating Martin Windsor. It seemed that every avenue I went down, however, Perkins had already been there. I decided I was wasting my time on that line of questioning and decided to get back to their personal relationship. "So, are you and Martin sleeping together?"

Fellows jumped to her feet and glared at me. "I think we're done here!" she spat.

I laughed. From her reaction, I'd got the answer to my question. Martin was a classic womanizer if I'd ever seen one—Cheryl's best friend and now his secretary. I wondered how many more there had been. Dozens probably. This interview hadn't been a waste of time after all.

Chapter 8

Field Trip

We decided it would be best to visit Cactus Island early on Saturday morning just as the sun came up, hoping that we would be mistaken for fisherman searching for one of those lunker bass who fed in the shallow waters around the island. Paula and Bart met us at Camp Comfort where we had arranged with Roger Dickens to take a couple fishing boats out to the island. It was still dark when we met in the mess hall over a pot of coffee and a sack full of doughnuts we'd picked up at a convenience store near Scuba Point. Possum Kingdom was a popular place for scuba divers as it was a very deep lake carved over thousands of years by the Brazos River. As the sky began to lighten outside, we cleaned up our mess and walked down to the dock.

"Well, this should be interesting," Rebekah said. "I haven't been exploring since I was a teenager."

"Don't worry, Mom," Peter said. "I'll watch out for you."

Rebekah laughed. "I'll be all right as long as there aren't any snakes."

Mark said, "Snakes are more afraid of you than you are of them. As long as you don't come up on one unexpectedly, they'll be long gone before you get there."

"Good. I'll follow behind you, Mark," Paula said.

Mark shot a dirty look at Paula. Then he smiled. "Sure, I'll take the point."

We all looked at Mark and laughed. I said, "Mark's our military man. He's already made friends with the neighborhood Marine Corps recruiter."

"Well, you were a Marine, Dad," Mark replied.

"That I was," I said. I'd never told the kids much about my disastrous military career. Fortunately, they were very young back then and didn't remember any of it. Rebekah's mother had mentioned recently that I had been a Marine and that got Mark on a military kick. I hadn't got up the courage to tell him the story yet, but one of these days I was going to have to do it.

The air was cool and a shallow fog clung to the surface of the lake. Visibility was only a few yards so we idled slowly out toward Cactus Island. Ten minutes out the sun broke over the eastern sky and illuminated the top of the island. It was an eerie sight seeing the island protruding out of the mist, littered with giant boulders, and surrounded by a rocky shore line. There were a few scrub oaks on the island but the primary vegetation was sage brush and every imaginable species of cactus.

Suddenly we heard voices and the hum of boat motors. As the mist quickly evaporated in the sun's early rays, we discovered we were in the middle of an armada of boats of every shape, color, and size. It reminded me of striper fishing at Lake Texoma when hundreds of boats would mass together searching for the schools of stripers that migrated between feeding grounds just beneath the surface of the lake.

Then we heard helicopters overhead and the sound of a distant bullhorn. "Stay back from the island," a stern voice commanded. We all turned toward the island, where two Texas Fish and Wildlife patrol boats were anchored near the shore. "Turn around and leave the area. The island is closed. Anyone trying to come ashore will be arrested."

I glanced at Paula. "I wonder what's going on."

"I guess we're not the only ones who want to inspect Cactus Island."

Just then a boat slipped up onto the shore and two men jumped out and started climbing toward the island's summit. Two sheriff''s deputies, whom I hadn't noticed before, began chasing after the men. It didn't take them long to catch them, throw them to the ground, and put handcuffs on them. We all looked on in shock. Then I spotted a man on the shore who I suspected was the Palo Pinto County Sheriff, judging by how everyone was hovering around him.

"Let's go talk to the sheriff," I suggested.

"Good idea," Bart said. "Maybe he'll tell us what's going

on."

We changed our course toward the small cove where the sheriff's boat was anchored. As we approached, a sheriff's deputy tried to wave us off, but we kept moving until we were within shouting distance. I yelled, "Permission to come ashore. We need to talk to the sheriff. It's official business. My name is Stan Turner." The deputy frowned and then motioned for us to wait. We stopped our engines as he conferred with the sheriff. A minute later the deputy returned and told us we could come ashore.

Once on the small rocky beach, Paula and I walked over to where the sheriff had set up a command center. He spotted us coming and turned to greet us.

"Mr. Turner. I didn't know you were coming out here today."

"We just wanted to take a look around. I figured we'd slip in early and leave before anyone saw us."

The sheriff laughed. "Well, thanks to you the island is closed. As you can see, every alien hunter in the country has descended upon Possum Kingdom Lake."

I shook my head. "I never imagined something like this would happen. I'm sorry for all the inconvenience this mess is causing you."

"Well, apologize to the taxpayers who are going to have to foot the bill for all the overtime I'm going to have to pay my deputies."

A helicopter flew over kicking up dust and debris. "Why the helicopters?" I asked.

"We've had several small planes try to land on the island. We're using the helicopters to keep an eye out for any more airborne sightseers."

"Since we're here and we have a good reason to inspect the island, may we look around?" Paula asked.

The sheriff turned to her and gave her a hard look. "So you must be the notorious Paula Waters."

Paula frowned. "Notorious?"

The sheriff smiled. "Well, that's as close to a compliment as I can give a defense attorney, if you know what I mean."

We all laughed.

"Sure, go ahead," the sheriff said. "Watch out for the snakes. I don't want to have to take anybody to the hospital."

Paula looked at Mark and gestured for him to lead the way. Mark eagerly started hiking up the rugged trail that led to the interior of the island. It was slow going as the path was lined with cacti and other prickly vegetation that we all wanted to avoid. Halfway to the top I looked back at the armada of boats and other vessels that were still lurking around the island. Why were all these people here? Surely they realized the aliens, if there were any, wouldn't be showing up today. Then I realized they were here for the same reason I was—to see if there was any evidence of extraterrestrial life. It was one of life's biggest mysteries—were we alone? As I started hiking again, I couldn't help but feel excited about the possibility that perhaps just a few yards up ahead we might find some answers.

Paula reached the top of the island, stopped and waited for the rest of us. As I walked up behind her, I couldn't believe what was below us. The very rugged terrain suddenly gave way to an almost perfectly level rectangular surface, sunken several feet below the outer rim. There was very little vegetation on the gravelly surface, which appeared to be quite suitable for use as a landing strip.

I looked at Paula. "Well, do you think that's a natural formation?"

She shook her head. "Somebody built this, and it sure as hell wasn't aliens."

"How do you know that?"

"Because I do. There aren't creatures from outer space running around building landing strips. Give me a break. This was done by bulldozers and a lot of human sweat."

"But there's no record of anyone ever doing this and nobody saw this airstrip being built. If this was done by men, it would have taken months to build. There would have been dust and noise that someone would have seen or heard."

"Let's take a look around," Bart said.

I nodded. "Good idea."

For the next thirty minutes we examined the surface of Cactus Island. We didn't find anything other than dirt and rocks so

I decided to take a soil sample for analysis. If an alien spacecraft had landed, surely some chemical residue would have been left behind. If a lab report did turn up something out of the ordinary, it might be just what we needed to corroborate Steven Caldwell's story.

Chapter 9

Mounting Evidence

Although the excursion to Possum Kingdom Lake was quite interesting and even exciting at times, I hadn't seen anything yet that made me believe that aliens had actually visited Cactus Island. What was fascinating though were the throngs of people from all over the U.S. who obviously did believe and whose belief was so strong they'd dropped everything to come to Central Texas hoping to witness history in the making—a Texas jury actually considering the possibility that an alien spacecraft had caused a fatal automobile accident. As much as I wanted this whole nightmare to go away, I knew now it wasn't going to happen. So, I'd have to set aside my personal feelings and give Stan as much support as possible if we were to save Steven Caldwell and preserve the reputation of Turner and Waters.

With that realization behind me, the next morning I put aside science fiction and dug back into my plain vanilla missing person case. Where was Martin Windsor? The next witness on my list to interview was Martin Windsor's administrative assistant, Barnard Lansdale. I'd called his office the previous week and been advised he was out of town. His secretary promised to have him call me when he returned. Earlier in the day he had finally called and we'd set an appointment for later that afternoon. He insisted the meeting take place at our offices. Before the appointed hour Jodie advised me that Cheryl was on the line.

"The police are here searching my apartment," she moaned. "They're making a wreck of the place. What should I do?"

"Just let them do their job and don't interfere. I'll be right over."

It didn't surprise me that Detective Perkins was having Cheryl's house searched. I wondered what he'd find. I'd suggested to

Cheryl several days before that she might want to ditch the stuff she bought at The Spy Shop, but I doubted she had got around to doing it. I wasn't prepared, however, for what Perkins shoved in my face when I walked in the door. He was holding a gun in a plastic bag.

"Looks like me might have a murder weapon," Perkins gloated.

"I'm sure she has a license for it," I said. "It's not a crime to own a gun. Even President Reagan has one."

"Yeah, but this one's been fired recently. I wonder if your client wants to tell us about that?" Perkins retorted.

I took a deep breath. Perkins threats were beginning to worry me. He still didn't have a body, but with Cheryl being the last person seen with Martin, a big insurance policy, and a potential murder weapon, he and Wilkerson were getting close to having a viable case. "I'm sure she has a good explanation for it. But I'll have to get back with you on the question of filling you in on the details. Since you seem to be obsessed with blaming Martin Windsor's disappearance on her, it doesn't make much sense, at this point, to be overly cooperative."

"It's all right, Paula. We're going to nail her ass whether she cooperates or not. Trust me."

"Who's we? Do you already have an assistant DA assigned to the case?"

"Yes, your old friend Rob Wilkerson."

My stomach churned. I felt sick. "Oh, wonderful." I couldn't believe out of all the assistant DAs in the Dallas County District Attorney's office, I'd managed to get stuck with Wilkerson again. Wilkerson hated female attorneys and didn't make any effort to conceal it. His cocky, arrogant personality was particularly annoying and he was pretty much an asshole to anyone who wasn't on his side. I'd drawn him in my last big murder case when I'd defended a man accused of killing savings and loan tycoon Donald T. Baker. The case was aborted in mid-trial when my client was murdered, so I guess you'd say that round was a draw. Now he was back for round two. I was sure there'd be a betting pool at the DA's office, and he, no doubt, would be the odds on favorite.

To keep Cheryl out of jail and avoid another vicious battle

with Rob Wilkerson, I needed to locate Martin Windsor, or at least prove he was still alive. I was hoping Barnard Lansdale would shed some light on his whereabouts. He finally showed up just before five.

"Thank you for taking the time to talk to me," I said.

"I want to find Martin as badly as you do. I'll help any way I can."

"Good. How long have you been working for Mr. Windsor?"

"About five years now. My father and he were friends. That's how I heard about the job."

"What do you do for him, exactly?"

"Whatever he needs me to do. I'm kind of a troubleshooter. If we have a problem with one of our investments, I'm the one who is sent to straighten things out. I do a lot of research and due diligence work, as well, to make sure our investments are sound."

"When did you last see Martin?"

"Monday morning. He came in about eight o'clock and left for lunch about one. He usually takes about an hour and a half, so we were expecting him by two-thirty. When he hadn't shown up by five, we started looking for him."

"Where did he go for lunch?"

"He said he was meeting his divorce attorney. There were some papers he needed to sign so they were going to get a bite to eat and then go over them."

"Do you know where they were going to meet?"

"At the Prestonwood Country Club, I believe."

"So, no one has heard from Martin since he went to lunch on Monday?"

"Right. I called his attorney to ask if he knew where Martin was going after their meeting. He said that during the meeting Martin got a telephone call that upset him. He cut the meeting short and left without any explanation. He said he'd call back and reschedule the appointment, but he never did."

After talking with Lansdale, I went back to Cheryl's apartment to see if she'd remembered anything. Unfortunately, she hadn't. I desperately needed an explanation as to why her gun had been recently fired, but she had no recollection of firing it at all. If she was lying to me, I had to get her to come clean. I told her about the mounting evidence against her.

"Perkins has a witness that saw you at his house Monday afternoon and we know you must have been there because of the surveillance equipment in the trunk of your car."

Cheryl shrugged. "I don't remember going to the house or seeing Martin, and I can't imagine why I'd be carrying a gun."

"Did it ever cross your mind that you'd be better off if Martin were dead?"

"No! Absolutely not!" Cheryl said, but her tone was not convincing. She sighed. "Okay, sure, the thought crossed my mind, but I'm not a murderer and I didn't kill Martin. I'm sure he's still alive. I can feel him out there watching me."

"Feel him?"

"Yeah, somehow Martin always knew what I was doing. I don't know if he had someone following me or we had developed some kind of psychic connection that allowed him to keep tabs on me. Whatever it was, I always felt that he was watching me." Cheryl looked around suspiciously. "I still feel that way, right now."

"Well, if you see him, or anyone suspicious, call me right away. In the meantime we've got to try to find you an alibi. What do you usually do on Mondays after you get your hair done?"

Cheryl thought for a moment and shrugged. "I usually run errands or go to the mall. It varies from week to week."

"You've got to try to figure out what you did Monday afternoon. Perhaps there are people who saw you and could provide an alibi."

"I wish I could remember, but my mind is a complete blank."

"Do you have your checkbook?"

"Why? Do I owe you some money?"

"No, look through the register and see if you wrote any checks on Monday."

Cheryl left to find her checkbook. As much as I hated to question a client's integrity, I was beginning to wonder if Cheryl didn't have something to hide. She came back with her checkbook and started flipping through the pages.

"Monday was September 10. Let me see. I wrote a check to

Southwestern Bell, TXU Gas, and apparently cashed one at Kroger for fifty dollars."

"Good. Maybe someone at Kroger will remember you coming in. Which Kroger?"

Cheryl suddenly became pale and her mouth fell open. "Two blocks from Martin's house."

"So you were within two blocks of the house on Monday. Did you remember having the gun with you in the car?"

"No. I don't remember the gun, cashing the check, or anything. Monday afternoon is a complete blank."

"Well, you're definitely not talking any more to Perkins and you won't be testifying if you end up going on trial for this."

"Trial? Do you think they'll arrest me?"

"To be honest with you, it's only a matter of time. If there was a body, you'd already be in custody. Perkins just wants to be sure Martin is dead. He'd be humiliated if he got you indicted and then Martin suddenly surfaced."

"I can't go to jail, Paula," Cheryl sobbed. "I've got children to take care of. You've got to do something. Find Martin. He can't be dead. I didn't kill him! I know I didn't kill him! I'm not that kind of a person. . . . You've got to help me."

"Okay, relax. If you did kill him, it might have been self defense. You may be suffering from traumatic amnesia. It's very common."

"What happens if it turns out I did kill Martin?"

"Then we'll just have to hope there was a good reason for it."

Chapter 10

Physical Evidence

The day after our visit to Cactus Island, I stopped by the campus of the University of Texas at Dallas where an acquaintance of mine, Dr. Bernard Walston, was a professor of geology. I wanted to show him my soil sample and have him analyze it. He was in class so I had to wait in his office for twenty minutes until it was over. While I was waiting, I couldn't help but notice he had a copy of the *Globe Inquirer* which featured the Steven Caldwell murder case and the alien landings on Cactus Island. I wondered if Dr. Walston was interested in UFO sightings or just this one in particular. When he returned from class, I asked him.

"When I told my teaching assistants that you were coming over to see me, one of them brought me this newspaper. I must say it was very amusing."

"Amusing? So you're not a believer?"

"No, not really," he chuckled, "but I have an open mind. Show me some proof and I'll become a fanatic just like all those people camping out at Possum Kingdom Lake right now."

"Okay. That's precisely why I'm here."

I handed the professor a bag which contained my soil sample from the surface of Cactus Island and asked him to analyze it for me. He agreed and said it would take a couple days to complete the task. He also suggested I not get my hopes up. From a cursory examination it looked like ordinary top soil.

When I got back to the office I called Susan Weber's mother and asked her if could talk to her daughter. I needed to get the full particulars around the breakup between her and Steven. This was a critical element of the DA's case and I needed to get Susan's take on the situation. Later that afternoon I dropped by her house and her mother showed me into the living room. When I saw Susan for the first time, my heart sank. She was a slim brunette with big brown eyes that I could easily see two teenage boys fighting over. When the jury saw her in tight jeans and a tank top, Steven's motive would be as clear as a glass of distilled water. The DA would argue that Steven couldn't stand the idea of losing Susan and set out to eliminate his competition.

"Hi, Susan. Thanks for agreeing to talk to me. I know it's only been a short time since Jimmy's death. I apologize for having to bother you about this now, but memories fade in time and it's important I know exactly what happened between you and Steven."

"It's okay. I understand," Susan replied softly.

"You've no doubt heard that the Palo Pinto County DA is alleging that the car wreck that killed Jimmy wasn't an accident."

Susan nodded, "Uh huh. I heard that."

"What do you think about that? You know Steven pretty well. Do you think he's capable of murder?"

"I don't know. It's hard to believe he'd do that, but he was pretty mad."

"Mad over your breakup?"

"Yes. He's very hardheaded," she said in an affectionate tone of voice. "He wouldn't accept the fact that it was over between us. He called me every day pleading for a second chance."

"I thought you two had drifted apart after Steven went off to college."

"We had, and Steven seemed okay with it until Jimmy and I began dating. I guess he got jealous and started having second thoughts about our breakup."

"How did you feel about ending the relationship with Steven?"

"It was hard at first but I got over him pretty quickly. I realize now I didn't love him. Jimmy was a lot more fun to be around."

"Did Steven ever threaten Jimmy, to your knowledge?"

She shrugged and looked away. After a moment she said, "Well, there was one time at our high school football game. I'd gone with Jimmy, but I ran into Steven during halftime. He wanted to take me to IHOP when the game was over. Of course, I said no. We were arguing about it when Jimmy showed up. He told Steven to get lost. Steven told him to mind his own business and continued arguing with me. That's when Jimmy grabbed Steven's arm."

"What happened then?"

"Steven looked at Jimmy and then back at me. He pulled his arm away from Jimmy's grasp and said, 'This isn't over, Jimmy. This isn't over by a longshot.' Then he stormed off."

"And that's the only time you know of that Jimmy and Steven ever fought over you?"

"Uh huh. That's the only time I can think of."

"So, does it surprise you that Steven and Jimmy were riding together in the Jeep the day of the accident?"

"Yes, a little, but Jimmy didn't have a problem with Steven so much. He knew it was over between us, so he wasn't jealous or anything like that. If Steven had just left me alone, Jimmy would have treated him just like anybody else."

"So what do you think about Steven's story about the spaceship?"

She rolled her eyes. "Steven has been known to exaggerate things. It's just his personality. UFOs have always fascinated him, so it doesn't surprise me that he'd say something like that. He was probably just trying to think of an excuse for the accident and that's the first thing that came to mind."

"So, you don't believe?"

"In aliens? No. It may have been an accident, but I doubt there were any aliens involved."

We continued to talk but nothing new came up before I finally got up to leave. I thanked Susan and her mom and left. It had been an interesting meeting and I felt I understood much better what had gone on between Steven, Susan, and Jimmy. It was also apparent to me that Susan didn't really believe Steven was a murderer, although she didn't come right out and say it. But I was bothered by the fact that Steven had told Jimmy that it wasn't over. I could just hear the DA reciting that little threat over and over again so the jury couldn't possibly forget it.

When I got back to the office Jodie told me Paula had been looking for me, so I went into her office.

She had a long face. "Hi, how did your interview go?"

"Fine. I learned what I need to know," I said. "It could have been worse."

"My day was a disaster," Paula moaned.

Paula briefed me on the evidence that was piling up against Cheryl Windsor and her total lapse of memory. She asked me if I thought hypnosis was an option.

"No. Not in your case. If your client is guilty, you don't want to know it. Innocent or guilty, you still have to defend her as best you can. If you find out that she's guilty your enthusiasm for her case could be dampened and she may end up being short-changed on her defense."

"I'm not so sure. If I know she is guilty I'll want to push for a plea bargain. Without a body their case is shaky at best. The DA may be quite reasonable."

"That's true. But first you better see how she feels about a plea bargain. If she's the slightest bit interested, we'll get her to a good therapist. Let's use the one that worked with us in the Sarah Winters' case, Norman Gerhardt. He is the best in the business."

Dr. Gerhardt had been very useful to me in my first murder case. Sarah Winters had been accused of killing her baby but she had no memory of even having a child. After being hypnotized several times she was able to piece together the night of her delivery and ultimately we were able to prove her innocence.

"I'll talk to her about it and see what she wants to do. I just wish I knew what happened to Martin. It's so strange that he disappeared the way he did. I can't believe Cheryl had anything to do with it, yet every day new evidence turns up pointing to Cheryl as the most likely suspect."

"I know how you feel," I said. "I can't believe Steven Caldwell is a killer either, yet the evidence keeps mounting against him as well. I guess we need to invest in a time machine so we can go back and see what actually happened."

"Yeah. Wouldn't that be handy?"

That night I dreamed over and over about Jimmy and Steven's confrontation at the football game. '*This isn't over, Jimmy. Not by a longshot. This isn't over, Jimmy. Not by a longshot. This isn't over, Jimmy. Not by a longshot.'* Each time Steven said this, I saw an image of him standing on the edge of the road at Possum Kingdom Lake looking down at the half-submerged Jeep. After he spoke these words, he turned and glared at me with blood red eyes and a demonic smile. I was bothered so much by the dream my tossing and turning woke up Rebekah.

The next day Dr. Walston called. He said the soil sample I'd brought him hadn't been adequate to establish anything conclusive. He wanted permission to send some of his students out to view the site, take photos, and bring back some more samples. I asked him if the sample I had brought him had told him anything at all.

"Well, yes. Your soil sample was quite interesting, actually."

"Really?" I said, feeling uplifted by his enthusiastic response.

"Yes. There was no trace of organic matter in the sample, which is unusual. This could have resulted from some sort of combustion or chemical residue left by an aircraft landing and taking off there. There was some evidence of iron, but the iron was not accompanied by chromium, manganese or nickel as would be the case if it were a steel residue. We found some evidence of polymers and traces of phosphate and zinc. These traces, which were visible as striations, may have been produced by a combination of mechanical and thermal effects."

"So, you think some kind of spacecraft landed there?"

"Something heavy landed there. I don't know if it was a spaceship, but visual and microscopic examination revealed that, apart from the striations, the soil had been compacted without major heating, since the structure of calcium carbonates was not affected."

"What does that mean?"

"Well, in the nutshell, whatever landed there was very heavy and compacted the soil causing the large crater or saucer shape on the surface of the island that you described to me. When the aircraft took off its combustion penetrated the soil killing all organic matter and leaving the chemical residue that I mentioned."

"So, something landed there and took off, but you don't know what it was?"

"Right, I'll need a lot more data to convince anyone a

spacecraft landed there."

"I'll call the sheriff and arrange for you to have access to the island."

"Good. My students are very excited about this project. In fact, I haven't seen them so enthusiastic about an assignment since I've been a professor here. I want to thank you for bringing this to me."

"Listen. I'm just glad you didn't throw me out of your office when I came by to show it to you."

He laughed. "Well, the thought occurred to me, but I've learned over the years that it's wise to keep an open mind."

"So, is there anything else you can tell me at this point?"

"Well, from what you told me, whatever visited Cactus Island took off and landed like a helicopter. There weren't any wheel or tire tracks, were there?"

"No, I didn't see anything like that. The entire area looked like it had been carefully graded to be a shallow tank or a pond."

"Well, the evidence so far indicates this is no ordinary soil. A bulldozer could level the land, but it couldn't have altered the molecular structure of the soil."

"Do you know if the Air Force or any private company has anything that could take off vertically and impact the soil the way it did?"

"No," Dr. Walston replied. "I did a quick check of all known aircraft and there isn't anything that even comes close."

Chapter 11

Parr Heating & Air

It had been two weeks since Martin Windsor's disappearance, yet I wasn't any closer to finding him. Apparently the Dallas Police Department hadn't been having much luck either. Detective Besch called to tell me that the FBI had been called in. Perkins apparently felt Windsor may have been kidnapped or killed as the result of his involvement in money laundering or drug trafficking. Perkins had been scrutinizing Martin's complicated business structure and had decided he was in over his head.

This was good news for Cheryl, because it meant the authorities were looking for other suspects. But it was also bad news, since it meant her community property could be tied up in court for years, and eventually forfeited if Martin had been involved in illegal activities. As I was pondering this new development, Jodie walked in and handed me a video tape.

"What's this?" I asked.

"I found this in the VCR. I guess Cheryl Windsor must have left it there."

"Oh, right. Hmm. We only watched forty-five minutes of it. I wonder what's on the rest of it."

"You want me to watch it?" Jodie asked.

I thought about Jodie's offer for a moment and almost took her up on it, but then decided she might not know if she saw something important. "Thanks, but I think I'd better do it. I appreciate your offer, though."

"No problem. Let me know if there is anything I can do. You know I like a little excitement once in a while."

I thought for a moment. "Actually, there is something you can do."

"Really. That's great. What is it?"

"How would you like to take a trip to Tobago?"

Jodie's eyes lit up. "Are you serious?"

"Yes, according to his secretary, Martin Windsor was thinking about going down there before he disappeared. One of his resort managers disappeared recently and he wanted to investigate what had happened and why the board of directors was having trouble replacing the manager. I've been wondering if Mr. Windsor might have taken that trip after all."

"So, you want me to check in at the resort and keep an eye out for Martin?"

"Yes, and bring a camera in case you spot him. We'll need pictures to convince Perkins Martin is alive."

"If I see him, do you want me to make contact?"

"No, I don't know what's going on with Mr. Windsor, so it's best not to approach him directly. I wouldn't want to put your life in danger. Just keep your eyes and ears open and let me know if you see anything unusual."

"Okay. When should I leave?"

"You should get an early flight tomorrow. It's a very long journey. You should be there by late afternoon. Call me when you get settled in at the resort."

"Great. This is exciting. Thank you, Paula."

It wasn't likely that Jodie would find Martin at the Cocos Bay Resort in Tobago, but even so the trip was a good idea for intelligence-gathering purposes. Since Cheryl would most likely be awarded some of Martin Windsor's investments, the more we knew about them the better. I particularly wanted to know if anything was going on down there other than entertaining tourists.

Bart had to work late that night so I went home early, ordered some Chinese take-out, and curled up on the sofa to watch Martin Windsor walk around his house for eight hours. It was probably a waste of time, but on the slim chance it might produce a clue to his whereabouts, I had to endure the agony.

After fast forwarding through several hours of inactivity, Martin came home and immediately got on the telephone. I could only hear one side of the conversation but it sounded like he was arranging a meeting with someone for that evening. Thirty minutes later he left. When he returned, he went to the front door, opened it, and a man in blue overalls came in. The patch on his uniform read Parr Heating & Air. The man carried a tool kit which he set down in the living room and then appeared to adjust the thermostat. Thirty seconds later he disappeared from the camera's view. I heard water running in the background and then the TV came on. There were voices and laughter.

Fifteen minutes later two men walked into the living room. The second man was taller and thinner than the first, but with his back turned I couldn't see his face. What were these men doing in Martin Windsor's house? Were they robbing him or were they friends waiting for Martin to return? When the second man finally turned toward the camera, I nearly choked on my fried rice. It was the man I'd seen in the elevator at Martin's office building, the man who'd vanished into thin air in the elevator only to suddenly reappear behind me. Who was this man and what was he doing in Martin Windsor's house?

Excited about what I'd seen on the tape, I called Cheryl to see if she could get together to look at the video tape. She agreed to come by the office in the morning. I was hoping she'd know the identity of the mysterious man. While I was talking to her on the telephone, I kept an eye on the video. Suddenly, I heard the front door open and Martin came into view. He didn't seem concerned about the two men in his house; in fact, they all acted like they were best friends—hugging each another, shaking hands, laughing, and messing around like fraternity brothers. It was a strange scene that I wanted desperately to understand.

When Bart got home, I showed him the tape and asked him for his take on what was going on. He was as mystified as I was but suggested Martin Windsor might be gay. That idea had occurred to me too, but I had dismissed it. Cheryl had told me about their active sex life and had bragged that Martin was an incredible lover. There had to be some other significance to the behavior of these three men and I was determined to figure it out.

The next day I called the Secretary of State's office to find out about Parr Heating and Air, Inc. It had been incorporated the previous year and listed a Raymond Sinclair as the registered agent.

I noted the address listed for the principal office of the corporation. It looked familiar. Then I realized it was Martin Windsor's home address. Why would Martin Windsor be running a heating and air-conditioning business out of his home?

When Cheryl showed up to look at the video, I filled her in on what I'd learned. She said she'd never heard of Parr Heating and Air, Inc. and had no idea why her husband would be running a company like that. I shook my head in dismay. It seemed with every new piece of information, came more and more questions. But I needed answers, not more questions, and I needed them soon. Cheryl's freedom depended on it.

Chapter 12

Two Critical Minutes

Steven was reluctant to go under hypnosis. He had read stories about how some unethical doctors had taken advantage of their patients by putting them under hypnosis and then instructing them to do something embarrassing or illegal. I told him that couldn't happen because a therapist could not make a person do something against their will. Then I assured him that Dr. Gerhardt was a renowned professional and would not do anything to hurt him in any way.

During the twenty-minute drive to Dr. Gerhardt's clinic in Plano, Texas I told Steven how the trial would proceed. "First we'll have to pick a jury, which will be very difficult due to the press coverage associated with your case. It's important that each juror be fair and impartial, but that might be difficult if they've been reading or hearing a lot about your case in the media or discussing it with family and friends. Most people quickly form opinions and beliefs that could impact their jury service, so the attorneys are allowed to question them about their backgrounds, employment, and beliefs or any other issue that might influence their service on the jury. Then if it turns out they can't be fair and impartial, we'll ask the judge to strike them."

Steven nodded. "How long do you think it will take to pick a jury?"

"I don't know. Usually it takes a day or two, but in a case like this it might be a week or better."

There was just one patient in Dr. Gerhardt's office when we arrived and he was leaving. The receptionist gave Steven a patient information sheet to fill out. Before he had it completed, Dr. Gerhardt came out to greet us.

"So, this is Steven, the young man I've been reading about

in the newspaper," he said.

"Yes, this is Steven Caldwell."

They shook hands and Dr. Gerhardt said, "It's a pleasure to meet you Steven."

"Steven's had a difficult couple of weeks so he's a little nervous."

"Ah! Don't be nervous. I won't bite you, I promise." He motioned toward the door, "Let's go back to the treatment room."

Dr. Gerhardt led us through the door and down a hall to a room that looked more like a study than a doctor's office. There was a desk, two side chairs, a sofa, an easy chair, a lamp, and a coffee table. Beautiful paintings adorned the walls and a bookcase held dozens of volumes of medical books and periodicals. He sat in one of the easy chairs and told Steven to sit on the sofa.

"Now, Steven, Mr. Turner tells me you can't remember what happened the night of the accident."

Steven nodded. "Well, I can remember some of it but not all."

"Tell me what you remember."

"Okay, well . . . ah, Jimmy and I were driving back to camp. I was driving a little too fast and as we were making the last turn before the camp entrance I heard a low-pitched hissing sound from above. I looked up and saw a gigantic object right above me moving slowly toward the lake. When I looked back at the road we were so close to the edge there was nothing I could do. The next thing I remember is waking up on the side of the road."

"How did you feel when you woke up?"

"Dizzy. Exhausted. Wondering what had happened. I remember looking around for the Jeep and smelling smoke. I struggled to my feet and edged toward the side of the mountain. The Jeep was sticking out of the water with its tail on fire. Then I heard a car approaching from behind me. It was a lady. She made me get in the backseat of her car and then we went for help."

"So, you're missing a couple of minutes, it sounds like."

"Yes, a very critical couple of minutes," I said.

Dr. Gerhardt got up and pulled a side chair next to where Steven was sitting. "Well, let's see if we can fill in the gap."

Dr. Gerhardt explained how hypnosis worked and told Steven to lie back on the sofa and relax. He asked me to dim the lights and then he removed a small pen light from his shirt pocket and told Steven to focus on it. He manipulated the light around Steven's eyes. "Now your eyes are getting heavy. They feel so, so heavy. You can barely keep them open. Now I'm going to count to ten and you're going to be back at Possum Kingdom Lake. It will be Monday the 10th of September 1990. You remember that date, don't you? It was the day of the tragic accident when Jimmy was killed. Now when we're finished reliving what happened that day, I'll count to three and tell you to wake up. When you wake up you will remember everything you just recalled. Okay?"

Steven took a deep breath barely able to keep his eyes opened. "Yes," he replied softly.

Dr. Gerhardt counted to ten slowly while he continued to manipulate the light around Steven's eyes. When he finished counting, Steven's eyes closed. "Are you there? Tell me what you see, Steven."

"Yes, I see it. It's dark and stormy. The road is very slick. I'm driving fast trying to impress Jimmy. He looks scared but forces a smile. I've driven this road a hundred times and this Jeep handles like a dream."

"Good. Very good," Dr. Gerhardt said. "Now, look around you. Tell me everything you see."

"It's daytime but it's dark from the thick clouds. It's hard to see much of anything but every few seconds a bolt of lightning lights up the sky just long enough to get a glimpse of what's around us. I'm making the turn now . . . Oh! What's that noise? . . . It's a loud, rattling, metallic sound from above me. I'm looking up and there's a— . . . What the hell? It looks almost like a spaceship. . . . Look at that, Jimmy. What is that?. . . Ah, shit! A blue light just exploded in my face. . . . I'm blinded! . . . I can't see a damn thing. The noise is like fifty pieces of chalk being scraped across a blackboard at the same time. 'What the hell is that noise, Jimmy? Oh, God! It's killing my ears. I can't stand it! Ahhhh!"

Steven held his hands over his ears and then began to toss and turn as if his eardrums were about to break. Dr. Gerhardt grabbed his hands and said, "All right, Steven. That's enough for now. On the count of three I'm going to snap my fingers and you're going to wake up. One. . . . Two . . . Three. *Snap!*"

Steven's body suddenly went limp. Dr. Gerhardt took his pulse and felt his forehead. Suddenly, Steven jerked, his eyes opened, and he looked around, seemingly disoriented. After a couple seconds he asked, "What happened?"

Dr. Gerhardt stood up and walked back to the easy chair. He asked, "Think back. Don't you remember what happened after you saw the object in the sky?"

Steven hesitated, still appearing groggy. "Yes, I remember the flash of blue light and that horrible piercing sound. I thought my eardrums were going to break."

"What happened after you heard the noise?" Dr. Gerhardt asked.

"That's all I remember. The blue lights and holding my ears trying to endure the pain. I must have passed out then, because I don't remember holding the wheel of the Jeep after that moment. Then I woke up on the side of the road."

"Well, you did very well, Steven. These things take time. If you come back next week, maybe we can recover another minute of your life—an interesting minute, no doubt."

"Yes, that would be cool. Thank you, Doctor."

"My pleasure. Stan, your boy did very well."

I said, "Definitely. Thanks a lot, Doctor. I really appreciate your help."

On the ride back we talked about the blue light and the intense, debilitating sound. We agreed that the flash of light and the horrible noise probably caused Steven to lose control of the Jeep, but we still had no explanation of how he ended up on the side of the road. I couldn't wait for our next session. An interesting minute, indeed—probably the most important minute of Steven Caldwell's young life.

Chapter 13

Cocos Bay

Jodie called me from the airport to tell me she had landed in Port of Spain, Trinidad. It had been a long flight via Miami and then Aruba and it had taken her quite a while to get through customs, find her luggage, and get a cab to the harbor. She indicated she was about to board a boat to the resort as it was on a separate island from the capital city. I cautioned her to be very discreet and not to let anyone know why she was there. We had randomly picked a travel agent out of the telephone book so there would be no way anyone could trace Jodie to the firm. She was even using her maiden name to make it doubly difficult for anyone to check her out.

After I hung up, I immediately started to have second thoughts about Jodie's assignment. What if she was a little too obvious in her spying? After all, she wasn't a trained private investigator. When I went into Stan's office to tell him that she had arrived safely, I mentioned my concern.

"Don't worry about Jodie," Stan said confidently. "She loves this kind of assignment and is very good at it. She knows how to be discreet. You saw how well she worked on the Dusty Thomas case."

Jodie had been with Stan since he started his law practice and she was more than just a secretary. Being very efficient at her job, Stan couldn't always keep her busy with ordinary secretarial work. As smart as she was she also got bored easily, so he started letting her do legal research, question witnesses, and perform investigative work. She was taking night classes at the University of Texas at Dallas where she was now a senior. After she graduated, she hoped to go to law school at SMU and continue to work for the firm until she graduated and became an attorney. Stan often told clients proudly that Jodie would be an attorney for the firm one day.

Since I'd known Jodie, I had become very fond of her too. She was a big help in planning my wedding and was someone I could talk to woman to woman. Although she was younger than I, Jodie was very mature and seemed to understand me more than anyone else I knew, other than Bart and Stan, of course. We had one big thing in common too—our love and concern for Stan. I say concern because Stan was so selfless and trusting of his clients that in the past many of them had taken advantage of him. That's why Jodie and I vowed not to ever let that happen again.

When I first came to the firm, I hired a temporary secretary but when he quit I didn't replace him because Jodie was so efficient she handled all our work without much trouble. When Jodie was sick, on vacation or on assignment we hired a temporary receptionist just to answer the phone and keep the filing up to date until Jodie returned. In the past the temp agency we used had sent us a girl named Brenda Watkins. She was great on the phone and didn't complain about the massive amount of filing there was to do each day, so we always asked for her.

When I got back to my office, Brenda's voice came on the intercom. "Detective Perkins is on line two."

A burst of adrenaline jerked me from my meditation. I had been dreading this telephone call. It could mean only one thing—more bad news.

"So, what's up?" I asked.

"Just wanted to update you," Perkins said gleefully. "Although there were no fingerprints on the gun, we found the blouse she was wearing when she fired the gun. It was at her cleaners. Even after it had been cleaned, we found a powder residue on it."

"So. . . . Have you found a body yet?"

"No, but along with the gun and the surveillance equipment we have just about all we need."

"She was using the surveillance equipment to get ammo for her divorce."

"I understand, but divorces are expensive and can drag on for months or years. Killing your husband and then hiring someone to dispose of the body is a much more expeditious solution."

"Give me a break. She didn't hire someone to dispose of her husband's body."

"Well, it makes sense. It's difficult and messy to get rid of a body. Why not hire professionals? Anyway, we've got a witness who saw her with two men leaving Mr. Windsor's house on Monday evening. They were wearing work uniforms and left in a van. The witness says he heard arguing inside the house."

"What? I don't believe that."

"It's true. I don't bluff. In due time I'll give you their identities and contact information so you can talk to them."

"Okay, is that it?"

"That's enough. The DA has authorized us to pick up your client."

"What! You still don't have a body."

"Like I said, we have enough. You'll need to bring in Cheryl in the next few hours or we'll send someone out to arrest her."

"Don't bother. Can I bring her in tomorrow morning at nine?"

"No, I said a few hours. Get her in here by nine tonight."

"She's got children, for godsakes. Give her some time to make arrangements for someone to take care of them."

Perkins sighed. "Okay, tomorrow morning at eight. Not a minute later."

"Good. Thanks for the call."

News of more witnesses claiming to have seen Cheryl at Martin's house on the day of his disappearance was devastating. It might be possible to discredit one witness, but if two or three were paraded before the jury it would be nearly impossible to overcome such testimony, particularly if the defendant didn't testify. Reluctantly, I picked up the telephone and called Cheryl to give her the bad news. She took it better than I expected. I told her I would call our bondsman and we would arrange the bond before we took her in. That way she'd only be spending a few hours in jail. She agreed to be ready at seven the following morning.

After I hung up with Cheryl, I called our bondsman and filled him in on Cheryl's impending arrest. He said he'd contact her to get financial information to secure the bond. A few hours later he called to tell me we had a problem. Because of the divorce and Martin's disappearance, there wasn't enough available collateral to fund a bond more than $100,000. In a murder case it was likely the bond would be much higher. That would mean Cheryl would have to remain in jail until her trial. As I began preparations for Cheryl's arraignment, I prayed hard that I could convince the judge that $100,000 would be an adequate bond.

Chapter 14

Corroborating Witnesses

The following week I decided to see if I could track down the two fishermen who'd been out with Doc Verner on Possum Kingdom Lake years back when he saw the spaceship land on Cactus Island. I called the two telephone numbers, but as I suspected, neither was good anymore. My next move was to check the telephone books to see if either man was listed. They weren't.

I had to go to a bankruptcy hearing one afternoon so, when I was done, I stopped by the Records Building to research the deed records. I had two addresses, so I checked the chain of title on both of the properties. The first fisherman was Earl Bullard. The records indicated he'd sold his house eight years earlier. The second fisherman was Jerry Kinder. When I pulled the records on his property, I was shocked to see that he still owned the place in Richardson, Texas. On the way home I went over there hoping to catch him at home. Unfortunately, he wasn't living there anymore, but the tenant was kind enough to give me his new address in Allen, Texas. Allen was out of my way, but I decided to go there anyway since I'd already wasted most of the afternoon.

Jerry Kinder was in his sixties and walked with a limp. He looked at my business card suspiciously and then invited me inside. He brightened when I explained that I was representing Steven Caldwell. "Oh, you're defending that boy who seen the flying saucer."

"Well, he saw something and that's why I'm here. I understand you saw something out a Possum Kingdom Lake yourself."

Kinder gave me another suspicious look. "How'd you hear about that?"

"Well, Doc Verner mentioned it."

"Ah, Doc Verner. Haven't thought of that old geezer in a

coon's age. I reckon he was the worst fishing guide I've ever hired. It figures he'd spill his guts. That man won't keep his flap shut for minute."

"So, what did you see?"

"Well, I don't rightly know what we seen. A terrible storm come up and nearly capsized us. Old Doc's not a very good seaman anyway, so when the storm come up he panicked."

"Really? So, what did you do?"

"You know. I don't exactly remember. I must have passed out. When I woke up, we were adrift in the lake."

"Hmm. What about the blue lights?"

"I don't know what that was," Jerry said, "some kind of crazy lightning, I reckon. You know, when there's dust in the air it can create all kinds of different colors. I imagine that's what that blue light was."

"Did you see something else in the sky?"

"Well, I know Doc thought we saw a spaceship but I'm not sure what it was. Coulda just been a cloud or a weather balloon. I never believed in spaceships and all that stuff so I can't say that's exactly what we saw. It could have been something entirely different."

"You did see something, though?"

He nodded, "I did. But like I say, I don't know what it was. I will say it was big, very big and moved across the sky very quickly."

"Did you hear a noise while the craft, or whatever it was, went by?"

"There was some kind of godawful, piercing noise. I remember that. I don't know what caused it, but it started during the storm."

"Could it have been the spacecraft?"

He shrugged. "I don't know. It was dark and we were very scared. There were times I didn't think we were going to make it off the lake alive."

"Did you take any pictures?"

"No, but Earl did," Jerry replied.

"Earl Bullard?"

"Yes, he's a good friend. We go way back."

"Do you know where I can find him?"

"Sure, he lives in Red Oak just south of Dallas. I've got his address if you need it."

"Yes, I would like to talk to him."

"He'll tell you just about the same thing I did."

"Doc Verner said you guys took off immediately after you returned to the marina and wouldn't talk to him about what had happened."

Jerry sighed. "Well, he damn near got us killed, so we weren't real pleased with the guy. Plus he was going on and on about seeing that there spaceship. We just didn't want to be around when he started spouting off about it."

"I can understand that. I know it's a lot to ask, but would you consider testifying about what you saw out on the lake that night?"

Jerry's eyes narrowed. "Well, I'd rather not. I don't want folks thinking I'm crazy."

"No, just tell it like you told it to me. Nobody's going to think any less of you because you had a strange experience on Possum Kingdom Lake. Weird things happen to just about everyone at one time or another."

"Well, I suppose, but I can't guarantee what I say will be of any help to your client."

"That's okay. All I want is the truth."

After Jerry reluctantly agreed to testify, he volunteered to go with me to see if his friend Earl would do the same. He called to make sure Earl was at home and then told me to follow him there. I got directions in case we got separated, which was good because he drove fast and I lost him at the first light signal. Forty-five minutes later I drove up in front of Earl Bullard's home. Earl and Jerry were talking on the front porch when I walked up. Earl was a big man with a red face and full beard. He smiled exuberantly when he saw me. Jerry introduced us.

"So, how's your case coming, Mr. Turner? I've been following it in the newspaper and on TV."

"I don't know. It's a pretty tricky case. Not too many people are buying Steven's story about the spacecraft. I've got to either

completely embrace that defense or come up with something entirely
different. I'm not sure what to do yet."

"You should believe your client," Earl said.

Earl's statement surprised me. Was he humoring me or just
playing along for fun? He seemed sincere, so I proceeded with
guarded optimism.

"So, you do believe that you and Jerry saw a spaceship?" I
asked.

He nodded. "You know, when it happened I was skeptical,
but in thinking about it over the years I'm convinced now it was a
spaceship."

"What made you change your mind?"

"Well, right after it happened I couldn't really remember
much. I was just happy to be alive. So I tried to shake off the whole
thing just like it had been a nightmare. But the next day I got curious
and checked with the weather bureau. They claimed there hadn't
been a storm on the lake that night and that there had only been a
light breeze from the south all day. That got me to thinking."

"But you have no memory of the spacecraft?"

"Well, I remember seeing something glide quickly across the
sky, but I can't seem to visualize it now."

"Jerry said you have photographs from that day?"

"Well, I should have had a full roll of pictures, but the film
was destroyed during the storm."

"You're kidding? Every photo?"

"Yes, not only the film but the camera as well."

"What do you mean?"

"The film didn't just get exposed, it melted right in the
camera and the gooey mess it left ruined it."

"Wow. That's weird, do you still have the camera?"

"No. I tossed it years ago."

"Too bad. I would have liked to have it examined."

This was all very interesting and Earl and Jerry seemed to
have some credibility, but I wasn't sure a jury would believe them.
There had to be more. "Is there anything else that makes you think
you saw an alien spacecraft that day?" Jerry looked at Earl and
raised his eyebrows. Earl shrugged.

Earl said, "Well, another odd thing was we both had burns on our left wrists."

"Burns?"

"Yes, apparently from the steel casing of our watches. Aside from the pain in our wrists, we noticed our watches had stopped at the same time. We took them to the jewelers for repair and the technician told us the batteries had exploded and the mechanism had been fried."

"I don't suppose you have the watches?"

"No, sorry."

"Is there a chance you were hit by lightning?" I asked.

"Maybe, that idea has occurred to us, but remember there wasn't a cloud in the sky according to the weather bureau."

"Right. Over the years have you told anyone about all this?"

"Just family. My grandchildren love for me to tell them about it, but I'm sure they just think it's a fisherman's tall tale."

"So, you haven't told any newspapermen or sold the story to the tabloids?"

"No, we don't know for sure what happened out there, so we agreed it would be best kept a secret."

"Well, how do you feel about going public with it now? It would really give Steven Caldwell a boost if you two would just tell a jury the same thing you told me."

"Before you got here, Jerry told me you had asked him to testify, so we were talking about that possibility when you drove up. In the past I would have declined, but now that Steven Caldwell and others have seen what we saw, the situation is different. Now might be the right time to tell our story."

I smiled gleefully. "That's great. Steven's a good kid. I know he's innocent and your testimony could help ensure he won't go to prison."

We talked a few more minutes, I got all the pertinent information from them so that I could contact them when it came time for trial, and then I left. Although I was excited that they were going to cooperate, I felt a little dazed. Now I was almost compelled to go ahead with Steven's seemingly ridiculous excuse that he lost control of the Jeep because he was distracted by an alien spacecraft.

I visualized myself before the jury explaining what had happened that fateful night, twelve men and women listening intently to my every word. Then one of the members of the jury cracked a smile and started to laugh. A lady in the gallery giggled. I glared out at her. Then another juror's laughter couldn't be contained. Soon everyone, including the judge, was laughing hysterically. I shook my head trying to dispel the image. How could I possibly pull this off?

Chapter 15

Setting Bond

Our bondsman Roger Rand met me at the foot of the stairs to the Dallas City Jail. He apologized again for having to limit the bond to one hundred thousand dollars. I told him he'd probably go home empty handed. I couldn't see Judge Richard Abbott letting Cheryl out for less than a quarter million. The judge shocked me, however.

"Well, since you don't have a body, Mr. Wilkerson, I'm reluctant to impose a large bond on Mrs. Windsor. Frankly, I'm surprised you've gone for an indictment this early. If I'm reading your pleadings correctly, it's been less than a month since Mr. Windsor disappeared."

"Yes, Your Honor," Wilkerson protested. "But we have a gun fired by the defendant on the day Mr. Windsor disappeared, and witnesses who will verify the defendant was the last person to see Mr. Windsor."

The judge leaned toward Wilkerson, his eyes narrowed. "Still, no body, right? And you want me to conjecture that this petite young lady was able to make a body disappear without a trace? How did she do that without her nosy neighbors seeing it?"

Wilkerson folded his arms and glared back at the judge. The two stared at each other for a moment and then the judge leaned back. "I'm setting bond at $50,000."

"Thank you, Your Honor," I said as I smiled gleefully at Wilkerson.

Wilkerson threw his file in his briefcase and stormed off. I congratulated Cheryl and told her we'd have her out of jail within the hour. She thanked me and then was led away by the bailiff. After she was out of sight, Roger and I left the courtroom and headed for the intake desk at the county jail to post Cheryl's bond. It was just a waiting game after that. The employees at the jail seemed to work in slow motion. There was no sense of urgency in their movement whatsoever. Two hours later I spotted Cheryl being led to the release desk. They handed her a bag with her personal belongings, made her sign a receipt, and then finally led her to a glass door. A buzzer sounded and the door opened.

I embraced Cheryl. "Sorry you had to go through that," I said.

"It's okay. Nobody bothered me," she replied. "Thanks for getting me out so quickly."

"Are you hungry? We can stop and get something to eat."

"No thanks," she said. "I just want to pick up the kids, go back to my apartment and take a bath. I feel dirty after being in that cell with all those drunks and homeless bitches."

I could sympathize. The Dallas City Jail was pretty old and dirty. The guests there were not the kind of people you wanted to hang around with either. I took Cheryl to get her kids and then took her home. On the way I told her about Jodie's trip to Tobago."

"That's a beautiful resort. Jodie will have a great time there."

"I hope she sees your husband."

"Me too. Wouldn't that piss off Wilkerson?"

"Yeah, he doesn't like you much."

"The feeling is mutual, believe me."

When I got back to the office, I got a call from Jodie. "This is a great place. You can send me here anytime," she said.

"So, have you seen our man?"

"No, a lot of people were expecting him, but they claim he never made it here."

"How did you find that out without telling them who you were?"

"I got chummy with one of the bartenders who knows everything that goes on here. He's cute too."

"Hmm. Be careful, Jodie."

"Oh, don't worry. I'm a big girl."

"Do they know about Martin's disappearance?"

"I don't think so. Jeff, the bartender, didn't mention it. He seems to expect Martin to show up at any time."

"Well. Did Jeff tell you why the manager quit?"

"No, that subject was a little too sensitive for the bartender. I'm not sure why, but I did find out from other sources that the manager didn't quit, he just didn't show up for work one day. The delay in replacing him seems to be due to the uncertainty as to what happened to him."

"Another missing person. That's very interesting. I wonder if there is a connection between the two men."

"I don't know."

"What was the manager's name?"

"Rubin Quinlin."

"Well, find out as much as you can about Mr. Quinlin. I'll call the local authorities there and see how the investigation is going. If we can show a connection between the two missing men that would be huge."

"Okay, I'll see you in a few days."

"Yeah, and don't forget this is an assignment. Don't come back with a great tan."

Jodie laughed. "Ah, you're a mean boss."

"Bye, Jodie. Be careful."

"I will. Piece of cake. Don't worry."

Don't worry. Right. That's all I seemed to be doing lately. Worrying about Jodie. Worrying about Cheryl. Worrying about Turner and Waters becoming the laughingstock of the legal community. I took a deep breath and tried to relax. The only thing that kept me from falling into a deep depression was the fact that the judge didn't seem to like Wilkerson's case very much. That was a sweet tune. I played back Wilkerson's annoyance with the judge's decision on the bond. I'd treasure the look of utter frustration on his face and his dramatic exit from the courtroom. That was a priceless memory that would help me through the tough days that I knew lay ahead. Several days later Jodie returned from Tobago. She hadn't seen Martin Windsor but she'd managed to acquire some valuable information that was bound to help us eventually locate him. I just hoped it wouldn't be too late.

Chapter 16

Mass Sighting
September 24, 1990

The image of laughing jurors made me rethink my trial strategy. I decided it would be wise to continue to develop a more traditional defense in addition to the alien spacecraft theory. There was no need to commit to one or the other until the last minute. Paula and I would have to evaluate the situation at the time of trial and make a decision based on what evidence we had been able to gather.

Steven's next appointment with Dr. Gerhardt was still a few days off, so I decided to check into the possibility that some sort of military aircraft had been flying over Possum Kingdom Lake on September 10, 1990. Dallas Naval Air Station was located not too far from Dallas, so I called out there and inquired if any of their aircraft might have been flying in that vicinity on that date. They declined to provide me that information over the phone so I made an appointment for the following week.

As I was hanging up the telephone, Jodie came rushing in. "Stan, you won't believe this. Someone just called to tell us that Channel 4 news is reporting that hundreds of people out at Possum Kingdom Lake just spotted an alien spacecraft!"

"What? Is it on the news now?"

"I think so."

We rushed into the conference room and turned on the television. Amy Tan was standing on the shore of Possum Kingdom Lake with Cactus Island prominently in the background. "Apparently a heavy thunderstorm went through here about an hour ago, and during the storm some sort of aircraft flew over Cactus Island. A lot of people saw it and believed they were seeing the same spacecraft that Steven Caldwell says caused his tragic accident three weeks ago. I have with me Laura Evans and Connie Marshall who are two of the witnesses who saw the craft just minutes ago."

Tan turned to the two women who looked to be in their twenties. "Laura, would you tell our listeners what you saw?"

Laura smiled at the camera. "Yes, it was so bizarre. We were cooking lunch over a fire and all of a sudden it got really dark like it was midnight. And uh, well, there was a bolt of lightning and then the wind got so strong it blew our tent clean off of the ground. There was stuff blowing everywhere and everyone was running for cover when I heard someone say, 'Look! Up in the sky.' "I looked up and there was some kind of aircraft gliding overhead going toward Cactus Island."

"Laura, could you describe the craft?"

"Well, it was so dark so, I'm not sure exactly, but I think it was dark green, thick, and shaped almost like a triangle."

"Was it an airplane?" Tan pressed.

"I don't think so. It wasn't like any airplane I've ever seen, but like I said, it was so dark and stormy I couldn't tell for sure."

What about you, Connie? What do you remember about the aircraft you just saw?

"It was huge—about the size of a baseball field," Connie replied. "It looked like a giant arrowhead."

The camera went back to Amy Tan. "So there you have it. Some sort of aircraft or maybe even an alien spacecraft, just flew over Possum Kingdom Lake, and this place is a buzz of excitement. Will this give credence to Steven Caldwell's claim that he was distracted by an alien spacecraft, perhaps the same one seen here tonight by hundreds of witnesses? Only time will tell. Now back to our studios."

Jodie turned off the TV. "Wow. What do think of that?"

I shook my head. "Jesus, just when the media attention is starting to die down, this shit happens. I can't believe it."

"What's wrong? I thought you'd be happy," Jodie said.

"No, I'm not. What happened tonight isn't necessarily relevant to what happened on September 10, and can you imagine how hard it's going to be to pick a jury now?"

Jodie shrugged. I turned to go back to my office when Paula walked in.

"You know what I just heard on the radio?"

I smiled. "Yeah, we just saw it on TV."

Paula shook her head. "I can't believe this. You know, I got a letter today from an inmate at Huntsville asking me to file a motion for a new trial because he's certain the evidence that convicted him was planted by men from Mars?"

Jodie chuckled. "It's not funny," Paula said. "We're the laughingstocks of the country."

"I don't know, Paula. Steven's defense is starting to shape up. I have three witnesses now who'll testify that back in 1958 they had a similar experience to Steven's. With what happened today, hell, we may have a viable defense."

"You should withdraw. Let Steven find local counsel in Palo Pinto County."

"Oh, come on. You know I can't do that."

"Well, it's going to be hell around here with two murder trials going on at once. How are we going to manage that?"

"I guess if we're sending Jodie out on foreign assignments, it's time to promote her to paralegal and hire a full-time secretary."

Jodie's eyes lit up. "Oh, wow. That's wonderful. No more typing or bookkeeping."

"Well, you certainly deserve it."

"Yes," Paula agreed. "A promotion is overdue. Stan and I will talk about your compensation too. Obviously, we'll have to give you a raise."

"We can get Paul Thayer to do any investigations we don't want to do ourselves and he can hire any help he needs."

"What about the media and all the fanatics who are starting to hang around? I had one following me around today," Paula said.

"Really? When did this start?" Stan asked.

"He was outside my apartment this morning in a blue Chevy Malibu," Paula replied. "I noticed him in my rearview mirror. He pulled out when I was about halfway down the street. I took two detours on the way to work just to be sure he was following me and sure enough he stuck to me like glue."

"I had someone following me too," Stan said. "I guess we'll have to have Paul provide us some security. No telling what one of these nut jobs might try."

"So, what do you want me to do?" Jodie asked.

I thought for a moment. "Well, I've made an initial inquiry with the military to see if any of their planes might have flown over Possum Kingdom Lake on the day of the accident. I've got an appointment at the Dallas Naval Air Station next week. You can take that for me and also check at Carswell Air Force Base in Ft. Worth. Ask them about today's incident as well. Check all the airports within 100 miles of Possum Kingdom Lake too, and see if anyone filed a flight plan that would have taken them over the lake on that day. Also ask them if they've seen any unusual aircraft coming or going lately."

Jodie nodded. "Fine, I'll get right on it."

I turned to Paula. "I'm sorry about this, but this case has a mind of its own. Every time I think I've got it under control weird stuff happens. Who would have thought—"

"I know it's not your fault. At least your defense seems to be getting stronger and stronger. My case is going the opposite direction."

"Maybe she's guilty," I said. "That's always a possibility."

"If she is, she's a damn fine actress," Paula said.

"If I can help in any way, let me know. In the meantime, show me the guy who's been following you. I'll call in his license number to Detective Besch and have him trace it."

Paula went to the window and pointed toward a blue Chevy parked at the side of the building across the street. I couldn't see the driver's face very well so I went into my closet and pulled out a pair of binoculars. I was able to see the license number on the car and get a look at the man inside. He was medium build, dark hair, and had a deadly serious expression on his face. Somehow I didn't think this man was hanging around out of curiosity. He obviously had an agenda.

Chapter 17

The Link

Another missing person in the Martin Windsor case intrigued me. There had to be a connection between the two disappearances. I did a little research on Trinidad and Tobago and discovered it was an old English colony that had been independent for only twenty or thirty years. The language of the island conveniently was English, so I called the American Embassy in the capital city, Port of Spain. The American diplomat who finally took my call agreed to check on who was handling the investigation into the disappearance of the manager of the Cocos Bay Resort, Rubin Quinlin. I was anxious to talk to him to see if there were any similarities in the cases.

Later that afternoon I got a call from Detective Shaw of the San Fernando Police Department who was the officer in charge of the investigation. He was a very polite man who spoke with an Indian accent. He seemed quite concerned with Rubin Quinlin's disappearance.

"You know, this has been the strangest case I think I've ever been assigned to investigate. I've interrogated every single person who had contact with Mr. Quinlin in the 72 hours before he was reported missing. But nobody has been able to tell me anything of value. He didn't tell anyone he was going anywhere. He didn't buy a ticket at the airport or charter a boat."

"Maybe he was kidnapped," I suggested.

"Yes, well, I thought of that, but there hasn't been a ransom demand. It doesn't make any sense at all."

"Were there any signs of a struggle or anything stolen?"

"No. In fact, Quinlin's suite was so perfectly clean that there wasn't a single strand of hair, no fingerprints, not even a spec of dust anywhere. Many of the hotel staff have told us that Mr. Quinlin was quite the ladies' man too, but there was not a trace of semen or sweat on the sheets, in the bathroom, or anywhere else in the room. Even the kitchen is so clean you could eat on the floor. There's not a particle of dirt or trace of any bacteria."

My heartbeat quickened as I listened to him talk. I had found the link between the disappearance of Martin Windsor and Rubin Quinlin. The signature of the perpetrator of the two crimes was to thoroughly clean the crime scene and erase all evidence that could tie them to the crime. But in their quest for perfection they had created the link that might ultimately bring them to justice. The only problem was that the link itself was not enough. It was just the beginning.

"Well, Detective. That's very interesting. You know. The crime scene up here was thoroughly cleaned as well. Our CSI team had never seen anything like it. They said whoever cleaned the place must have used chemicals and cleansing solutions that weren't on the market. My people had nothing in their files to explain how the kidnappers were able to clean the crime scene the way they did."

"This must be a professional job—maybe organized crime?"

"I suppose so. The FBI has been called in, which could be because of the possibility of kidnapping or because organized crime is involved. Unfortunately, they won't talk to me. They might talk to you, however. Why don't you contact them and tell them about the similarities between the two crime scenes? If they got involved, it could help both of us."

"Good idea, Ms. Waters. I'll contact your embassy and see if I can get them to contact me."

"Great. It's been nice talking to you."

"Likewise. I'll let you know if I discover anything of interest."

I couldn't wait to tell Stan and Cheryl what I had discovered. Now the only problem was to find out what Martin and Rubin had gotten themselves into and who would have benefitted by their death or disappearance. My head was beginning to ache just thinking about that daunting task. It was time to call in Paul Thayer. It was going to take a lot of manpower to get to the bottom of this mess.

Paul agreed to meet me for lunch to discuss the case. We met in a little café in Ola Podrida across the street from our offices.

We took a seat in a quiet corner in the back of the restaurant. Paul had worked on several cases for us in the past and had been instrumental in many of our successful verdicts. Paul was a quiet, thoughtful man who had worked for the FBI in his earlier years. He looked more like an accountant than a private investigator.

"That is a strange signature," he said thoughtfully. "The crime families I've dealt with in the past have used a much simpler method of sanitizing a crime—gasoline and a match."

I smiled. "Well, this job must have taken hours, and a lot of people must have been in the house to pull it off."

"What I don't understand," Paul said, "is why go to all this trouble? What were they trying to hide?"

"You know, I'm thinking this might be the work of the CIA or the military," I suggested. "It's just too clean a job for a criminal organization."

"Maybe. I'll check out that angle. If that's true, though, you better be careful. I'd hate for you to be the next person to disappear."

A jolt of fear shot through me. I hadn't thought through the implications of our investigation. If I discovered why Martin and Rubin had been kidnapped, I would become a threat to the abductors. Nevertheless, I couldn't let that possibility deter me. I owed it to Cheryl to diligently defend her even at my own peril. I'd just have to be careful and take measures to protect myself. I decided it was time to bring Bart up to speed. I hadn't wanted to worry him, so I hadn't mentioned that I was being followed. But now with Paul's warning I decided I had to tell him.

That night after dinner, Bart and I got a couple drinks and went out on the balcony to talk. I told him about my meeting with Paul Thayer and the situation with Rubin Quinlin. Then I told him about Paul's warning. His eyes widened. "You're being followed?"

"Yes, I think it's just a tabloid reporter looking for a scoop. They've been following Stan around too."

"You need to stay in the office and let Paul do the leg work from now on. No more amateur PI crap," Bart said.

"I can't sit around the office all day. I need to talk to witnesses, go to court, and follow up on leads."

"From now on you need take a bodyguard with you whenever you go out. It's too dangerous for you to be alone with all those lunatics hanging around and people following you. Have your witnesses come to you. Remember you're a lawyer, not a detective."

I took a deep breath. "I didn't mean to scare you. I'm probably not in any danger. The guy following me is most likely harmless."

"I don't care. Promise me you'll keep a bodyguard with you at all times."

I hated the idea of having a bodyguard hanging around constantly. I liked my freedom and my privacy. Unfortunately, Bart was right. It was too dangerous and I was beginning to worry about what I might uncover if I continued to dig.

"Okay, I promise. It's going to be a royal pain in the ass, but I'll do it for you. I don't want you to worry about me."

"I do worry about you," Bart said. "I don't know why you always have to get involved in these high-profile murder cases. Why don't you take on more routine cases, or better yet, find a new specialty?"

I sighed. "Come on, you know I'm living my dream. I'm not going to do anything else and I'm not going to let anyone intimidate me."

Bart put his drink down and put his arm around me. "I know, honey. But I love you and I'd die if anything happened to you."

I smiled softly and we embraced. "Don't worry," I said. "I won't do anything foolish. I love you and our life together too much to jeopardize it."

With that Bart stood up and led me to the bedroom. It was only eight o'clock but I didn't put up a fight. Making love to Bart was wonderful, but what I loved the most was cuddling with him after our passions had died. In his arms I felt relaxed and safe. All my fears and anxieties melted away and for a few moments that night I was at peace with the world.

Chapter 18

A One Way Ticket to Seattle

The day of Steven Caldwell's second appointment with Dr. Gerhardt finally came. I don't know who was more nervous about it, Steven or myself. The missing two minutes were critical and could make or break our defense. Dr. Gerhardt explained again how the session would proceed and asked Steven if he wanted to continue. He said he did. He wanted to know how Jimmy had died. Dr. Gerhardt handed Steven some cotton balls. Steven frowned. "You will probably need these," Dr. Gerhardt said. Steven shrugged and took them from him.

As Steven lay back and relaxed on the sofa, Dr. Gerhardt began slowly waving his small flashlight back and forth in front of Steven's eyes. "Now your eyes are getting heavy. They feel so, so heavy. You can barely keep them open. Now I'm going to count to ten and you're going to be back at Possum Kingdom Lake. It will be Monday the 10th day of September 1990. Now when we're finished thinking about what happened that day, I'll count to three and tell you to wake up. When you wake up you will remember everything. Okay?"

Steven took a deep breath and focused on the small light, "Okay," he replied.

Dr. Gerhardt counted to ten slowly while he continued to manipulate the light around Steven's eyes. When he was finished counting, he said, "Are you there? Tell me what you see, Steven."

Steven grabbed his ears. "Ah! What's that noise? I can't stand it."

"Put the cotton balls in your ears, Steven," Dr. Gerhardt commanded. Steven crammed a cotton ball in each ear. His face calmed. "Now look around you and tell what you see."

Steven took a deep breath. "There's a flash of bright light. I'm looking up at the dark sky. Whoa! Look at that. What the hell?

The car is starting to shake and rattle—Oh, Jesus! I'm driving off the road. I'm slamming the brakes hard but it's too late.   Now I'm reaching for my seatbelt. It pops open. We've got to jump, Jimmy! We're going off the cliff! I glance at Jimmy. He's fumbling with his seatbelt—it won't release. I want to help him, but there's no time. I have to jump now or it will be too late. I look again at Jimmy frantically scratching and clawing at the seatbelt. It won't open! 'Help me!' Jimmy yells. 'Please, Steven! Help me!' I hesitate, but there's nothing I can do. I open my door and jump and as I hit the ground hard and start sliding down the mountain, I can still hear Jimmy screaming."

Steven's head nodded like he'd fallen asleep. Dr. Gerhardt snapped his fingers but nothing happened. He picked up a stethoscope and listened to Steven's heart, took his pulse, and called in his assistant to take his blood pressure.

"He's unconscious but his vital signs are fine, Dr. Gerhardt said. He must have hit his head when he jumped from the Jeep. We have to wait for him to wake up then I'll bring him out of hypnosis."

"You mean he's even reliving unconsciousness?"

"Apparently. He should wake up here momentarily."

Steven's head jerked, and he tossed and turned on the sofa. Dr. Gerhardt said, "Now at the count of three I'm going to snap my fingers and you're going to wake up. One. Two. Three." Snap.

Steven's eyes opened. He looked pale and was sweating profusely. "I remember now," he said. "Jimmy couldn't get his seatbelt opened. I told him to jump, but he panicked and couldn't get it unbuckled. We only had a split second to jump. There was no time. I just couldn't help him."

Steven began to cry. "I tried to help him, I really did, but he went crazy. He must have known he was about to die. He grabbed my arm as I was trying to jump. I had to jerk it away to get free. Poor Jimmy. I'm sorry. I'm so sorry."

Dr. Gerhardt put his hand on Steven's shoulder. "It's okay, Steven. It wasn't your fault. It was just Jimmy's time to go. It wasn't your fault. It was his fate."

"But why couldn't he release his seatbelt? I don't understand what happened. He shouldn't have died."

"I know. Death never makes sense. But you can't blame

yourself for this. It was out of your control."

I said, "Well, at least now we have a rational defense. I think I can convince a jury this was just a tragic accident. You were distracted by something—we don't know what exactly—but the bottom line is that Jimmy's death was just an accident. You were able to jump from the Jeep but unfortunately Jimmy couldn't get free of his seatbelt in time to jump."

Steven wiped a tear from his eyes. "You really think the jury will understand?"

I nodded. "I'll convince them. Don't worry. This was just a terrible accident. Nothing more."

Steven took a deep breath and tried to smile. I looked at Dr. Gerhardt. "Thank you, doctor. This was great work. We owe you one."

Dr. Gerhardt shook his head. "No, Steven is the one to be congratulated. He let us into his subconscious mind so we could find the truth. I'm just glad I could help."

I couldn't wait to get back to the office to tell Paula about the breakthrough. I felt as if a great weight had been lifted from my shoulders. For the first time in weeks I was starting to feel confident about the trial and keeping Steven out of prison. Now all I had to do was downplay all the spaceship hoopla and get the jury to focus on the accident itself. Sure, Steven had been speeding and driving recklessly, but he was just being a teenager and had no intention of hurting anyone. Had Jimmy been driving it could have been Steven at the bottom of the mountain. It was just a horrible misfortune.

The next day Steven was scheduled to appear in court in Palo Pinto. It was standard procedure for the court to require a defendant out on bond to appear from time to time just to make sure he hadn't fled the jurisdiction. The notice I had received also advised us that a scheduling order would be worked out as well. This meant we would be given a trial date and the clock would start ticking.

Since we were traveling all the way to Mineral Wells, I decided Steven and I should meet with our accident reconstruction expert after the hearing. He would need to spend some time at the crash site and talk to Steven about what had happened there. From his interview with Steven and our inspection of the site, he'd be able to construct a video simulation of the accident. This would be critical if I was to convince the jury that the crash was just an unfortunate accident.

Up until now I hadn't had any communication with the Assistant DA assigned to the case outside of our meeting at Jimmy's funeral. I wondered how they were handling all the publicity the trial had been generating. They had so far been unusually quiet particularly considering their outspokenness at the funeral.

Since Palo Pinto was several hours away and the hearing was in the morning at nine, we decided to drive up the night before and stay in a motel in Mineral Wells, close to Palo Pinto. Unfortunately Jodie discovered there were no vacancies because of all the press and tourists who'd been pouring into town after the UFO sighting. That meant we would have to leave Dallas at five to get to court on time. Since I was a night person, I dreaded the thought of getting up at four to be ready at five. As I was agonizing over this development, Jodie indicated someone from the mayor's office in Mineral Wells was on the phone. I picked up the receiver.

"This is Stan Turner."

"Mr. Turner. This is Ruth Zelle. I'm the mayor's secretary. We heard you were trying to get lodging in town tonight."

"Yes, I've got a hearing early tomorrow morning and I'd like to come up tonight, but I guess the town is overrun with tourists."

"Yes. Thanks to your client, business is certainly booming. That's why the mayor told me to find you a place to stay."

"Oh, that's okay. I understand. We'll just get up early—"

"Nonsense, I've made arrangements for you to stay with one of our distinguished citizens, Robert Swanson. He's the President of the Chamber of Commerce and owns several businesses in the area."

"Oh, no. That's too much trouble."

"It's no trouble. He has a big house and his wife Lauren loves to entertain. When I told her you needed a place to stay she volunteered immediately. She's been following the case with great interest and would love to meet you and Steven."

"Well, then, we wouldn't want to disappoint her."

"Good. Give me back to your secretary and I'll give her directions."

After transferring the call back to Jodie, I contemplated this unexpected hospitality. Did Lauren Swanson really care about

Steven? Would the rest of the community be as sympathetic?

I got the answer to my question when we drove into Mineral Wells late that afternoon. The first marquis we passed on the main road into town read, **'Good Luck, Steven. We know you're innocent.'** Later on we passed other signs and banners indicating support for Steven Caldwell. When we drove by the courthouse in the center of town, a lot of the people mingling around carried placards with a variety of messages—**We are not alone!**—**The End Is Near!**—**Steven, We Believe!**—**Love Thy Aliens**.

Mrs. Swanson must have alerted the media that we would be staying at her house because there was a huge welcoming party when we arrived. The police were there directing traffic and clearing a path for us into the Swanson mansion. Steven seemed shocked and amazed at all the attention he was getting. As we got out of our car the cameras started flashing and the spectators began chanting, **"We believe! We believe! We believe!"**

Lauren was a tall, elegant, articulate woman I guessed to be in her late 30s. I wondered what a woman like this was doing in a small West Texas town. I pictured her at home in Boston or New York but not Mineral Wells. Once inside Lauren greeted us and told us how pleased she was to have us as her guests. She advised us the cook was preparing a special dinner and that she had invited some guests who were due at seven. I cringed at the thought of having to make conversation with a room full of strangers. No doubt, they had but one thing on their mind: Had Steven really seen an alien spacecraft?

A maid led us through an enormous sitting room, up a flight of winding stairs, and down a hallway to our rooms. I counted six bedrooms just in this part of the house alone. My bedroom was the size of our family room at home. Since we had a couple hours before dinner, I decided to call Rebekah and then take a short nap. Judging from what I'd seen so far it would be a long evening. Rebekah is a worrier, so she was glad to hear from me and expressed great relief that we had arrived safely. I told her about Lauren, her beautiful home, and the special dinner she was having for us. She asked when we would be returning. "It will be late," I said. "Now that his memory has returned, I want to take Steven back to the crash site and have him walk me through everything that happened."

"Do you think that's a good idea? It may be too traumatic for him this soon after the accident."

"Maybe. But we don't have any choice. Judge Applegate is going to set a trial date tomorrow and it probably won't be that far off. Since we're so close to Possum Kingdom Lake, we need to do this now."

"Well, you're going to miss Peter's soccer game."

"I know. Tell him I'm sorry."

I flicked on the TV in the corner of the room. The six o'clock news was on. Mineral Wells didn't have its own TV station but it was close enough to pick up the Ft. Worth station. After kicking off my shoes, I lay down on the bed, closed my eyes, and listened to the newscast. The voices on the TV started to fade as I dozed off . . .

I was steering a bass boat through rough water. The wind was strong and the boat was rolling with the waves. In the dim light I could see the rocky shore of Cactus Island dead ahead. As I neared the shore, I cut the engine and drifted up to the dock. A gust of wind nearly pushed me off the dock as I struggled to the secure the boat.

In front of me was the steep trail to the island's summit. Above me clouds partially concealed a full moon that was casting eerie shadows over the island. Then a blue light from the eastern sky came toward the island. With a surge of adrenaline and an unexplained yearning to reach the summit, I started climbing quickly up the trail. With surprising speed I made it to the large flat surface of Cactus Island.

As I walked slowly toward the center of the island, the blue light hovered overhead. A strange peaceful feeling came over me. I felt no fear or anxiety over what was about to happen, but a willing acceptance of my fate. I took a deep breath and suddenly a warm beam of light engulfed me and I became buoyant, like I was in a swimming pool. My body began to rise toward the blue light. Then—

"Tomorrow morning in Palo Pinto Steven Caldwell is scheduled to make his first court appearance since his indictment for the alleged murder of Jimmy Falk at Possum Kingdom lake in September," the reporter said. "But tonight Caldwell and his attorney, Stan Turner, are the special guests at a gala dinner hosted by socialite Lauren Swanson."

Hearing Steven's name jolted me from my nightmare. I sat

up feeling a little dazed. The dream had seemed so real, yet I knew it was simply my overstimulated imagination reacting to the strange events of the past few weeks. But even so, I immediately regretted being awakened. It reminded me of my childhood when I went to the movies and the film broke right in the best part. That made me so mad. Luckily the projectionist always spliced it back together quickly so nothing was missed. A dream, however, wouldn't necessarily start up again if you went back to sleep. I wondered what my mind would have conjured up as an ending to my mental flick. I knew it would have been good.

I turned my attention to the TV news. "Since Steven Caldwell's claimed encounter with a spacecraft in September and last week's sighting of a similar UFO by hundreds of tourists and local residents, interest in the murder trial has soared. At tomorrow's hearing the court is expected to set a trial date and impose pleading and discovery deadlines.

"Channel 4 News reporter Amy Tan met up with assistant District Attorney Carla Simms and asked her what impact all this publicity would have on the trial."

The steps of the Palo Pinto County Courthouse appeared on the screen. Simms replied, "It will make it harder to pick a jury obviously, but aside from that, I don't think it will have any impact on the trial. No sane person believes there are alien spaceships flying around. I doubt any of our fine jurors will believe Steven's Caldwell's preposterous defense."

"But Ms. Simms," Tan said. "If what you say is true, why have so many people descended on Possum Kingdom Lake in the last few weeks? Don't you think it's an indication that many citizens believe in extraterrestrial life?"

"No. I think the people camped out at the lake are a bunch of lazy, no-good drifters who are desperate for a little excitement. The hard-working citizens of Palo Pinto County, on the other hand, have too much common sense to give credence to Steven Caldwell's ridiculous excuses."

"Is the state going to continue to prosecute Mr. Caldwell for Jimmy Falk's murder in the wake of what seems to be an outpouring of support for him?"

"Absolutely, "Simms replied. "We have no intention of

letting defense counsel's theatrics interfere with our prosecution of Steven Caldwell. He must be held accountable for taking a human life."

"Do you think Steven Caldwell's attorneys are orchestrating all this publicity?"

"I don't know if that's true, but I do know Stan Turner is well known for his trickery and deception. I believe he's done a little jail time for it, and I guarantee Judge Applegate won't put up with any of it."

The image of Carla Simms faded from the screen and Amy Tan's image appeared. She said, "Well, as you can see, tensions are rising here in Palo Pinto in anticipation of Steven Caldwell's murder trial. As you heard, Assistant District Attorney Simms gives no credence to Steven's Caldwell's claim that he was distracted by an alien spacecraft while driving his Jeep near Possum Kingdom Lake in September. But many tourists and local residents apparently disagree with the prosecutor and they are making their feelings known in a very vocal way here in Palo Pinto. This is Amy Tan reporting for Channel 4 News."

I looked at my watch and saw it was time to go to dinner. On the way downstairs I knocked on Steven's door. He opened the door immediately and stepped outside.

I paused. "Listen. Don't talk about the case tonight, and for godsakes, let's not get into a discussion about UFOs."

"What can we talk about, then?"

"School, politics, the weather—I don't care. Just don't comment on your case or what you saw on the date of the accident."

"Okay," Steven replied. "Let's go."

We walked down the hallway and started down the stairs. I was surprised to see dozens of people mingling around. Lauren, spotted us and met us at the bottom of the stairs.

"Gentlemen. Just in time. Come meet our guests."

Lauren took both our arms and led us to the first group of people. "I'd like you to meet my husband, Robert and his business associates, Cliff Stewart." Robert was tall and distinguished looking. Cliff was short and obviously loved his pasta. We shook hands and Cliff introduced his wife Elaine. Lauren took us around and introduced us to the rest of the guests and then showed us to our seats in the dining room. The table was an ornate display of fine china, silverware, crystal, and floral arrangements fit for a head of state.

Everyone sat down and Robert bowed his head to say grace. "Thank you, Lord for all our family and friends who are gathered here today, for this bountiful food and all thy many blessings. Thank you for safely bringing our guests here tonight and please, Lord, see that justice prevails in Steven Caldwell's trial and that Jimmy Falk finds his way to life eternal. Amen."

"Amen," the guests replied in unison and then Robert sat down. Lauren nodded to the head waiter and the staff began serving salads.

"So, Steven, are you nervous about tomorrow?" Lauren asked.

Steven shook his head. "No, Mr. Turner says tomorrow is just a formality. The judge just wants to see me and make sure I'm going to show up for the trial."

"Aren't they setting the trial date?" Cliff asked.

"Yes," I replied. "It's a scheduling conference just to agree on discovery deadlines and a trial date. It shouldn't take but thirty minutes."

"What do you think of the alien spacecraft that everyone saw over the lake last week?"

I forced a smile. "Pretty amazing. I wish I'd have seen it," I said, honestly wishing I'd been there. Knowing Steven was telling the truth would take the uncertainty out of our trial strategy.

"Well, *I* saw it and I'd be happy to testify if you need me," Elaine said.

"Really. So, you work over at the lake?"

"I'm a realtor and I was showing a piece of property to some clients when it happened."

"Wow. Maybe we can talk later. I did want to interview some of the witnesses who saw it."

Elaine smiled triumphantly. I took a bite of my salad but was interrupted when Robert asked, "So, Mr. Turner. How did the sessions with Dr. Gerhardt go?"

My stomach tightened. How did he know about Dr. Gerhardt? Nobody should have known about Steven's sessions with him. Had someone followed us to Dr. Gerhardt's office? I stared at him for a long moment trying to contain the anger that was swelling within me. "I'm afraid we can't go into any of the details of the case," I finally said. "I hope you understand."

Robert nodded. "Yes, of course."

I took another bite of salad and was interrupted again, this time by Cliff who asked, "Well, if we can't talk about Steven's case, how about telling us how you and Dr. Gerhardt managed to get that girl up in Sherman off—what's her name?"

"Sarah Winters," I replied. I didn't really want to talk about Dr. Gerhardt but, unfortunately, I couldn't think of a good way to avoid the topic.

"Yes, Sarah Winters. Tell us about her. How'd you ever get the idea to put her on the stand while she was under hypnosis?"

"Well, it was an act of desperation, actually. She had no memory of what happened to her and the babies, so Dr. Gerhardt hypnotized her and was able to get the truth out of her. Unfortunately, just as soon as Sarah came out of hypnosis she lost her memory again. We asked the judge to let me examine her under hypnosis, but he refused."

"So, the judge put you in jail for putting her back on the stand under hypnosis in violation of his ruling," Cliff stated.

"Yes, he did, but it turned out to be my first vacation since I started practicing law. I just sat around the jail for four weeks watching TV, reading, and drinking beer. I actually gained eight pounds."

Everyone laughed. I added, "But as much as I liked shooting the bull with the sheriff and his deputies, I missed my wife and kids, so it wasn't an ideal vacation."

"Have you figured out how Steven ended up on the side of the road and poor Jimmy fell to his death?" Cliff asked.

I glared at Cliff. Was he deaf? I had just explained we couldn't talk about the case. I took a deep breath. "Well, you know I had a dream about that very thing," I said. "The alien spacecraft must have shot an anti gravitational beam down to the Jeep which allowed Steven to float up to the spaceship. Of course, he doesn't remember anything, so I'm just speculating."

Steven's mouth dropped and there was dead silence in the

room. I continued, "They must have only had one anti gravitational beam on board or they would have saved Jimmy too, I'm sure."

Still dead silence. I smiled and said, "Just kidding."

Everyone started laughing. Cliff said, "Oh, you really had us going, Mr. Turner."

I smiled and dug back into my salad. I wasn't interrupted again. After dinner everyone moved to the den and I spent a few minutes talking to Elaine. She told me in meticulous detail about her close encounter the previous week. Her account was similar to the other witnesses, however, she didn't recall any noise coming from the spacecraft. Her recollection was that it moved silently across the sky.

About nine o'clock, Steven and I excused ourselves and went upstairs. We had a big day ahead and needed a good night's sleep. The next morning we got up early and ate a quiet breakfast with just Lauren and Robert and then headed for the courthouse. As we approached Palo Pinto from the east, the big courthouse stuck out from the trees like a sore thumb. In the town square a large crowd had gathered and the media was present in full force. I looked for a side entrance to the courthouse but since it was in the middle of the square there was no way to totally avoid the press. There were no parking places near the courthouse either, so we had to park on a side street two blocks away. We tried to avoid the crowd by walking down an alley and dashing for a side entrance, but a reporter saw us and the stampede began. Soon we were in the midst of a mass of humanity with a dozen microphones shoved in our faces.

"Mr. Turner. When do you think the trial will be set?" a reporter asked.

I shrugged. "I have no idea."

"Is it true Steven was beamed up into the spacecraft?" another reporter asked.

I looked at the reporter. Obviously my joke at dinner the previous night had leaked out. He looked at me with great anticipation. "No," I said. "He has no recollection of being beamed aboard a spacecraft"

"But we were told you—"

"No, I repeat. He has no recollection of being beamed aboard a spacecraft. That was a joke. I'm sorry, but we have no more to say today," I said as Steven and I pushed our way through the crowd. As we got closer to the courthouse, we heard chanting from the crowd.

"We believe! We believe! We believe!"

Finally we made it into the courthouse and were met by two sheriff's deputies who escorted us up to the courtroom. The gallery was packed with spectators who'd probably be disappointed since our appearance and conference with the court would take only a few moments. We sat down at the defense table. When I saw Assistant DA Carla Simms sitting alone at the prosecution table, I went over and we shook hands.

"Nice to see you again," I said. "Quite a crowd here today."

"Yes, you're up to your usual tricks, I see."

"My usual tricks?" I asked.

She shook her head. "You know what I mean. Did you learn them from Snake?"

Snake was the nickname of my law professor at SMU. He had a reputation for underhanded tactics and a willingness to do anything, no matter how unethical or reprehensible, to win a case. He was also a drunk and a womanizer. Simm's remark was a calculated slap in the face.

"No. The only thing I learned from Snake was not to be intimidated by overzealous prosecutors."

Simms snickered. "Don't underestimate me, Mr. Turner. Despite all your cheerleaders out there, your client's going to spend the best part of his life behind bars."

I shrugged and went back to the defense table. Arguing with Simms at this point didn't make much sense.

After a few moments the bailiff stood up. "All rise for the Honorable Andrew P. Applegate."

Everyone stood up as the judge walked in and took his chair.

"Be seated," the judge said and everyone sat down.

He continued. "In the matter of the State vs. Steven Caldwell, cause number 90-2373-22, are there appearances?"

I rose. "Stan Turner, counsel for the defendant and Steven Caldwell, present, Your Honor."

Simms rose and replied, "Carla Simms for the prosecution, Your Honor."

"Very well," the judge said, looking down at his calendar. "I guess we need to set a trial date. Since there is so much public interest in the case it probably should be sooner rather than later, don't you think?"

"That would be my inclination, Your Honor," Simms said. "All of the tourists and media are stretching the county's resources. We need to get this matter resolved soon so things can get back to normal."

"Exactly," the judge said.

"I'm sure that's a concern, Your Honor," I said, "but I don't think it's wise to fast track a case simply because there is a lot of public interest. We need adequate time to prepare. This is a complicated case and I don't think rushing it would be in the interest of justice."

The judge peered down at me. "I'll decide what's in the interest of justice, Mr. Turner. And let me make something very clear to you—this court will not tolerate any attempt to manipulate it or circumvent its rulings. You may have gotten away with that kind of behavior in other courts, but don't try it here. Our jails are not equipped with refrigerators and TVs."

A chill darted through me. It seemed the Judge had done some research on me. That was unusual and didn't bode well. "Excuse me, Your Honor," I replied. "I thought you were soliciting our opinions as to when to set a trial date."

"Your opinion is noted. However, I agree with Ms. Simms. We need to move this case along quickly. Trial is set for January 7 at nine a.m. I've prepared a scheduling order, and please note the deadlines carefully as there will be no extensions."

"Yes, Your Honor," I replied.

"And Mr. Caldwell, let me remind you about the terms of your bond. You are not to travel outside the state of Texas and definitely you're not to go into outer space."

The gallery erupted into laughter.

"And your attorney must know your whereabouts at all times. Do you understand?"

"Yes, Your Honor," Steven replied.

The judge dismissed us and called his next case. The moment we left the courtroom, Steven and I were immediately surrounded by spectators and the press. It was a friendly crowd who had got their money's worth watching our first courtroom encounter. They were happy and barraged us with questions. Ordinarily I wouldn't have answered any of them, but since the assistant DA had already chosen to use the airwaves in their prosecution of the case, I decided to do so as well. "Just a few questions then we have to get going."

"Mr. Turner. Will you be calling Elaine Stewart or any of the others who saw the UFO last week as witnesses in this case?"

"Possibly. I'd have to show the relevance of that sighting to our case which, I'm sure, the prosecution would challenge."

"Mr. Turner," a second reporter said. "Is it true you've been abducted by aliens yourself?"

I laughed. "No, where did you hear such nonsense?"

"Well, it's been reported that last night you admitted to having frequent dreams about being beamed aboard an alien spacecraft. Is that true?"

"It was just a crazy dream. It didn't really happen. I made that clear."

"But isn't it true that many alien abductions are remembered as dreams? The aliens want you to think you're dreaming. You may have—"

"Hold on. This was just a dream pure and simple. Let's not go off the deep end here."

Why I had agreed to answer a few questions suddenly escaped me. I kept forgetting reporters were always looking for something sensational that would sell newspapers, and get them promotions and job security. Reporting the truth was only incidental to their jobs. I raised my hand. "That's all, folks. Let us through. We've got an appointment to get to." As we drove out of the town square, I could hear the chants, **"We believe! . . . We believe! . . . We believe!"**

"Boy. I'm glad that's over," I said to Steven. "I can't believe the press jumped on my little joke the way they did."

Steven turned to me excitedly. "Do you think what the reporter said was true?"

I frowned. "What are you talking about?"

"You know, like when you dream of being abducted by

aliens that it's not a dream at all. The aliens mess with your mind so you think it was a dream but it really did happen."

I shook my head. "No. I don't believe that."

Steven sat back in his seat and stared at the road ahead. "I do."

"You do?" I said, glancing over at him.

"Yes, because last night I had almost exactly the same dream you described at dinner last night."

"You did?"

"Yes, except I don't think it was an anti gravitational beam that they used to bring me aboard. It was more like a presser cylinder where the air was as thick as water and I just floated up to the ship."

I looked at Steven in disbelief. "You had this dream last night?" I asked. Steven nodded.

I shook my head in dismay. "Well, I guess we'll have to talk to Dr. Gerhardt about that. I'm sure there is a rational explanation." Steven nodded again and then looked away. How could we have had the same dream? Had we become so close that we'd developed some kind of psychic connection? It had to be something like that because the alternative was surely not possible.

Steven and I didn't talk much on the way to Possum Kingdom Lake. I guess we were both mulling over the events of the last twenty-four hours. The whole trip seemed surreal. I couldn't get my mind off Steven's claim that he'd had a dream identical to mine. Was he pulling my leg? Was he hoping his story would make me a believer, like all his fans who had flocked to Possum Kingdom Lake and to the courthouse to offer their support? I wondered.

As we left Mineral Wells, we entered the North Texas Hill Country. Most of Texas is as flat as a chess board but around Possum Kingdom Lake there are a few hills and we had to climb one of them to get to Camp Comfort. As we turned left off the main highway we passed Scuba Point where the road narrowed, and I saw to the left a steep drop of forty to fifty feet down to the lake. As we neared the camp, the road curved sharply to the left and then back again to the right. In my mind's eye I saw what must have happened—the Jeep had swerved left and then was unable to make the hard right turn necessary to stay on the road. I just hoped we'd find something that the sheriff and his detectives had missed—something to help us make sense of this whole bizarre case.

The accident reconstruction expert, Carl Loftus, was waiting for us when we arrived at the accident scene. According to Paul he was one of the best in Texas and apparently came across very credibly with juries. When we approached, I noticed he was writing something in a notebook. We got out of the car and introduced ourselves. While he and Steven were going over the accident scene, I decided to take a look around.

Looking down the mountain, there weren't any buildings or structures within eyeshot, so I walked across the road and climbed up to the top of the hill on the opposite side of the road. From there I looked in every direction but saw nothing but trees and underbrush. As I was about to leave, I spotted an oil well in the distance, maybe a quarter mile away. The area around it was clear of vegetation, as if it had been recently bulldozed. I decided to go check it out.

Sure enough, it was a new well. A sign indicated it was called 'Possum Kingdom NW #7'. Memories of a big oil rig in action flashed through my head. I had been to one of these rigs years earlier. The promoters had invited me to a comin'-in party. They were sure they were going to hit oil in a certain geological formation, so they invited all the investors out to be there when it happened. When they reached the targeted formation, sure enough, they struck oil and it was a day I'll never forget—but that's another story. What intrigued me about finding a newly drilled oil well here, so close to Steven's accident site, was his insistence that the spacecraft had created a piercing noise so intense that he'd had to cover his ears. I thought back to the comin'-in party and remembered the noise that big rig was making. It was so intense everyone had to wear earplugs.

When I got back to the accident scene, a sheriff's car was parked next to my Nissan 300ZX. What was the sheriff doing here? I looked around and saw Steven and Carl Loftus talking to a deputy. As I approached, the deputy turned Steven around and cuffed him. "What's going on here?" I asked.

"Oh, Mr. Turner. I'm deputy Fry. I'm sorry, but I've been instructed to bring Steven in."

"Why? He appeared at the hearing this morning."

"We got a tip from an airline employee at American Airlines. It seems your boy here booked a one way ticket to Seattle for next Saturday. I guess he was planning to slip into Canada where he could hide out."

I glanced at Steven to get his reaction. He looked down and avoided eye contact. "Steven, why would you do that?"

He shook his head angrily. "Nobody's going to believe me. You don't even believe I saw a spaceship, but I did! I swear to God! I should have just lied. Damn it! Look where being honest has gotten me. I didn't want to spend the rest of my life in jail. I had to do something."

I shook my head. "Oh God, Steven. This is going to make everyone think you *are* guilty. You've just made my job twice as difficult. We've been making some real headway in your case and now—shit, I don't know what will happen now."

His head hanging, Steven was led to the deputy's squad car and put in the back seat. Carl and I watched silently as they drove away. I turned to Carl and said, "Shit, the kid really thinks he did see a spaceship. Can you believe that?"

Carl shook his head. "Hell, maybe he did. I don't know what else would explain this accident scene."

"What do you mean?"

"Well, if he jumped from the car as it went airborne he would have fallen eight to ten feet and his momentum would have carried him at least thirty yards down the mountain. After he hit the ground, he would have rolled another ten or fifteen yards. So, how is it that he even survived that kind of trauma with all the trees, sharp rocks, and boulders in his path, let alone come out of it with hardly a scratch?"

I shrugged. "You're the expert. You tell me."

Chapter 19

Liquidation

It seemed both Stan's and my murder cases were getting more complex and difficult each day. Stan confided in me that he was very concerned now that Steven had planned to escape. I wasn't feeling much better about Cheryl. Her convenient lapse of memory was a big problem, particularly as the DA gathered more and more damning evidence against her. In the movies the sage old detectives always said follow the money and the answer to the puzzle will be revealed. In this case I had good reason to follow the money since at least half of it belonged to my client. So, I decided it was time to do exactly that.

I contacted Paul Thayer and told him to locate Martin Windsor's parents or his siblings, if he had any. My thinking was to have one of them petition the court to be appointed guardian of his estate. Then together we could start tracking down the money and taking possession of it. Unfortunately, Paul called me back with the surprising news that he couldn't find any relatives at all in the United States. That bothered me considerably, but then I remembered he was an immigrant from Hungary so it was possible he was the first of his family to come to America. Before he hung up, Paul also told me about the car that had been staked out in front of our offices. It was owned by Globe Information Group, Inc., the parent corporation of the *Globe Inquirer*. No surprise there.

Next I contacted the Immigration and Naturalization Service to get a copy of Martin's file which would contain information about his family back home. Unfortunately this would take time, so I also decided to pay a visit to his company and see what I could find out there.

What I found at the headquarters of Village Drugstores, Inc. was even more disturbing. The offices were empty. It suddenly occurred to me that Windsor may have intentionally disappeared in order to avoid having his assets divided by the divorce court. That thought infuriated me. I couldn't let him get away with that.

With a little sweet charm and twenty bucks I convinced the building manager to let me into the empty suite to look around. The place was neat and tidy. I complimented the manager for what a good job they'd done cleaning the place. "Actually," he said, "this is the way they left it."

"Really? Did they give you notice that they were moving out?"

"No, actually they moved out in the night without us even being aware of it. I was quite surprised to find the office vacant, particularly since the rent was paid a month in advance. Often when a tenant gets a few months behind in the rent this kind of thing happens. But Village Drugs always paid the rent in advance and was never behind."

"Hmm. Was there anything unusual about them?" I asked.

"Well, they always paid in cash—thirty-three one hundred dollar bills every month. That's rare."

"That's rare," I replied. Martin Windsor was in direct violation of the temporary injunction that the court had issued. He'd been directed not to sell or encumber any community property pending division by the court. I normally would have contemplated filing a contempt motion, but since he was missing that would have been a useless exercise.

Totally frustrated, I visited one of the Village Drugstores to see if I could find out where they had moved their corporate headquarters. When I finally was able to talk to the manager, he hit me with another jolt.

"All the Village Drug Stores were sold to a competitor two weeks ago. We are now owned by VDS, Ltd."

All this was starting to annoy me. Martin Windsor appeared to be liquidating all his assets to thwart the divorce court's jurisdiction over the parties' community property. The manager gave me the name and address of VDS, Ltd.'s corporate counsel. I drove over to talk to them.

"Yes, it was rather sudden but the price was so good we could hardly pass it up."

"Didn't you know Mr. Windsor was in the middle of a divorce and enjoined from selling any of his property?"

"No. I'm sorry. He didn't tell us about that. If we'd have known about it, we obviously wouldn't have proceeded."

"Did Martin Windsor attend the closing?"

"No. The papers were sent by Federal Express to New York for his signature."

A ray of hope finally shone through and lifted my spirits. If Martin Windsor had signed papers just a few days earlier, that would be proof that he was alive and get Cheryl off the hook.

"Did you get the papers back?"

"Of course, we couldn't have closed the deal without them."

My heart leaped for joy. Finally, I'd gotten a break. "Can I see the closing papers?"

"Well, I don't know."

I glared at the attorney and said, "My client owned an undivided one-half interest in these drug stores. Now, you can either let me look at the documents or I'll get a court order directing you to do so."

The attorney shrugged and buzzed his secretary. "Betty, would you bring me the Village Drugs file?"

A moment later a secretary walked in with a thick file. After examining it the attorney pulled out a document and handed it to me. My pulse quickened as I flipped through the pages until I got to the signature page."Martin Windsor didn't sign this," I said.

The attorney took a deep breath. "Right. It was signed by the Vice President. Apparently Mr. Windsor was unavailable."

"Yeah. He was unavailable because he's been kidnapped."

"Well, I had no idea."

"Sure you didn't. Let me tell you something. In the next couple days I'll be filing a fraudulent conveyance suit to have this whole transaction set aside, so tell your client not to get too comfortable running the stores."

The attorney's eyes narrowed. He said, "Well, you've got to do what you've got to do, but we are bonafide purchasers and paid a lot of money for these stores. I can't really see any court setting the sale aside."

"It doesn't matter. The sale was in violation of a direct court order. It's void as a matter of law."

After storming out of the attorney's office I drove over to Martin's house to be sure it hadn't been disturbed. I had a sick feeling inside me that something would be awry there as well and I was right. A new owner had moved in!

Livid, I went back to the office to talk to Stan. I needed help and I needed it fast. What was going on? When I arrived at the office there was more bad news. Paul Thayer had called and left a message that the INS had no record of a Martin Windsor immigrating from Hungary! I rushed into Stan's office and told him what had happened.

"He must have been here illegally," Stan said. "Windsor probably isn't even his real name."

"So, what do I do now?" I asked.

"Didn't you say the FBI had been called in?"

"Yeah, that's what I was told."

"Well, let's find out who's in charge of the investigation and see if they'll talk to us. Cheryl has a right to know if they've made any progress. I'm surprised they haven't contacted her yet. How can you conduct a kidnapping investigation without questioning the victim's wife?"

"I'll call Perkins and see if he'll tell me who's in charge," I said.

"Good idea. Tell him Martin Windsor is obviously alive if he's liquidating his assets. That ought to shake him up a bit."

When I got back to my office there was a message from Detective Shaw saying he'd contacted the FBI about the similarities in Martin's and the Cocos Bay Manager's kidnappings. I dialed his number but he was out of the office. I wondered what he had found out. Had the Cocos Bay Resort been sold too? With any luck someone had seen Martin Windsor. He had to be alive. Then a sinking feeling came over me. How was I going to tell Cheryl Windsor that in the last few days millions of dollars in community assets had disappeared?

Chapter 20

Tracking the Money

It felt weird driving home from Palo Pinto alone. I kept looking over in the empty passenger seat expecting to see Steven sitting there. It didn't seem right leaving him behind, but there was nothing I could do. There was no motion I could file or appeal I could lodge. The courts had no leniency for defendants who couldn't be trusted to appear for trial.

I dreaded having to face Steven's mother. She'd be devastated. The long drive home gave me time to try to make sense of Steven's plan to flee just before his trial began. Did he really think he could just hop on an airplane and escape this whole ordeal? I finally decided it was predictable behavior for a naive teenager. If I'd have been in his shoes, I might have done the same thing.

When I got home, I told Rebekah what had happened and asked if she'd go with me when I told Jenny Caldwell her son was in jail.

"You didn't tell me there was a chance Steven wouldn't come home," Jenny sobbed.

"I know. It was a total shock to me too."

"I can't believe my boy is in jail again. Jails are such horrible places. I'm so worried about him. Do you think they'll mistreat him?"

"No. There's too much media attention on this case for them to allow any funny business."

"He must be scared to death."

"He's a tough kid. He'll be all right," Rebekah said.

"I don't know."

"Did he ever mention running to you?" I asked.

"Yes, his father went to Canada during the Vietnam War to escape the draft. He mentioned doing that a few times, but I thought he was joking. I never thought he would actually do it."

"Dodging the draft and fleeing to avoid a trial for murder are not exactly the same thing."

"To Steven they were," Jenny said.

Steven Caldwell's plan to flee just before trial was the lead story in the *Ft. Worth Star Telegram* the following morning. While I was staring at the headline and lamenting the events of the previous day, Jodie walked in.

"I saw the headlines. I couldn't believe it. What a day, huh?"

I nodded. "To say the least."

"Well, I've got some good news for you."

"Really? I could use a little good news. What do you have?"

"Well, I went to your meeting at the Dallas Naval Air Station yesterday and they agreed to check all their flight logs to see if any military aircraft were near Possum Kingdom Lake on September 10. I should have that report by week's end. I also called all the civilian airports within a hundred-mile radius of Possum Kingdom Lake, as you requested."

"So, any luck?"

"Yes, as a matter of fact, I found out that several members of the Confederate Air Force have been using a private airstrip in Weatherford to practice for some of their stunts."

"Is that right? Did you talk to any of them?"

"No, but I have a couple names if you want to question them. The airport manager indicated they're usually there practicing on the weekends. He said one of their common flight patterns is to fly over Possum Kingdom Lake on their way to their headquarters in Midland," Jodie replied.

"Did he say what types of planes they fly?"

"Mainly old World War II aircraft that have been preserved or restored. There's a Confederate Air Force Museum at Dallas Love Field if you want to go check it out."

"That's a good idea. I might do that at lunch."

After Jodie had left, I stopped by Paula's office to fill her in on what had happened in Mineral Wells and to see if there had been any new developments in her case. She told me she hadn't heard from Detective Shaw as yet and there was still no word from the FBI.

"You know. I could call Mo at the CIA," I said. "He might

be able to help us out on this since the case has obvious international connections. Hell, the CIA may be involved somehow. Isn't that what Paul thought?"

Mo was an ex-client and friend I knew who worked for the CIA. I had handled his bankruptcy several years earlier and he had referred a number of clients to me over the years. Since these cases were often delicate and a little dangerous, he had offered to assist me with some unofficial intelligence services whenever I needed it.

"That'd be great. I'll take all the help I can get," Paula said appreciatively. "I just need some answers right now. I have no earthly idea what is going on in this case. I feel totally helpless. Cheryl's assets have just evaporated overnight and I haven't been able to do a damn thing about it."

Paula's frustration concerned me, so I went straight to my office and called Mo at his contact number. He never answered that telephone, but I usually got a call back within a couple of hours, no matter where he was in the world. This time it took just forty-five minutes.

"Hi, Stan. It's been awhile. What's up?"

"Oh, struggling with a couple murder cases as usual."

"Yes, I heard about one of them—the Cactus Island sighting."

"Oh, really. You guys have a name for it?"

"Sure," Mo said. "Whenever there's a major UFO sighting it gets a name. This one is of particular concern since your murder trial is creating so much media attention."

"I didn't know the CIA got involved in UFO cases."

"We usually don't, but some cases everyone gets involved in. The government can't afford a general panic over a UFO sighting."

"Well, if you learn anything that would help me defend Steven Caldwell, let me know."

"Right. So far we haven't learned a whole lot, but the island is somewhat of a mystery. None of our scientists can figure out how the surface of the island was leveled the way it did, and some of the chemical compositions on the island don't make any sense."

"That's what my geologist said, too, and there's no record of any construction on the island."

"So I've been told."

"Anyway," I said, "Cactus Island isn't the reason I called. What I need help with is our other murder case."

I told Mo about the Martin Windsor case and how his assets were being systematically liquidated in violation of the temporary injunction in place in the divorce proceeding. We talked about the Tobago connection and the similarities between the two cases. He said he'd look into it and see if he could track the money. If he had any luck, he'd give me a call.

After lunch I stopped by the Confederate Air Force Exhibit at Dallas Love Field. I was particularly interested in the types of planes that were being flown over Possum Kingdom Lake. Most of the planes I saw were small combat aircraft like the Curtis P-40 Warhawk and P-39 Aircobra. None of these planes could have possibly been mistaken for an alien spacecraft. There were some bigger aircraft like the big B-25 Mitchell Bomber and the B-29 Superfortress but even those were clearly conventional looking aircraft that wouldn't likely be mistaken for a spaceship. As I was about to leave, a photograph on the wall of an unusual looking plane stopped me in my tracks. It was the P-38 Lightning. Now this had possibilities, I thought. It didn't look like any plane I'd ever seen before. It almost seemed like two planes had been welded together. This made it appear rectangular. I closed my eyes and imagined seeing that plane at twilight during a thunderstorm. I bought a photograph of it and took it back to the office to show Paula.

"That is weird looking," Paula said.

"If that baby flew overhead during a storm what would you think?"

"I'd freak out."

"Well, let's hope somebody was flying her to Midland on September 10. Wouldn't that be sweet?"

"I'll keep my fingers crossed."

"Oh, by the way, the CIA's been monitoring Steven's case."

"You're kidding."

"No, I think the government is worried about a general panic if we prove that Steven actually saw a spacecraft," I said.

Paula raised her eyebrows. "Then why don't they help us come up with a better explanation of what happened? The military hasn't been busting their ass getting us information."

"That's for sure. Mo also said he'd try to track Martin Windsor's money. He'll let us know what he finds out."

"That's good because I'm at a dead end."

Paula's face grew pale. I thought I knew what she was thinking. If Martin Windsor was actually alive, he might try to take his children. Paula picked up the telephone and dialed a number. She waited a minute and then hung up the telephone. "There's no answer," she said as she started to dial another number. "I'll try her on her cell." She put the telephone receiver to her ear and waited. Finally, she hung up. "Damn it! Why doesn't she answer?"

"Don't panic," I said. "She might just be in the bathroom."

Paula sighed. "Oh, Stan. What if she's been kidnapped too?"

Chapter 21

Kidnapping

Cheryl had given me the numbers of several of her friends. I called them all but was only able to reach one, Sarah Long. Sarah said she hadn't talked to Cheryl for a couple days and had no idea where she might be. She suggested I call her children's school to see if her three kids were in class. The kids went to a private school in North Dallas called the Hillcrest Academy. When I called over there, they refused to give me any information, so I decided to visit the school when classes ended that day to see if Cheryl came to pick them up.

Alex Garcia, my new bodyguard, insisted on accompanying me. It was weird dragging a stranger along everywhere I went, but Stan and Bart insisted I do it. Alex was in good shape and nice to look at, but he'd be a distraction that I didn't need now that I was married. He was too young anyway—barely 21. He told me he'd worked part-time for a security firm while he was training at the Dallas Police Academy and could handle anything that might come our way. I didn't have reason to doubt him.

Five minutes before dismissal we parked across the street from the school that Cheryl's kids attended. "What kind of armor are you packing, Alex?" I asked.

Alex smiled and said, "A Smith & Wesson 342D. I like as much power as I can get without sacrificing compactness and light weight. It's just 10.8 oz., yet packs a major wallop. It's a significant step up in ballistics from the .380."

"Yeah, so I've heard," I said. I didn't know a lot about weapons but had picked up a little training while working as an assistant DA. I heard the bell ring and children starting pouring out of the school. There was a line of cars waiting in front and cars parked along the main street and adjacent cross streets. I didn't see Cheryl's car, but breathed a sigh of relief when I spotted her walking up to the school's entrance. Her children came running out and gathered around her. They immediately began walking back to her car. As I started to cross the street to intercept her, two men jumped out of a big tan Suburban and grabbed her and the kids. I recognized one of the men. He was the guy from the elevator in Windsor's office building. I screamed for help and started running toward the Suburban. The men pushed Cheryl and the kids into the backseat and then jumped in the car and took off.

"Shall we go after them?" Alex screamed.

"Absolutely, let's go! We can't let them get away!"

We ran back to my car and took off after them. Alex was at the wheel and we were traveling north on Hillcrest Boulevard going about fifty-five. I could barely see them about a half mile ahead. When the road dipped downward, we lost sight of them and when we came up on the other side of the hill they were gone.

"Where are they?" I screamed.

"I don't know. They probably went right toward Central," Alex said, taking a right onto Forest Lane.

Our wheels squealed as we made the turn and accelerated to 70. As we crossed the bridge near the EDS campus, I saw the Suburban turning onto the access road to Central Expressway. "There they are!" I screamed. Alex floored it. The tires squealed and the car swayed violently as we turned right onto the access road. Looking ahead I saw the road was a dead end and the Suburban had come to a stop. We slowed the car and approached it cautiously. It appeared to be abandoned.

Alex pulled out his Smith and Wesson as we got out and approached the car. I peered through the tinted windows, but there didn't seem to be anyone inside. Then I heard someone coughing. I pulled open the back door and saw Cheryl lying in the backseat. Her eyes were half open and she looked disoriented.

"Cheryl, are you all right?" She grimaced and tried to get up. I took her hand and helped her out.

"Where am I?" she asked, looking around curiously. She turned and gave me a hard look. "Paula? Why are you here?"

"You and the kids were kidnapped."

"Huh?"

I put my hands on her shoulders and looked her in the eyes. "They've taken your children, Cheryl. I'm sorry. "

"What?"

I shook her hard. "Your children! They grabbed you and your children when you were picking them up from school."

She twisted her head as if I was speaking another language. "My children?" She looked at her watch. "It's time to pick them up. Oh, God! I'm late." Cheryl pulled away and rushed toward the Suburban. "Whose car is this?" She looked back at me with panic in her eyes. "Where are my children?"

"You don't remember anything that happened?"

"No. What happened? Where are my children?"

"They've been kidnapped."

"No!" she said, grabbing her head with both hands. Tears began to run down her cheeks. "I can't remember. What's happening to me? I can't remember anything."

"You came to the school to pick up your children and, after you got them, two men grabbed all of you and forced you into this car. We chased you here just now."

Cheryl fell to her knees. "No! God! No! Not my children!"

I bent down, put my arms around her and stood her back up. "Come on. Come sit in my car while we wait for the police."

I turned to Alex. "Call the police. Detective Perkins. Tell them to get over here now! There's a cell phone in my purse."

While Alex called the police, I tried to calm Cheryl. It blew my mind that she couldn't remember what had just happened. I'd heard of people having short-term memory problems, but this took the cake. As we were waiting, I scanned the area for escape routes, but saw nothing. Why had the kidnappers abandoned their car? Where could they have gone on foot? Why hadn't they just gotten on the freeway and escaped? After a few minutes I heard sirens and soon we were surrounded by police cars. Out of one of them came Detective Perkins.

"What happened here, Paula?" Perkins asked.

"Someone kidnapped the Windsor children," I replied.

"Jesus. You're kidding."

"I wish I were."

I filled Perkins in and he said he'd call the FBI. Soon an ambulance came and the EMTs checked Cheryl out. Since she had amnesia, they assumed she'd suffered head trauma, so they took her to Medical City Hospital. Once she was gone, Alex and I began to survey the area. We saw Perkins over near the Suburban so we joined him.

"She's on her way to Medical City," I said. "Where do you think the kidnappers went? We couldn't have been more than a minute behind them."

Perkins pointed over to an alleyway behind a shopping center that fronted Forest Lane. "We think they had a getaway car in the alley."

"It looks to me like Martin Windsor's alive and he hired these men to get his children," I said. "He couldn't risk the divorce court dividing up his property and giving custody to his wife."

Perkins looked at me thoughtfully but didn't respond. I told him about the Windsor fortune being liquidated and the money evaporating like the morning dew. He shook his head. "You know, your client's loss of memory is awfully convenient. First she can't remember what happened the night her husband disappears, and now she can't remember her children being kidnapped."

"True. That is strange but it's consistent with her mental state. I think it's called traumatic amnesia."

"Yeah. I know what the shrinks call it, but it's all bullshit to me."

I laughed. "So, you think she hired someone to kidnap her own children?"

"Sure. Why not? Like you say, it makes it look like Martin's alive and that takes her off the hook for his murder."

I shook my head. "That's ridiculous."

"No. It's actually brilliant," Perkins replied. "Your client is one smart cookie."

Perkins smirked and walked away. It was all I could do to keep from screaming at him. I motioned to Alex and we went back to the car. "Let's go to the hospital," I said. "It's time to check on Cheryl. I want to be there when they finish checking her over." If her memory came back, I wanted to be the first to hear what she had to say. I was also worried about Perkins or the FBI coming to talk to her since they had the crazy idea that she might have hired someone to kidnap her children. I had to protect her and reassure her that somehow we'd find her three kids and bring them back to her.

Chapter 22

October 18, 1990

It was our 22nd wedding anniversary, so I left work early to pick up some flowers and get ready for a night of celebration. It was a tradition to spend the night of our anniversary at the Adolphus Hotel. It was a romantic place to get away for an evening and we looked forward to it every year. We had just finished an elegant dinner at the French Room and were planning to get a cab to the Majestic Theater to see the musical *City of Angels*. As we were sitting there happily, I looked into Rebekah's eyes and remembered the day I had proposed to her. Suddenly I got the urge to tell her how much I loved her, but in a way she'd never forget.

I called the waiter over and ordered a glass of champagne for everyone in the restaurant. He looked at me oddly, but nevertheless carried out my instructions. Rebekah watched all this curiously wondering, I'm sure, what I was up to.

When everyone had been served, and all were looking around curiously for an explanation as why they had been given champagne, I stood up and said. "Ladies and Gentlemen. Excuse me for this intrusion on your evening, but many years ago I proposed marriage to this wonderful woman who is with me tonight. When she said yes, I bought everyone in the restaurant a glass of champagne and proposed a toast in celebration of our engagement. Our marriage and our life together have been so blessed that I felt compelled tonight to repeat that toast to a room full of strangers."

Everyone laughed. I smiled and lifted my glass. "So, here's to my bride, who is just as beautiful and wonderful as she was the day I married her. Thank you for twenty-two wonderful years, four precious children, and most of all, for putting up with me all these years."

Rebekah looked at me and shook her head. A tear ran down her cheek as she raised her glass to mine. Then I took her hand and helped her out of her chair. We kissed and I heard applause and then laughter as we lingered in each other's arms. I let Rebekah go and turned to the hundred smiling strangers. "Thank you. Thank you all very much. Now dessert is on me!"

The door to the kitchen opened and a gigantic anniversary cake was rolled out by a chef in a white hat. Rebekah looked up at me again and we embraced once more. There was more laughter and I heard a lady behind me sobbing.

"Oh, this is so nice!"

I smiled at her and then the music began. An hour later we left in a cab to go to the theater. The musical was great and Rebekah seemed to be as happy as any woman could be. I knew I was the luckiest man alive to have someone like her. When we got back to the hotel I turned on the TV to watch the news while Rebekah drew us a bath. Much to my shock and dismay, the headline story was all about Paula and Cheryl Windsor. My heart pounded as I paced back and forth wondering what I should do. I considered not telling Rebekah and ignoring the story until morning, but I was worried about Paula and Rebekah would sense something was wrong.

When I told her what had happened, she insisted we go straight over to the hospital. It was nearly midnight, but Paula and Alex were still there. They looked very tired.

"We just heard the news," I said. "Are you two okay?"

Paula nodded. "Yeah, physically we're fine. Emotionally . . . well, that's another story."

"Where's Bart?"

"He's helping out the DA down in Houston this week."

"Oh. So you're all alone?"

"Yeah. Well, I've got Alex my bodyguard here with me."

A wave of concern swept over me—or was it my own jealousy? I knew Paula hated to be alone and with Bart out of town she would be vulnerable—particularly to a young hunk like Alex. I considered intervening, but then decided it wasn't any of my business.

"Good. I won't have to worry about you getting home safely."

"No," Paula said. "I'll be fine." She smiled at my obvious concern and then began giving us a detailed account of the kidnapping and the chase that ensued. She said that they had only been allowed to talk to Cheryl for a few minutes since she'd been admitted and at the time Cheryl still had no recollection of the kidnapping. I suggested calling Dr. Gerhardt to see if he might be able to help Cheryl regain her memory.

"Even if she regained her memory, I doubt she could tell us anything we didn't already know," Paula said. "Alex and I saw just about everything she did except where they went when the left the Suburban."

"Have you talked to Perkins or the FBI about the man you recognized?" I asked.

"Yes, Alex and I are supposed to go to FBI headquarters tomorrow to give a statement and work with a sketch artist."

"That's good. If they can get a picture out on this guy, someone is bound to know who he is."

"How is Cheryl?" Rebekah asked. "She must be devastated losing her children."

"She was so traumatized, they had to sedate her. Can you imagine your husband disappearing, being accused of his murder, and then having your children kidnapped?" Paula asked.

Rebekah shook her head. "No, I can't. You'd have to send me to the looney farm if that happened to me."

Paula's face suddenly lit up. "Oh, happy anniversary! I hope this mess tonight hasn't ruined it for you."

"Well," Rebekah said. "We were about to hop into a hot tub at the Adolphus."

Paula glanced at me and then back at Rebekah."Oh, no. I'm so sorry."

"It's okay," Rebekah said with a smile. "We had a wonderful evening anyway."

"Yes, but this was your night away from the kids and I ruined it for you. I feel terrible."

"Forget it," I said. "I can always book another night for us at the Adolphus."

Rebekah rolled her eyes."You better book us somewhere else. I'm not sure I can go back there."

Paula's confusion showed on her face. "What happened? What did you two do tonight?"

"Nothing," I said. "Just a quiet little dinner."

Rebekah turned away, suppressing a smile. I said to Paula and Alex, "So, you two have had a long day. Why don't you both go home and Rebekah and I will stay here and look after Cheryl? You can relieve us in the morning."

"You sure?" Paula asked. "It's your anniversary."

"Not anymore. It's after midnight. Our anniversary is over so, don't worry about it. Go home. You need to get some sleep."

Paula gave us a look of great relief and said, "Thanks. We'll be back by eight, okay?"

"Fine. See you then."

After Paula and Alex left, I put my arm around Rebekah and gave her a squeeze. "Well, I bet you never figured you'd be spending our anniversary at Medical City Hospital."

"It's okay," Rebekah replied. "As long as it's not you or one of the kids in the hospital, I can handle it."

I took her hand and looked her in the eyes. "Hey, I think I saw an empty room down the hall. You want to— "

Rebekah gave me a provocative look. "Hmm. . . . What if we get caught?"

I shrugged. "So, they'll charge us for using the room. Hell, the room rates here are probably cheaper than the Adolphus."

Chapter 23

The Trap

Stan and Rebekah's offer to stay with Cheryl was much appreciated as I was so tired and upset over the events of the day. When Alex and I got back to my car, I told him I'd take him back to the office where his car was parked.

He thought for a moment. "Well, actually I don't have a car back at the office. A buddy dropped me off this morning. Would you mind taking me to my apartment?"

I sighed, a little perturbed that I couldn't go straight home. "I guess. Just tell me how to get there."

While we were driving to his place near White Rock Lake, he told me now much he'd enjoyed working with me and how much he admired me as a defense counsel. When he said he had heard how beautiful I was, I started to get nervous. When we got to his apartment he said, "Hey, you must be exhausted. I've got an extra bedroom. Why don't you come up and crash here tonight?"

I gave him a hard look. I was tired, there was no doubt about that, but I knew what was on his mind. "No, thanks. I should get back to my place. Bart might call."

"Come on. It will take you an hour to get back to your condo. What if you fall asleep at the wheel and get into an accident? I'd feel terrible."

It had been a long day and there was a certain logic in his pleas, but I knew I had to say no. Then he leaned over and took my hand. My heart quickened as I felt the warmth of his grasp. He gave me a boyish smile and my resolve crumbled. "Please," he said, "I can't let anything happen to you. I'm your bodyguard, remember. . . . And what a body!"

That was it. Before I knew it, I was scampering up the stairs to his apartment with the excitement of a high school cheerleader escaping to a sleazy motel with the varsity quarterback. Alex opened the door and yanked me inside. We embraced and kissed passionately. The route to Alex's bedroom was strewn with clothing before we finally fell hard onto his bed. The exhaustion we had felt just moments before evaporated as we launched into in a sexual frenzy that lasted for hours. When it was over, I looked at the digital numbers on the clock radio and saw it was 3:03 a.m.

As I lie awake, a strange feeling suddenly came over me. It was one I'd never felt before or, at least, not in a long time. Before I met Bart, I had been a free and independent woman. I had casual sex with men whenever I felt like it with no regrets. Now suddenly, I regretted having sex with Alex even though it had been by far the best night of carnal delight I'd had in months. A shroud of guilt was choking me and I didn't like it.

I got up, slipped on my clothes, and made my escape. What had I done? I was a married woman in the public eye and I'd just slept with my bodyguard. Not only was he an employee but he was ten years younger than me. And, then suddenly I remembered the reason for hiring Alex in the first place. I was being followed. Now the person watching me knew what I had done. Oh, Jesus. How could I have been so stupid? I looked around nervously. Maybe they'd taken the night off. They had to sleep. They couldn't watch me 24 hours a day—unless there were more than one of them.

My car was parked on the street outside Alex's apartment—another mistake. As I pulled out of my parking space, I heard another engine turn over. I looked in my rearview mirror and saw two ominous headlights behind me. It was dark along the lake, and clouds concealed a full moon. I accelerated, hoping to distance myself from my stalker, but the car remained a hundred yards behind me. When I got to Northwest Highway, I was relieved to see there was a little traffic. I nestled myself between two cars and stayed between them all the way to Central Expressway. Once on the freeway, I drove fast, hoping I'd be pulled over by a state trooper, but no such luck. Those menacing lights were still directly behind me. When I got back to my condo, I hit the remote control for the gate into the development. The door slowly opened. I waited so I could dash through just as it was starting to close so my stalker wouldn't be able to follow. It worked. The door closed behind me and the two headlights were locked outside the gate. I breathed a sigh of relief and continued on to my condo. After I parked in the garage, I went inside and fell onto the sofa exhausted.

I woke up after eight, my body sore from lying on the couch all night. I groaned as I got up, put on a pot of coffee, and started the water for a shower. As I was taking off my clothes, I heard a noise in the bedroom. My stalker! Had he come onto the property by foot or slipped in behind someone who came in after me? I looked around for something to use as a weapon but the best I could come up with was a heavy marble pot full of flowers. I picked up the pot and edged toward the doorway.

Suddenly the door sprang open and I raised the pot over my head to crush the skull of the intruder. As I started to swing with all my might, I realized the intruder was Bart. "Oh, shit! What are you doing home?" I pulled the pot back and held it meekly at my side.

Bart gave me a sour look. "The defendant decided to take the deal we were offering, so I got to come home early. Where the hell have you been?"

"Oh, . . . well. I've been at the hospital. Did you hear about Cheryl?"

"No, what about her?"

"Uh . . . her children were kidnapped. She was in really bad shape so they took her to the hospital. We stayed with her."

"We?"

"Alex and I. You know. . . .The bodyguard. You insisted I have one at all times."

Bart gave me a hard look. "Right, the bodyguard."

"After Stan and Rebekah relieved us, I took him home and then came straight here. Along the way, I noticed a car following me. It stayed on my ass all the way up to the outside gate. Luckily it didn't get in. When I heard you, I thought whoever had been following me had broken in."

Bart looked at his watch. "But it's almost eight-thirty! When did you leave the hospital?"

"I don't know. It was after midnight. I was so tired I crashed on the sofa just as soon as I made it inside. If I'd have known you were home, I'd have made an extra effort to make it all the way to the bedroom."

Bart seemed to be buying my story. I gave him my most seductive look. He frowned. "Why in the hell did you have to take your bodyguard home? He should have followed *you* home and made sure you got in safely."

"Oh, honey. Don't be too hard on him. His car was in the shop or something. A friend brought him to work. I'm sure it will never happen again."

"I don't care. In the security business mistakes like that can get people killed. We're going to have to replace him."

I felt a little sorry for Alex, but he must have understood sleeping with me could jeopardize his job. I was just relieved Bart hadn't discovered my little indiscretion. My only worry now was my stalker. He knew what I'd done and he was sure to find a way to use it against me.

Chapter 24

Confederate Air Force

A little after nine, Paula made it back to the hospital to relieve us. Alex wasn't with her. She said he'd join her soon, so we went home and crashed. It was early afternoon when I woke up. Since the day had been pretty much wasted, I decided to run out to Weatherford and see if I could talk to someone about the Confederate Air Force and the P-38 Lightning. I asked Rebekah if she wanted to come, but she turned over and went back to sleep.

It was a beautiful day and the ride out to the small airport was very relaxing. By the time I got there at four I was fully recovered from the previous day's ordeal. As I approached the hangar, I noticed several World War II planes parked inside. They were all in mint condition and quite impressive. A mechanic was working on one of them.

I parked my car outside and entered a door with a sign in the window that read, "Airport Operations."

Inside, a young woman was working on some paperwork. Her badge read: Rose Brewer—Flight Operations. She looked up. "Hi. Can I help you?"

"Yes, I'm Stan Turner. I'm an attorney and—"

Her eyes lit up. "Oh, Mr. Turner. I've heard about you on TV. What are you doing out here?"

I chuckled. Rose was making me feel like a celebrity. "I'm interested in the Confederate Air Force. I heard they kept some of their planes here."

She nodded enthusiastically. "Yes, they do. There are some of them in the hangar right now."

"Yeah, I saw that. Is there anyone here with the Confederate Air Force today?"

"Yes, Roberto. He's their chief mechanic," she replied. "You can go out there and talk to him, if you want to."

"Great. He must be the one I saw working on one of the planes."

She broadened her already wide smile. "That's him."

"Good. I'll just go and say hello."

"Fine," she said.

I started to walk away. "Oh, Mr. Turner," she called after me."I just wanted to tell you—"

I turned around and looked back at her. "I just wanted to tell you . . . well . . . that . . . I believe."

"Great. I appreciate that. Thanks a lot," I said and continued on.

"If I can help you with anything, please let me know."

I waved without turning around and continued on. Roberto looked up warily when I approached. I introduced myself, but unlike Rose, he didn't seem impressed. "So, I understand you handle the maintenance for the planes in the Confederate Air Force."

"Me and a half dozen other mechanics," he replied.

"Well, I visited your museum in Dallas and was very much intrigued by some of your planes."

He perked up a bit. "Well, we have quite a collection. Anything you like in particular?"

"Yes, the P-38. It's got such a unique design."

"It's a beauty, ain't it?"

"Oh, yes. Do you have one around here anywhere?"

"Well, we did but it crashed the other day. It's a real mess right now."

"Oh, that's a shame. I was hoping to take a look at it."

"I'm afraid it will be a while before we'll be able to raise the funds to fix it."

"Oh, that's too bad. Where is it now?"

"In a hangar in Midland."

"How did it crash?"

"One of our pilots took it out and didn't check the weather reports well enough, I reckon. He got caught in a bad thunderstorm."

"Do you remember the date?"

He frowned. "The date?. . .Why does that matter?"

"Oh, just curious."

"I'm not sure, but you can check with Rose inside. She may have a record of it."

"Okay. I'll do that. A couple more things. Who were the pilots?"

Roberto frowned again. "What difference does that make?"

I laughed. "Well. . . . Uh. . . . I just thought one of them might know where there might be another P-38 I could take a look at. I really wanted to see one up close."

He shrugged. "Uh, well Adam Peterson and Carl Brooks are our main pilots. I'm pretty sure they took 'er up the day she crashed."

"Were they hurt at all in the crash?"

"Adam wasn't but Carl got scraped up a bit. They were lucky. They were able to set 'er down. It was a hard landing, but they weren't seriously injured."

"Do you have addresses or telephone numbers for them?"

"No, but you can find them at the Chevrolet dealership in town. They work there during the day."

"Good," I said."Thanks a lot for your help."

"No problem," Rob said and went back to what he had been doing.

I went back inside and asked Rose if she knew the date and location of the crash site of the P-38 and she gave it to me without even looking it up. "It was September 22 and the location was 6.8 miles west of Possum Kingdom Lake." She looked like she had more to tell me, but I wasn't sure what it was so I decided to hang around awhile and talk.

"What do you do as flight operations assistant?" I asked.

"Well, this is a very small airport so it's not all that glamorous. You know, . . . there's lots of paperwork, logs to keep up, and reports to do."

"Do you happen to have a log that shows when the P-38 might have flown?"

"Sure, that's one that I keep."

"Can we take a look at it? I'm interested to see if the P-38 went up on September 10. Since you've been following the Steven Caldwell case, you know he was distracted by what he thought was a spaceship, but a P-38 is a pretty strange looking aircraft. If he had seen that plane—"

"Sure, that's possible. Let's check it out."

Rose started looking through a journal. She looked up and frowned. "That's weird. The page for September 10 has been torn out."

As we were contemplating this new development, the door opened and a tall man wearing a blue suit and a red silk power tie walked in. He nodded at Rose, then looked at me. "You must be Stan Turner."

I nodded. "Yes, that's right."

He extended his hand. "Well, I'm Adam Peterson. Roberto called and said you were looking for me, so I decided to come out and see if I could be of any assistance."

"Well, that was nice of you. I would like to talk to you."

He grinned. "Roberto said you were interested in the P-38."

"Yes, it's a pretty unique looking plane. I was sorry to hear it had been crashed. It was a miracle you weren't hurt."

He sighed. "Tell me about it. I was damn lucky, but my copilot Carl was busted up a bit. They just released him from the hospital."

"Really. Well, I guess just to survive a plane crash is pretty lucky."

"Absolutely. So, we're looking for donations to get her repaired. Any assistance you might provide would be greatly appreciated."

"Well, actually I was wondering if there were any other P-38s around."

He shook his head. "No, this is the only one in these parts that I know of."

"I'm curious. Did you take the P-38 up on Monday, September 10?"

Adam stiffened. "I don't know. Why do you care?"

"Well, are you familiar with the murder case I'm working on?"

He nodded. "I've heard something about it, but I haven't really been following it."

"Well, I won't bore you with the details. I just need to know if you took up the P-38 on September 10. That date seems to be missing out of the traffic logs."

Adam looked at Rose and frowned. "Really. Hmm. Let me think. What day of the week was that?"

Rose rolled her eyes. "It was a Monday."

"No, we wouldn't have taken it up on Monday. I'm a working man, you know. Gotta be there at the lot when the customers come in."

"Right. Do you keep a personal log book you could look at just to double check? It's pretty important."

"Sure. . . . Oh! Damn, I just remembered. I lost my log book in the crash. Jesus. I'm sorry."

Rose shook her head and walked away. Adam impressed me as the typical used car salesman that would say whatever it took to make the sale. I didn't believe a word he had told me but I couldn't figure out his motivation for lying. Rose rolled her eyes every time Adam told a lie and I could see she was anxious to spill her guts if I could get her alone. But I didn't want to get her fired or put her life in jeopardy, so I decided to terminate the interview and contact her later.

On the way home I thought about the P-38 and how it would play into Steven Caldwell's defense, assuming I could prove it flew over Possum Kingdom Lake on September 10. What I needed—or the jury needed—was to actually see the big plane flying over head. It occurred to me that there must be old newsreels of the plane in flight. If I could find one, I could give it to our accident reconstruction expert and he could create a simulation of the plane flying in a thunderstorm. I decided that would be a good project for Jodie to start working on.

It was late when I got home. Rebekah met me at the door with the news that Mo had called. She said he'd call back at ten. I looked at my watch and saw it was 9:30. Curiosity began eating at me. What could he have found out that would be so important that he would call me now? He usually called me at the office. Precisely at ten the telephone rang.

"Stan. You're back," Mo said.

"Yes, I just got in. What's up?"

"Bad news, I'm afraid."

"Oh God. What did you find out?"

"It seems all of the proceeds from the liquidation of the

Windsor assets are being wired into a BVI bank account under the name of Zorcor, Inc. Walter Johansen is listed as the sole officer and registered agent."

"BVI?"

"British Virgin Islands."

"So who is Walter Johansen?"

"He's a banker who acts as the sole officer and director of offshore corporations, and puts his name on the accounts for persons who want their identity kept secret."

"So, do you have any idea who has hired him to maintain the account?"

"Well, yes. He does business with the Agency and I was able to call in a favor to find out who owns the account."

"Okay. Don't keep me in suspense. Who is it?"

"You're not going to like this, but it turns out the account is being maintained for Cheryl Windsor."

Mo's words hit me like a jolt from a stun gun. "Shit! That's exactly what Perkins predicted. Damn it! How am I going to tell Paula?"

"I don't know, but at least now you know she can afford to pay your fee. There are more than three million dollars in that account."

"What? Three million?"

"And change."

"Huh. It still doesn't make sense. If she set up the kidnapping of her children, why didn't she just stay with them? Everyone would have figured they all had been kidnapped and when they were missing long enough, they'd be presumed dead. She could have taken her kids anywhere in the world with that kind of a bank roll and no one would have ever found them."

"I don't know, but she's one clever lady. I've never seen assets liquidated so fast and moved around the world as deftly. It took me hours to track it, and I do this for a living."

"From what Paula tells me she's not a financial wizard. I doubt she's behind it."

"So, you think her husband is alive and he's orchestrating all this?"

"That's my gut feeling."

"But what about the money? That's a lot of cash to throw away just to get rid of your wife."

"Not if he's worth ten times that much and doesn't want a divorce court splitting it up fifty-fifty. He had to wire enough money into the account to make it look plausible. A few hundred grand wouldn't do it."

"Probably not. Anyway, good luck sorting it all out. If I can do anything else for you, let me know."

"Thanks, Mo. I appreciate it."

Now I had a headache. Paula's case was getting more complicated with each passing day, and Cheryl was looking more and more guilty. Yet, killing her husband didn't make any sense to me. A divorce court would have been quite generous to her, in my estimation. Why risk life in prison? But then it occurred to me. Maybe she knew Martin Windsor wouldn't let her live long enough to enjoy whatever the divorce court awarded her. It was a matter of survival. She had to kill Martin before he killed her.

Chapter 25

Intimate Confessions

Alex and I arrived at FBI headquarters within minutes of each other. He gave me a sly smile when he saw me in the reception area. He was in such good spirits. I didn't have the heart to tell him he was about to get canned. After we announced our arrival to the receptionist, we took a seat to wait. He told me what a wonderful night it had been and about his disappointment when he woke up and found me gone. I told him about my ride home and the car that followed me. He apologized for not being there to protect me. I didn't tell him about finding Bart at home or that it was over between us.

After a few minutes, the receptionist led us back to a small conference room and told us to take a seat. She asked us if we wanted a cup of coffee. Alex declined, but I accepted as I needed the caffeine boost. As soon as she had left, Agent Doug Barnes joined us. He appeared to be in his late 20's, medium height, a crew cut, and intense brown eyes—probably ex-military, I thought. I wondered if his partner was watching us through a two-way mirror. He sat down across from us and smiled. "Quite a day you two had yesterday."

I nodded. "Yes, it was. Any word on the missing children?"

"No. They seem to have vanished. We've had every law enforcement agency in Texas looking for them, but so far no luck."

"What about the car? Did you find any prints or other evidence that would tell you the identity of the kidnappers?"

"No. The car was wiped clean."

"But how could that be? They didn't have time to wipe down the car. We weren't two minutes behind them."

"I don't know how they did it, but there isn't a print anywhere in the car. In fact the car looks like it was just detailed—not a speck of dust, lint, hair, or anything."

"Well, that consistent with their signature. Whoever these people are, they're very clean and tidy."

"If that's all your questions, I'd like to ask you a few."

"No problem, shoot," I replied.

"How was it that you two just happened to be at the school when the kidnapping took place?"

"I wanted to talk to Cheryl, so I called her at home and on her cell phone. She didn't answer, so I got worried. She always has her cell phone with her. One of her friends suggested I catch her at the school when it let out."

"So, did you recognize any of the kidnappers?"

"Yes, the bald one. I'd seen him once in the elevator at Martin's office building and a second time in a video tape of his living room." I told Barnes about the bald man disappearing in the elevator and Cheryl's video surveillance of Martin's home. "That's why I'm quite sure Martin is behind the kidnappings and the liquidation of assets."

"I'll need those video tapes," Barnes said. "I'll send someone over to your office to get them."

I shrugged. "Sure, why not. It doesn't look like I'm going to need them."

Barnes continued to question me. I walked him through the kidnapping and the ensuing chase in as much detail as I could remember. When he was finished asking me questions, he told me he'd been in contact with Detective Rupert Shaw of the San Fernando police department in Trinidad.

"What do you think of the similarities between the two kidnappings?" I asked.

"At first I just thought it was a coincidence, but now I'm not so sure."

"What changed your mind?"

"Well, it seems that yesterday Mr. Quinlin's two children disappeared."

"You're kidding!" I replied. "Damn. What do you think it means?"

"I don't know. When children disappear, it's usually one parent trying to deprive the other of their visitation rights. That happens all the time. But usually the parent and children disappear at the same time. What's unique with these two cases is the disappearance of the husband first and then the children several days later."

"That is strange, isn't it?"

"Yes, quite so. I've been doing a little research to see just how strange it is."

"So, what did you find out?" I asked.

"Well, in the last six months I've found 23 similar scenarios in Texas and most of them are in the Dallas-Ft. Worth area."

"Why, I wonder? Is someone kidnapping children so they can sell them?"

"Yes, and killing the father so it appears he's run off with them. If the police believe a parent is involved in the disappearance they're not likely to refer the case to us, and their own efforts to locate the missing persons will be downgraded."

"You mean it's possible Cheryl had nothing to do with her husband's disappearance?" I asked, finally seeing a ray of hope. "That would explain why they didn't take her along with the children. They just needed her to get access to them."

"It's just a theory," Agent Barnes said. "I wouldn't bet the store on it quite yet."

"No. I understand. I really appreciate you sharing it with me. Let me know if anything else develops along those lines."

"I will if you'll keep me abreast of anything new you come up with."

"Sure," I said, amazed at Agent Barnes' openness.

My spirits were high as I drove back to the office. In my previous encounters with the FBI, I had found them to be rather closed-mouthed and uncooperative. This was a very refreshing encounter, particularly considering Barnes's promise to share information with me in the future. I was excited about his theory too. It was simple, yet very credible. A jury would eat it up.

When I got back to the office, Stan was in the reception area talking to Jodie. He looked up but didn't smile. "I need to talk to you, Paula."

I didn't like the look on his face or the tone of his voice. "What happened?"

"You'll want to be sitting down," he said. "Let's go to my office."

I took a deep breath and followed him into his office. We sat across from each other at a small table. "I got a call from Mo last night," he said solemnly. "He traced all the money from the Windsor assets that were liquidated."

"Oh, wow. That was fast."

"That's his business and he's really good at it. Anyway, it seems the money was wired here and there but finally ended up in an account at the British Virgin Islands' branch of VP Bank. Normally it's impossible to know who controls an account because they are held in the name of a nominee."

"Uh huh."

"But Mo knew the nominee and got the identity out of him."

"Jesus. That's great. Who is it?"

"You won't believe this, but it's Cheryl Windsor."

"What? No!" I said, shaking my head. "That's impossible. She wouldn't outright lie to me. I just can't believe it. It can't be true."

Stan shrugged and leaned back in his chair. "Well, that was my reaction too. Maybe she's being set up."

"By whom?"

He laughed. "Martin Windsor, I guess, assuming he's alive."

I told him about Agent Barnes's theory. He liked it a lot and said I should explore it some more. We decided we needed to confront Cheryl with the information about the VP bank account and see how she reacted. If she continued to claim a lack of memory, then we'd ask her to let Dr. Gerhardt put her under hypnosis. We had no other choice. The evidence against her was mounting and we had to get some answers soon. If she refused to be hypnotized, then we'd know she didn't want the truth to be known and we'd have to do the best we could without her help.

"So, how's Alex working out?" Stan asked.

The question surprised me and the intensity of Stan's gaze was unsettling. "Fine," I finally replied.

"Did he take you home last night?"

The question also alarmed me. Had Bart already talked to him about Alex? I hesitated a little too long.

Stan continued, "I was a little worried about you two."

"Worried?" I asked, feigning innocence.

"Well, I knew Bart was away, and well—Alex is young and

good looking."

I didn't know what to say. Stan knew me too well. He didn't wait for a response because he knew he'd hit pay dirt. "Well, I figured as pretty as you are there was a ninety percent chance Alex would be hitting on you before the day was over, and I wasn't sure if you could handle that. You know, you mix fire and oxygen and what do you get?"

I sighed. "I didn't plan for it to happen. If the jerk's car hadn't been in the shop, I wouldn't have had to take him home."

"Are you sure it was in the shop?"

My pulse quickened. "Sure. . . . I mean. . . . Yeah, he wouldn't have lied about it."

Stan raised his eyebrows. "It's not that it's any of my business, but I care about you and Bart. I'd hate for anything to split you two apart."

"It's just that I'm used to doing what I feel like. I hate looking back and feeling guilty."

"I can understand how that might be difficult. I got married young, so I never had that kind of freedom."

"Do you regret getting married young? You don't seem to have any problem resisting temptation."

Stan smiled. "Oh, I've had my share. You haven't been my only challenge."

"Oh, is that right?" I smirked.

"Fortunately the man upstairs kicks my ass whenever I start to stray."

"How's that?"

"Well, there was the time out in West Texas when we were celebrating an oil well coming in. I'd drunk a little too much champagne and found myself in the caretaker's cabin with the chairman's wife. Sheila had a crush on me so things got a little out of hand. Fortunately, in our haste to get our clothes off, I knocked over a lamp and set the cabin on fire."

I laughed hard. "That's so funny."

"Yeah, the Lord really went out of his way to protect me from Sheila. She liked to sail, so her husband, Bird, bought her a big yacht. Bird was prone to getting seasick, so he wouldn't go out with her. When I came down one time to do some legal research at the courthouse, she insisted I go out on the yacht with her. Bird didn't seem to mind, so I went. After awhile she got hungry and wanted to stop at a little island in the middle of Corpus Christi Bay to have a picnic lunch. Well, after eating, she pulled off her top to do a little sun bathing. That was a little more temptation than I could handle, and I'd have no doubt broken two of the ten commandments had the Lord not conjured up a huge thunderstorm right there on the spot."

"Well, that makes me feel better. You're not such a saint after all."

"No, the flesh is weak. I'll admit that."

"Do you really believe God was watching over you?"

"Sure, He does it all the time."

"I don't know. I don't see how he could watch out for everyone. Why didn't He kick my ass before I slept with Alex?"

Stan raised his eyebrows. "Hmm. I don't know."

"I don't think you really wanted to screw Sheila, so subconsciously you found a way to stop yourself. But, subconsciously I probably did want to screw Alex, so I did."

"I don't think my subconscious mind can create thunderstorms," Stan replied.

"Maybe not. Who knows? So, what do I do now? Bart wants to can Alex for not following me home last night."

"Don't give him the chance. Call Paul and tell him to replace Alex. Tell him you need somebody older and more experienced. He'll understand. That way Bart and Alex don't have to have it out."

That advice seemed sound. It was great to have someone I could talk to honestly and confidentially. I knew Stan wouldn't reveal my secrets or judge me either. "Thank you, Stan. You're such a good friend. I could never have this conversation with Bart. He'd get all jealous and angry."

"I know. Rebekah is the same way. It's nice for me to have someone to confide in too. I've never really had a close friend that I trusted enough to tell all my secrets."

"You mean, there are more?" I teased.

Stan smiled. "Yeah, I'm afraid so. I doubt you've told me all yours either."

"No. Not by a long shot."

When Stan had left, I called Paul and told him I didn't feel comfortable with Alex and wanted him to replace him. As Stan had predicted, Paul took it in stride and said he'd take care of it. I hoped Alex would blow off our relationship since we'd only been together one night. I didn't want to have to face him again. I had more serious problems to deal with, namely a client who was either a liar or had the worst memory of anyone south of the Red River.

Chapter 26

Setback

Jodie got right on her project of finding some camera footage of a P-38 Lightning in action. Within a few days she'd found a documentary on World War II aircraft that included a little over a minute of footage of the P-38. Out of that there was about 13 seconds showing the plane flying overhead.

Carl Loftus, our accident reconstruction expert, was excited about the project and promised us something in about a week. When he called and said it was ready, I called Steven and asked him to come watch it with me. Paul Thayer, Jodie, and Paula also had told me they wanted to see it, so I invited them as well. Carl set up his video equipment in the conference room and when he was ready we all came in.

"Now I've recreated this flyover in several weather and light conditions," Carl said. "First I'll show you the raw footage so you'll have a little perspective."

Carl turned on his video player and pushed a button. In the footage, which appeared to be in Great Britain, the P-38 was sitting on the ground with a pilot climbing aboard. The scene changed to a shot of the plane taking off. It was a big plane but even with the double fuselage, it clearly was an airplane. My hopes started to dim. The scene changed again to the overhead flyby. It was an odd-looking bird, but still clearly an airplane. I smiled, trying to hide my disappointment.

Carl said, "Now, I'll show you the same plane at twilight."

This time the plane looked different. The clarity of the double fuselage was more difficult to see and at first glance it looked like a square object in the sky. But I wondered what a teenager driving too fast on a mountain might think of it. I looked at Steven and saw a glimmer of recognition.

"Steven," I said. "What do you think?"

"I don't know," Steven replied "I don't think that's what I saw."

"Don't be hasty now," Carl said. "Let's take a look at it in a thunderstorm. I've taken actual footage of the site during a thunderstorm and spliced in the P-38 flyby. Take a look at this."

Carl pushed a button and the scene changed to the road to Possum Kingdom Lake. The camera panned the road and the cliff where the Jeep had catapulted over the side. The camera moved upward and the P-38 came into few. There were flashes of lightning and rain was falling. The P-38 looked even less distinct and more difficult to see.

"That's not it," Steven said. "That's not what I saw."

"Not at all?" I asked.

"It looks a little like it, but it was traveling slower and it was a rectangular object. I can still tell that it's an airplane."

We all watched the videos several more times, but unanimously agreed the P-38 didn't quite look like a spaceship. I thanked Carl for his efforts as he was packing up and he left. The rest of us lingered in the conference room for a while, trying to figure out where our failure had left us.

"It was still a great idea, Stan," Paula said. "We can still use it since Steven isn't going to testify. Even if one juror buys it, we could hang the jury."

"No, I want to figure this thing out. Steven saw something and we need to find out what it was. That's the only sure way to get him acquitted. If we throw a bunch of garbage at the jury, it could just make them angry."

"So, what now?" Steven asked.

I shook my head. "If the P-38 isn't what Steven saw that night, then why did everyone get all uptight when I asked about it out at the airport in Weatherford? They're hiding something. I just know it."

"Then go with your instincts," Paula said. "Keep digging until you find what they don't want you to know."

"I plan to do just that," I said. "Paul, I want to know everything about that airport and the people who run it."

"No problem. I'll get right on it," he replied.

"You haven't talked to the other pilot yet, have you?" Jodie asked.

"No, I need to do that," I said.

"Why don't you let me talk to him? He's expecting you to contact him so he'll be ready for you. If I happen to bump into him, who knows what he'll tell me if I turn on my charm."

"Hmm. I like that idea," Paula said. "You should let her do that, Stan."

"Okay. You're probably right. I feel sorry for the guy already."

Everyone laughed. Jodie smiled and said she'd do a background check first to help her develop a good approach. She was obviously very excited about the assignment and left immediately to start working on it.

"Stan, what are you going to do while Paul and Jodie are out doing their investigation?" Paula asked.

"I'm going out to the airport again to see if I can talk to Rose. She seemed anxious to talk to me but we were interrupted by the pilot. Maybe I can get her alone or catch her at lunch or something."

"Be careful. If the pilot doesn't want you to talk to her, he might hurt you if you try."

"I can't let that possibility deter me."

"You better take your gun."

I stared at Paula. "Really? You think that's necessary?"

During our last case my life had been threatened, so I asked Detective Besch to help me pick out a weapon to carry around with me. He not only did that, but he also took me to the gun range and showed me how to use it.

"Yes, we don't know what we're dealing with here, so it's better to be safe."

"But I haven't picked up the Beretta since—"

"Since you shot Earl Modest?"

"Yeah, I didn't think I'd ever need it again."

"Well, it saved your life once, so I'd take it with you just in case."

Earl Modest was the first and only man I'd ever shot. Fortunately, I hadn't killed him. He'd come at me with a knife and might have killed me had I not grabbed the Beretta that was strapped to my ankle. I made a mental note to go to the bank and get it out of my safety deposit box. Rebekah wouldn't let me keep it at home with four kids roaming the house. She was a worrier, so I'd agreed to lock it up. She'd be very upset if she knew I was carrying it again.

The following day I went back to the airport to see if I could make contact with Rose. I got there before noon and waited in the parking lot hoping to see her leave for lunch. My plan was to follow her and try to make contact when she was alone. Around 12:20 p.m. she left the office alone and got into her dark-blue Chevy Malibu. As she drove off, I followed her at a safe distance. She took the road that led into Weatherford and stopped at the local Dairy Queen. I watched her through the window to be sure she wasn't meeting anybody and then parked next to her car. She was ordering when I walked up beside her. She turned to me and did a double-take.

"Mr. Turner?"she said.

"Oh, hi . . . ah . . . Rose, isn't it?"

She frowned a moment. "What are you doing back in town?"

I smiled. "Well, I must confess I'm here to see you. I would have called and asked if I could take you to lunch, but I didn't want anyone to know we were meeting."

After we had ordered, we found a booth in the corner and sat down to eat. Her face was brimming with excitement."Is this social or business?"

That question threw me a little. She was a cute young lady but couldn't have been a day over twenty-one. I studied her a moment trying to determine if she was sincere. "Business, but if I were fifteen years younger, well—who knows?"

She smiled broadly. "But I like a mature man, particularly one who leads an exciting life like you."

I laughed. "Okay, quit teasing me. A girl as pretty as you must have a dozen young guys tripping over each other trying to get her attention."

She rolled her eyes. "Now you're teasing me."

"Not really."

She took a deep breath. "Okay, what can I do for you? It must be something very important for you to sneak out here to meet me."

"Yes, it is. I sensed you had something to tell me the other day when I was out at the airport, but we were interrupted and I never got an opportunity to find out what it was."

"Gee. I can't remember what that would have been."

"It was right after you discovered the missing page in your log book and Adam Peterson showed up."

"Oh, right. You were talking about the P-38 crash."

"Uh huh."

"Well, I'm not so sure that it actually did crash."

Rose told me that Adam and Carl, his copilot, had reported that the plane had crashed and been destroyed, but that she'd not seen an accident report even though she'd asked for it several times. When she'd called the NTSB to ask them for a copy of their report, they didn't have a record of the crash. She later confronted Adam about it, but he claimed it was just a paperwork snafu and said not to worry about it. As I listened to this bizarre story, I wondered where the P-38 was and why Adam and Carl didn't want me to see it.

Chapter 27

Manipulation

Since Cheryl's trial had been set for early March and Stan would have to be up to speed on all aspects of the case in the event something happened to me, I asked him to join me when I confronted Cheryl about the bank accounts. He said that was a good idea, so I set up a meeting. It would be a tricky meeting because Cheryl, if she was telling the truth about all that had happened, would be grieving and I certainly didn't want to cause her any more heartache. I would have to be very delicate in the way I questioned her.

As I was thinking about our meeting, Jodie walked in with a Hispanic young lady at her side. She said, "Paula, this is Maria, our new secretary."

Stan and I had decided it would be better if we let Jodie hire her replacement as she obviously understood the job better than we did. Nor did Stan or I have the time to interview applicants and check their references. Maria was short with dark hair and big brown eyes. She had a cheery smile yet seemed sophisticated enough for the job. I extended my hand. "It's so nice to meet you."

"She's very smart and types 95 words a minute," Jodie advised.

"Wow! That's pretty impressive," I said.

"And she has four older brothers so she's not easily intimidated."

"Jes," Maria said. "I don't take any chit for anybody."

I laughed. "You sound perfect for the job."

"She speaks Spanish, of course, which will really come in handy since we have so many Hispanic clients."

"Right. Well, welcome aboard, Maria. I'm looking forward to working with you."

"Me too," Maria replied.

"Oh," Jodie said. "Cheryl is here."

"Okay. Tell Stan and show her in."

Maria brought Cheryl in and she sat across from me in a side chair. A minute later Stan joined us. I asked her if she'd heard anything about her children and she said the FBI talked to her every day but there hadn't been any new developments. I told her that there actually had been a few developments that the FBI didn't know about.

"Like what?" she asked.

"I can't tell you exactly how we know this, but Stan's sources have been able to trace the money from the liquidation of your assets."

Cheryl looked at Stan, "Really? So who has it?"

"Before I answer that question, I want to remind you that whatever you tell us is confidential and cannot be used against you in a court of law. It's very important that you tell us everything that happened to you. If you don't it will only harm you in the long run."

Cheryl stiffened. "I don't understand. I've told you everything."

"Have you? According to our sources all your money is neatly tucked away in a bank account in the British Virgin Islands. Have you ever heard of the VP Bank? It's a German bank, I believe, but they have several branches around the world. One of them is in the British Virgin Islands."

"No," she replied indignantly. "I don't even know where the British Virgin Islands are."

"Well, I'm sure you could have found them when the time came?"

"What do you mean—when the time came? Are you insinuating—"

"Cheryl, our sources say you control the account. It's in the name of a Walter Johansen. Does that ring a bell?"

She shook her head vigorously and glared at me. "No. I swear, Paula. I've never heard of Walter Johansen. This must be one of Martin's sick jokes. He disappears and then frames me for his murder. It's just like him, the dirty bastard. You've got to help me, Paula. You can't let him get away with this."

I raised my hands in surrender. "Okay. . . . Okay. I believe you. I just had to be sure. We figured it was probably a set-up." I sighed. "Now all we have to do is prove it. We'll need your help to do that."

"What kind of help?"

"Cheryl," Stan said, "I know a doctor who can put you under hypnosis to help you remember what has happened to you. We need to know everything so we can properly defend you."

Cheryl's body became rigid, her face turned pale, and she shook her head vehemently. "No. I can't go under hypnosis."

Stan and I exchanged glances. He shrugged. I asked, "Why not?"

"I just can't. It's out of the question. I won't do it."

Looking her directly in the eye, I said, "Cheryl, explain to me why you won't. It doesn't make any sense unless you're afraid of what we'll find out."

"I can't do it. I'm sorry. No hypnosis."

"Cheryl, I understand you won't do it, but why not? Don't you think we're entitled to an explanation?"

Cheryl looked out the window. There was a look of fear in her eyes. Finally, she turned and said, "Martin told me if I ever went to a shrink and allowed myself to be hypnotized I'd die a horrible death."

"What?" I asked, incredulous. "When did he tell you this?"

"The day we separated. He said shrinks are evil people who manipulate you and make you think people have harmed you when they haven't. He hates them and he's especially against hypnosis. He says when you're under hypnosis you're very vulnerable and can be made to do and think anything. He said he'd let me divorce him, but only on the condition that I'd never go to a psychiatrist or allow myself to be hypnotized. It seemed a little paranoid at the time, but I had no plans to ever be hypnotized, so I didn't really see that condition as being significant. I had forgotten all about it until you just now mentioned it. But Martin was quite serious. He'll kill me if I allow myself to be put under hypnosis."

"But he's gone. He can't hurt you now."

Cheryl shook her head. "No, he's out there somewhere. He had the children kidnapped and he'll kill me in an instant if I do anything to threaten him."

"But how will he know you've been hypnotized?" Stan

asked.

She sighed. "He's watching us. He knows we're in here right now. I'm sure of it. He's always been very aware of everything I ever did. It annoyed me at first, but after a while I got used to it. You can't hide things from Martin. I promise you. If you try, you'll regret it."

A horrible chill swept through me. Who was this man who had cast such a powerful spell over Cheryl Windsor? Even in his absence he controlled her. What had happened to the woman I had first met who was determined to extricate herself from the grip of this evil man? I looked at Cheryl and said, "Okay, Cheryl. We'll try to put up the best defense we can with what we have. But if you change your mind, let us know."

"I will," she said. "I'm sorry I haven't been much help. Please forgive me."

After Cheryl left, Stan and I sat in silence for a while. Finally, I said, "Well, that went well."

"Yeah, didn't it?" Stan replied.

"Why do you think Martin doesn't want her to be hypnotized?"

"Well, it's one of two things. He's either afraid of what she'll remember if she's put under hypnosis, or—"

"Or what?"

"She's under hypnosis right now."

Stan's observation jolted me. Cheryl had been acting oddly as of late. She seemed different from when I first met her. I thought back to when her personality had suddenly changed. It was about the time of Martin's disappearance. What had happened that day? Had Martin hypnotized her or had someone at the house done it for him? That might explain her loss of memory.

"Let's see if we can get Dr. Gerhardt on the line. Maybe he can shed some light on the situation."

I buzzed Maria and asked her to call Dr. Gerhardt for us. A few minutes later she buzzed back that he was on line two. Stan explained to him what Cheryl had just told us.

"It's possible that she was hypnotized and told to forget certain events," Dr. Gerhardt said. "She must have consented to being hypnotized, however."

"Maybe he made a deal with her," Stan said. "Cooperate or

you'll never see your children again. He didn't trust her enough to be satisfied with just a promise, he wanted to take it one step further—hypnotize her so her conscious mind wouldn't remember any of it."

"Fear is a great motivator," Dr. Gerhardt said. "It's possible she consented out of fear."

"So, she's not in a hypnotic state right now, she's just acting under a hypnotic suggestion?"

"Yes, that's possible," Dr. Gerhardt said. "That may be why she doesn't remember the details of her children's abduction. When she was hypnotized, she may have been told to cooperate with the kidnappers and that after it was over she wouldn't remember anything."

"Jesus. This is mind boggling," Stan said. "So, Martin may also have told her not to cooperate with us?"

I rubbed my temples. "I'm so confused," I said. "How am I ever going to try this case if my client is programmed to torpedo her own defense?"

Stan shook his head and said, "I'm glad it's you and not me."

"Ah! Thanks a lot," I said.

Stan laughed. "I'm joking. Don't worry. We'll figure this out. Just take a break for now. We have a lot to digest. Tomorrow it may not look so bleak."

Stan's reassurances didn't make me feel any better. Not only was Martin Windsor in control of Cheryl's life, but it seemed he was controlling us as well. What was he up to and what did he have in store for us down the road? Somehow, I knew I wouldn't like it.

Chapter 28

Scandal

When I looked at my calendar, it suddenly hit me that Steven's trial was less than a month away. Time was running out and I needed to settle on a defense strategy very soon. The frenzy over the possible alien aircraft landing on Cactus Island had subsided for the moment, but as the trial drew closer it was bound to flare up again. My indecision was over the P-38 Lightning. Could it have been mistaken for a spaceship? Should I be spending the precious little time left before trial continuing down that path or was it just a rabbit trail? My brain told me to forget about it, but my gut told me to stay on it. In cases like that my gut instinct usually prevailed.

Late one afternoon Jodie brought me some of the reports we had ordered. I eagerly looked through them. There were reports on the Weatherford Airport, the Confederate Air Force personnel who worked at the airport, and the drilling report on the Possum Kingdom NW #7 Prospect. According to the first report, the Weatherford Airport was a privately owned facility that had been in operation about fifteen years. It catered to the needs of the local business community and the general public. There was no commercial traffic going in and out of the facility, hence little federal interference with its operations.

The facility was owned by a company called Weatherford Aviation, Inc. of Mineral Wells, Texas. While quickly scanning the nine member board of directors, Robert Swanson's name caught my attention. He and his wife, Lauren, had hosted the very interesting dinner party before Stephen's first court appearance. Was it a coincidence that he was a part owner in the Weatherford Airport?

Glancing through the report on the Possum Kingdom NW #7 Prospect, the well that had been drilled near the accident site, I discovered that drilling had begun on precisely the same day as the accident. The operator of the well was listed as Gary Queen. I buzzed Maria and asked her to track down Mr. Queen for me.

In the Weatherford Airport personnel report I reviewed Adam Peterson's employment history which further piqued my curiosity. It seemed the automobile dealership that Adam worked for was also owned by Robert Swanson. I started to wonder if the little dinner party the Swansons had thrown for us was part of some kind of plan. What was going on between Adam Peterson and Robert Swanson and how did the P-38 fit in? That made Jodie's assignment to make a connection with Adam's copilot that much more important. I called her into my office.

"How are you coming with your investigation of Carl Brooks?" I asked.

"Oh, well, I've read over the background check that Paul sent me and I've done some research on Weatherford so I can pretend to be a local girl. Now I just need to run into him at one of his hangouts."

"Where does he hang out?"

"Well, he's divorced so he usually goes to a restaurant and bar named the Stockyard Stampede. It's kind of a hangout for cowboys and ranch hands. He usually eats dinner there and then hangs around for an hour or two."

"I need you to concentrate on locating the P-38 Lightning. I think it's going to be critical to our case."

I told Jodie about the connection between Adam Peterson and Carl Brooks and Rose's suspicion that the P-38 may not have crashed after all. She said not to worry, if it was still in one piece she'd find it. Then she changed the subject.

"What's going on with Paula and Alex?"

"What do you mean?" I said, feigning ignorance.

"Well, I know Alex was reassigned, but Maria says he's been calling her several times a day."

"Jesus. You've got to be kidding."

"No. I'm afraid not."

"You don't think her and Alex are—?"

"Well, it doesn't look good."

"Oh, my God. Does Bart know?"

"I don't think so and let's hope he doesn't find out. I think it was just a moment of weakness on her part, you know, with Bart out of town and everything. She doesn't have any feelings for Alex. I'm sure."

"What should we do?" Jodie asked.

"Just tell Maria not to put any of the calls through to her. I'll tell Paul to talk to Alex. Hopefully that'll be the end of it."

Jodie nodded and left. Maria poked her head in. "I've got Gary Queen on the line."

"Oh, good," I said and picked up the phone. Queen confirmed that his production company had started drilling Possum Kingdom NW #7 on the day of accident, but that neither he nor his men even knew that an accident had taken place since they were on the opposite side of the road working on the noisy rig.

After hanging up with Queen, I called Paul Thayer and asked him to do a background check on Robert Swanson. I needed to learn as much as possible about him if I was going to figure out what he was up to. I also asked Paul to have a talk with Alex.

"Alex quit," he said. "I doubt he'd listen to me even if I were able to talk to him."

That bit of news disturbed me. Now I'd have to track Alex down myself and tell him to lay off Paula.

I tried the number Paul had given me for Alex but the line was busy. I tried again five minutes later and it was still busy. When I heard the busy signal again ten minutes later, I decided to go pay Alex a visit. I dreaded confronting him, but I knew I had to put a stop to his apparent obsession with seducing Paula, before it destroyed her marriage.

Thirty-five minutes later I stood in front of Alex's apartment. I knocked, but there was no answer. I could hear people talking inside so I knocked again. Finally, the door cracked open and Alex peered out warily.

"Stan? What are you doing here?"

"I need to have a talk with you for a moment. Can I come in?"

"Well, I'm busy. We'll have to talk later."

"Listen, I tried to call you by phone but you either have long telephone conversations or your phone is off the hook."

"It's off the hook for a reason. I'm busy and I don't want to be disturbed."

"Listen, I'm sorry to bother you, but I came all the way over here because it's important. I need to talk to you now. It won't take but a minute. It's about Paula."

"What about her?"

"Let me come in or step outside. It's kind of awkward talking through the door."

"Just spit it out or I'm closing the door."

"Okay," I groaned. "You've got to stop calling Paula. You know she's a married woman."

"Hey, it's a free country and I'll call whoever I want."

"No, you won't. You violated your duty and trust as a security officer when you seduced Paula. If you ever want to become a police officer, you'd better back off."

Alex stepped outside wearing only boxer shorts. "Are you threatening me?" he said angrily.

"No, I'm advising you of the likely result of stalking a former client."

"Stalking?"

Suddenly the door flew open. Paula, clad only in a T-shirt, glared at me angrily. "What the hell are you doing here?"

My eyes were drawn to her long sexy legs and bare feet. I didn't know what to say. "Paula? . . . Shit. . . . I thought you were done with Alex."

"Stan, just leave. This is none of your business."

"Yeah, get the hell out of here," Alex said. "Before I kick your ass."

I turned to Alex. "You'll never make it through the academy. You're not fit to be a police officer."

Alex's fist came out of nowhere landing a right punch to my face that sent me sprawling onto the pavement. Pain resonated through my head and I felt dazed as I tried to pull myself up. Paula ran over to me and pulled me into her bosom. "Stan, are you okay?" She turned to Alex. "You son of a bitch! What's wrong with you? Are you some kind of animal?"

Alex gritted his teeth."Leave him there! Come back inside."

"No. He needs medical attention. Call an ambulance."

"No, that won't be necessary," I moaned. "I'll be okay."

Paula stroked my hair and looked into my eyes, "I'm sorry,

Stan. I never dreamed something like this would happen. Are you going to be okay?"

"Yes," I said trying to get up. I was feeling a little dizzy but I made it to my feet. I rubbed my sore eye and when I pulled my hand away I saw blood. "Okay, maybe I will need to see a doctor. I think I saw a Primacare not too far from here."

Paula helped me to the car then went back inside Alex's place to get her things. I heard them screaming at each other inside. When it seemed to take her too long to come out, I started to go in after her, but then she suddenly walked out the door. Forty minutes later the Primacare doctor was suturing the gash over my right eye. My vision seemed okay although the pain was intense. The doctor said I was lucky, the blow could have blinded me in that eye.

Paula repeatedly expressed her regrets about the incident and concern for my health.

"Don't worry about it. My eye will heal and the pain will subside. I'm sorry I interfered"

"No. I'm glad you did. From the first day I met Alex he's been hitting on me. I tried to ignore it, but he was very persistent. When I took him home the other night, I was so tired I just didn't have the strength to resist him."

"Don't worry. Alex will never bother you again."

On the way home I got to thinking about the wisdom in being truthful about what had just happened. It would be very difficult to explain to Bart and Rebekah and if the press got wind of it, well I didn't even want to think about that. "Listen. Maybe we should keep what just happened to ourselves," I said. "I don't want you to get in trouble with Bart and I don't know what I'm going to tell Rebekah."

"Sounds good to me, but how are you going to explain your face?"

"I don't know—I tripped and fell down some stairs?"

"Hmm. I don't know, maybe you could say you got into a barroom brawl."

"I don't frequent bars too often. Besides, in a bar there'd be witnesses. The press would probably want to talk to one of them, and in the process figure out I had lied."

"Didn't you get hit in the face one time when you went with

Reggie to the batting cages?"

"Right. I got distracted about the time a fast ball was coming in high and tight."

"There you go."

"But I don't usually go to the batting cages alone. I usually go with one of the boys."

"What the hell—you were stressed out and decided to work it out with a bat and a ball. Who could dispute that? There are a lot of batting cages around so you could have gone to any one of them."

"Okay. I guess that'll work. I've been known to go bowling during the middle of the day when I'm stressed out. Why not go to the batting cages?"

When I got home and told Rebekah what had happened she seemed skeptical but didn't challenge my explanation. I felt bad about lying to her, but I couldn't handle the interrogation that would follow if I told her the truth. The whole incident was better forgotten. Unfortunately, that wasn't going to happen. When we turned on the nightly news, my altercation with Alex was the lead story.

"Good evening. This is Amanda James with the Metroplex Evening News. Tonight's top story: Are Stan Turner and Paula Waters more than partners in their law firm of Turner & Waters? That's the question many people are asking today after Stan Turner was decked by Ms. Water's apparent new boyfriend, bodyguard Alex Garcia. According to Garcia, Turner showed up while the two were alone together and threatened Garcia if he continued to date Ms. Waters. The two apparently came to blows and Turner ended up in a local Primacare facility for treatment.

"Channel 7 News also learned that Alex Garcia is a reporter for *Globe Inquirer* who was trying to get the inside scoop on the defense of Steven Caldwell. Channel 7 News this afternoon attempted to talk to Ms. Water's husband, Collin County Assistant District Attorney Bart Williams but he declined comment."

Rebekah stood up. "You son of a bitch!"

"This is bullshit," I said. "Don't believe a word of it."

"You lied to me!"

I took a deep breath and said, "Yes, but—"

Rebekah stormed off, leaving me struggling to breathe.

Paula and I had been set up, and with one quick blow Alex Garcia may have destroyed us both and imperiled Steven Caldwell's defense. My mind whirled trying to fathom all the implications of what had just happened. How could Paul Thayer have allowed Alex to infiltrate his organization?

Chapter 29

Damage Control

The evening news jolted me. Alex was a reporter? We'd talked a little about the case but he didn't seem all that interested in it. He was clever. He knew if he questioned me too much, I'd get suspicious. Besides, he didn't need to ask me anything—all he had to do was keep his eyes and ears open. He and his editor must have got a good laugh at how easy it was. Yet, in retrospect, Alex had actually screwed up. He had made it to the firm's inner circle, poised to get the biggest story of his career, but he'd let his dick blow his cover.

I cringed at the thought of facing the media, not to mention Bart. *Damage control.* I hated those words. I used to hear them all the time at the DA's office. When a case went south, everyone in the office focused on *damage control.* What would Bart's reaction be? I looked at the clock. He was due home any minute. Should I just shoot myself now and avoid his wrath? There was a gun in the bedroom drawer, but I knew that wasn't an option. This was all too much fun.

There was a noise at the door. I stepped into the living room and saw it was Bart fumbling with his keys. I held my breath as he walked in. He wasn't smiling.

"So, I guess you heard the news." I said.

He raised his eyebrows. "Yeah, the press has been calling every ten minutes wanting my reaction."

"So, what is your reaction?" I asked. "Is it over between us?"

Bart swallowed hard. "Well, Paula. I don't know what to think. Is that what you want? Is that why you slept with that bastard?"

"No. I love you. It just happened. I didn't plan it. I let him seduce me. I know I shouldn't have, but I was weak. I'm not used to having to worry about who I sleep with."

"Well, since we're being honest, I kind of expected it."

Bart's statement knocked the wind out of me. "You expected it?"

"Well shit, you slept with half the DA's staff. I knew marrying you would be a gamble, but I thought it was Stan I'd have to worry about, not some goon off the street."

Bart's words were drawing blood, but it was no time to fight back. I had it coming and I just prayed Bart's anger would subside if I let him hammer away at me. "You don't have to worry about Stan. He tried to stop me from seeing Alex. He thinks you're good for me and didn't want anything to screw up our marriage."

"Yeah, and look where that got him. Now everyone thinks you and he have been sleeping together."

"I know. I know. I've really screwed everything up," I said as I rubbed my temples. My head was throbbing. I took a deep breath trying to relieve the pain. It was slowing moving to my neck and shoulders. I closed my eyes.

"Have you learned anything from all this? Are you going to be able to change your ways?"

I opened my eyes. "Yes. It was stupid," I admitted. "I'll never let it happen again. I promise. Just don't leave me. I really do love you."

Bart sat down on the sofa and sighed. "So now what? How do you plan to extricate yourself from this mess?"

I went over to Bart and sat next to him. After thinking for a moment, I said, "Well, I guess I need to talk to the press and tell them what happened. I've got to get Stan off the hook and take responsibility for my stupidity. We can't let this little bump in the road impact the law practice. If I lash out at the Globe Inquirer, you know, threaten a lawsuit and stuff, I think it will take the heat off the firm. I'll never file the lawsuit of course, and hopefully in a couple of weeks the whole mess will be forgotten."

"Okay, that might work," Bart said softly. "In the meantime, what should I tell the press?"

"Just tell them I'm going to make a statement in a day or two and that everything will be explained then. I'll call a friendly reporter and grant an interview." I put my hand gently on Bart's knee. "Don't worry, we'll survive and I'll never put you through anything like this again. I promise."

Bart turned to me and said, "You're just lucky I'm obsessed with you, otherwise I wouldn't put up with this bullshit."

I sighed. "Yes, I am very lucky. I know that."

The next day I called Jane Witherspoon, a reporter from the *Dallas Morning News*, and told her I wanted to explain to her what had happened with Alex. She said she'd be right over. After I had detailed my relationship with Alex, I launched into a tirade about the *Globe Inquirer* and their underhanded tactics. I said I was thinking about filing a criminal complaint against Alex, and that a civil suit against the *Globe Inquirer* was in the works. After Jane had left, I called Rebekah.

"Listen, don't believe a word you heard on the TV last night. It wasn't like that at all."

Rebekah listened without comment to my explanation. I told her everything.

"Deep down I didn't think any of it was true, but Stan lied to me about it," she said finally. "If he had just told me what was going on, I'd of understood."

"He was just trying to protect both of us. Don't be too hard on him."

"Well, thanks for the call. I'll think about what you said."

Once I'd completed my damage control for the day, I started thinking about Cheryl Windsor again. With her trial less than sixty days away, it was time to focus on trial strategy. The biggest weakness in the prosecution case was their lack of a body. This had to be the major thrust of our defense. I had to convince the jury that Martin Windsor was still out there somewhere. The liquidation of his assets, the kidnapping of the children—all pointed to him still being alive. Cheryl's loss of memory wouldn't be a factor since she couldn't be forced to testify. I just prayed that Detective Perkins and the FBI wouldn't find out about Cheryl's VP bank account. Hopefully they weren't as proficient at tracking money as Mo had been.

"Rob Wilkerson is on the line," Maria said. That was a surprise. Wilkerson rarely called. Usually he'd write a letter or have one of his assistants call. I picked up the phone tentatively.

"Hello. This is Paula Waters."

"Ms. Waters. This is a courtesy call. A body has been found

in the woods a few miles east of Dallas. There is a strong likelihood that it is the body of Martin Windsor. The coroner is on the scene and if you want to visit the site I suggest you get on over there immediately. When the coroner has completed his work, the body will be removed and taken to the morgue for an autopsy."

My mood quickly changed from cautious optimism to utter depression. This was the worst possible development. If the body turned out to be that of Martin Windsor, Cheryl's defense would be ten times as difficult. I mumbled, "Oh, shit."

"What was that?" Windsor asked.

"Uh. . . . Oh, I said I'll be right over. Don't let them move the body until I've seen it."

"Okay, but we're not waiting all day."

I hung up the phone. My heart pounded from an overdose of adrenalin. My hands shook and my shoulders ached. "Damn it!" I moaned.

Jodie walked in. "I heard Wilkerson called. What did he want?"

"They found a body," I said. "Can you believe this?"

"Oh, my God," Jodie said. "I'm so sorry."

I shook my head. "Call our forensics expert and get him over to the crime scene. Our only hope is that it's not Martin Windsor. If it is, it's going to be damn near impossible to get an acquittal."

I drove to the crime scene in a daze. Cheryl was doomed. The thought of losing a case mortified me, but the way things were shaking out that would surely be the final outcome. But despite all the mounting evidence against Cheryl, I couldn't believe she had murdered her husband. Could my gut instinct be that wrong?

As I drove up to the crime scene, I noticed that the center of attention was the burnt remains of an automobile. My spirits jumped as I realized the body was probably burnt as well. A burned corpse couldn't always be identified. Was there hope after all?

I got out of the car and noticed our forensics expert, George Gabbert, standing by the medical examiner watching him work. I walked over to him. "George. You got here fast."

He nodded. "Well, fortunately, I wasn't too far from here when I got the call."

"So, what does it look like?"

"The body is burnt to a crisp. I doubt they'll get DNA from it. Of course, they might be able to identify it by dental records."

"I don't think so," I said. "According to Paul Thayer, Martin Windsor never went to a dentist in the U.S. and nobody knows where in Hungary he lived."

"Well, the size and weight of the body are about right, and this is Windsor's car, I've been told."

"It is? Are you sure of that?"

"Yes. I heard a police officer call in the vehicle identification number and it apparently matched Windsor's car."

"They could still read it after the fire?"

"Yeah, the number is etched into a steel plate and welded onto the dash. It's almost indestructible."

"Damn. I thought maybe we were going to catch a break here, but I guess not."

"I'm sorry, Paula."

"Well, keep your eyes open. Call me later and let me know what you find out."

"I will. Where are you going?"

"Back to the office. There's not much I can do here. I've got to call Cheryl and give her the bad news. She may want to go to the morgue. Stan needs to be apprised of this new development as well. We're going to have to rethink our entire defense."

When I tracked Cheryl down, she seemed genuinely shocked by the news. When I mentioned going to the morgue, she declined. She said she didn't want to see Martin's burnt body as the image might haunt her for the rest of her life. She wanted to remember him as a living, breathing person. It made sense to me and she wouldn't be able to tell if the charred corpse was Martin anyway.

Stan was nowhere to be found, so I finally gave up and called it a day. On the way home my mind quickly flipped back to Bart. I wondered what kind of mood he would be in. It was going to take awhile for things to get back to normal, if they ever would. But I needed him now more than ever. I prayed he would eventually forgive me.

Chapter 30

Plane Ride

Rebekah barely talked to me for several days. Even after Paula called her and took the blame for what had happened, she still hadn't warmed up at all. I didn't blame her considering the media attention and the humiliation she must have felt. My black eye was a constant reminder of what had happened and, unfortunately, it would take weeks to heal, so the tension in the house wasn't likely to let up anytime soon.

It was late one night about a week after my encounter with Alex and I was expecting a call from Jodie. She had been in Mineral Wells all day trying to make a connection with Carl Brooks. She had promised to call me just as soon as she got back to Dallas. It was after 9:30 p.m. and I was worried that I hadn't heard from her.

Earlier in the week I'd received the background check on Robert Swanson from Paul Thayer. Paul was embarrassed about having let Alex infiltrate his organization. He promised to do a thorough investigation to see how it happened and make appropriate changes to make sure it never happened again. He promised to make it all up to me somehow. I told him I was going to hold him to that.

The report on Robert Swanson showed he had an interest in twenty-six businesses in Weatherford, Mineral Wells, Palo Pinto, and Possum Kingdom Lake. The thought occurred to me that he had a lot to gain by the influx of tourists into the North Texas Hill Country. Not only had his exclusive Brazos Country Resort at the lake been sold out every night since Steven Caldwell reported seeing an alien spacecraft, but all the motels, restaurants, and gift shops in Palo Pinto, Graham, and Mineral Wells were packed as well. Swanson was clearly cashing in on all the media attention from the trial and the sightings.

Jodie's call finally came in at 10:15 p.m. Rebekah had already gone to bed without talking to me. I picked up the phone quickly so it wouldn't wake her up. Jodie apologized for calling so late.

"Don't worry about it. So, tell me what happened," I asked.

"Well, I hung around the Stockade Stampede for a long time waiting for Brooks to show up. He finally came in about 3:00 p.m. I didn't want to be too obvious, so I didn't approach him immediately. I watched him and when he looked over my way, I smiled like he was my best friend. After about the third smile, he came over."

"So, what was your impression of him?" I asked.

"He seemed to be a nice guy—kind of laid back"

"So, did you get him to talk?"

"Yes. Once he got going, he wouldn't shut up. He talked for a while about the Cowboys, the weather—you name it. I didn't want to make him suspicious, so I didn't come on too strong. I just listened. He bought me a couple drinks and then I casually asked him about his business. He told me he worked as a finance manager for Western Chevrolet in Weatherford. I think it's the one Swanson owns."

"Right."

"Anyway, he eventually mentioned he was also a pilot. He talked about the Confederate Air Force and flying the P-38. He said his father had flown that plane in World War II. I asked him if he'd flown it lately and he said he had. He didn't mention anything about crashing it."

"So, did you find out where it was being stored?"

"No, but I'll know on Saturday."

"How's that?" I asked.

"He's going to take me up in it."

"You're kidding! So, it didn't crash! That's fabulous. Nice work."

"Well, I wanted to impress my boss."

"He's impressed, believe me. I'll want to be close by when you take up the plane. Maybe when you two are up in the air, I'll be able to take a look around the hangar. No telling what I'll find."

"Sounds like a good plan. He's going to call me Friday night and tell me where to meet him. I'll call you then."

After I had hung up the telephone, Rebekah walked in and

sat down.

"Did I wake you?" I asked. "I'm sorry."

"No, I couldn't sleep. Who were you talking to?"

I told her about Jodie's assignment and what she had just told me.

"Are you coming to bed?" she asked.

This was the most she had talked to me in a week, so I was greatly relieved. "Yes, I'm tired. It's been a long day." She got up and I followed her to the bedroom. As she walked through the bedroom door, she turned and embraced me.

We kissed for a long time, then she pulled away and looked me in the eyes. "Don't ever lie to me again. And don't try to protect me. I'd rather know what's happening, no matter how horrible it might be. That's all part of marriage."

I nodded. "I know. It was stupid, but—"

She put her finger over my lips. "No buts."

On Friday Jodie called me and said she got a call from Brooks. He told her to meet him at the Dairy Queen in Grafford, a little town about half way between Mineral Wells and Possum Kingdom Lake at 9:30 a.m. the next morning. I called Paul Thayer and he arranged for a photographer to come out with me to film the flight and take some pictures inside the hangar. He said he'd do some checking and see what airfields there were around Grafford and find out who owned them.

On Saturday morning Paul, the photographer, and I waited at a coffee shop across the street from the Dairy Queen where Jodie was to meet Brooks. Paul had found three landing strips in the vicinity of Grafford and had the details on each. At 9:30 a.m. a red Ford pickup pulled into the Dairy Queen lot. Jodie was standing next to her car and Brooks pulled up. She got in and they drove east out of town. We followed some ways back to avoid detection. About three miles out of town Brooks turned down a dirt road.

"Shit!" I said. "We can't follow him on a dirt road. He'll notice all the dust and debris we'd be kicking up."

Paul looked at his notebook and said, "You can hold back. I know where he's going."

We pulled over for a moment and Paul told me about the landing strip Brooks was headed for. It was a small strip used by several independent oil companies that operated in the area. One of the companies was owned by none other than Robert Swanson. After waiting for Brooks to be out of sight, we continued down the dusty road. After awhile, we saw a large hangar and several buildings in the distance. We parked out of sight and surveyed the situation.

Brooks' truck was parked outside the hangar next to a silver Corvette, but we didn't see any other cars or persons around. In the distance we heard the sound of an engine turning over. Paul told his photographer to get his camera ready. After a minute the big P-38 came lumbering out of the hangar and taxied to the runway. We watched it take off and then made our way to the hangar. Inside a few small planes were parked and one World War II fighter. I went over to where I figured the P-38 had been parked earlier and looked around while the photographer panned the interior of the building. Paul stood guard at the door just in case someone came by or the P-38 returned.

Several rolls of canvas were stacked along the hangar wall. After close inspection I determined that they were banners that small planes sometimes drag behind them for advertising. I thought back to sitting in Texas Stadium and seeing planes fly by with signs advertising the local strip clubs, or a desperate man's proposal of marriage to a girlfriend sitting next to him in the stands. I wondered if ever a young lady had turned down such a public proposal. That would be embarrassing.

There were cans of paint as well that looked like they'd recently been opened. It looked to me like the P-38 had been painted recently. As I was trying to understand what I was seeing, Paul yelled. "They're coming back!"

The photographer and I immediately ran over to where Paul was standing. We could see the P-38 in the distance turning to make its final approach. We dashed across the parking lot to our car which was hidden behind some trees.

"Do you think they saw us?" the photographer asked.

"No," Paul said. "They were too far away. I think we're okay."

We watched the P-38 land and taxi back into the hangar. There was talking and laughter. Apparently Jodie was putting on a good act. After a minute the hangar door closed and Jodie and two men emerged from a side door. I recognized the second man as Adam Peterson. He drove off in the Corvette and Brooks and Jodie got in his pickup. They drove off and after awhile we headed back to town. When we got there, Jodie's car was still parked at the Dairy Queen. Now I was worried.

"I wonder where they went," I asked.

"Well, Brooks probably took her to lunch," Paul said. "You didn't think he'd take her up in his plane and not expect her to spend some time with him, did you?"

"No, I guess you're right. I just hope he doesn't suspect anything. I'd die if Jodie got hurt."

"From what I've seen of Jodie, she can take care of herself."

I sighed. "I know, but we don't know much about Brooks or Peterson or what they're up to. We can't leave here until I know Jodie is safe."

"Maybe they went back to Weatherford to the Stockyard Stampede," Paul said. "Isn't that where they met?"

"No, that's too far away. Jodie would have taken her car and met them there."

"This isn't much of a town, I'm sure if we look around we can find them."

That seemed like a good idea, so we drove through town keeping our eyes open for Brooks' truck. I said, "Well, I wonder why they wanted everyone to think the P-38 had crashed? It looked just fine to me."

"Didn't you say they were trying to raise money to fix the plane?" Paul asked.

"Right."

"Well, it could be just a scam to rip-off some unsuspecting philanthropist," Paul said.

"I doubt it. I think Robert Swanson wanted people to think there was a spaceship flying around Possum Kingdom Lake, so he hired Peterson and Brooks to make the plane look strange enough to be mistaken for a spacecraft."

"Maybe, but it didn't look much like a spacecraft to me," Paul noted.

"True, but when people want to see something, it doesn't take much to fool them."

As we turned onto Dallas Avenue, we noticed Brooks' truck in front of a diner called Alice's Home Cookin'. We drove down the street and parked in a church parking lot to wait. About thirty minutes later, Jodie and Brooks came out. They tore off in his truck in a hurry. We followed them and when they sailed past the Dairy Queen, I got really nervous.

"Where is he taking her now?" I mumbled.

"According to the map there's nothing down this road for twenty-five miles," Paul said. Brooks' pickup slowed down and signaled. We drove past and saw they were pulling into a stockyard with a rodeo arena. "It appears they're going to the rodeo."

We doubled back, stopped on the side of the road, and watched Brooks and Jodie for awhile. It didn't appear she was in any distress, but I was still worried. Finally, she looked over our way and gave us a thumbs up. A rush of relief came over me. She was fine and actually enjoying herself. Her cover hadn't been blown after all.

On the way back to Dallas, I realized that everything was at long last coming into focus. It was clear now what my defense strategy should be. But I'd keep it to myself. I didn't want anyone, particularly Paula, second guessing me and eroding my confidence. If I didn't whole heartedly believe my theory, how could I convince the jury it was the truth? I just prayed I was right—because if I wasn't, Steven Caldwell would spend the rest of his life in prison.

Chapter 31

Finishing Touches

With Steven Caldwell's case approaching quickly, I put Cheryl's case on the back burner to work full time with Stan to get ready for trial. I drove to Palo Pinto and found that the media had already arrived and were setting up camp. I heard that Robert Swanson had graciously arranged for a hospitality suite for them to make their stay more enjoyable and we'd been told the food and booze was flowing. Lauren Swanson had offered to let us stay at her place, but Stan didn't think that was a good idea, so I arranged for a half dozen rooms at the local Best Western. Although these accommodations wouldn't compare, we would be too busy to notice.

The weekend before trial Palo Pinto was inundated with spectators. Most of them were UFO fanatics who believed Steven Caldwell had seen a spacecraft and wanted to support him. Many claimed to have seen UFOs themselves and thought if a jury believed Steven Caldwell and let him go that they too might somehow be vindicated. My greatest fear was that Stan would get caught up in this UFO euphoria and actually try to prove Steven Caldwell saw an alien spacecraft. He had assured me that wouldn't happen, but with Stan you never knew.

One of my jobs before trial was to research the judge and our opposing counsel. Stan needed to know their general demeanor and what to expect from them. Stan had already seen Judge Applegate in action and had been warned not to pull any stunts in his courtroom. His short temper was well documented and I was worried how Stan would fare in front of him. Further research at the county law library revealed that the judge had lived his entire life in Palo Pinto County, graduated from St. Mary's University Law School, and had only practiced law five years before taking the bench in 1977. While I was snooping around the library, I bumped into a local attorney. He told me that Judge Applegate had a close friendship with Carla Simms and would go out of his way to accommodate her.

I also discovered that Carla Simms was born and bred locally and was the daughter of a local bank president. A look at the shareholders of the bank indicated that Robert Swanson was a 20 percent owner. This bothered me, but probably wasn't enough to challenge her role in the trial. Simms had attended Texas Tech law school and graduated in the top 10 percent of her class. She had practiced as a sole proprietor specializing in family and criminal law for three years before joining the DA's staff. Simms was married to a local investment banker and had an eleven-year old daughter. Local counsel indicated she was confident, capable, often rude to opposing counsel, and seemed to have a perpetual chip on her shoulders. Bottom line, it didn't appear the trial of Steven Caldwell would be a pleasant experience.

Before the trial began, we had promised to give my friend at the *Dallas Morning News* an interview. This was unusual in criminal cases, but since this case was getting so much media attention, we thought it would be wise to try to keep the speculation to a minimum. Jane Witherspoon had been a college acquaintance and we had become good friends over the years. I felt we could trust her to conduct a fair interview. It was Sunday, the day before the trial was to begin, and we had arranged to talk to her in a conference room at our motel. We agreed the meeting would be restricted to Stan, myself, Jane, and her photographer.

As the interview began Jane asked, "Stan, what do you think of all the attention this trial is attracting? I've been told the population of this town has tripled in the past two weeks. Do you think all this attention will impact the trial and, if so, how?"

"Well Jane, the attention *will* affect the trial. There is no doubt about that. The first problem will be in picking a jury. How are we going to find twelve impartial jurors? As you know, the court denied our motion for a change of venue. Since neither Steven nor Jimmy Falk was from this area the judge didn't feel the venue needed to be changed, and frankly I can't argue with him on that point. But the media will impact the trial in other ways as well. Unfortunately, I can't delve into that without revealing our trial strategy."

"Can you give us a hint?"

Stan smiled. "No, sorry. That's all I can say."

"Okay, the big question: Will you try to prove an alien spacecraft landed on Cactus Island?"

"No. I don't need to do that. All I have to show is that Steven was distracted by something that caused him to lose control of his Jeep."

"But your client says it was a spacecraft. Are you going to deny that?"

"We can't deny that he believed he saw a spacecraft, but people often perceive things incorrectly, particularly when they just glance at something for a split second."

"So, what do you think Steven saw if it wasn't a spacecraft?"

Stan smiled, "Well, that will all come out in the trial. I really can't discuss that now."

"I understand," Jane replied. "So, how is Steven holding up? Has his incarceration been difficult for him?"

"Yes, it's been very hard for him and his mother, and they'll both be glad to get this trial over with."

"What do you think made him to want to run? Is that an indication of his guilt?"

"No, not at all. He got scared and depressed like anybody would if they were wrongfully accused of murder. He panicked and bought some airline tickets. I don't think he would have gone through with it."

Jane turned to me. "Paula, what's going to be your role in this case?"

"I'm here to help Stan in any way I can. It's his case but if he needs me, I'm here."

"She's good at picking juries," Stan said. "So, I'll be relying on her expertise in that area and, of course, her women's intuition."

"Women's intuition? Is that true or are you joking?" Jane asked.

"No, I'm quite serious. Paula has great instincts and if she feels strongly about something, I usually go with her gut feeling."

"So, Paula, do you believe in alien beings?"

"No, I don't," Paula said.

"Stan, how about you?"

"Well, Jane, I have an open mind on the subject. If there's

one thing I've learned over the years, it's that we know very little about the universe. I think it's quite possible, if not likely, that intelligent life does exist. Personally, I haven't seen an alien or an alien spacecraft, but if you read the newspapers and popular magazines they report that thousands, if not millions, of Americans believe they have seen UFOs at one time or another. The interest in this trial is proof of that, so I don't think you can just dismiss Steven's claim."

My mouth dropped. Stan had promised he wasn't going to say anything to encourage the UFO fanatics that were using the trial to promote their ridiculous beliefs. I rolled my eyes and forced a smile. Jane noticed my anxiety. "So, Paula, you don't share Stan's view?"

"Well, I guess I'm the skeptic."

"Which is good," Stan added. "Paula plays a good devil's advocate. She makes me do my homework."

"Well, I want to thank both of you for talking with me, and I wish you and Steven Caldwell the best of luck."

We thanked Jane and, after her photographer took a few pictures, they left. I couldn't wait to see Jane's story which would be coming out just as the trial was getting underway. It was bound to create a frenzy amongst the tourists and make it even more difficult to conduct the trial. Although Judge Applegate had refused to allow the case to be televised, since there were far more spectators wanting to see the trial than there were seats in the courtroom, he'd consented to a closed circuit feed into a large room in the basement.

That evening we were told the ABC affiliate in Ft. Worth was airing Amy Tan's interview with Carla Simms. Stan was busy working on his trial outline, so he asked me to watch it in case she revealed any case strategy during the interview. I poured a glass of wine and got some snacks from the motel refrigerator. The trial was the big news on TV and the station was in the middle of a historical account of Possum Kingdom Lake, and in particular, Cactus Island. I shook my head at all the nonsense about spaceships using the island as a landing site. Video footage of the island showed that the armada of boats around the island was still there, and in even greater numbers than when Stan and I had visited the island weeks earlier. Finally, the interview of Carla Simms began.

"Ms. Simms. Has there ever been a trial like this one in Palo Pinto County?"

"No. I've got to hand it to Stan Turner and his girlfriend—partner—or whatever their relationship might be. They know how to choreograph a murder trial."

If Simms was trying to make me mad, she'd succeeded. I gritted my teeth as the interview continued.

"Do you think you have enough evidence against Steven Caldwell to overcome the tide of support for him shown by the crowds that have gathered?"

"Absolutely. There is no doubt in my mind that Steven Caldwell is guilty and we have plenty of evidence to prove it. It doesn't matter what the spectators believe, it's the jury that counts."

"Can you tell us more about this evidence you have?"

"A lot of it's been reported in the newspapers. The rest will be presented at the time of trial."

"But you're confident of a conviction?"

"You bet. The citizens of Palo Pinto County want justice, and they have too much good sense to believe crazy stories about alien spacecrafts. Steven Caldwell is going to pay for his crimes against Jimmy Falk and the citizens of this county."

"What about the second sighting? How do you explain that hundreds of people saw the spacecraft a second time?"

"You've got to understand, Amy, that these people came specifically to Possum Kingdom Lake to see an alien spacecraft. They desperately wanted to see one, so when they saw an object in the sky they couldn't identify, because of a lack of experience, bad eyesight, or whatever, they jumped to the erroneous conclusion that it was an alien spaceship. They may actually believe they saw one, but they didn't. We all know that."

Simm's interview continued on for some time but nothing was said we didn't already know. I called Stan when it was over. "The bitch intimated that we were lovers. Can you believe that?"

"You're kidding? . . . Damn it! . . . Rebekah was probably watching it to. . . . Oh, well. She's just trying to distract us before trial. Don't worry about it."

"It just makes me so mad," I groaned.

"I know. Just let it go. We've got to focus on the trial."

"Right. . . . How's the trial outline coming?"

"It's done. I'm as ready as I'll ever be."

"Good. I talked to the court coordinator on Friday and she said the jury list would be available at eight tomorrow morning. We should get it as early as possible, so we'll have time to study it."

"Come by at 7:30 and we'll grab a little breakfast at the diner across the street. We may not have time for lunch, so we better have a good breakfast."

"Okay. I'll have them give us both a wake-up call."

"Good idea. Has Jenny arrived?"

"Yes, she and her mother checked in about an hour ago. They stopped by the jail to visit Steven first."

"How's Steven doing?"

"She said he's nervous, of course, but he's a tough kid. He'll be okay."

"Yeah, I think so. Well, I'm going to crash early. I don't want to be yawning tomorrow during Simm's opening statement."

I laughed. "What about your opening statement? Don't you want to practice it with me before you go to bed?"

"No. I think I'll wait until we put on our case to do the opening statement. It'll probably take us a couple days to pick a jury and then a couple more days for Simms to put on her case. I probably won't be giving it until next week. No use memorizing it now. I'll just have to do it again next weekend."

"Okay. I'll see you in the morning?"

"Sleep tight," Stan said and the phone went dead.

Stan seemed quite cool and confident for the eve of a high-profile murder trial. I'd hoped he'd practice his opening statement with me, as I wasn't even sure what our defense strategy was. One moment he was saying the whole thing was just a terrible accident and the next moment he was talking about the possibility of intelligent life in outer space. The thought occurred to me that perhaps he hadn't decided which way to go yet and that was why he was putting off his opening statement. God, that was a scary thought. I hoped it wasn't true. Either way, I was just glad he was first chair and not me.

Chapter 32

Brilliance or Blunder

The first ray of light into my motel room awakened me from a shallow slumber. I'd been periodically waking to look at the clock since 4:00 a.m. No need for a wake-up call today. Steven's trial was just a few hours away and there was nothing I could do now but let fate take its course. There was no time to analyze evidence, seek out new witnesses, or research salient points of law. It was game day, ready or not.

A hot shower had always been my ritual on the opening day of a trial. There was nothing like it to relax me and clear my head before I faced the day. After putting on my suit and gathering my things together I sat down and called Rebekah. I wanted to be sure she and the kids were okay, of course, but I also needed all the encouragement I could get. She came through as usual and I left the motel feeling fresh and confident.

Paula seemed a little nervous and out of sorts when I picked her up to go to breakfast. She said she hadn't slept well either. After we had eaten breakfast and were enjoying one last cup of coffee she asked me about our jury strategy. "If I'm going to be of any help in picking the jury," she said, "I need to know what our defense strategy is."

That made sense, but I was still reluctant to divulge this information even to Paula. "I don't think it's going to matter that much who's on the jury," I said casually.

"What? That's crazy. Of course it's going to make a difference. People have prejudices—racial, economic, social—you've got to find out what drives each juror. You don't want someone on there who is obviously going to be against you."

"Well, I'm not sure in five minutes of questioning that much could be determined about a juror anyway. It's all pretty much a guessing game. I know a lot of people spend thousands of dollars on jury consultants, but personally I think it's a waste of money. I'd take your gut instinct over a jury consultant anytime."

"Well, I'm flattered you think so highly of my instincts, but I don't think you're being very realistic."

"Nevertheless, just pick me a jury of good honest citizens who don't have any hidden agendas, okay?"

Paula shook her head. "Whatever."

As we left the diner and began our short walk across the city square to the courthouse, a swarm of reporters surrounded us. "Mr. Turner. There's a story in the *Globe Inquirer* that you've listed a Mr. X on your witness list."

"Mr. X?" I chuckled.

"Yes, rumor has it that Mr. X is . . . well . . . an alien who was left behind by the mother ship."

Paula laughed. I smiled and shook my head. "No. I don't know of any Mr. X, sorry."

"What about Professor Walston from UTD? Is it true he has confirmed an alien landing?"

Did this reporter know something or was he just fishing? I hadn't heard from Professor Walston for several weeks. He'd sent some students out to Cactus Island to inspect the crater, take pictures, and gather more samples. The last time I had talked to him he indicated he couldn't explain how the crater was formed or the condition of the surface soil. When I asked him if he would testify as to what he'd found, he seemed reluctant, but said he would if it were critical to Steven's defense. I understood where he was coming from. He didn't want to risk the ridicule of his colleagues at the university by supporting our alien landing theory.

"Sorry, I can't comment on a witness' testimony," I replied.

Another reporter asked, "Do you think with this circus atmosphere that Steven Caldwell can get a fair trial?"

I turned and looked at the reporter who asked the question. I thought for a moment and replied, "Sure he can. It may be a circus out here, but inside that courtroom it will be just like any other trial. Twelve good men and women will weigh the evidence and render a verdict, and that's good enough for me."

More questions were thrown at us, but this was no time for a news conference so I held up my hand. "Sorry, we don't have time to answer any more questions. We've got to get inside and pick a jury. We'll be happy to talk to you later."

A couple of sheriff's deputies came over to our rescue. They cleared a path, escorted us across the street to the courthouse, and showed us a private staircase that led to the upper floor where the courtroom was located. Carla Simms and her assistant were setting up at the prosecution table. We made our way to the defense table and set down our briefcases.

"I'll go get the jury list," Paula said and walked back toward the court coordinator's office. A few moments later she came back with a stack of seventy-two juror questionnaires with basic information on each juror. From these we'd be picking twelve jurors and three alternates. Paula immediately began studying each questionnaire and jotting down notes.

As she was working, I began unpacking my briefcase and surveying my surroundings. This was an old courtroom dating back to the 1920s and was much more dramatic than the modern courtrooms that were now being built in Dallas. The gallery took up approximately two-thirds of the room and there were three sections of wooden seats. The bench and counsel tables were separated from the gallery by an ornate wooden barrier about three feet high. The court reporter sat to our left and the witness stand was on our right. The judge's bench was dark oak and quite elegant looking.

By nine the courtroom was packed with spectators. The first three rows of the gallery had been roped off for the jury panel. Paula and I were discussing potential jurors when the bailiff yelled, "All rise for the Honorable Andrew P. Applegate."

Everyone got to their feet as the judge appeared, walked briskly to the bench, and took his seat. He shuffled through some papers, made a note in the file, and then looked up. "All right. Be seated. This is case number 90-0321, the State of Texas V. Steven Caldwell. The bailiff will please bring in the defendant."

The bailiff stepped into the back hall a moment and then reappeared with Steven at his side. He pointed to the defense table and Stephen came over and sat down. He looked tired and scared. Paula smiled at him and gave him a hug. "Can I have appearances?" the Judge asked.

Carla Simms stood up. "Carla Simms for the prosecution,"

Your Honor.

I stood up. "Stan Turner for the defense, Your Honor."

The judge looked at the bailiff. "Bring in the jury panel."

The bailiff nodded and went to a side door and opened it. He stepped inside and a moment later prospective jurors began filing in. They were directed to the empty rows in the gallery where they took their seats. After they were seated, the judge explained to them why they were there and what their role would be if they were selected as jurors. He then told them how the *voir dire* would work. After he had concluded his remarks he said, "Ms. Simms, you may begin your *voir dire*."

Simms stood up, introduced herself, and identified everyone in the courtroom by name. She asked if any of the jurors knew any of us. Nobody raised their hands so she began telling them briefly about the case, supposedly the undisputed facts, so the jury panel would know enough about the case to field questions designed to elicit how they would perform as jurors. Some prosecutors abused *voir dire* by misstating the facts or drawing conclusions from them. I hoped Simms wouldn't do that.

Simms walked in front of the gallery, faced the prospective jurors, and begun. "On Monday, September 10, 1990," she began. "Steven Caldwell and Jimmy Falk were at Camp Comfort, a Boy Scout camp located at Possum Kingdom Lake. They were working on preparations for the evening meal when they discovered they needed some supplies. Steven Caldwell offered to drive to town to get what was needed and he asked Jimmy Falk to go with him. They took the camp Jeep to drive into town which was located about five miles away. To get to town they had to travel on a winding mountain road."

Simms' eyes jumped from one juror to another. Eye contact was important in trying to develop a rapport with the jury. Simms had been well trained and the jury seemed to be listening to her intently as she continued. "On the way back from town it was getting dark. It began to rain as a line of thunderstorms was crossing the lake. Despite the rain and strong winds, Steven took the road at a high rate of speed. As he was taking the last curve before the entry to Camp Comfort, the Jeep suddenly, and without warning, went off the road, fell down the mountainside into the lake, and exploded into a fiery inferno with Jimmy Falk still strapped in his seatbelt.

"Sometime later Steven was found dazed but alive on the side of the road where the Jeep had left the roadway. Jimmy Falk's charred remains were later found still strapped into the front seat of the Jeep. When the motorist who found Steven questioned him as to what had happened, he told her he had been distracted by a spaceship that had suddenly appeared overhead."

One of the panel members snickered and there was laughter in the gallery. The judge banged his gavel and demanded order. Simms smiled at the panel member who had interrupted her and jotted something down on a notepad she had with her. She looked up and continued. "Now, I know the facts I have given you are sketchy, but unfortunately there are no eye witnesses to what happened. These are the undisputed facts and from these facts and the evidence produced at trial you will have to determine the defendant's guilt or innocence.

"Now we, the prosecution, contend that this was no accident but actually an elaborate plot to murder Jimmy Falk. You see Steven Caldwell and Jimmy Falk had one thing in common. They both loved a pretty, young girl named Susan Weber.

"The defense will claim that this was nothing but a tragic accident and that there was no animosity between Steven Caldwell and Jimmy Falk, or certainly not enough to drive him to murder.

"These are the facts, and the issues that you will have to deal with. Now I have to ask you some questions to be sure you can serve as fair and impartial jurors. When I am done, Mr. Turner will have some questions as well. It's important that you be as honest and responsive as possible so that we can be sure that you don't have any preconceptions about this case."

Simms asked again if any of the jurors knew the plaintiff or defendant or were related to them in any way. She then went through the witness list and asked if anyone knew any of the witnesses. Next she asked if anyone had ever seen a spaceship over Possum Kingdom Lake. There was more snickering and then someone yelled, "Shut up!"

"Screw you!" another voice replied. Two men began to scuffle in the back of the courtroom. The judge banged his gavel and demanded order. The bailiff walked quickly their way to put an end to the ruckus. Both men were escorted out of the courtroom. The judge shook his head in anger. "Any more outbursts," he said, "and I'll clear the courtroom."

Simms waited for things to quiet down and then continued, "Another question I must ask is whether you've read about this case in the newspaper, the tabloids or watched the news reports on TV. If you have, raise your hand."

All hands went up.

"Well, that's what I expected. Is there anyone who's been so influenced by these news stories that you've already made up your mind as to Steven Caldwell's guilt or innocence?"

Three jurors raised their hands. Simms looked down at her notes and then addressed a Hispanic woman who had raised her hand. "Mrs. Lopez. I take it you have been following this case pretty closely in the papers and on TV?"

The lady nodded. "Yes."

"And you've already made up your mind on Mr. Caldwell's guilt or innocence."

"Yes, he must be guilty. Why else would he come up with such a story?"

"You mean about seeing a spaceship?"

"Yes, anyone with half a brain knows there is no such thing."

"You don't think you could listen to the testimony and consider the evidence that is presented with an open mind?"

"Sure, I can listen, but there are no spaceships flying around the lake. Everyone knows that."

Simms nodded and looked down at her notes again. Paula put a big check mark by Lopez's name to denote she was a likely strike. After a moment, Simms addressed a middle-aged black man. "Mr. Morris. I noticed you raised your hand indicating you'd made up your mind already in this case."

"Yes, I have. I believe. I believe Steven saw the spaceship."

The courtroom erupted in chants of "I believe! I believe!"

The judge pounded his gavel and glowered at the gallery. "Stop that! Stop that now!" he growled. "I'll not tolerate cheerleading in this courtroom. This is not a football game. Keep your emotions to yourselves."

Simms scratched her head and looked at the judge for permission to continue. The judge nodded. "Mr. Morris. You believe Mr. Caldwell saw a spaceship and that caused him to lose control of the Jeep?"

"Yes, I do. . . . I believe!"

"Amen, brother," yelled someone in the gallery.

The judge pointed to the man. "Bailiff, escort that man out of the courtroom and hold him for contempt of court." The bailiff walked over and yanked the man out of his seat. The judge looked around the gallery. "Anyone else want accommodations compliments of the county sheriff?"

Nobody responded, so the judge nodded again at Simms. "So, you don't think you could sit back and listen to what the witnesses have to say and follow the judge's instructions?"

"No. Like I said. I know they are out there and I really believe Steven Caldwell saw their ship."

Simms rolled her eyes and then looked back at her notes. She addressed a short blond woman next. "Miss Warner. You raised you hand. Do you have an opinion as to Mr. Caldwell's guilt or innocence at this time?"

"Yes. Many people saw the spaceship just a few days after Steven saw it, so he obviously didn't make it up," she said.

"Well, if the judge instructed you that what other people might have seen at a different time and place was irrelevant and not to be considered, would you honor the judge's instructions?"

"How could I ignore what hundreds of people saw?"

"The court will instruct you that you can only consider evidence introduced at trial by myself or Mr. Turner. Are you saying you couldn't obey that instruction?"

"Well, I'm not sure."

Simms shook her head and wrote something in her notebook. She then continued. Her questioning lingered on for two solid days as she questioned each juror thoroughly about their background, employment, hobbies, activities, and personal beliefs. Although it was arguably necessary to uncover any bias or prejudice a juror might have, it was very tedious and I saw more than one of the prospective jurors doze off. When Simms was finally done Wednesday morning, the judge recessed the case for lunch and advised me that I could question the jury panel when we returned.

Paula wanted to work through the lunch hour going over what we had learned about every person on the jury panel. I told her I already knew more than I wanted to know about the jury pool. She protested but when I didn't back down, she handed me a list. "These are the people who I seriously doubt will ever believe Steven's story. They are all well educated professionals or scientific types who are going to require actual proof of the alien flyby in order to vote in favor of Steven's acquittal."

"Okay, great," I said.

Paula handed me a second list of names and said, "These are the ones who would most likely be sympathetic to Steven. They include the very young jurors who are into science fiction and fantasy, workers, laborers, and anyone associated with the tourism industry. We need to get as many of these people on the jury as possible."

"See," I said, "You've already got it figured out. Let's get some lunch."

At lunch we ran into Lauren Swanson. She said she was watching the trial on one of the closed circuit TVs located in the basement of the courthouse. She reiterated her invitation for me and Paula to stay at her place during the trial. We thanked her, but said we didn't want to impose on her. I wondered if she knew what her husband had done. She acted like a high school girl before the prom, all excited about the trial and the media covering the trial. In my mind's eye I could see her putting a plaque on the wall—Convicted murderer Steven Caldwell slept in this room on October 3, 1990.

After lunch the judge turned over the jury panel to me. This was my chance to score some serious points with the jury. I knew they were sick and tired of being interrogated and I frankly couldn't think of a question that Simms hadn't already asked. It was time to end this and get on with the trial. I said, "Ladies and Gentlemen of the jury. I want to thank each and every one of you for your patience these last few days. I know Ms. Simms has asked a lot of questions and pried mercilessly into your private affairs. Let me assure you that the intrusion is over." One of the jurors started clapping and the others laughed in response.

"Seriously, I've watched and listened these past few days to all of the questions and your responses, and I feel I've really gotten to know all of you very well. And I want you to know that I don't have a problem with any one of you. I think each and every one of you would make an excellent juror. Therefore, I have no questions."

There were many smiles amongst the prospective jurors and a general sense of relief swept over them. As I was walking back to my seat Simms was sneering at me and Paula looked like she was in shock.

The judge shrugged. "Very well, please make your strikes."

Paula put the jury list in front of me and said, "Okay, who gets the axe?"

I looked at her. "Didn't you hear what I said? Nobody."

"Nobody? Are you nuts?"

A jolt of fear shot through me. Paula rarely questioned my judgement. The muscles in my neck and shoulders began to ache and my pulse quickened. Was I doing the right thing? My gut feeling was *yes*, but obviously Paula didn't think so. Should I give in and make the strikes? . . . No! I couldn't. It was too late. I'd lose face with the jurors. There was no going back now.

"Maybe I am crazy," I replied, "but as I said, I like *all* the jurors."

Paula shook her head and sat down. Steven looked at her and she shrugged. The bailiff collected the juror lists and took them to the judge. After a moment the judge looked up."Mr. Turner. Where are your strikes?"

I stood up. "We have none, Your Honor. This is a fine-looking jury panel. I'd be proud to have any of these folks on the jury."

The judge mumbled something to himself. "Very well, then. The following persons will take a seat in the jury box."

The judge read the names of the jury members and three alternates and each took a seat. Then he excused the remainder of the jury panel, and the bailiff allowed spectators to fill in the vacant seats in the front of the courtroom. When all that was done the trial began with the reading of the indictment. At 2:30 p.m. Carla Simms stood before the jury box and gave her opening statement.

"Ladies and gentlemen of the jury. Thank you for bearing with me during the *voir dire*. I know it must have seemed like I was unnecessarily prying into your affairs, but that wasn't it at all. It's my duty to be sure that each of you can be fair and impartial jurors. Since I don't know any of you, the only way I can do my job is to ask a lot of questions. So, if I have offended anyone, I apologize. That wasn't my intent." Simms took a deep breath and then smiled. "Anyway, now the housekeeping is done and we can move onto the job at hand—that is to determine whether or not Steven Caldwell is guilty of murder on account of the death of Jimmy Falk on September 10, 1990."

Simms paced a few steps to her left, stopped, and then faced the jury with a very serious look on her face. "As the judge told you, the prosecution has the burden of proof. That means we must prove beyond all reasonable doubt that Steven Caldwell intentionally or knowingly caused the death of Jimmy Falk. We intend to meet that burden by calling a number of friends and acquaintances of Steven Caldwell and Jimmy Falk who will testify that Steven was in love with Susan Weber, that they had talked of marriage, and that he was devastated when Jimmy Falk stole Susan away from him. These witnesses will testify to Steven's unwillingness to accept the loss of Susan and his obsession with getting Susan back at any cost.

"We will call other witnesses such as Steven's scoutmaster Roger Dickens; Sylvia Bassett, the woman who found Steven on the side of the road; Freeman Fry, the first sheriff's deputy on the scene; and detective Ben Swenson who will testify as to the sequence of events of September 10, 1990 which led to the death of Jimmy Falk."

Simms looked over at me. "Now the defense will be cross examining our witnesses and calling their own witnesses trying to show that this was all just a tragic accident caused by an alien spaceship on its way to Cactus Island where it supposedly was going to land. We all know this is nonsense, but unfortunately there are a lot of people in this country who believe or want to believe that intelligent life does exist in outer space, so they will be using this trial to validate their beliefs. But we cannot let these people take this trial hostage."

There was an audible sigh from the gallery. The judge looked up and glared at the person responsible. Steven looked at me and smiled.

"You as jurors cannot abrogate nor delegate your

responsibilities as jurors in this case," Simms said. "Only you can determine Steven Caldwell's guilt or innocence. It doesn't matter what the people out front picketing, or those out on the lake, or in the campsites think. Only the twelve of you have the right and the duty to decide whether Steven Caldwell will be set free or go to jail for five to ninety-nine years, which is the punishment for murder in the State of Texas.

"Now during the course of this trial you're going to hear what a fine young man Steven Caldwell is and that his record and accomplishments are exemplary. We don't dispute that, but leading a perfect life doesn't give a person the right to commit one heinous crime. In this instance, we will show that Steven Caldwell, due to his jealousy and rage over Jimmy Falk taking his true love, made a conscious decision to cause Jimmy Falk's death. Once he made that decision he then diligently began planning and plotting how to accomplish that ill deed without getting caught.

"I must say his scheme was brilliant. Steven knew Jimmy couldn't survive the Jeep plummeting down the mountainside particularly if his seatbelt was jammed. He knew that if he jumped out just as the Jeep left the roadway he wouldn't be seriously hurt but it would make it appear as an accident. Don't be fooled. Steven Caldwell is a very clever young man. You will find out that he's an amateur magician and very knowledgeable about how magicians fool their audiences. One of their techniques is distraction. That is why Steven Caldwell claimed to have seen a spacecraft. He knew that revelation would be sensational and distract everyone's attention from his crime to the alien encounter.

"Don't let him manipulate you as jurors. Take a good look at him and see him for what he is—a cold-blooded murderer who must be brought to justice. Thank you."

Simms sat down.

"Mr. Turner," the judge asked. "Would you like to make an opening statement?"

I stood up and replied, "No, Your Honor. I'll reserve my opening statement until we put on our case in chief."

The judge nodded, "Very well. Ms. Simms, call your first witness."

Simms stood up. "The state calls Freeman Fry."

William Manchee

Fry, a sheriff's deputy, took the stand and testified that he was about five miles from the scene of the accident when he got a call from his dispatcher. He said he went to the accident scene and another sheriff's deputy went to the diner. Fry testified that at the accident scene he saw tire tracks running off the road, and when he went to the ledge he saw the partially submerged Jeep burning below. After securing a fire extinguisher from his trunk, he made his way down the mountainside to the Jeep and tried to extinguish the flames. Unfortunately, the fire was too intense and he was unable to put it out. A couple minutes later the fire department arrived and extinguished the fire. That's when they found Jimmy's body, or what was left of it.

When Simms was finished with Fry, I cross examined him but there wasn't much I could challenge about his testimony. He saw what he saw. I did have two questions that hadn't been addressed.

"When you got to the Jeep was Jimmy's seatbelt still fastened?"

"Yes, it was."

"Did you examine the seatbelt?"

"Yes."

"Did it appear to be working properly?"

"Well, it was damaged and we had difficulty getting it to unfasten."

"So, you couldn't get it unfastened, perhaps Jimmy couldn't either."

"Well, that depends on when it was damaged. I believe it was jammed from the accident."

"But you don't know that for sure?"

"No."

"Was it noisy at the accident scene when you got there?"

"Well, I don't know. What do you mean?"

"Was there a drilling rig operating near the accident scene?"

"Yes, as a matter of fact there was. Those rigs do make quite a racket."

"Thank you, Deputy Fry. I have no further questions."

Simms next called Sylvia Bassett who recounted her discovery of Steven Caldwell lying on the side of the roadway dazed and confused. When she recalled Steven's statement that he had seen a spaceship the gallery buzzed with excitement. The judge banged his gavel and demanded order. Simms asked Bassett if she'd seen the spaceship and she replied she had not, but that there had been reports of UFO sightings at Possum Kingdom lake for years. On cross examination I asked her if she had heard the drilling rig in operation when she found Steven on the side of the road. She said she had not and didn't know there was a drilling rig in the area. After Sylvia Bassett had been excused the judge recessed the case until Thursday morning.

Unfortunately, we couldn't go out to a restaurant without getting mobbed by the press or tourists, so we ordered Chinese to be delivered to our motel room. Paul, Jodie, Paula and I were enjoying our fare when the evening news came on. Of course our trial was the lead story and Amy Tan was on the courthouse steps with the report.

The news anchor said, "Will Rogers once said, 'I've never met a man I didn't like.' Today, Stan Turner said he's never met a juror he didn't like—or at least in Palo Pinto County. Amy Tan is in Palo Pinto County to tell us about that surprising story."

"Yes," Amy Tan said, "I've been following the Steven Caldwell murder trial here at the Palo Pinto County Courthouse in Palo Pinto, Texas. The trial is in recess after a jury was finally seated, Assistant District Attorney Carla Simms made her opening statement, and testimony began. The most shocking event of the day was defense counsel Stan Turner's apparent attempt to win favor with the jury by cutting short what had been two and a half days of grueling *voir dire* conducted by Carla Simms. Turner told the judge he was quite happy with the jury panel and wouldn't subject them to any more questions. In fact, when the Judge asked for the six strikes each side was allowed, Turner didn't have any, stating again there wasn't a jury member on the panel he didn't like.

"Whereas the jury seemed to appreciate Turner's sensitivity and belief in them, many courthouse observers are questioning Turner's strategy. They say failing to remove the panel members who were obviously not likely to be sympathetic to Caldwell's defense was brash, dangerous, and bordering on malpractice.

"As far as the testimony we heard today, there wasn't much brought up that we didn't already know. Sheriff's deputy Freeman Fry testified that he arrived on the scene and seeing the Jeep on fire tried to extinguish it. Turner on cross examination honed in on the fact that Jimmy Falk's seatbelt may have been jammed preventing him from jumping from the vehicle or getting out of it when it caught fire. It was unclear from testimony whether of not the seatbelt was working properly before the accident.

"Testimony will resume tomorrow at nine when Carla Simms is expected to call the mother of the victim, Barbara Falk. This is Amy Tan reporting from Palo Pinto, Texas."

Everyone looked at me when the report was over. "Well, if my gamble doesn't pay off, Steven will have a great incompetent counsel argument for appeal."

"Why did you do that?" Paula said. "I don't understand your thinking."

"Well, I know you have your theory on what makes a good juror just as Carla Simms has hers. The fact is, nobody really knows who's right. I think that the only thing to be accomplished at *voir dire* is to get rid of the extremists one way or the other. What I want is just twelve honest, decent people who don't have hidden agendas. After listening to Simms interrogate the jury panel for two and half days I realized there were only three or four prospects on the jury panel who were what I call extremist and they were all UFO nuts who I knew Simms would strike. So, why not use this fact to gain some leverage with the jury?"

Paula stared at me for a moment and then shook her head. "Well, I hope you're right."

"Me too," I replied. "If Steven goes to jail because I screwed up, I'll be feeling like shit."

"Don't worry," Jodie said. "I think everything is going fine. You did a good job today. Just keep it up."

Jodie's words did little to cheer me. Now I was worried. Had I made a fatal blunder that would ultimately lead to Steven's conviction for murder? It seemed like the right move at the time, but my stomach suddenly was in knots and I had a headache beyond belief. I excused myself and went back to my room to take some aspirin and go over my cross examination questions again. Somehow, I had to get Steven Caldwell off, otherwise he'd get five to ninety-nine years and it would be all my fault. I couldn't live with that. It just wasn't an option.

Chapter 33

Surprise Witness

I stood up and said, "I'm going to bed." Stan looked up but didn't say anything as I walked past him and out the door. I slammed it hard. Stan's cavalier approach to picking a jury really pissed me off. I had worked hard to determine which prospective jurors should be stricken and he had just blown it all off as a waste of time. He'd said he believed in my instincts and wanted me to help him, but I guess that was just talk to make me feel good. I thought Stan was different but he was just a typical male, self-centered and thoughtless.

But I couldn't let my anger and disappointment in Stan's behavior affect my performance as second chair. Steven Caldwell's freedom was at stake, and if we'd made a mistake in jury selection, we needed to make up for it somehow during the remainder of the trial. We couldn't give up over one mistake. It was the final result that was important, not how you got there.

When Stan knocked on my door to go to breakfast on Thursday morning I felt like giving him the cold shoulder, but my plan quickly evaporated when I saw him. His disheveled appearance made it apparent he hadn't slept all night.

"You look like shit," I said.

"I'm not feeling so well," Stan replied.

"Why? What's wrong with you?"

"It might have been the champagne."

"The manager's complimentary bottle? I got one too. So you're hung over? Hmm. That's not like you."

"I couldn't sleep. I thought it might help."

"Why couldn't you sleep?"

"I don't know what got into me yesterday. I was just feeling so confident there in front of the jury. I know it was stupid not to take our strikes, but it just seemed like the right thing to do. Do you think I could get disbarred over it?"

"Oh. So that's it. . . . No. It was a judgment call. You watched the jury, listened to them, and felt it was a good strategy. You may be criticized for it by some, including me, but it was your call and it's water under the bridge now."

Stan took a deep breath. "I'm sorry I ignored you yesterday. I'm still not used to having a partner. I've always just done what I felt was right without consulting anyone."

"I can imagine it's a tough adjustment, but I can't help you if you don't tell me what's going through your head. I have no idea what your trial strategy is in this case. I'm flapping in the wind here, Stan. Help me out."

Over the next thirty minutes Stan finally revealed his trial strategy and I was pleasantly surprised. Now I could see why he had acted the way he had. He was setting a trap for Carla Simms and she was stepping right into it. When I told him I thought his strategy was brilliant, his color started to come back.

"You still look like shit. You better go back to your room and sleep for a couple of hours and then take a shower. I'll tell the judge that you had a bad reaction to something you ate, but you expect to be okay by afternoon. I'll cover for you until then."

"Are you sure? I can take a shower and be there by nine."

"No. We're partners, remember. We cover for each other."

Stan smiled. "Thanks, Paula."

There wasn't time for breakfast so I went straight to the courthouse. Several members of the press inquired as to Stan's whereabouts, but I didn't feel the need to respond to their inquiries since I'd be soon explaining it to the judge. Steven was already seated at the defense table when I arrived, so I joined him.

"Good morning," I said.

"Hi, Paula. Where's Stan?"

"Oh, he had a little allergic reaction to something he ate. He'll be okay by this afternoon."

Steven opened his mouth to respond when the bailiff yelled, "All rise. The 993rd Judicial District Court is now in session!"

The judge took the bench and looked over at me. "Ms.

Waters, where's Mr. Turner?" He didn't look happy with my explanation but he told Carla Simms to call her next witness. Barbara Falk walked slowly to the witness stand. She looked thin and worn out from her ordeal. I wasn't looking forward to cross examining her. The judge administered the oath and then Simms began asking her all about Jimmy. A junior in high school, he was a smart boy with dreams of going to Rice University when he graduated. She didn't know much about the alleged conflict between Steven Caldwell and her son, but she suspected there was a problem when Steven called their home a couple of times.

"Can you tell us about those phone calls?" Simms asked.

"Well, the first one took place about two weeks before the accident. Steven called and asked if Susan was there. He seemed angry and was short with me when I told him that I hadn't seen her. I thought it was rather odd for him to be calling our house since I knew Jimmy and Susan were dating."

"Did you ask Jimmy about it?"

"Yes, but Jimmy didn't like to talk to me about his social life. He just told me not to worry about it."

"You said there was a second time?"

"Yes, a few days before the accident Steven called and asked if Jimmy was going to Camp Comfort for the weekend camp out. I said I thought he was and asked why he wanted to know. He didn't respond right away but finally said he was working on a duty roster and needed to know if he could put him down or not. Again he sounded a bit hostile and I didn't believe that he was being honest about the purpose of the call. I didn't mention this call to Jimmy since he had told me not to worry about the previous call and, obviously, didn't want to talk to me about any problems he might be having with Steven. That probably was a mistake."

Simms continued to question Barbara Falk but there wasn't much she really knew about the events of September 10˙ so I only asked her a couple questions on cross-examination.

"Mrs. Falk. Steven never said anything derogatory about Jimmy, did he?"

"No."

"And he never directly threatened him, did he?"

"No."

"And Jimmy didn't tell you there was a problem between Steven and him, did he?"

"No."

"Now, when Ms. Simms asked you to tell the court about the phone calls, you said the first one took place about three weeks before the accident. Isn't that right?"

"Yes?"

"So, you believe it was an accident and not murder?"

A thoughtful look came over Mrs. Falk's face. She looked up at the judge and then she shrugged."Well, I don't know what to think."

"Thank you. No further questions."

The judge excused Barbara Falk and Ms. Simms called Susan Weber. This was the witness who could really hurt us and I wished Stan were here to cross-examine her. I looked at my watch and saw it was 10:30 a.m. There was a good chance the judge would recess for lunch before I had to begin my cross examination. With a little luck Stan would be back in the courtroom by then and could take over for me. Susan Weber looked sad, alone, and a little scared when she took the stand.

Simms took Susan through her relationship with Steven, the drifting apart, the breakup, her new relationship with Jimmy. Then she asked how Steven had taken it when she and Jimmy started dating.

"He was very upset and jealous when he found out. He called me every day wanting to hang out or do something together. When I said I had other plans he demanded to know what they were and if I was going out with Jimmy."

"When you continued to spurn him, what happened?"

"He got angry and wanted to know what he'd done to make me mad at him. I told him he hadn't done anything but that I was just bored with him."

"How did he take that?"

"I think it really hurt him. All he said after that was that he didn't believe me and that I'd change my mind."

"Did you?"

"No, Jimmy and I were having a lot of fun together. Jimmy was much more talkative and exciting to be around. I would have never gone back to Steven after I'd met Jimmy."

When Simms indicated she had no more questions of Susan, it was about 11:45 a.m. The judge looked at the clock on the wall and said, "All right. We'll recess until 1:30 p.m. at which time you can begin your cross examination, Ms. Waters."

"Yes, Your Honor," I nodded, breathing a sigh of relief.

Although Susan wasn't entirely hostile to Steven, she had portrayed Steven as an angry, jealous, and obsessed ex-boyfriend who had plenty of motive to kill Jimmy Falk. The fact that she obviously still had some affection for him, made her testimony even more effective. It wouldn't be easy for Stan to discredit her.

When I got back to the motel, Stan had ordered us pizza for lunch and looked much better than when I had left him. Since I hadn't eaten breakfast, I was famished and didn't waste any time digging in. While we ate, I briefed him on what had transpired during the morning session and told him he'd be cross-examining Susan Weber when he returned. He said he had gotten a couple hours sleep, taken a hot shower, and felt much better. He apologized again for the previous day and thanked me again for covering for him.

When we got back to the courtroom, Steven was obviously relieved to see Stan. That didn't bother me too much as I knew that Steven had known him for several years and trusted him. Susan took the stand and the judge told Stan he could begin his cross examination.

Stan smiled. "Miss Weber. I know you've suffered a horrible loss and I don't want to make you suffer any additional agony over Jimmy's death. Unfortunately, I do have to ask you a few questions since Steven's life is now on the line."

Susan replied, "It's okay."

"At one time you and Steven were in love, is that not correct?"

"Well, we thought we were."

"I understand you later realized you were not in love with Steven. You've said that, but don't you think Steven still loves you?"

"Yes, and I feel bad that my feelings changed, but—"

"That's all right. All I'm getting at is that Steven loved you and probably still loves you, right?"

She nodded. "Yes."

"In the time that you were together did you ever see Steven do anything violent?"

"No. I can't think of anything."

"How would you characterize his temperament?"

"He was kind, gentle, and easy-going."

"Didn't you say he was boring?"

"Yes, compared to Jimmy."

"So, do you really think Steven would be capable of murder?"

"No, I wouldn't have thought so, but he changed after I left him. He was angry and couldn't let go."

"Yes, he loved you. He was hurting. It's not easy to let go of someone you love. Did he really act that abnormally under the circumstances?"

"No. I guess not."

"Wouldn't you have done the same thing, had the tables been turned?"

She shrugged. "Maybe."

"Is it possible that when Steven asked Jimmy to go into town with him to get supplies, that he was finally accepting the fact that it was over between you and him, and moving on?"

"Yes. I suppose that's possible."

"And from your intimate knowledge of Steven, isn't that much more likely than Steven concocting a sinister plot to murder Jimmy Falk?"

Susan shrugged again and took a deep breath.

Stan didn't wait for an answer. He said, "Thank you. No further questions."

On redirect Simms went through the altercation between Steven and Jimmy at the pep rally and asked Susan to repeat Steven's parting words. She replied, "This isn't over, Jimmy. Not by a longshot." After Susan had been excused, Simms examined detective Ben Hayden. He added little to the testimony we'd already heard. Simms next called the troop's scoutmaster, Roger Dickens.

"Mr. Dickens. Can you tell us how your troop is organized?"

"Well, I'm the scoutmaster, Steven Caldwell is . . . was the junior assistant scoutmaster. He had worked his way through the troop, became an eagle scout, and when he was too old to be a scout any longer, we invited him to be our junior assistant scoutmaster. We also have an assistant scoutmaster and three parent advisors who come to meetings and sometimes go on camping trips as well."

"As a junior assistant scoutmaster what were Steven's duties?'

"To assist me and take over whenever I couldn't personally handle an activity."

"Have you given him any specific tasks to assist you when you're at Camp Comfort?"

"Yes, he was in charge of the mess hall and the campfire."

"Does that mean he arranges the entertainment for the campfire?"

"Yes."

"And did that entertainment usually include a magic show?"

"Yes, Steven's hobby was magic and he always put on a little show at camp. He was quite good, you know, making things disappear and later reappear."

"He was a smart kid then?"

"He was an Eagle Scout," Dickens replied. "You have to be very smart and very determined to earn that award."

"And what was Jimmy Falk's position in the troop?"

"He was one of our veteran members, a Life Scout working on his Eagle."

"So Jimmy and Steven Caldwell had been together in the troop a long time?"

"Yes, about three years."

"How did they get along?"

"Just fine, as far as I can remember. Steven and Sam, that's Jimmy's brother, were good friends."

"Did you ever notice any disharmony between Steven and Jimmy?"

"Well, at our last meeting, before the camp out at Possum Kingdom Lake, they had an argument. I didn't realize what it was about at the time. I just thought it was Jimmy rebelling against something Steven wanted him to do. I only found out later it was about Susan."

"Did Steven strike Jimmy during that argument?"

"Well, you know, he might have pushed him a little like boys do. Jimmy certainly wasn't hurt, that's for sure."

"Did anything else happen between Jimmy and Steven that alarmed you?"

"Well, at the camp out Steven was picking on Jimmy and teasing him a little more than I thought appropriate, so I pulled him aside, told him to lighten up, and keep his personal issues to himself."

"What was his reaction?"

"He said he was sorry and he'd figure out another way to deal with Jimmy Falk."

The courtroom went deadly silent. Carla Simms looked over at the jury and said, "So, he said he'd figure out another way to deal with Jimmy Falk."

"Yes."

"What was the tone of his voice?"

"It was a little intense, so I told him to grow up and act like a man."

"Intense? You mean threatening?"

"Perhaps. I didn't like his attitude so I told him to go take a walk and come back when he was in control of his emotions."

"Did he take your advice?"

"Yes, and when he came back twenty minutes later it was like nothing had happened. In fact, that's when he asked for a volunteer to go to town with him to pick up supplies."

"So, what happened then?"

"Jimmy volunteered. The boys love to ride in the Jeep, so they always fight over who gets to go to town with Steven."

"I see. So, Steven selected Jimmy?"

"Right."

"When they left, did you think everything was okay?"

"Yes."

"Pass the witness, Your Honor," Simms said.

The judge nodded. "Mr. Turner."

Stan stood up and stepped a few feet in front of the defense table. "Mr. Dickens. You said Jimmy and Steven seemed to be over their differences when they left for town, is that right?"

"Yes."

"And you testified that Jimmy, in fact, jumped at the opportunity to go with Steven, correct?"

"Yes."

"So, he couldn't have felt very threatened by Steven—"

"Objection, calls for speculation," Simms said.

"Let me rephrase," Stan replied. "In your opinion, did Jimmy seem at all concerned about being alone with Steven?"

"No, not at all. In fact, I heard them laughing and joking while they were getting ready to go."

"So, in your experience as a scoutmaster, were skirmishes like the ones between Steven and Jimmy unusual?"

"No, not really. Kids are kids. They don't always get along and tempers flare on occasion. It's not that unusual."

"One last question. You testified Steven was an Eagle Scout, right?"

"Yes," Dickens replied.

"Isn't one requirement for being an Eagle Scout to have a high moral character?"

"Yes, absolutely. If there was any question about a scout's moral character, he wouldn't get the award."

"Isn't it also true that Steven was awarded the God and Country Award?"

"Yes, he got that the same year he made Eagle Scout."

"That's a religious award, isn't it?"

"Yes, it requires the scout to pass a very rigorous course of study of his particular religion. His priest, minister, or rabbi must participate and certify that he qualifies for the award."

"So, along with being very smart and determined, wouldn't you say Steven Caldwell was of the highest moral character by virtue of his being an Eagle Scout and a recipient of the God and Country Award?"

Dickens smiled broadly. "Yes, I would. There's no doubt in my mind about that!"

"Thank you, Mr. Dickens. Pass the witness."

I felt better. Stan had done some damage on cross. Sure there was a fight over Susan Weber, that had been established, but it didn't seem to me that Carla Simms had come close to convincing anyone that it was enough to trigger the intricate plot to kill Jimmy Falk that she was trying to sell. But she still had a few more witnesses, so I wasn't breathing easily as of yet. Her next witness was Steven's best friend and Jimmy's brother, Sam Falk. This would be interesting.

As with Susan Weber, Sammy Falk was caught in the middle of this teenage love triangle. Obviously he would be torn between his best friend and his brother. I could see the torment on his young face as he took the witness stand and was sworn in. He was shorter than I expected with dark brown eyes and black hair.

"Sammy," Simms began. "You are Jimmy's brother, right?"

Sammy nodded and replied, "Yes, Ma'am."

"I'm sorry about your brother. I know this must be hard for you testifying today, but it's very important that you tell the jury everything you know about what happened between Steven Caldwell and your brother."

"It's okay. I understand."

"Now, you were good friends with Steven Caldwell, isn't that right?"

"Yes, ma'am."

"Tell us about Steven's relationship with Susan Weber before she met your brother."

Sammy looked inward for a moment and then smiled, "They were in love. I thought they were going to get married. They hung out together all the time and couldn't be away for ten minutes without calling each other."

"So did that change at all?"

"Yes, Steven and I graduated and went to junior college, but Susan had another year in high school. They didn't see as much of each other after that. They still hung out on weekends for a while but even that began to taper off."

"So tell us how Susan and Jimmy met, would you?"

"Yes, ma'am. They met at our house one day. Steven, Susan, and I were messing around one Saturday afternoon when Jimmy came home. Jimmy knew Steven but hadn't met Susan, so I introduced them. Later Jimmy told me he thought Susan was hot. I didn't think much about it at the time, but a few weeks later I mentioned that Susan and Steven seemed to be drifting apart and Jimmy said he was going to call her. I didn't think he was serious but before I knew it they had set up a date."

"Did Steven find out about it?"

"Yes. I overheard Susan telling Jimmy that Steven was very upset that she was dating him. Jimmy asked her what she was going to do, and she said it was over between Steven and her, so not to worry about it."

"Did you observe anything else as a result of the breakup between Steven and Susan?"

"Yes, Steven asked me to talk to Jimmy and tell him to back off."

"Did he say what he would do if he didn't?"

Sammy looked down and took a deep breath.

"It's important, Sammy," Simms persisted. "Tell the jury what Steven told you he would do if Jimmy didn't leave Susan alone."

Sammy looked up at Simms. "He said he'd kill him."

"What? I don't think the jury heard that," Simms pressed.

Louder, Sammy said, "He said he'd kill him if he didn't stay away from her."

The gallery erupted into excited chatter. The judge banged his gavel and demanded order. As the room quieted, all eyes were on Carla Simms, who had a smug look on her face. "Thank you, Sammy," she said. "No further questions."

The judge looked at his watch. "Okay, we have just enough time to finish up with this witness and then we'll break for the day. Mr. Turner, your witness."

Stan stood. "Thank you, Your Honor. Sammy, what did you think when Steven said he would kill your brother if he didn't back off?"

"It bothered me a little."

"A little? Not a lot?"

Sammy shrugged.

"It didn't bother you a lot because you didn't take it seriously, did you? You didn't really believe Steven would kill your brother, did you?"

"No, sir."

"Isn't it common for kids to say they're going to kill someone if they do something they don't like? For instance, I'll kill you if you eat any more of my popcorn?"

Simms stood up. "Objection, counsel is testifying."

Judge Applegate shrugged. "I'll allow it."

"Go ahead, Sammy. You can answer my question," Stan said.

"Yes, I've heard people say that before."

"So, is that why you were only a little upset when Steven said he would kill your brother if he didn't leave Susan alone?"

Sammy nodded. "Yes, sir."

"Thank you, Sammy. Pass the witness," Stan said.

Simms stood up. "Jimmy. Now that your brother is dead, how do you feel about what Steven said."

"Objection!" Stan said. "Irrelevant and intended to inflame the jury."

"Withdrawn," Simms said. "Let me put it this way. If you didn't think Steven would kill your brother, what did you think he would do to him?"

"I don't know. I never thought he'd do anything. I just assumed it would blow over."

"Thank you, pass the witness."

The judge frowned. "Are we done with this witness?"

"Yes, Your Honor," Stan replied.

"Very well then, we are in recess until 9:30 tomorrow morning."

As soon as the judge left the bench the gallery erupted in spirited conversation. It was obvious that Sammy's testimony had hurt us. I could see it in the dejected look on Steven's face and the worry in Stan's eyes. Fortunately, by my calculation Sammy was the prosecution's last witness so I thought the worst was over. But I was wrong. Simms walked over to Stan and handed him some papers. "Oh, here's an addition to our witness list."

Stan snatched the paper out of her hand and began reading it. Suddenly his eyes widened and he looked up at Simms angrily, "You're calling Peter? You can't do that. He's my son."

"I don't care if he's your son. He knew Jimmy and Steven and he's fair game."

Stan glared at Simms and said, "There are ten other members of the troop you could just as easily call. There's no need to call my son. You're doing this just to irritate and harass the defense."

"Take it up with the judge," Simms said as she walked off.

Stan stared at her as she left the courtroom. For a moment I thought Stan was going to chase after her, but he didn't move. I went over to him and put my hand on his shoulder. "Don't worry. The judge won't allow it. She has no justification for adding Peter to the witness list at the last minute. She's just trying to upset you and distract you while you're preparing to put on our defense. Just forget about it, let me handle this."

"Shit!" Stan yelled, throwing his legal pad down on the table. "Rebekah is going to have a stroke when the constable shows up with a subpoena. I can't believe that bitch would do something like this."

"I'm sorry, Stan. I'll call Rebekah and warn her. You just concentrate on getting your case ready. You'll have to give your opening statement before noon tomorrow, I'm sure. You can't be distracted by this."

Stan agreed to let me handle Simm's last-minute ploy, but I feared he'd still be quite distracted. It was a very clever move and I had to admire Simm's timing, but I couldn't let her get away with it. It would be a late night researching case law at the Palo Pinto County Law Library. I had to find some legal authority for keeping Peter off the witness stand. I just prayed I'd find some.

Chapter 34

Campfire Tales

Calling Peter as a witness was a low blow and I couldn't understand why Carla Simms would resort to something so cold. Could Peter know something important about the case that he hadn't told me? I couldn't imagine it. When I got back to my motel room, I called Rebekah to warn her Peter was about to be subpoenaed, but it was too late. The constable had already been there.

"Peter has school tomorrow. He can't go to Palo Pinto."

"He has to, honey. He's been served with a subpoena."

"But he doesn't know anything." Rebekah complained. "This is so ridiculous."

"I know. It's just trial strategy. She's trying to piss me off so I'll lose my focus."

"That's not right. You can't let her get away with this."

"We won't, but Peter will have to show up just in case. The problem will be in getting him here. I can't really afford the five or six hours it will take to come get him."

Rebekah sighed. "I'll have my father bring him. Do you have room for them at the motel?"

"I'll have to make room. There aren't any other accommodations in town."

"Don't let that bitch be mean to my boy," Rebekah said. "I'll never forgive you if Peter is traumatized by all this."

"Don't worry. He's a tough kid. He can handle it."

Peter was a tough kid—he had to be with two older brothers. He was very independent and had a mind of his own which had made raising him a challenge. His counselor said the problem was that his IQ was through the roof and he saw the world differently than the average student. He wasn't satisfied with just living and having fun like most teenagers. He wanted to understand the world and how everything fit together. Despite his high intelligence and inquisitive mind, he was still a teenager who spent countless hours playing video games and watching football on TV. The difference between Peter and his friends, however, was that Peter had actually designed and built his own video game and could explain to you the intricacies of the NFL compensation system. But above all, he was a good kid with a kind heart who'd go out of his way to help out a friend or even a stranger, if he thought it was the right thing to do.

After Rebekah had hung up, I started to review my trial outline and work on my opening statement. By now the jury knew the facts of the case pretty well and I didn't want to bore them with a bunch of redundant testimony. I planned to pick up where Carla Simms had left off. The main difference between Simms' case and mine was the interpretation of what had happened the afternoon of September 10, 1990. I didn't have a big quarrel with what the witnesses had said so far, but I needed to show the jury that the facts weren't what they seemed.

By the time Peter arrived with his grandfather, it was nearly midnight. I asked him what he knew about the love triangle between Steven, Susan, and Jimmy. He claimed to know nothing about it. That puzzled me because I couldn't imagine Carla Simms calling him up to the stand without a long list of questions to ask. But it was too late to worry about that now. After getting a cot from the housekeeping staff for my father-in-law, we all turned in for the night.

The next morning at breakfast, Paula advised me that through her research she hadn't found any definitive law on the subject of calling a relative of defense counsel as a witness. It was apparently totally within the discretion of the trial judge. The controlling issue was whether or not the witness had some direct knowledge of facts material to the case. I felt better at hearing this because I couldn't imagine that Peter had any such knowledge. When Paula pointed this out to the judge before he brought in the jury and the trial recommenced, Carla Simms protested.

"Your Honor. If you will indulge me, I can assure you Peter Turner does have some very relevant testimony to give in this case."

"Very well," Judge Applegate said. "Let's hear it, and it better be relevant." He turned to the bailiff. "Bring in the jury."

Simms didn't flinch at the judge's admonition. Instead, as

soon as the jurors were seated, she turned and said, "The state calls Peter Turner."

The gallery buzzed as Peter walked briskly up to the witness stand. The judge banged his gavel demanding order while Carla Simms glanced over at me, a smug smile on her face. The judge told Peter to raise his right hand and then swore him in. Carla Simms stood and began her direct examination.

"Peter, I know this is kind of weird, calling you as a witness in a trial in which your father is defense counsel, but you know something that could be very important in determining whether Steven Caldwell is guilty or innocent."

"I do?"

"Yes. I believe so. I understand you're in Roger Dickens' scout troop?"

"Yes, ma'am."

"And Steven Caldwell is your junior assistant scoutmaster?"

"Yes, ma'am."

"So, were you friends with Jimmy Falk?"

"I guess. We knew each other."

"Were you aware that Jimmy Falk was dating Susan Weber?"

"Not back then. I heard about it later."

"Were you at Camp Comfort the night of Jimmy's death?"

"Yes, ma'am."

"Were you in the mess hall when Steven Caldwell asked Jimmy to go to town with him?"

"Well, he didn't ask him. He asked for volunteers and Jimmy said he'd go."

"Did you hear any strange noises on that day?"

Peter grimaced. "Strange noises?"

"Right, any sounds out of the ordinary?"

He thought a moment. "Yeah, there was an oil well being drilled across the road. It was very noisy."

"Anything else?"

"Oh, yes. Earlier that day I heard a banging noise coming from the parking lot."

"Really? Did you find out what it was?"

"Not exactly. I went to check it out, but it stopped before I got there."

"So, you don't know what made the banging noise?"

"No, Ma'am."

"What kind of sound was it—wood on wood, metal on metal?"

"It sounded like metal on metal."

"Did you see anyone in the parking lot when you got there?"

"Yes. Steven was getting out of the Jeep."

"Did you see what he was doing in the Jeep?"

"No, Ma'am."

"Was he carrying anything when you saw him?"

"He had his tool box."

"Could the sound have been Steven banging on the seatbelt in the Jeep?"

"Objection!" Paula said. "Counsel is leading the witness."

"Sustained," Judge Applegate replied.

"Do you have any idea what Steven was banging on?"

"Objection!" Paula said. "Assumes facts not in evidence. Your Honor, Ms. Simms is deliberately misstating prior testimony. Peter said he didn't know where the sound came from."

"Sustained."

"Did you talk to Steven when you saw him?"

"Yes. I told him I'd heard someone banging on something and wondered what was going on."

"What was his response?"

"He just shrugged and said he hadn't heard anything."

"So, what did you do then?"

"Nothing. I just followed him to the mess hall."

"Pass the witness."

Paula rose. "Peter. Do you know where the banging sound came from?"

"No, ma'am."

"Do you know who was making the sound?"

"No, ma'am."

"Did you tell Ms. Simms you didn't know anything about this case?"

"No, ma'am. I've never talked to Ms. Simms."

Paula looked over at Carla Simms incredulously. "Peter, who

did you tell about hearing the banging noise?"

"I think I told one of the sheriff's men a long time ago."

Paula shook her head angrily. "Your Honor, I move that Ms. Simms be sanctioned for dragging Peter Turner out of school and all the way from Dallas when he had no material information to provide this court."

"Your Honor!" Simms screamed. "This is outrageous and clearly calculated to prejudice the jury—"

Judge Applegate stood up. "In chambers, now!"

The judge stormed out, leaving a courtroom full of stunned spectators. In chambers the judge chastised Simms for calling Peter as a witness and Paula for her oral motion for sanctions. He warned them both that any further breaches of proper courtroom behavior would be dealt with harshly. He asked Paula if she was sure she wanted to press her motion for sanctions. Paula said no, she'd withdraw it. He asked Simms if she had any more witnesses. She indicated she did not. He said when we got back in the courtroom he'd take any motions before the defense put on their case.

Back in the courtroom and before the jury was brought in Paula stood. "The defense moves for a directed verdict, Your Honor," Paula said. "The prosecution has rested without meeting their burden of proof as to each of the elements of murder as set forth in section 19.02 of the Penal Code."

"Motion denied," the judge said. "We're going to let the jury decide this one."

With that we were dismissed with instructions to be ready to proceed with the defendant's case in thirty minutes. During the recess I talked to Peter to be sure he was okay. He said he was. I was about to send him and his grandfather back to Dallas when I got an interesting idea. I asked him if he'd like to tell the jury a campfire tale. He said he would.

The trial resumed and Judge Applegate told me to present my case. I stood up to give my opening statement. "Ladies and gentlemen of the jury. You haven't heard much from me or my partner, Paula Waters, during the course of this trial. That is because the prosecution gets to put on their case first. This custom, in part, is followed because the prosecution has the burden of proof in a criminal trial. That is, they must prove beyond any reasonable doubt that the defendant is guilty of the offense for which he is charged. In this case they must prove beyond any reasonable doubt that Steven Caldwell knowingly or intentionally caused the death of Jimmy Falk. What Paula and I will show over the next few days is that the prosecution has failed to meet their burden and that there is reasonable doubt as to whether Steven Caldwell is guilty of murder.

"We will be calling a number of witnesses to show reasonable doubt, but before we do that let's consider the facts that have been established thus far. First, we know that Steven Caldwell and Jimmy Falk both dated Susan Weber. That's no big secret. We know that Steven was upset, as any jilted lover would be, when Jimmy started dating Susan. We can't deny that. The big question, however, is whether these events caused Steven Caldwell to concoct a complex and risky plot to kill Jimmy Falk. We think not.

"What we will show in the next few days is clear evidence that Steven Caldwell is a decent, gentle, and a moral person who would never even consider taking the life of another human being. We will show that death of Jimmy Falk on September 10, 1990 was the result of a string of tragic events over which Steven Caldwell had little or no control. Specifically, we will show that Steven and Jimmy were returning from an amicable shopping trip into town. The weather was bad as a line of thunderstorms was moving through the area. There were strong winds, lightning, thunder and heavy rain. Steven admitted to the police that he was trying to impress Jimmy and was probably traveling too fast. When he rounded the bend just before the entrance to Camp Comfort he was distracted, took his eyes off the road for a split second, and lost control over the Jeep. When he realized the Jeep was going off the cliff, he screamed to Jimmy to jump as he was preparing to do himself. Unfortunately, Jimmy's seatbelt jammed and he was unable to escape.

"As you know, Steven jumped to safety while Jimmy fell with the Jeep to his death. If we convince you that these are the facts of this case, then you must find Steven Caldwell not guilty because he wouldn't have intentionally or knowingly caused the death of Jimmy Falk. Even if we don't convince you 100 percent you still could not find Steven Caldwell guilty of murder if there was any reasonable doubt as to whether he intentionally or knowingly caused the death of Jimmy Falk.

"Now I know some of you might have already made up your minds in this case, but I want to remind you that you have a duty to listen to all the evidence before you make a decision. So, please keep your minds open. Listen carefully to the remaining witnesses, consider the rest of the evidence that I will be introducing, and then, and only then, consider all the evidence that has been presented to you in its entirety. Thank you."

Judge Applegate said, "You may call your first witness."

"The defense calls Peter Turner," I said.

The judge frowned. Carla Simms looked at me like I was a drunken lunatic. "Your Honor, Peter Turner was just on the stand."

"Yes," I said. "Now that he's testified for the prosecution I'd like him to testify for the defense."

"Your Honor," Simms pressed. "This witness is not on the defense's witness list."

"Since he's here, Your Honor, and already sworn in, we've decided to call him as a defense witness. He has valuable information that the jury needs to hear. I don't see how the prosecution can complain since they subpoenaed him."

The judge raised his eyebrows and tilted his head thoughtfully. Finally he said, "You've opened the door to Mr. Turner testifying, Ms. Simms. I'm going to have to allow it."

Simms shook her head in dismay and sat. I looked over at Peter and nodded. He got up and made his way to the witness stand once again. He looked up at the judge and smiled. The courtroom was as quiet as the library on Christmas Day. I began.

"Peter, how many years have you been going to Camp Comfort for camping trips?"

"This was my fourth trip."

"And were Steven Caldwell and Jimmy Falk with you each of these times?"

"Yes, they were."

"Now, what do you do at night on these camp outs?"

"At night there's always a campfire."

"What do you do at these campfires?"

"Well, we sing, have contests, tell jokes, give out awards and tell stories."

"What kind of stories are told at these campfires?"

"Ghost stories, stories about cowboys and Indians, and stories about Cactus Island."

"Who tells these stories?"

"Our scoutmaster and sometimes the scouts themselves."

"Have you ever told a story at one of these campfires?"

"Yes."

"Which one?"

"Last camp out I told the story about the alien landings at Cactus Island."

"How do you know that story?"

"Someone tells it at every campfire. I heard it the first year I went to camp. It's kind of a tradition."

"Could you tell the story to the judge and the jury?"

"Objection!" Simms yelled. "Your Honor. This is totally irrelevant, prejudicial, and a waste the court's valuable time."

I replied, "Your Honor. I beg to differ. Steven Caldwell's state of mind is an issue in this trial. If he heard this story four or five times, it could go a long way in explaining his behavior on the day of Jimmy's death."

The judge smiled. "Actually, I would like to hear the story, and I think everyone in the courtroom would like to hear it as well. Am I right?"

The gallery responded with screams of approval and applause. Peter started to laugh. Simms glared at the judge who finally picked up his gavel and banged it a few times. "All right. Let's get on with it."

"Go ahead, Peter," I said. "Tell us the story of the landings on Cactus Island."

Chapter 35

Closing Arguments

Peter wiggled in his chair and with a deadly serious look on his face began. "Shortly after World War II two veterans and their fishing guide were out on Possum Kingdom Lake fishing near Cactus Island. It was late afternoon and the men were about to call it a day when a terrible wind came up, creating monstrous waves that nearly capsized their boat. They held on for dear life as the small bass boat was tossed up and down by the waves and spun around by gale force winds. Then the sky got very dark and they saw blue lightning in the distance and heard a noise so shrill it nearly busted their eardrums.

"They held their ears trying to protect them from the noise, but it didn't help. Finally, the noise died down and they noticed the blue lightning coming closer and closer. They wondered what was causing it as they'd never seen anything like it before. They watched it until it was directly overhead.

"Then they realized the blue lightning was coming from a huge spaceship the size of a football field. Both of the men had seen some pretty strange things while fighting in the war, but nothing like this alien spacecraft that was hovering over Cactus Island. As they watched in sheer terror the spaceship began to drop lower and lower until it had landed on the island.

"Although they desperately wanted to stay and watch the spacecraft, they feared for their lives so they tried to start the outboard engine and get away as fast as they could. Unfortunately, the motor wouldn't start and they found themselves dead in the water. Lucky for them the aliens paid no attention to them and went on about their business.

"As the two fishermen watched, the spacecraft's huge side doors opened and out came what seemed like ten thousand huge frogmen. They looked like humans except for their pale green colored skin and webbed hands and feet. The frogmen, each over six feet tall, dived into the lake and began to feed.

"The fishermen were panicked now with swarms of frogmen all around them, swimming, diving, jumping, and churning the water like a beater in a mixing bowl. It was all the men could do just to keep the small boat afloat.

"Finally, the frogmen began to move away from the island as the schools of fish around it began to flee from their new predators. With the frogmen gone the fishermen decided to go ashore and take a closer look at the spacecraft. They didn't think anyone was on the ship, but before they reached the shore they saw people running around the spacecraft like mechanics or pilots checking out the condition of the ship. The men all wore a dark blue uniform with a yellow triangle on their chest. There was some kind of writing within the triangle but it was not a language the fishermen had ever seen.

"The fishermen hid behind some rocks and watched the aliens at work. When they appeared to be finished with their preparations, a giant drill dropped from the belly of the ship and began to turn and drill deep into the island. The men watched in wonder until they heard the frogmen returning. The fishermen jumped into their boat, got it started, and made their escape. From a distance they watched the huge spacecraft take off, flashing its blue lights over the landscape as it glided toward them.

"When the big ship passed over them and they were engulfed by the blue light, a strange thing happened. The fishermen forgot what they'd seen and only had a vague recollection that something unusual had transpired that day. Within a few weeks it all just seemed like a bad dream, except one odd thing they remembered, not a single fish was caught in the lake for weeks after that fateful day.

"Even though the blue lightning made it difficult for people to remember what they'd seen, over the years the spaceship returned many times and people began to piece together what was happening at Cactus Island. When the fish quit biting for a week or more, they knew they had been visited by the alien spacecraft. The fishermen called it the Blue Tide.

"Many believe that the big drill that came from the belly of the spaceship created a shaft down to a cave that lies under the lake and surfaces on dry land. Some believe the aliens wander around at night looking for women and children to kidnap and take back to their dying planet. Some say the frogmen, if the fish don't satisfy them, will come on land at dusk and feed on dogs and small children."

"Objection, Your Honor!" Simms protested. "This is—"

"Okay, okay," Judge Applegate said. "I think that's enough. Objection sustained. Thank you, Peter. That was quite a story, but I think we get the picture."

Peter shrugged. "Yes, sir."

"Do you have any further questions, Mr. Turner?"

"No, Your Honor."

"Ms. Simms. Would you like to cross?"

Simms gave Peter a hard look. "Peter. Do you believe that what you just told us about is true?"

Peter thought for a moment. "No, I guess not. I've never seen the aliens so I can't say that they exist."

Simms smiled. "Pass the witness."

"Redirect?" the Judge asked.

"Yes," I said. "Peter, you say you don't believe the stories about Cactus Island, but when you are at Camp Comfort do you or the other scouts ever keep an eye out for the frogmen or look up in the sky hoping to see the spaceship?"

"Yes. All the time. That's the best part of coming to Possum Kingdom Lake—to hunt for frogmen and humanoids."

"Have any of the other scouts told you they believe in the Cactus Island landings?"

"Sure. Lots of them do."

Simm's didn't have any more questions, so Peter stepped down. As he walked down the aisle of the courtroom many spectators smiled and whispered. "Great story, Peter. . . . Way to go, boy. . . . Thank you, Peter. . . . That was far out." Peter basked a moment in the limelight and then his grandfather escorted him out of the courtroom. The judge asked me to call my next witness.

"The defense calls Carl Loftus," I said.

Carl Loftus took the stand, was sworn in, and told the jury he had been hired to analyze all the evidence at hand and then prepare a video recreating the accident. I asked him if he would play the video.

"Certainly," Carl said and pushed a button on the remote. The big TV came to life and a roadway where the accident took place came into view. The camera angle was from above and far enough away so the jury could see exactly what happened. An animated Jeep suddenly came around the corner traveling very fast. An object passed overhead and the driver's head moved to follow it. Instead of turning with the curve, the Jeep slipped off the pavement. The driver looked ahead again and tried to bring the Jeep back onto the roadway, but the Jeep sailed over the side of the cliff. Just as the rear tires left the pavement, the left driver's door flew open and the driver jumped out.

The scene faded, and when it reappeared the camera angle was from the bottom of the mountain. On the right side the driver was seen hitting the ground and rolling to a stop while the Jeep sailed over the cliff, landed on its front tires, flipped over vertically, hit a rock and rolled over and over on its side. Just before it reached the lake, it exploded into a fiery inferno and finally came to rest in three feet of water.

People in the gallery moaned and groaned during the video. A lady screamed. The judge looked at her, but didn't bang his gavel. When the smoke and steam had cleared, the scene faded away. Carl played the video again, this time in slow motion, then he went into a scientific explanation of the dynamics of the accident.

"Now, you're aware that the prosecution contends that Steven Caldwell intentionally took the Jeep over the cliff and bailed out just as it plummeted down the mountain, right?" I said.

"Yes, that's what I understand."

"How risky a strategy would that have been?"

"Very risky. You saw the video. It's a miracle that Steven Caldwell is alive today."

"So, in your opinion was this an accident or did Steven Caldwell intentionally cause the Jeep to go off the road?"

"Everything I saw was consistent with an accident. Jumping out of that Jeep had to be an act of desperation. Intentionally driving it over the cliff and jumping out of it would be tantamount to committing suicide."

"Thank you, Mr. Loftus. Pass the witness."

The judge said, "Ms. Simms. Cross?"

"Yes, Your Honor," Simms said, rising slowly from her seat. "Mr. Loftus, is there anything in your investigation that would categorically disprove the prosecutions contention that Steven Caldwell intentionally drove the Jeep off the cliff?"

Loftus shrugged and replied, "No. It's possible he did it intentionally."

"And, in fact, teenagers often don't think through what they plan to do, wouldn't you agree?"

"True."

"And teenagers often don't appreciate the danger they routinely put themselves into—i.e., driving on a mountain road at an excessive speed?"

"Uh huh."

"So, although, to you or me, jumping out of that Jeep may have been suicidal, to Steven Caldwell it may not have seemed like such a big a deal?"

"I suppose that's true, but I—"

"No further questions, Your Honor."

My next witness was a gamble. I planned to call Robert Swanson. I doubted he would admit to anything, but I needed to set him up and then hope Adam Peterson or Carl Brooks would tell the truth and contradict him. If not, the whole thing could be perceived as an act of desperation and hurt our case. I noticed Carl Brooks sitting in the gallery and I didn't want him to hear my direct examination of Robert Swanson, so I stood up and said, "Your Honor, I'm invoking the rule and request that Carl Brooks be removed from the courtroom." The rule I was referring to was the option of either prosecution or defense to object to any potential witness hearing another witness' testimony. If I wanted Brooks to contradict Swanson's story, I didn't want him to know how Swanson had testified.

"Bailiff. Please escort Mr. Brooks outside until we need him," the judge said.

"Thank you, Your Honor," I said. "The defense calls Robert Swanson."

Simms stood up. "Your Honor. I see another person on Mr. Turner's witness list in the courtroom—Rose Brewer. I'd ask that she be removed as well."

"Very well," the Judge said. "Ms. Brewer, you'll need to go with the bailiff too."

Rose stood up. I hadn't even noticed her in the courtroom. She was on our witness list but I hadn't planned on calling her unless it was absolutely necessary. She had been very open and helpful in the investigation, so I didn't want her to lose her job for testifying against her boss. We made eye contact, but she didn't give me that big smile that she had in the past. There was an anxious look on her face and I knew instantly something was wrong. As she left the courtroom, I noticed she had a tight grip on a rolled-up magazine. She held it against her bosom like she was afraid someone might try to take it from her.

"All right, Mr. Swanson. Please raise your right hand," the Judge said. "Do you swear to tell the truth and nothing but the truth so help you God."

"I do," Swanson said.

I stood and began asking him questions about his background, education, family, and employment. He gave us a complete rundown of his many business enterprises and admitted he owned a majority interest in the Weatherford Airport and the Brazos Country Resort. I asked him how he came to own an airport.

"I was a pilot in the Navy during the Vietnam War and when I came off active duty, I flew for Braniff Airlines for a few years. As an airline pilot I had a lot of free time and I got involved in several business ventures with other pilots. When the Weatherford Airport came on the market, I was intrigued by the idea of owning an airport, so I put together a limited partnership and bought it."

I nodded. "So, you must be a very happy man with all the visitors in town and at the lake."

"Well, we always encourage tourism. It's good for business."

"I bet. For nearly six months now your businesses have been booming. I bet you're rolling in dough."

"Well—"

"It almost makes you wonder if you didn't invite the aliens to Possum Kingdom Lake."

Laughter broke out in the gallery and the judge frowned. Swanson smiled. "If I'd have known how to contact them, I probably would have invited them."

"But since you didn't know how to contact them you did the next best thing, right? You staged an alien landing."

"What?" Swanson chuckled. "How could I do that?"

"Isn't it true you support the Confederate Air Force?"

"Yes. I let them use a hangar out at the Weatherford Airport. What of it?"

"And haven't you had a Lockheed P-38 Lightning parked out there?"

"Well, yes but—"

"Would you describe that plane for the court?"

"Sure, it's an old World War II bomber. It's got a twin fuselage with two propellers."

"It's a big plane, right?"

"It's a bomber. Of course it's big."

"Now, Carl Brooks and Adam Peterson fly that plane, isn't that correct?"

"Yes."

"And it just so happens that they work for you, right?"

"Sure, a lot of people work for me. I own—"

"Isn't it true you hired them to disguise the P-38 as an alien spacecraft and then fly it over Possum Kingdom Lake so that people would think there had been another landing?"

The gallery erupted in conversation. The bailiff stood up and glared at the crowd.

"No. That's ridiculous," Swanson protested. "The P-38 crashed six months ago."

"Is that right? I must remind you, Mr. Swanson, you're under oath."

"I know that."

"So, did you report the crash to the FAA?"

"No. That wouldn't be my place. I don't get involved in CAF operations. I just let them use my facility because I believe in the importance of preserving history."

"Would it surprise you to learn that there hasn't been a report of that plane having crashed?"

He shrugged and said, "I wouldn't know. I'm not really sure what the proper protocol would be for a crash like that." Swanson turned a little pale and swallowed hard. I waited as he twisted uncomfortably in his seat. Finally he said, "You'll have to ask them about that."

I continued, "Well, actually I won't. There is no such report and I have a witness who took a ride in the P-38 just a few weeks ago. . . . I could call her up here if need be."

He laughed. "That's not possible. I mean—" Swanson looked up at the judge and forced a smile. "It was my understanding—" Chatter broke out in the courtroom and the judge banged his gavel. "It was my understanding that the plane crashed. I didn't actually go out to the crash site, but I can't believe Adam and Carl would lie to me."

"So, you deny that you hired them to fly the P-38 Lightning over Possum Kingdom Lake?"

He laughed. "Yes, absolutely. Why would I fly the P-38 Lightning over the lake? It doesn't look anything like a spaceship."

"You're right. It doesn't unless you disguised it."

"Disguised it?"

"Yes, didn't you stretch canvas between the two fuselages so the plane would appear to be rectangular. In the darkness of a thunderstorm it could be mistaken—"

"No, that's crazy. That never happened."

"Do you deny that there are rolls and rolls of canvass in the hangar where the P-38 is kept?"

"What hangar? What canvas? I don't know what you are talking about."

"You haven't been to the airport east of Grafford where the P-38 is currently stored?"

"No. It was my understanding the remains of the P-38 had been taken to Midland."

I looked at Swanson and shook my head. He was either a good liar or didn't know anything about the fake P-38 crash. It was time to get Peterson and Brooks on the stand so we could get some answers. "Pass the witness," I said.

Simms took Swanson on cross and he scoffed at my suggestion that a P-38 could be mistaken for a spaceship. She led Swanson through all his community activities, his awards, and other accomplishments. She apologized for my suggestion that he had done something illegal or unethical. When she was done, Swanson sat tall in the witness stand with a smug look on his face.

"Pass the witness," Simms said.

"No questions at this time," I replied, "but I may want to recall Mr. Swanson later on in the trial."

The judge nodded. "Mr. Swanson, you may step down, but please remain in the courthouse in case you're needed later."

Swanson stood. "Yes, Your Honor," he said and then left the courtroom.

"Mr. Turner. Call your next witness."

"Thank you, Your Honor," I said. "The defense calls Adam Peterson."

The bailiff went into the hallway and brought Peterson in. He didn't look thrilled to be a witness. He took the stand and ran his large hands through his thick black hair. Fortunately, he hadn't heard Robert Swanson's testimony about the P-38, so he wouldn't be expecting my line of questioning. I stood and smiled.

"Mr. Peterson. You work for Robert Swanson, don't you?"

"Not directly. I work at his auto dealership. It's a corporation, I think."

"You're also a pilot, right?"

"Yes, I fly for the Confederate Air Force, sometimes."

"Have you ever flown a P-38 Lightning?"

"Sure. That's usually what I fly."

"When was the last time you flew the Lightning?"

Peterson swallowed hard. "Ah. . . . It's been quite some time. It crashed a month or two ago and it hasn't been restored yet."

"When did it crash?"

"Back in September. I forget the exact date."

I pulled an envelope out of my briefcase and dumped a pile of photographs on the defense table. Peterson's eyes narrowed.

"Do you know what I have here?" I asked.

Peterson shrugged. "No. Can't say that I do."

"Well, these are photographs of you, Carl Brooks, and a pretty, young lady taking a ride in the P-38 Lightning."

Peterson squirmed in his seat and ran his hands through his hair again.

"Do you know when these pictures were taken?" I asked.

He shrugged. "Can I see them?"

"Absolutely," I replied and gathered them up into a neat pile. I looked at the judge. "May I approach the witness, Your Honor?"

Simms stood. "I'd like to see those first, Your Honor."

Without waiting for a response from the judge, I handed the pile of photographs to Simms. She glanced through them and then shook her head. "Your Honor, I object to Mr. Turner showing the witness these photographs. There hasn't been a proper predicate laid."

"Your Honor," I replied. "I've got three witnesses who can authenticate these photos, but unless Mr. Peterson disputes their authenticity there's no reason to waste time doing that."

"Objection overruled. The witness may view the photographs."

I handed the pile to Peterson and his face grew pale as he flipped through the photos one by one. Finally, he looked up and said, "I don't remember this."

"Do you dispute that you and Carl Brooks are in those pictures?"

"No. It looks like us. Like I said, I just don't remember when that was."

"Do you dispute that the plane in the photographs is the P-38 Lightning."

"Yeah, it is, but those must have been taken before the crash."

"So, you're going to make me call the three witnesses to testify that those pictures were taken several weeks after the alleged crash?"

Peterson didn't respond.

"Did Robert Swanson know about your restoration scam?"

Peterson frowned. "I don't know what you're talking about?"

"Do you remember the first day we met? It was after the crash, remember?"

"Yeah."

"Didn't you ask me if I wanted to contribute to the fund to restore the P-38?"

Peterson took a deep breath. He was sweating now and wouldn't make eye contact. The courtroom was quiet as everyone was straining to hear every word.

"Did you and Carl pocket the money or did you cut Swanson in on the deal?"

Peterson just looked at me with his mouth half open. "I guess I should take the fifth," he finally said.

I shrugged. "That is your right, but I doubt it will help much now. If we call up to Midland, I'm pretty sure they'll confirm the P-38 isn't there."

Peterson drew in a long breath and then sighed. "All right. I guess I'm screwed. . . . No, Swanson didn't know about the scam. It was Carl's stupid idea. I can't believe I let him talk me into it."

"It was actually quite clever. It was just bad luck that I happened onto it."

Peterson shrugged.

"Did Swanson pay you to fly the P-38 over Cactus Island?"

"No. After we told everybody it had crashed, we kept it out of sight."

There was no doubt Peterson was telling the truth. He'd have no reason to lie now that he'd admitted in open court to committing a felony. My heart sank as I realized I'd gone down a rabbit trail and now was at a dead end. My gut told me Swanson wasn't the outstanding citizen that Simms had made him out to be, yet I had nothing on him now but suspicions. An old law professor of mine once said good luck was too unpredictable to be relied upon. He said you had to create your own good fortune. I was sure that was the case with Robert Swanson, but what had he done? I had to figure it out—and soon. Time was running out.

Before I called my next witness, the judge gave the jury a short break. I took that opportunity to find Rose. She was always so upbeat, I figured she'd boost my spirits. She was seated at a bench in the hallway. I walked over and sat next to her.

"Sorry I had to drag you down here. Hopefully I won't need to call you. I hate for you to get fired."

She smiled. "It's all right. I understand. If I get fired, I'll probably just go back to school. I was thinking about doing that anyway."

"Yeah, but–"

"Don't worry. It's no big deal. How's the trial going?"

"Terrible," I said. "I thought sure Swanson had hired Peterson and Brooks to fly the P-38 over Cactus Island, but I was wrong."

"Maybe not entirely."

I looked up and saw Robert Swanson looking at us. "Oh, God. There's your boss. I'm sorry. I better leave you alone." I got up.

"Here," Rose said and then handed me the magazine she'd been holding so tightly. I took it from her and frowned.

"What's this?"

"There's an article in there you ought to read."

Swanson started walking toward us, so I said, "Thanks. I'll check it out."

Members of the jury were starting to go back into the courtroom, so I knew it was time to go back inside. Paula gave me a funny look when she saw me clutching the magazine as I approached her. "What's that?" she asked.

"It's a magazine Rose gave me."

"Why?" Paula asked taking it from me. She started leafing through the pages. The magazine was called *Aviation Weekly*. The date on the cover was May 11, 1990. Paula let out a gasp. "Oh, my God!"

"What?" I asked.

"There's an article in here about Robert Swanson. Check out what he's standing next to."

I looked at the photograph and suddenly everything started to make sense. When the judge took the bench, I stood.

"Your Honor, I'd like to recall Robert Swanson."

The judge nodded. "Very well. Bailiff, bring in Mr. Swanson."

Swanson looked surprised that he'd been called back to testify again. He reluctantly took the witness stand.

"Mr. Swanson," I have just a few more questions."

"Okay," he said.

"You testified you were a pilot, is that right?"

"Yes. I've flown for more than twenty years."

"Are you currently employed as a pilot?"

Swanson didn't respond. He closed his eyes and sighed.

"It's a simple question, Mr. Swanson."

"I know. It's just that I can't answer that question."

"Your Honor, please instruct the witness to answer the question."

The judge leaned forward and gave Swanson a hard look. "Mr. Swanson, you will have to answer the question."

Swanson looked over at the judge, "I can't, Your Honor. What I do is classified."

"So you are employed as a pilot?" I said.

Swanson frowned and shook his head. "Okay. Yes, I'm a test pilot. How did you find out about that?"

I ignored his question and continued. "Tell us about the B-2 Spirit."

"No. The B-2 program is classified. I can't discuss it."

"You're under oath, Mr. Swanson. You don't have a choice," I said as I opened the magazine to a photograph of Swanson standing in front of a B-2 Spirit. I asked the judge if I could approach the witness.

"You may," the judge replied.

I put the magazine in front of Swanson so he could see the picture. "Is this the B-2 Spirit you flew over Possum Kingdom Lake?"

Again Swanson didn't respond. He just looked at the photograph then looked away gritting his teeth. I took the magazine back and studied the photograph. "I must say it was a brilliant plan to stage a fake alien landing. The B-2 does look like a spaceship." I held it up so the jury could see it.

"Objection!" Simms screamed. "That photograph hasn't been admitted into evidence."

I closed the magazine quickly and set it in front of Swanson. "Sorry, Mr. Swanson, can you identify this photograph. I assume you were there since you're in the picture."

Laughter broke out in the gallery.

Swanson glared at me. "Yes, I was there."

"So, that is a B-2 Spirit—an experimental airplane."

Swanson nodded.

"You must have been elated when Jimmy Falk was killed and Steven Caldwell blamed it on a spaceship—your experimental airplane actually. That brought in the tourists by the droves."

Swanson stiffened, looked at the Judge, and shook his head. "I can't talk about this. I told you the project is classified."

"Your Honor," I replied. "We don't need any details about the aircraft or Mr. Swanson's assignment. All I want to know is if he flew the B-2 Spirit over Possum Kingdom lake."

The judge nodded. "Answer the question, Mr. Windsor."

Swanson twisted in his seat. "Yes, but the flyover was after—" He stopped in mid-sentence, a look of despair on his face.

"The flyover was after what?" I asked.

"It was just a joke, for godsakes. I never thought anyone would actually think the Spirit was a spaceship. It certainly had nothing to do with Jimmy Falk's death. I didn't get the idea to fly the Spirit over the lake until after the crash and all the UFO nuts came here looking for an alien spacecraft."

There were gasps from the gallery, then bedlam. Simms stood up to object but nothing came out of her mouth. Cameras flashed. Reporters ran out of the room. The judge banged his gavel repeatedly but nobody cared. It was several minutes before the room quieted.

"So, how did you get access to the B-2?"

"The manufacturer hired Airtran to provide test pilots for the B-2. I'm a part owner in Airtran and one of their test pilots. The plane is still in the experimental stages and they needed pilots to take it up from time to time. On September 24 I happened to be near Possum Kingdom Lake so I did a flyover just for the heck of it."

"Did you fly the B-2 on September 10, 1990?"

"No. I told you. I only did it on the 24th."

Frustrated, I shook my head and said, "Pass the witness."

The Judge looked at his watch and then recessed for lunch. Paula put her arm on my shoulder and congratulated me, but I wasn't feeling all that satisfied. Swanson had admitted to faking the second alien landing, but he denied staging the first one. We may have dealt a fatal blow to the myth of the alien landings at Cactus Island, but unless we could prove the B-2 had flown on September 10, Swanson's admission was irrelevant to Steven's defense.

Hollow victory or not, the press mobbed Paula and me when we left the courtroom. One reporter asked, "Do you believe Swanson when he says the B-2 didn't fly on September 10?"

"I don't know and since it's a classified project, we may never know for sure."

"Why do you suppose Mr. Swanson would admit faking the second landing, but not the first?"

"Well, perhaps he's worried about some culpability in Jimmy Falk's death," I replied and then continued on through the crowd of reporters. "That's all for now. Thanks."

Paula and I met Jodie at the Pizza Hut on the outskirts of Mineral Wells. As I was eating my meatball sandwich, I noticed a lot of traffic heading out of town.

"I guess we ruined the party," I said. "There go the UFO junkies."

Paula nodded. "Well, it was just a matter of time. I just can't believe Swanson thought he could get away with flying that experimental plane over the lake."

"Well, he pretty much runs the town, so I'm sure he's used to doing whatever he wants," I replied.

"I bet he'll take some heat from his employer for taking the plane off course," Jodie said. "Maybe they'll fire his ass."

"If we could prove the B-2 went up on September 10, do you really think Jimmy's family might have a cause of action against Swanson?" Paula asked.

"It would be a stretch," I said, "but a creative personal injury attorney could probably come up with a viable theory."

"Good. I hope that arrogant bastard gets what's coming to him," Paula said.

"Okay, enough of Swanson. We need to focus on the rest of the trial. Do you think I need to call the two fishermen and Doc Verner?"

"I thought we were trying not to focus on the alien spaceship." Paula said. "You got the story into evidence with Peter's testimony and everyone has read the newspaper accounts of the landings."

"True. Okay, we'll scratch them and finish up with Gary Queen."

"I agree," Jodie said. "I think we have the momentum on our side right now so we should wrap up our case and let it go to the jury."

The courthouse looked deserted when we returned. The crowd of spectators that had been hanging around all week was gone. Only half the media vans were still parked on the side streets around the town square and we were able to walk into the courthouse without being mobbed by reporters. The spectators in the hallways all had long faces and avoided making eye contact. When we walked into the courtroom, disappointment hung in the air. Although I hadn't been the one who betrayed the people, I was the messenger and could feel the contempt of the crowd. I was afraid this might happen and had counted on Simms using her strikes to get rid of the UFO fanatics on the jury panel. Luckily, she hadn't disappointed me.

The judge took the bench and I continued questioning Robert Swanson. He claimed he'd gotten the idea to fake a UFO sighting after Jimmy's death and altered his flight plan so he'd fly by the lake. When he got close to the lake, he went off course and flew directly over Cactus Island. Later he blamed the altered course on an instrument malfunction. On cross examination, Simms hammered on the fact that the second UFO sighting was irrelevant and had no bearing on the case at hand and she was right.

When Swanson stepped down, I called Gary Queen. He explained that he operated an oil rig and had been hired to drill a well near Camp Comfort. It just so happened the drilling was to begin on September 10, 1990. I asked exactly when it started.

"According to my log, drilling commenced at 4:47 p.m."

"Were you aware of an accident on the road to Camp Comfort about that same time?"

"Not then. I've heard about it since."

"Did you know that the accident was first reported at 4:58 p.m.?"

"I've heard that, yes."

"And once you started drilling did it continue all day?"

"Well, actually, no. Just after we started drilling, a wrench was dropped into the hole and we had to stop and fish it out. "

"When did you stop drilling?"

"The log says 4:55 p.m."

"So, when Steven Caldwell and Jimmy Falk came around the curve just before the entrance to Camp Comfort, they would have heard your drilling rig."

"Oh, yes. Absolutely."

"But when Sylvia Bassett came upon the scene at 4:58 p.m. you had stopped drilling and it was quiet except for the wind and the thunder."

"Yes. That's correct. It was a very windy and stormy day."

"Mr. Queen, is a drilling rig very noisy?"

Queen nodded. "Yes. Extremely noisy, almost deafening. The men have to wear special earplugs to prevent permanent injury to their eardrums."

"Does that noise carry any distance?"

"Oh, yes. That's one of our biggest public relations problems. If we drill anywhere near a home or business the occupants are sure to be complaining about the noise."

I motioned to Jodie and she brought up a big boom box and set it in front of the witness. I said, "Did you bring a tape to play to the jury?"

"Yes, I did," Queen replied.

"Objection!" Simms said. "This is totally irrelevant."

"I don't think so, Your Honor. There's been testimony that Steven Caldwell said he'd not only been distracted by an object in the sky, but a loud noise as well. I believe this oil rig was the source of the noise in question."

"Overruled," the judge said. "Proceed."

"Thank you, Your Honor. Now, Mr. Queen, would you play the tape for us?"

"Sure," Queen said and slipped the cassette into the boom box.

I turned to the jury. "Be prepared to cover your ears. This will be pretty loud."

Queen pressed the play button and an intense, high-pitched grinding sound filled the courtroom. It was so deafening almost everyone covered their ears immediately. The judged banged his gavel and yelled, "That's enough!" Queen hit the stop button.

I smiled. "I'm sorry about that. I hope everyone's eardrums are still intact. So, Mr. Queen, is that the sound that would have confronted Steven Caldwell and Jimmy Falk when they come around the curve where the accident took place?"

"Yes."

"In your opinion would that sound have distracted them for at least a second or two?"

"Yes, I think it would have startled them if they hadn't been expecting it."

"Do you think the sound alone could have caused the accident?"

"Objection! Mr. Queen is not an expert."

"True. Withdrawn. Thank you, Mr. Queen. Pass the witness."

Simm stood up. "Mr. Queen. How far away was the oil rig from the road?"

"About a hundred yards."

"Isn't the sound a lot less intense 100 yards away rather than right next to the well site?"

"A little less intense, I guess, but still pretty loud."

"Where was this tape made? At the site or near the road?"

"It was near the site, but I—"

"No further questions."

On redirect I asked Queen to finish his answer. He said he didn't think the sound was much less intense a hundred yards away. He said it was common to get complaints from people a mile or two away from the drilling site that they were so distracted by the sound of the drilling they couldn't think, let alone sleep. I was pretty sure the jury had gotten the message.

If we were going to allow Steven Caldwell to testify in his defense, now was the time. I asked the judge for a short recess to discuss the issue. He granted us ten minutes.

"What do you think, Paula?"

"It's too dangerous. Right now we have a good chance of acquittal. If we let Steven testify and for some reason the jury doesn't like him, or Simms tears him up on cross, we'll be sunk."

"That's what I was thinking, but I just wanted to be sure."

"Besides, I think you've effectively moved us away from the UFO defense and we don't need Steven muddying the water on that issue."

"Okay, then. I guess it's time to rest."

When the judge came back, we rested our case. Then Simms recalled Deputy Freeman Fry and Detective Ben Hayden to dispute our contention that the noise from the oil rig could have been enough to cause the accident. On cross I pointed out that neither of the witnesses was there when the accident happened, so they couldn't possibly know whether the noise was enough of a distraction to cause the vehicle to go out of control. When Simms was done with these two witnesses we both closed and the judge asked for closing arguments. Since Simms had the burden of proof, I gave my closing argument first.

"Ladies and gentlemen of the jury, I want to thank you for your patience and attention throughout this long trial. I know it's difficult to sit there day after day doing your civic duty while your own lives have been put on hold. Well now it's time for you to digest what you've seen and heard and render a verdict. Before you start that process I want to remind you that when this trial started, Steven Caldwell was presumed innocent. The burden in this case rests with the prosecution. To win they must prove beyond any reasonable doubt that Steven Caldwell intentionally and knowingly caused the death of Jimmy Falk. Well, let's face it, they haven't met that burden.

"They've proved there was some animosity between Steven and Jimmy over Susan Weber, sure, but not the hatred and bitterness that would be necessary to drive someone to commit murder. You heard the testimony of Roger Dickens that Steven and Jimmy were laughing and kidding around before they took off in the Jeep. You heard the testimony of Carl Loftus who, after carefully studying the accident scene and preparing a video simulation, concluded that for Steven to intentionally jump out of the Jeep after it left the roadway would have been suicide.

"The prosecution's case against Steven Caldwell is speculation at best. Sure, there were words between Steven and Jimmy—angry words and empty threats—but nothing sinister or calculating. Steven was frustrated over losing the woman he thought he loved, yet there was testimony that Steven and Susan had been drifting apart before Jimmy came on the scene. Steven's jealousy was normal adolescent behavior and nothing more.

"What happened on September 10 was simply a tragic accident, an unfortunate twist of fate that neither Steven nor Jimmy could have done anything to avoid. It was a dark, stormy day with lightning, thunder and strong winds. You can imagine what happened as Steven sped around the sharp curve in the open Jeep. First he saw a strange object in the sky and then was jolted by the piercing screams of an oil rig. You heard the testimony that the scouts talked incessantly about the landings on Cactus Island, the frogmen and the humanoids. They spent hours looking, watching, waiting for signs of the alien visitors. Certainly you can understand how Steven could have mistakenly believed he'd seen the long-anticipated spacecraft when he rounded that curve. There was a strange object in the sky, the wind, the darkness, the lighting, and the piercing noise—all the elements of the story that had been told over and over again year after year.

"In that split-second of wonder, he lost control of the Jeep and Jimmy Falk died. It was a tragic accident that will haunt Steven for the rest of his life, but it wasn't murder. You've heard witness after witness characterize Steven as a hard-working, honest, decent young man. No one has come forward with any evidence to the contrary, not even Susan Weber or Sammy Falk who had good reason to be angry with Steven. No one has shown us any evidence that Steven Caldwell is the kind of person who could commit murder.

"So, again. The prosecution has the burden of proof and it simply hasn't met that burden. Therefore, you must find Steven Caldwell not guilty. Thank you and may God be with you as you decide the fate of Steven Caldwell."

"Thank you, Mr. Turner," Judge Applegate said. "Ms. Simms. You may proceed."

I took my seat much relieved that my job was over. Jodie gave me a thumbs up from the gallery and Paula whispered congratulations. Then I noticed two of the jurors looking at me and smiling. I wondered what it meant, if anything.

"Yes, Your Honor," Simms said. "Thank you, ladies and gentlemen of the jury, the State too thanks you for your diligence in acting as jurors in this very important trial. I've watched you carefully this last week and have been impressed with the close attention you have been giving to me and Mr. Turner. I am confident that you will do what's right here today.

"It is true the State has the burden of proof in this case and I think you will agree we have more than met that burden. The defense admits that Steven was angry with Jimmy over taking Susan Weber away from him. It is undisputed that Steven made threats to get even, to make Jimmy pay for stealing the woman he loved.

"I can't tell you exactly when Steven began to concoct his murderous plot, but you probably remember Sammy Falk testifying that Steven had called over to their house to make sure Jimmy was going to be at the camp out. Why did he want to know if Jimmy was going to be there? Because he was making plans to kill him.

"Recall the scene in the mess hall when it was discovered supplies were needed. You heard the testimony that everyone volunteered to go to town with Steven, but Steven picked Jimmy. Why was that? I think you know.

"Think back to the testimony of Peter Turner when he heard a banging noise coming from the parking lot and ran into Steven Caldwell there with a tool box. What was he doing in the parking lot? I think you know. He was hammering on the seatbelt to damage it so Jimmy wouldn't be able to open it quickly enough to jump from the Jeep.

"Then he came up with the story of the alien spacecraft. That was quite an effective tactic as you all have observed these past few weeks. He knew the focus of this trial would be shifted away from him, to the larger picture, the age-old question: Is there intelligent life in outer space?

"But the one thing that nobody has talked about, but is common knowledge to anyone following this trial, is that while out on bail Steven Caldwell made plans to flee the country. What does that tell you? It tells you he's knows he's guilty. It's tantamount to an admission of guilt.

"Ladies and gentlemen, don't fall victim to Steven Caldwell's tricks. He is a highly intelligent young man who was insanely jealous and angry over the loss of Susan Weber. In order to exact revenge he very cleverly plotted and planned the murder of Jimmy Falk and executed that plan with precision and cold calculation. Please don't let Steven Caldwell get away with his heinous crime. Look beneath that calm, collected veneer. See him for what he is and find him guilty of murder. Make him pay for his crimes against Jimmy Falk and people of the State of Texas. Thank you."

The judge thanked Simms and then gave his instructions to

the jury. He answered their questions, wished them good luck, and asked them to retire to the jury room to deliberate. After the court deputy had escorted them out, the judge recessed the trial for the duration of jury deliberations. Steven looked scared as the bailiff cuffed him and took him back to the county jail. I offered him words of encouragement, but they didn't seem to lift his spirits much. I think he sensed that it was a close case and the jury could go either way. A huge sense of relief washed over me as my responsibility was over. Now it was just a matter of waiting, hoping, and praying that Steven would be found innocent and the jury would set him free.

Chapter 36

Tortola

By 5:00 p.m. on Friday the jury had yet to reach a verdict so I went back to Dallas. Stan didn't need any help waiting on a jury verdict, and I had plenty to do to get ready for Cheryl Windsor's trial that was fast approaching. Just before Steven Caldwell's trial began the police had found Windsor's car with a charred body in the driver's seat. I called my forensics expert to get an update.

"George. Hi. I'm back from Palo Pinto."

"Any verdict yet?"

"No, the jury is still out. . . . I was just wondering if you've heard anything more about the body?"

"Yes. As I suspected there is no viable DNA. The fire must have been very intense."

"Thank God. How about dental records?"

"None. I guess he never went to the dentist. His mouth was perfect. No cavities."

"Lucky for us. . . . All is not lost after all."

"It's still going to be pretty hard to convince the jury that the corpse isn't Martin's."

"I know, but at least I have something to argue about."

Feeling a little relief after talking to George, I worked on my trial outline, sifted through what evidence I had, and considered additions to my witness list. As I worked, I started to get depressed again realizing what an uphill battle we were facing—Cheryl having no recollection of what had happened on the night of Martin's disappearance, witnesses who placed her with Windsor before he disappeared, assets being liquidated and funneled into her account, and now a charred body. How in the hell was I going to successfully defend her? Of course, there was a slim chance that Perkins wouldn't discover the VP bank account, but I had to prepare for the worst and assume he would.

After sleeping on it that night I settled on the two theories that made the most sense. The first was that Martin was alive and had set Cheryl up so he'd get all the community property and the children. If she was in jail, she'd be out of the way and wouldn't be a threat. The second was that there was a criminal organization dealing in children who camouflaged their crimes by disposing of the parents at the same time they took the children. That way the children's disappearance would look like the work of a disgruntled spouse refusing to accept a divorce court's custody decree.

To prove that Martin Windsor was still alive we'd need to prove that he orchestrated the liquidation of community assets and set up the account at VP Bank in the British Virgin Islands. Maybe Cheryl could contact the bank and attempt to access the account. If they refused to allow her access that would be pretty good evidence that Martin was still alive and had control of the community assets. The problem was Cheryl couldn't leave the country since she was out of jail on bond, and we didn't have account numbers and passwords to access the account by telephone.

After thinking about it for some time, I decided the prudent thing to do was to get Cheryl to give me a power of attorney and then I'd go to the British Virgin Islands and see if I could access the bank account on her behalf. I was pretty certain I'd hit a brick wall, but it was her money and, if it was there, she should have it. I called Cheryl and explained my plan and when she agreed it was a good idea, I called my travel agent and had her check on flights and accommodations there.

The VP Bank was located in Tortola. I had never been to the Caribbean so I didn't have any idea where the British Virgin Islands were located, but my travel agent said it was nearly a seven-hour flight from DFW with a stop in San Juan, Puerto Rico. I tried to call Stan and tell him what I planned to do, but I couldn't get through to him. I explained my plan to Jodie and Maria and told them to fill Stan in when he called. Jodie thought I should wait a few days and talk to Stan about what I was going to do, but since Cheryl's trial was fast approaching I didn't think I could afford the delay.

Early Monday morning Cheryl came by and signed the power of attorney and I was off to DFW Airport. My flight was at 10:31 a.m. and I was due in Tortola at 6:57 p.m. My travel agent booked me at the best hotel on the island, the Sugar Mill Resort. She said she had stayed there once and didn't want to come home. Somehow, I didn't think I'd enjoy the stay as much. The flight was long and tedious, but it gave me a lot of time to think about the case and what I was going to do when I arrived. It would be too late to go to the bank by the time I got there, so I'd have the evening to get the lay of the land and talk to some of the local people.

When the plane touched down at the Tortola Beef Island Airport, I was exhausted and anxious to get to my hotel. Unfortunately, going through customs, finding my luggage, and getting a cab to the hotel took over an hour. It was nearly nine o'clock when I finally made it to my room. After taking a shower and putting on a short red dress with matching sandals, I ventured out to the dining room. Although it was late, the staff was very friendly and attentive and fed me well. After finishing off some homemade ice cream to die for, I wandered into the bar to see if I could learn anything useful about BVI banking.

There were far more men in the bar than women, so my appearance turned a few heads. I walked up to the bartender and ordered a rum and coke.

"Where are you from?" he asked.

After he poured my drink, I replied, "I'm from Dallas. I'm in town to do some offshore banking."

"Well, you've come to the right place," he said. "The laws here were written to attract money. There are strict bank secrecy laws that made BVI banking very attractive to foreigners."

I asked him if there were any bankers in the bar. He pointed to two men sitting at a table across the room. I noticed they were checking me out, so I smiled. A few minutes later one of them came over and invited me to their table. Of course, I accepted.

They introduced themselves as Ted and Winston. They were both loan officers at Scotiabank. I told them I was in town to set up some trust accounts for some clients who were concerned about an imminent financial disaster that was certain to cause them serious liability exposure. I confessed that I was new to this game and had planned to spend a few days getting up to speed on all available options. That got them talking.

"Your best bet is to set up an IBC," Ted said.

"What's that?"

"An International Business Corporation. It's very flexible and protects the identity of its officers and directors. If you set up an account in your actual name, the account can be traced, but with and IBC the account is anonymous."

"What about the IRS or the FBI? Can't they find out who the officers are?"

"No, the law is very clear. No one, not even the IRS or FBI, can force the bank to divulge the identity of the stockholders or directors of an IBC."

"Hmm. What about security? My clients want to be sure their money is safe."

"Well, the British Virgin Islands has a very stable government protected by Great Britain. And each account is insured up to 20 million dollars by reputable insurance companies rather than the measly one hundred thousand at U.S. banks."

"So how does the IBC operate?"

"Well, our bank will set it up and act as registered agent and provide a local address, which is required. The account works just like any other account."

I lifted my drink and took a sip. "Well, thanks for the short course on offshore banking. Now I won't seem like a complete idiot when I talk to Walter Johansen."

"Walter Johansen?" Ted said. "That's who you're here to see?"

"Yes, it is. Is that a problem?"

Winston shook his head. "Well, he doesn't have a great reputation. He claims to be legit, but a lot of people are quite sure he's mixed up with organized crime, drug cartels, rogue government operatives—you name it."

"Really? Wow. I didn't know that."

"I'd find someone else. We can introduce you to one of our account reps. You'd be much better off with them."

"Well, I appreciate that, but I'm kind of committed to Mr. Johansen."

Tom raised his eyebrows. "Well, that's too bad. I'd hate to see anything happen to you or your client's money. You best be careful."

I thanked Tom and Winston and went back to my room. It was after midnight and I was beyond exhaustion, so I went straight to bed. As I took off my robe and slipped into bed, I started to worry about meeting Walter Johansen. If he was associating with criminals and drug dealers, he'd be a dangerous man to deal with. But I was too tired to even worry, so I drifted off to sleep.

Chapter 37

Verdict

The judge asked the jury to come in on Saturday and continue their deliberations. This meant I'd be spending the weekend in Palo Pinto. Paula and Jodie had left after closing arguments on Friday so I was alone and had decided to catch up on my sleep. It was about 10:00 a.m. when the telephone awoke me. It was Rebekah wanting to know how I was and if I had heard anything. I told her the jury was still out. We talked awhile about what she and the kids were going to do for the weekend and then I asked her how Peter was doing."

"He was as high as a kite. I can't believe you let him tell his story to the jury."

"I can't believe the judge let me, but I'm glad he did. It was good for the jury to know what Steven had been hearing at the campfires all those years. I think he really believed there were spaceships landing at Cactus Island."

"I heard on the news that all the tourists left town."

"Yeah, it's almost like a ghost town now. The media is still here to get the verdict, but that's about it."

"Have you seen the news since the jury went out?"

"No."

"Apparently you're not too popular with the UFO fanatics right now."

"I don't know why. I didn't prove Steven didn't see a spaceship. I just explained how he could have been distracted by the drilling rig or something other than a spaceship."

"I know. But you made it look like that businessman was behind the whole thing."

"Robert Swanson?"

"Uh huh. I'd hate to be in his shoes right now."

"Yeah. He's in deep shit, I'd say."

"Oh, Jimmy's mother called. She wants to talk to you. She said she's left messages at the motel but you haven't returned her calls."

"Well, I haven't checked my messages since yesterday after the jury went out. I was so tired, I told them at the desk to hold my calls, except for you and the office, of course. I'll call her."

After she hung up, I took a hot shower, got dressed, and called the front desk for my messages. There were a lot of them, mostly from people I didn't know. First I called Barbara Falk and apologized for not calling her back promptly.

"It's okay. I know it's probably strange to be getting a call from me, but I just had to talk to you."

"It's okay. Listen. I'm really sorry about Jimmy. I know you may not think so, but I am. The fact that I'm defending Steven doesn't diminish the way I feel. This was just a—"

"I know. I know. You're just doing your job, and that's why I wanted to talk to you. I'm worried about Steven."

"Steven? Why?"

"I don't think he's responsible for Jimmy's death and if he gets convicted, I don't know if I'll be able to live with myself."

"What makes you feel this way?"

"I don't know if you know this or not, but my ex-husband is Martin Windsor."

Her words didn't compute. I shook my head wondering if I was fully awake. "Excuse me. What did you say?"

"My ex-husband is Martin Windsor. You know, the one who is missing and presumed dead—your partner is defending his wife, Cheryl Windsor."

"What? How could that be?"

"It's a long story, but you need to hear it."

"You've got that right. I'm listening."

"Sixteen years ago Martin and I had a fling and I got pregnant. When he found out I was pregnant he was ecstatic and insisted we get married. So we did, right after Jimmy was born, and we lived together happily for about six years."

"Uh huh."

"Then things began to unravel. Martin wanted me to get pregnant again, but I couldn't. There were some complications with the first pregnancy that prevented it."

"I see."

"So we began to drift apart and then I discovered Martin was having an affair. He didn't try very hard to hide it. I think he wanted me to find out about it so I'd divorce him."

"That doesn't make sense. If he was guilty of adultery he could lose everything."

"He didn't care about money," Barbara said. "He had so much of it and was so good at making it, he wouldn't have cared if I got it or not. His main concern was maintaining his relationship with Jimmy."

"Really? Okay. So you gave him the divorce?"

"Yes, and he agreed to support us very nicely until Jimmy was 18. After the divorce I went back to my maiden name, Falk. Since Jimmy was born before we had been married his name was Falk on his birth certificate."

"Martin didn't have a problem with that? I would think he'd want Jimmy to have his last name."

"He didn't care about names. He was kind of a strange man."

"Okay, so what's bothering you about this?" I asked.

"Jimmy's death and then Cheryl's children being abducted."

"I see. You think there's a connection?"

"Yes. You see, I didn't take Jimmy's death well, so I went to a therapist. I'd been having nightmares and couldn't sleep. He suggested hypnosis."

"Really. So, he hypnotized you?"

"Yes, and since then I've remembered some things that are quite disturbing."

A tingling sensation came over me. This was all becoming very bizarre. I suddenly remembered Cheryl telling us about Martin Windsor's aversion to hypnosis. He had told her that if she let herself be hypnotized, she'd die a violent death. I was afraid to hear what Barbara Falk was about to tell me, but I had no choice.

"Go on, " I said.

"When Martin found out I was pregnant, he made me change doctors immediately. He took me to this clinic that I'd never heard of before. I wasn't comfortable there at all. The doctor was very secretive, and he and Martin would go off and whisper to each other in a corner."

"Hmm."

"When my delivery date got close, Martin insisted I check in at the clinic until the baby came. I protested but he said the doctor had told him it was absolutely necessary because the baby was not positioned correctly in the womb and there could be complications. The strange thing is, after I checked in the hospital, I have no memory of the delivery."

"What? How could that be?"

"The doctor said it was traumatic amnesia, and I believed that up until I was put under hypnosis."

I'd heard all this before from Cheryl—the same bizarre story. It couldn't be a coincidence that they both had a loss of memory. Martin or the doctors had obviously drugged them or did something to impede their memory. They must have. "What happened then?" I asked.

"Now I remember bits and pieces of the delivery. I see flashes of many men hovering over me. Some of those men were very strange and talked in a language I'd never heard before."

"Was it Hungarian? I think Windsor was Hungarian."

"No. It wasn't a language I'd ever heard."

Barbara told me more, but it wasn't anything I could use for an appeal. It was all too bizarre and I knew nobody would believe it. After I hung up, I called Paula to tell her about the conversation with Barbara. I knew she'd be interested to hear that our cases were related. I wondered why Cheryl hadn't mentioned that Barbara Falk was her husband's ex-wife. Paula's answering machine picked up and I listened to the message, but then another recording came on stating that the mailbox was full. That didn't surprise me since Paula had been in Palo Pinto all week and probably hadn't had a chance to clear her answering machine. I knew I'd have the same problem when I got back to the office. I called her cell phone but there was no answer there either.

On Sunday I was really bored so I decided to go pay a visit to Doc Verner. After hearing Peter's version of the Cactus Island landings, I wondered about the alleged tunnels under the lake linking it to the shore, and wondered why he hadn't mentioned them to me. His dogs quit barking as soon as they saw me. They were happy to see me. Doc Verner wasn't.

"What are you doing here? Haven't you done enough damage already?"

"What do you mean? Why am I the bad guy?"

"You singlehandedly destroyed my life's work. Nobody believes in the Cactus Island landings now because of you."

"But I didn't disprove the landings. All I proved was that Robert Swanson is a greedy bastard."

"I know that, but the public won't see it that way. If part of it's a fraud, all of it's a fraud."

"I'm sorry. I didn't mean—"

"So, what do you want?" Verner barked.

"Well, you never told me about the caves under the island. I was curious if there's any evidence to back that up."

"Why do you care?"

"Just curious, I guess. I hadn't heard that part of the story and it surprised me."

Verner stared at me like I was crazy. "Yeah, there were some reports of caves that went under the lake and made a connection to Cactus Island, but nobody to my knowledge has ever found them."

"Where did the reports come from?"

"From seismic testing done by a wildcatter about ten years ago. He claimed he had hired a geologist to do some testing of potential well sites and one of the reports showed a system of caverns that started north of the lake and went underneath it. Of course, it would have cost a lot of money to verify the claim, so nobody ever did."

"Did you ever go looking for an entrance to the caverns?"

"Damn right. I spent days searching the north side of the lake, talking to people, and looking through public records hoping to find evidence that it existed."

"Do you remember the name of the oil operator? I'd like to take a look at those geological studies."

"I don't know. It's been a long time."

"Well, if you can find out for me, I'd appreciate it."

"Why? I didn't think you were a believer."

I shrugged. "I don't know what I believe anymore, but I do know one thing—I don't like loose ends. I still don't know what

Steven saw on September 10 and if he's convicted, I'll need to find out."

Doc Verner didn't seem convinced that I was serious about solving the mystery of Cactus Island, but he did promise to try to recall the name of the oil operator. I thanked him and left. What I said was true. If Steven was convicted, I'd have to do a lot more digging into the Cactus Island landings, but even if he wasn't, it would be a fun hobby to work on with Peter. He was getting older and it was getting harder to find things to do together. His older brothers might get a kick out of it to. That night I slept well, despite the nagging worry about Steven's verdict. Somehow, I knew it would all work out.

At 11:31 a.m. Monday morning, in the middle of a late breakfast, the telephone rang. It was the court clerk. The jury had reached a verdict. I got dressed quickly and drove to the courthouse. Reporters were scurrying inside and a handful of tourists crowded the hallway leading to the courtroom. The gallery was already full when I walked in. Carla Simms and her assistant were at the prosecution table and the bailiff was just bringing Steven in the side door. I nodded at Barbara Falk as I walked by and then made my way to the defense table. Steven's mother intercepted me and asked, "What do you think?"

I smiled. "I don't know. I felt good when the jury went out, but I just don't know."

I got to the defense table as the bailiff was taking off Steven's handcuffs and we shook hands.

"Well, good luck," I said. "I hope you've said your prayers."

Steven nodded. "I have, and I just wanted to say that, no matter what happens, you did a great job and I appreciate everything you've done for me."

I shrugged. "I just wish I could have found those aliens. Everyone would have been a lot happier with me."

We laughed and then we embraced. The bailiff said, "All rise."

Judge Applegate came in and took the bench. "All right. Bailiff, please bring in the jury."

The jury filed into the courtroom and took their seats.

The judge looked at Steven. "The defendant will rise."

Steven and I stood up. The judge looked at the jury and said, "Has the jury reached a verdict?"

The first juror rose. "Yes, Your Honor. We have."

The judge nodded. "What is your verdict?

The juror looked at a single sheet of paper in his hand and said, "We, the jury finds the defendant, Steven Caldwell, not guilty on the charge of murder."

Jenny Caldwell screamed and the crowd buzzed with excitement. Carla Simms shook her head in disgust and whispered something to her associate. I shook Steven's hand and then he ran over and embraced his mother. I looked over at Barbara Falk and saw she was smiling.

"Thank you, ladies and gentlemen of the jury," the judge said. "You are excused. This case is adjourned. Bailiff, you may release the defendant. He is free to go."

The press mobbed me as I left the courthouse. A reporter asked, "Mr. Turner. Were you pleased with the verdict?"

"Yes. I felt Steven was innocent and I'm just glad the jury felt the same way."

"Was there ever a moment that you felt you might lose?"

"Yes, there were many moments like that, and this morning when I heard the jury was ready to come in, I got very scared. You just never know what the jury is thinking until the verdict is announced."

"What do you think the deciding factor was in this case?"

I laughed. "Why don't you ask the jurors that? They probably could answer that question better than me. I'm just glad Steven is free and can get on with his life."

When I got back to the hotel I called Rebekah to tell her the news but she'd already heard about it on TV. Then I called the office to tell Paula because I knew she wouldn't be watching television. Jodie answered.

"That's wonderful news. Steven must be ecstatic."

"Yes, he and the family were on cloud nine. They're having a party tonight. We're all invited."

"Sounds like fun."

"Can I talk to Paula?"

"Well, no. She's on her way to Tortola."

"Tor what?"

"Tortola. It's in the British Virgin Islands."

"Why in hell is she going there?"

Jodie explained to me Paula's mission and said she'd be calling us first thing in the morning before she met with the banker. I couldn't believe she had left the country without talking to me about it first. I immediately began to worry. The Martin Windsor case was an enigma if I'd ever seen one and there was nothing more frightening than the unknown. I was disappointed that I couldn't tell her about Steven's acquittal, but more importantly I wanted her to know that Barbara Falk was Martin Windsor's ex-wife. I didn't know exactly what it meant and how it would affect her case, but I knew it would be important. It was just too much of a coincidence.

Chapter 38

The Setup

The sunlight streamed into my room without mercy. It seemed like I'd just gone to bed. I rolled over and tried to cover my head with my pillow but it was no use. It was too light to sleep. The clock said 8:38 a.m., time to get up and get ready for my meeting with Walter Johansen. At least I hoped there was a meeting. Jodie was supposed to have set it up for me. There weren't any messages for me when I checked in, so I assumed she hadn't had a problem.

My head was aching. I figured it was a mild hangover. How many Mai Tai's had I drank? As I was taking my shower, I began to think about the warnings from my drinking buddies about Walter Johansen and the company he kept. My only solace was the fact that VP bank was an old reputable bank and presumably wouldn't tolerate any aberrant behavior by its bank officers.

The bell captain called me a cab and within fifteen minutes I was walking into the lobby of VP Bank. It had an impressive but conservative decor and the receptionist who greeted me was very polite and businesslike. She said Mr. Johansen would be five or ten minutes and offered me coffee.

I sat on the sofa to wait. The bank appeared extremely normal and I scolded myself for being so paranoid. A tall man with thinning brown hair walked up to me. He said, "Ms. Waters?"

I stood up and extended my hand. "Yes, Mr. Johansen?"

"That's right," he replied, shaking my hand politely. "Please come this way."

He led me down a long corridor and into his office. It was very nicely decorated with an assortment of sculptures and abstract art. He took his seat behind his desk and pointed to a side chair. His desk was busy but everything was neatly stacked in piles. He looked me over and said, "So, what brings you to Tortola?"

"Well, I'm an attorney from Dallas and apparently we have

a mutual client, Cheryl Windsor."

Johansen didn't show any recognition of the name and seemed a bit preoccupied. "Her husband is Martin Windsor," I continued. "Apparently he set up an account here for Mrs. Windsor. We understand the account is in her name."

"Do you have an account number? We deal with thousands of accounts."

"Well, actually we don't. You see, Mr. Windsor is missing. That's another reason we need to locate this account and take charge of it until we find him."

"Missing? Where is he?"

"We don't know. That's the problem, but in Texas a husband and wife's money is community property and either party can manage it for the other. If you will locate the account I think you'll see that Mrs. Windsor has the right to control and access. I have her power of attorney if you need it."

"We don't like to deal with powers of attorney. They can be revoked and we have no way of checking to see if they are still effective. Why didn't Mrs. Windsor make the trip with you?"

"Ah, well . . . she's not able to leave the country right now. I assure you this is a Texas durable power of attorney and is totally legal. The bank has no duty to check its validity under Texas law."

"This is the British Virgin Islands, Madam, not Dallas, Texas."

"I know. I know. If you can't accept the power of attorney, we can FedEx the paperwork to Dallas and she can sign it and overnight it back."

Johansen stood up. "Let me get the file, maybe we can work something out. I'll be right back."

While I was waiting, I sipped my coffee and wondered if there was any chance in hell Cheryl would ever see that money. If the bank found out that Cheryl was being charged with Martin's murder they'd freeze the account and nobody would get the money for years.

A few minutes later Johansen returned with the file and a computer printout. He sat down and started going through the file and checking it with the printout. He looked up. "You said Martin Windsor set up this account?"

"Well, that's what we thought," I replied. "She's been kind of left in the dark about her husband's finances. We're just trying to piece it together."

"Well, according to our records your client came in two weeks ago, set up an IBC, and opened an account to receive funds. Since then there have been nine wire transfers into the account totaling $3.7 million."

"That's impossible. My client never left Dallas."

"We obtained two forms of identification, I assure you."

"Can I see them?"

Johansen shrugged. "Of course."

He opened the file and pulled out copies of a Texas Driver's license and a U.S. Passport. I examined them closely. They appeared to be genuine and the picture was definitely Cheryl Windsor.

"Who met with Mrs. Windsor when she set up these accounts?" I asked.

"I did."

"You did?"

"Yes, now that I've looked at the file, I remember the transaction quite well."

I shook my head and pointed to the picture. "You're telling me this woman came in here and set up this account."

"Yes," he replied emphatically.

Either somebody was lying or Cheryl Windsor had an identical twin sister. I knew for a fact that Cheryl Windsor had turned in her passport and couldn't have possibly come to Tortola. If Martin Windsor was setting Cheryl up to take the fall for his death he was doing a good job. Now what should I do. If I tried to take possession of the account on Cheryl's behalf, it would look like Cheryl had set up the account all along and used it to stash her money after she killed her husband. Before I did anything, I had to talk to Cheryl and Stan. The situation was getting complicated and one false move could be disastrous.

"Okay. I guess I need to confer with my client. Apparently there has been a misunderstanding. I'll have to get back with you."

"Certainly."

"I would like to get a copy of the corporate papers and an account statement to take back to my client. Do you have her correct address?"

Johansen showed me the address and it was correct. He made me copies of the Articles of Incorporation of the Beef Island Trading Company as well as the minutes of the organizational meeting. They were all signed by Johansen as the bank's representative. I felt sick when I left the bank. This was the worst possible scenario, but I did need to know what I was up against. At least I wouldn't be blind-sided by this at trial. I'd have time to try to come up with a strategy to deal with it.

It was noon and I hadn't eaten any breakfast, so I decided to walk around town a bit and find a good place to eat. It was an interesting town and as long as I had come all this way, I decided I ought to explore it this afternoon since my flight home wasn't until the next morning. Luckily it was a small town on a small island, so I could explore a good portion of it before dark.

I found a little café with a good view and ordered soup and a salad. As I ate, I noticed a man looking at me. When I made eye contact, he turned away. A strange feeling came over me. I had seen that face somewhere before. When I tried to sneak another glance at him, he was gone. I looked around expecting to see him walking off, but he had vanished. Suddenly I remembered who he was—it was the man I'd first met in the elevator at Martin Windsor's office, the man I'd seen on the video tape, and one of the men who had abducted Cheryl's kids. The man who had vanished into thin air before my very eyes in Dallas had done it again 2500 miles away. A coincidence? I thought not.

After lunch I hurried back to the hotel to call Stan. Seeing the disappearing man again had me rattled. As I walked into the lobby, I ran into Ted. "What are you doing here? Do you live in the hotel?"

"Yes, just temporarily. My place was severely damaged by a recent hurricane and is being fixed up."

I nodded. "Oh. Well, it's nice to see you again."

"How did your meeting go with Johansen?" he asked.

"Not so well, I'm afraid."

"Sorry to hear that. Perhaps I can buy you a drink tonight and try to cheer you up."

I didn't feel like being alone with the disappearing man

lurking about, so I said, "Yes, that would be nice." On the way up the stairs to my room an ominous feeling came over me. I looked around, but saw nothing. I continued on figuring it was just my rattled nerves.

As I approached the door to my suite, I dug into my purse and found my keycard. I slipped it in the slot and pulled it out. The green light came on and I pushed the door opened. Suddenly a hand grabbed my arm and yanked me inside. I screamed in protest, but was rudely pushed to the floor. A knee pinned me down and I felt the sharp sting of a needle penetrating my arm. Someone said something in a language I'd never heard before. There was a flash of blue light, then the room began to fade away.

Chapter 39

Incarceration

When I got back to the office late Monday, Jodie advised me that Paula had left a message with Maria that she had arrived safely in Tortola and was going to do some research for her meeting with Johansen. I really wanted to talk to her, so I tried to call her at the hotel but the desk clerk said she wasn't in. My desk was overrun with neglected work, unopened mail, and stacks of phone messages. I considered ignoring it and going home, but I knew I'd regret that in the morning, so I took a deep breath and started sorting through it. Before she went home, Jodie brought me in an extra Jumbo Jack and fries she hadn't eaten at lunch. I thanked her and she left me hard at work.

The next time I looked up I was startled to see it was nearly nine o'clock. I called Rebekah and told her I'd be home soon. Before I left, I tried Paula at her hotel one more time, but she still didn't answer. I was starting to get worried. It was 11:00 p.m. in Tortola. I couldn't imagine her still being out at that hour when she had a morning appointment the next day. Reluctantly, I shut down my computer and went home.

Peter met me at the door. He had just returned from Steven Caldwell's acquittal party and wanted to tell me about it.

"I thought you were going to come," Peter said.

I shrugged. "Yeah, I'm sorry. I forgot about it. I got so wrapped up in work it just slipped my mind."

"I wish you'd have been there. It was a great party. Mrs. Falk went all out. You should have seen the food."

"Well, she almost lost her son. I'd be celebrating too."

"You must be tired. Why did you work so late?"

"Unfortunately, there wasn't anybody at the office doing my work while I was gone."

"Hmm. That sucks."

"Tell me about it. . . . Hey, I've got a proposition for you."

"What's that?" Peter asked.

"I'm intrigued by your Cactus Island story. Oh, and by the way, you did a great job telling the story to the jury. Thank you for doing that."

Peter smiled proudly. "No problem. It was cool. All my friends said they heard about it on the TV. Even Michelle talked to me and before I testified she didn't know I was alive."

"Wow. Your popularity rating went up, huh?"

He grinned and replied. "I guess."

"Anyway. I'd like to find out if there really is a cave that leads from the shore to Cactus Island. It seems that some oil operator a few years back claimed one showed up on a geological survey he commissioned."

"Really? But I thought you didn't believe in the alien landings," Peter asked.

"I don't know. Like I said, I'm intrigued now, so I thought maybe you and I could check into it."

"What do you want me to do?"

"I'm trying to locate a copy of the geological report showing the caves. If I get it, we'll have to go out to Possum Kingdom Lake and try to find it."

"But what if there *are* aliens landing at Cactus Island and they don't like us messing around in their caves?"

I laughed. "I thought you didn't believe in aliens."

"I don't but—"

He shrugged and went up stairs to his room and I continued on to the living room where Rebekah was watching TV. She looked up and smiled. "Well, the stranger returns."

"Yeah, the tired stranger. I think I'll just sleep straight on through until dinner tomorrow night, okay?"

I sat down next to her and took her hand in mine.

"Speaking of dinner, did you eat?" she asked.

"Yeah, I had a hamburger and some fries."

"If you'd have come home, I'd have cooked you something more nutritious."

"I know, but I wanted to clean off my desk and make sure

there wasn't anything critical that needed to be done."

"Are you going to take a couple days off now that the trial is over, I hope?"

"Yeah, I think I can take tomorrow off at least. We can sleep late and go out for breakfast."

Rebekah smiled. "That sounds good. I've missed you."

"Me too," I said leaning over and kissing her.

It felt good to be home after spending a week and a half away. I was so glad the Cheryl Windsor trial would be in Dallas, so we didn't have to live out of a suitcase and eat take-out. Rebekah stood up and led me into the bedroom. I was too tired for sex but Rebekah wanted to make up for lost time. So we did. Afterward Rebekah fell asleep quickly, but I lay awake worrying about Paula. I wondered if she was back in her room yet. I prayed she was.

The next morning I called Paula's hotel again only to find out that she'd left in a cab to go downtown. That made me feel better. At least I knew she was safe. After the kids were off to school, Rebekah and I went to Poor Richard's Café in Plano which was one of our favorite places for breakfast. We ate too much as usual. In the afternoon we went to a matinee and spent some time at the mall. When we got home, I called the office to see if anyone had talked to Paula. They hadn't.

"I'm worried about Paula," I said to Rebekah as I hung up the phone.

"She's a big girl. She can take care of herself."

"Sure she can, but if Martin Windsor is alive and trying to play dead, he may not like Paula snooping around. I wish she'd taken Paul with her."

"Don't worry. She'll be fine."

When the kids got back from school, we discussed taking the whole family out for dinner. We were having trouble getting a consensus on where to go when the telephone rang. It was a long distance call from Tortola.

"Yes, this is Stan Turner."

"Mr. Turner. This is Art Wright. I'm calling from the American Embassy in Tortola, British Virgin Islands. I'm afraid we have a situation involving your partner."

"Paula? Is she all right?"

"Well, I think she's physically okay, but she's in custody."

"In custody? What do you mean?"

"Well, the local authorities found her passed out in her room this afternoon. She apparently had a reaction to some drugs she took. There were needle marks in her arm."

"What? You've got to be kidding. I guarantee you Paula does not do drugs. This has got to be some kind of a mistake."

"Well, the drugs aren't the real problem. I understand she's representing a Cheryl Windsor in a murder case in Dallas."

"Yes, that's right."

"Well, it seems the authorities found a briefcase containing $500,000 cash and all the account and access information for another $3.2 million that belonged to Martin and Cheryl Windsor. Your prosecutor in Dallas has asked the local authorities to detain Ms. Waters."

"But why? She was just picking up the money for our client!"

"Yes, but it seems they also found an airline ticket to Santiago, Chile. Your prosecutor, Mr. Wilkerson, believes Ms. Waters planned to help Ms. Windsor escape the country."

"That's ridiculous. This has got to be a set up. I know Paula. She would never dream of doing something like that."

"Nevertheless, Mr. Wilkerson has asked us to hold Ms. Waters so they can initiate an extradition proceeding."

"Oh, Jesus! . . . Okay, thank you for contacting me. I'll start working on something from this end. I may fly down there later today or tomorrow. Are you sure Paula is okay?"

"Yes, she has a few cuts and scratches but aside from that she appears to be fine."

My hand shook as I hung up the phone. I refused to believe Paula was helping Cheryl skip the country. That didn't make any sense. What was going on? My heart pounded and I could feel my blood pressure rising. Rebekah gave me a concerned look. "Are you all right?"

I told her the news. She was nearly as shocked as I was. I told her we'd have to take a rain check on dinner and then called Paul Thayer and Jodie. We agreed to meet at the office and try to analyze what had happened and come up with a strategy to deal with it.

Cheryl's trial was less than two weeks away and now with Paula in custody I'd have to shoulder the burden of Cheryl's defense alone. I grabbed my briefcase, kissed Rebekah goodbye, and drove to the office. All I could think about was Paula in some filthy, rat infested jail cell. I had to get her out of there—and fast.

Chapter 40

Rude Awakening

When I opened my eyes I saw blinking lights, and heard buzzing sounds and a steady bleep . . . bleep . . . bleep. A man lay in a bed a few feet away with tubes down his throat and an empty expression on his face. I was in a hospital, obviously, but what was I doing here? I felt okay except for a little lightheadedness and a pain in the small of my back. I tried to remember what had happened to me, but my mind was as blank as the look on my roommate's face.

Who are you? What day is it? Do you know where you are? That's what the doctors would ask me. Let me see. I'm Paula Waters, attorney at law, all the way from Dallas, Texas. I have no clue what day it is. Sorry about that. Where am I? Hell if I know. Wait a minute. I'm in the Caribbean somewhere. What was the name of that city? Torta something. Tortola, that's it. I remember now—the British Virgin Islands.

I heard a voice out in the hall, so I started to get up to go talk to whoever was out there. Unfortunately, my left arm wouldn't move. What the hell? I tugged again, a little harder this time, and then realized I was handcuffed to the bed. Fear shot through me like a jolt of electricity. What was going on? Had I been kidnapped? The voices got louder and louder and then the door opened. A nurse and an orderly walked into the room stood at the end of my bed.

"Hey! What's with the handcuffs? " I demanded.

"Ah. You're awake," the nurse said.

"Yes, I am and I want to know what's going on. Why am I handcuffed?"

"I'm just a nurse. You'll have to ask the detective outside who's guarding you."

"Guarding me?"

"Right. I'll go get him. Hang on."

A short, stout man with dark brown hair walked in the room and introduced himself as Detective Pollock. "The Tortola police got an anonymous phone call last night that someone had overdosed at the Sugar Mill Resort," he said. "The caller gave them your room number. They found you in your room unconscious from an apparent drug overdose. While you were being rushed to the hospital, they searched your room and found a lot of money and financial documents. When they discovered you were from Dallas they checked with the Dallas Police Department and were told you were an attorney representing Cheryl Windsor. A Detective Perkins suggested you might be planning to help Ms. Windsor flee the country."

"That's absurd!" I said. "I would never do something like that."

I could understand how he might see it as a plausible scenario, but it was totally untrue. The idea of helping Cheryl flee the country had never even crossed my mind. I wondered where the money had come from. I had only brought a few hundred dollars with me and I would certainly remember if I had a briefcase with a half a million dollars in it. I tried to think back to the last thing I remembered. I was having lunch downtown. I remembered taking a cab back to the hotel, but after that it was a blank. What had happened to me?

"Nevertheless, we're going to have to hold you until we check a few things out. You'll be transferred to the central jail just as soon as the doctors release you."

I shook my head in disbelief. "I need to call my partner," I said.

"I believe Detective Perkins called your office and advised them of the situation."

"Perkins! You told Perkins about this? Shit!"

He shrugged. "I must go. I believe there is someone from the American Embassy waiting to see you. I'll send him in." A few moments later a middle-aged man in a grey business suit walked in. He nodded and then introduced himself as Art Wright.

"So, how are you feeling, Ms. Waters?" he asked.

"I was feeling just fine until I realized I was chained to my bed. This is a set up. I guarantee you I know nothing about the drugs or the money. The only reason I came down here was to investigate a report that some of my client's money had been wired here."

"That's not my primary concern, Ms. Waters. My job is to

make sure you are treated fairly and in accordance with local and international law as well as the treaties that exist between our countries. That's why we made sure your office had been notified that you were in custody, so you would have the opportunity to retain an attorney if you chose to do so."

"Can you recommend a good one? Someone you know very well and trust?"

"Yes, the embassy has a list of reputable attorneys who handle these types of cases. I'll send a list to your Dallas office. In the meantime, is there anything else I can do for you?"

"Do you know anything about a banker named Walter Johansen?"

The smile disappeared from White's face. "Sure, he's a regular at the embassy parties," he said carefully. "What does he have to do with your case?"

I told him that Johansen had set up an IBC and bank account purportedly for Cheryl Windsor, but I didn't think she had authorized it nor signed any of the paperwork. He shrugged and suggested I tell that to Detective Pollock who could look into it. Somehow, I didn't think he'd run very fast with that information. I'd just have to wait until Stan arrived. In the meantime, I just needed to relax and try to remember what had happened.

In the next few hours I didn't remember anything new about my predicament, but I did finally realize something about the case that had to be significant. The one thing many of the witnesses complained of was a complete loss of memory—a memory gap of sorts—lasting several critical minutes. Cheryl couldn't remember what happened to her husband when he disappeared, although witnesses said she was with him just before it happened. She couldn't remember her children's kidnapping, although she was there when they were taken. She couldn't even remember the births of her own children for godsakes. Finally, there was Rubin Quinlin, the hotel manager in Tobago. Although he was abducted in a busy hotel, nobody could remember anything about his kidnapping. And now I was sitting here accused of taking drugs and possessing a half million in cash and I had no recollection of how it all happened. It almost seemed like Martin Windsor, or somebody associated with him, had developed a new invention—some kind of short term memory eraser—one that worked on anyone in the vicinity of where it was used.

It was pretty far fetched, but with the rapid advances of technology nowadays I suppose it wasn't beyond the realm of possibilities. I thought awhile about the ramifications of such a device. In the hands of a criminal, money, jewels, almost anything could be stolen with impunity. For the psychiatrist it would be a powerful tool to rid people of painful memories. As a weapon its effectiveness would depend on how it was administered, of course. Was it a drug? I'd been injected with heroin, according to the local police, but not when Cheryl's children were kidnapped. A gas, maybe? I wondered how much memory could be erased.

The old man in the bed next to me woke up. His eyes came alive and for the first time I saw a little color in his face. I looked at his wrist and saw that he too was handcuffed to his bed. I laughed to myself. The cuffs were a bit of overkill. I doubted if he could have made it to the door without collapsing had he wanted to escape. The door opened and an orderly came in with a tray of food.

"Hi there, Ms. Waters. Are you hungry?"

Up until that moment the last thing on my mind had been food, but now that I thought about it, I was famished. I nodded. "Yes, actually I am."

He put the tray down next to me and then rolled a portable table across the bed in front of me. He put the tray on the table and lifted the lids that covered the plates of food. The main dish didn't look half bad—some kind of fish, boiled potatoes, and a medley of vegetables. Underneath another lid there were two fresh rolls with butter. Finally he poured me a cup of tea. All and all it wasn't bad for hospital food—or prison food, I wasn't sure which.

After I finished eating, I was bored so I turned on the TV. I didn't usually watch it back home because I worked such long hours and had little time for it. Bart watched the news in the morning and just before bed, but that was about it. Suddenly, I felt lonely. I wondered if Bart had heard about my arrest. How embarrassing this was going to be for him. He was a patient man but my wayward life was getting ridiculous. I doubted he could stand much more.

Outside I heard footsteps—very familiar footsteps. Could it be? The door opened and my heart jumped for joy!

"Bart. Oh, my God! I was just thinking about you. I'm so glad to see you."

He rushed over to me and we embraced. Tears gushed down my face. "How did you get here so fast?"

"As soon as I heard, I took the first plane. What is going on? Why did they arrest you?"

I related to Bart all that had happened since I'd left Dallas and I told him my crazy theory about a memory eraser. He looked skeptical but heard me out. Then he told me that Stan wanted me to know that Barbara Falk was Martin Windsor's ex-wife.

"What? You've got to be kidding! So, Jimmy Falk was Martin's son?"

"That's right. Apparently Barbara called Stan to tell him that while the jury was out. I guess she was worried Steven might get convicted and was feeling guilty that she hadn't brought it up. It certainly raises a lot of questions."

"Yes, it does," I said still trying to process this new bit of information. "You know, Steven complained of a memory loss when he saw the spaceship and the fishermen who Stan interviewed said the same thing. Do you think there's a connection here?"

"It's a hell of a lot of coincidences," Bart replied.

I swallowed hard. "So, are you going to be able to get me out of this mess or am I going to be a resident of the British Virgin Islands for a while?"

"No. We're going to get you out of here soon. Stan met with Wilkerson and Judge Abbott today to try to work out a deal. He's hoping the authorities here will drop the charges against you and let the Dallas District Attorney's office press charges if they think they have a case. Since the money you had belonged to Cheryl Windsor and her husband, they can't get you with theft. The only thing they could charge you with would be possession of a controlled substance, which would be a relatively minor offense."

"Are you going to stay with me tonight? I don't want to be alone."

"I wish I could, but the policeman guarding you only gave me an hour to be with you. I've checked into your room at the hotel. I've got all your luggage. The money and account documents are being sent to Dallas."

"Damn. I hate being in here alone with that corpse."

"He's a serial killer, I've been told. The cops shot him five times. It's a miracle he's still breathing at all."

"A serial killer? Isn't that my luck?"

After Bart had left, I started thinking about Barbara Falk being Martin Windsor's ex-wife and Jimmy being his son. Why hadn't Cheryl told me that? She must have known. What did all this mean? Was there a connection between Jimmy's death and Martin's disappearance? I wondered.

Chapter 41

Continuance

Jodie was at the office when I arrived and she had already made coffee. She told me that Paul was running late. On the way over I had contemplated just scrapping the meeting and heading for the airport, but I knew it wasn't my place to go to Paula's rescue. I called Bart and told him what had happened. He said he'd pack a bag and get on the next flight out.

When Paul arrived, we all huddled in the conference room and began to discuss our very delicate situation. It was bad enough that Paula had been arrested, but with a murder trial looming in the horizon we had some serious problems to overcome. It wasn't just a question of whether or not Paula was locked up or not, it was quite likely she'd be disqualified from defending Cheryl since the allegation against her was that she was aiding Cheryl in fleeing the jurisdiction of the court.

"Bart is on his way to the airport," I said. "I told him to call me just as soon as he got there. I know Paula didn't do what they say she did, so the question is, who is responsible?"

"None of this makes sense," Paul said. "If Windsor was alive he would have just taken the money. He already has the children."

"Or, somebody does. We don't know for sure who has them."

"I'd bet on Windsor. Who else would want them?"

Jodie replied, "Paula said something about a criminal organization that bought and sold children. Do you think—?"

"They wouldn't go to such elaborate lengths to frame Paula," Paul said. "How would they know how to liquidate all of the assets? The only persons who could do that would be Martin or Cheryl."

"You don't think Cheryl orchestrated this whole thing, do you?" Jodie asked. "Why would she frame Paula?"

"Like I said, none of it makes any sense," Paul repeated.

"Well, one thing is clear," I said. "We don't have a clue what actually happened, so we better just worry about our immediate problems. I guess I need to file a motion for a continuance. If Paula is charged, the judge won't let her try the case. I'll have to do it and I'm frankly not up to speed enough for the task. We need more time—a lot more time."

"How much time are you going to ask for?" Paul asked.

"Six months is what I need, but if I get ninety days I'll be happy. In the meantime, Paul, I need you to get somebody down to Tortola and find out exactly what happened. We've got to figure out who's trying to set Paula up and why."

"I'll take care of it."

"And check with Bart and see if he needs any help finding Paula a good honest lawyer."

"What can I do?" Jodie asked.

"I need you to go through Paula's case files and notes and see what's been done and how everything is organized. Get Maria to help you. Then you and I will have to sit down and go through it all. I've got to get up to speed as quickly as possible. There's no guarantee that Judge Abbott will grant us a continuance."

The next morning I called Rob Wilkerson and told him I was filing a motion for continuance and taking it to the judge immediately. He said he'd meet me down at the courthouse at 11:00 a.m. At 10:30 I was in the clerk's office filing the motion. Word of Paula's arrest had already spread through the courthouse. Several people stopped me and asked if she was okay. I told them I didn't know. At 10:45 Wilkerson walked into the clerk's office with a short brunette woman in her late 20s. I hadn't seen her around, so I figured she was a new recruit at the DA's office. They came over to me.

"Stan, this is Veronica Simpson. She'll be assisting me during the trial. I think the judge is ready to see us. He said for us to come directly into his chambers when you got here."

I nodded and we all filed into Judge Abbott's office. He looked up and smiled. Sit, gentlemen, Ms—?'

"Oh. Judge, this is Veronica Simpson," Wilkerson said. "She's new to our staff."

"Hi, Ms. Simpson. . . .Okay, who filed this motion?"

"I did, Your Honor," I replied. I don't know if you heard but my partner, Paula Waters, was arrested last night in Tortola, British Virgin Islands."

The judge nodded. "Yes, I heard something about that—seems hard to believe."

"Exactly. Paula detests the use of drugs. She used to prosecute drug dealers for the DA's office for godsakes and she wouldn't think of helping a client flee the jurisdiction of the court. She's obviously been set up."

"Well, a half million dollars in cash and another 3.1 million ready to be wired anywhere in the world is quite a temptation," said Wilkerson. "I understand she had a power of attorney, maybe she was going to leave Cheryl Windsor to rot in jail."

"Give me a break," I said glaring at Wilkerson. "Paula doesn't give a damn about the money. She loves being a defense counsel and kicking your ass every chance she gets."

Wilkerson jerked around at me, tightening his fists.

"All right. That's enough," the judge said.

Wilkerson relaxed a bit but didn't take his eyes off of me. The judge said, "So, does the DA's office have any plans to charge Ms. Waters?"

Wilkerson took a deep breath. "We don't have enough information yet, Your Honor, to make that determination, but I would say that's likely."

"Then I'll have to grant the continuance. Obviously, Ms. Waters will not be able to defend Cheryl Windsor if she's under indictment. How much time will you need to prepare for trial, Mr. Turner?"

"Six months, Your Honor. I really don't know that much about the case. Paula's been pretty much handling it."

"What do you say about that Mr. Wilkerson?"

"Your Honor. The state is ready for trial now. We oppose any continuance. Mr. Turner is quite capable of defending Mrs. Windsor, and despite his protests, I am sure he is very familiar with the case."

"Your Honor, I just finished a murder trial. I haven't even looked at the Cheryl Windsor file in three weeks. It's going to take some time to get this case ready."

"Well, you can't have six months. I'll give you thirty days."

"But, Your Honor. I couldn't possibly—"

"If you can get Ms. Waters out of jail, she can sit with you during the trial as an assistant, but not as co-counsel."

Wilkerson jumped in. "But, Your Honor, we may need her as a witness."

"Not at this trial you won't. If there was a conspiracy to flee the jurisdiction, it would have occurred after the murder and wouldn't be relevant to this trial. I'd suggest, Mr. Wilkerson, if you decide she is culpable, that you wait until the trial is over to indict her. That will make life easier for all of us."

Wilkerson didn't look happy, but he shut up. Was he really that anxious to go to trial or was he just trying to be a prick? His new assistant rolled her eyes and gave me a wry smile. I wondered what that was about. Had she already developed a disdain for Rob Wilkerson?

Once we were out of the judge's chamber, I asked Wilkerson if he'd support our suggestion to the Tortola authorities that they let Paula come home to Dallas where she'd surrender to the sheriff. He said he'd talk to his bosses about it, but by the look on his face I seriously doubted he wanted to. He was obviously having too much fun watching us twist in the wind and didn't want to lift a finger to ease our pain.

Solving the Cheryl Windsor case in thirty days seemed a daunting task. The case defied all logic and was as bizarre a case as I'd ever seen or even heard of. When I got back to the office, Jodie had all the case files and evidence in neat little piles in the conference room. Paula organized her cases much differently that I did. She was an organization freak and had files for everything. My style was much more basic. I usually had a medium sized trial notebook with everything I needed at my fingertips. The evidence of course was separate but it was organized by exhibit numbers and I had an index of all the exhibits in the trial notebook. My task now was to go through all the evidence, and decide what I needed to introduce at trial and then make an index. I got right to work.

Later that night Bart called and said he'd seen Paula and she seemed physically fine with the exception of a few bruises to her back and the lingering effects of the drug overdose. I told him Paul was sending someone there to help him find a barrister and to do some factual investigation. He thanked me and said he'd call me the next day with an update.

It was very late that night when I got home. Rebekah was already in bed asleep when I eased under the covers. Despite my exhaustion, I couldn't sleep. Every time I closed my eyes, I thought of Paula in jail surrounded by thugs and perverts just waiting for an opportunity to hurt her. Lawyers were universally loathed by inmates almost as much as cops. We had to get her out of there before she left the hospital. My stomach was in knots just thinking about it and I tossed and turned for a long time before I finally fell into an uneasy slumber.

Chapter 42

Rescue

On Thursday my nurse advised me that they were planning to move me to a detention facility that afternoon. That scared me because that meant I would soon be in the general population with other prisoners, most of whom were dangerous criminals who might relish the idea of doing a little attorney bashing—and not the verbal kind that was so popular nowadays. I had taken a few self defense courses, but I wasn't exactly a black belt. If there were a betting pool on the odds of me winning a prison yard brawl, I'd bet against me.

As I was staring out the window contemplating my fate, I remembered what Stan had said to me on more than one occasion. When things go wrong, don't panic. It won't help. Have faith that God will somehow take care of you. Stan was always so calm even when things went to hell. I needed to be strong too and have faith that somehow I'd get through this nightmare. I closed my eyes and said a silent prayer. A second later I heard footsteps in the hallway. I opened my eyes and watched as the door opened. It was Bart and Paul Thayer. I would have jumped for joy had I not been handcuffed to my bed.

"Hey. You brought reinforcements," I said grinning broadly.

Bart nodded, "Yes, I picked him up this morning at the airport."

"I hope you have some good news," I said to Paul. "I've been told they're transporting me to the local jailhouse this afternoon."

"That's not going to happen," Paul said. "You're booked on a six o'clock flight to Dallas."

"Oh, thank God! How did you manage that?"

"Stan worked it out with the judge and Wilkerson. The local authorities aren't going to press charges here in Tortola. I'm afraid you're going to have to go back to Dallas in handcuffs, though."

I shrugged. "That's okay, I guess, but what's going to happen when I get to Dallas?"

Paul replied, "You'll be released on your own recognizance with the stipulation that you won't leave Dallas County until after Cheryl's trial. At that time you'll either be indicted or no-billed."

"Well, that's not so bad."

"There is one thing. You won't be able to represent Cheryl anymore. You can help Stan, but you won't be able to act as co-counsel at the trial."

"Damn it! That's exactly what they wanted. Whoever set me up wanted to compromise me and they succeeded. We can't let them get away with this."

"Don't worry. They haven't succeeded yet. We're going to figure this thing out," Paul said. "Bart and I paid a visit to Walter Johansen today and we've started interviewing staff at the hotel. Someone is bound to remember something."

"Not if their memory has been erased," I replied. I told them about my theory that Martin or someone had invented a memory eraser.

"Well, Johansen doesn't seem to have a memory loss," Paul replied. "He gave us a complete account of your meeting."

"That should be interesting. What did he tell you?"

"He said you met with him and told him you were closing out Cheryl's account and wanted to move the money immediately to an account in Chile. He said he advised you against it because there were stiff penalties for withdrawal of funds within one year of deposit. According to him, you said you didn't care about that, you just wanted the money moved immediately."

"Bullshit! " I replied. "He's involved in this somehow. He's either working for Martin Windsor or the organization who stole her children. You've got to thoroughly investigate him and find out who he's working for. He's the only lead we have right now."

"I've got a man watching him as we speak," Paul said. "I'm going to stay here for a few days after you leave and find out as much as I can about him. If he contacts the people he's working for we'll know it."

After Bart and Paul left, I was giddy over the news of my evening flight back to Dallas. Stan had been right. My prayers had been answered after all. It was just a matter of hard work and a little faith. The fact that I couldn't be first chair at trial was disappointing, but I wasn't going to dwell on that right now. Hopefully, Paul would find something on Johansen that would clear me and things would get back to normal.

At 4:00 p.m. Bart and Detective Pollock came to pick me up to go to the airport. Pollock uncuffed me and let me get dressed, then we went outside where a police car was waiting. Pollock and I went in the police car and Bart took a cab. It was complicated going through customs with lots of paperwork and conferences between Pollock and numerous customs' agents. Finally we made it through and boarded the airplane.

It was embarrassing to be handcuffed to Pollock. People looked at me like I was the two-headed lady at the circus, but I didn't care. I was on my way home and soon all of this would be but a distant memory. Bart found us and sat in the aisle seat next to me. He took my hand and squeezed it. I smiled up at him and thanked God again for saving my butt.

The flight back to Dallas seemed to take forever with two stops along the way. At the U.S. Customs office at DFW Airport Pollock turned me over to Detective Perkins and a uniformed officer who escorted me to the downtown Dallas Police Station. There I was booked and then released on my own recognizance as had been agreed. I nearly cried when I came out and saw Stan and Bart in the waiting room. Stan gave me a big hug.

"How are you? I've been so worried about you," Stan said.

"I'm okay now that I'm home. It got a little scary there before Bart and Paul showed up."

"Yeah, I bet. I'm sorry I didn't come with them, but I figured I could do you more good from this end."

"Yes, I heard you cut a deal with the judge. Thank you so much."

Stan shook his head. "It was nothing. I'm just so sorry you had to go through all of this."

"Well, it's water under the bridge. Now we have to focus on the trial coming up. I heard you got a short continuance."

"Right. So, just as soon as you've recovered, I could use your help getting back on track."

"I'll be at work first thing Monday morning," I said.

"Well, that's all right. You should take a day or two off. You've been through quite an ordeal."

I shrugged. "I've been lying around for three days in a hospital bed. I don't need much more rest. I'll be at my desk at 8:00 a.m. ready to work on Monday."

"Okay, I'll see you then."

Bart and I drove home and all the way I kept rubbing my wrists thankful that the handcuffs were gone. When we got home, I took a good look around the condo. It was nice to be back home where I finally felt safe again. Although it had been less than a week since I had left for Tortola, it seemed like a month. After a late dinner and a couple of drinks, Bart led me to the bedroom to show me how much he'd missed me. I soon discovered he'd missed me a lot.

Chapter 43

Unanswered Questions

I should have been delighted with Steven Caldwell's acquittal, but I wasn't. An uneasy feeling had settled over me almost immediately after the verdict was announced. Even after months of investigation, the case was still a mystery. When Barbara Falk had revealed to me that Martin Windsor was her ex-husband that blew my mind and got me thinking about other unsettling facts. The first was that Steven Caldwell had stuck to his story about seeing an alien spaceship, even though that could have cost him his freedom. Then I realized Martin Windsor had disappeared the same night his son, Jimmy Falk, had been killed. Finally, there was the fact that we hadn't really explained what Steven saw on September 10. There were no military aircraft flying that night, no commercial flights, no blimps or weather balloons, so what had Steven seen? I had to find out because I had a gut feeling that knowing this information would be important to Cheryl Windsor's defense. Of course, I couldn't tell Paula or anyone else that.

I'd begun to believe that aliens were responsible for Jimmy Falk's death as well as the disappearance of Martin Windsor and Cheryl's kids, among others. It was such a radical idea, I didn't dare breathe a word of it to anyone until I was absolutely sure it was true. Even then it would be a hard sell to even the most open minded of listeners. My investigation had to be completely secret and off the record. That's why I had enlisted Peter's help in creating a cover story for our covert operation.

To prove that aliens had used Cactus Island for a landing strip, we'd have to discover the caves that supposedly linked the island to the shore. Without such a passageway, it wouldn't have made sense to land on the island. Ferrying the ship's crew back and forth across the lake on a barge or a boat wouldn't have been practical and such activity would have been slow and easily detected.

If the caves did exist, they might contain evidence of the alien visits to the island.

My efforts to find the geological study showing the caves finally bore fruit. Doc Verner called with the name of the firm that had prepared the report. But when I called them they admitted they'd done the survey but advised me that the operator who had commissioned it had never paid for it. So, if I wanted it, I'd have to pay the bill of $1,500. After a little haggling we finally agreed on $750.00 and I had the report on my desk via Federal Express the next morning.

With the report in hand, Peter and I drove to Possum Kingdom Lake. What we'd do if we actually found the caves, I had no idea. Exploring them would be perilous work, so I didn't have any plans to do anything but find them for now. Exploration would be a task for another day.

We drove to the north end of the lake where the caves were supposed to begin, and then got out on foot and started walking along the shore. We didn't know exactly what the entrance to the caves would look like, so we just kept our eyes open for anything out of the ordinary. After awhile, we came across two fishermen working the shoreline. We asked them if they knew of any caves in the area. They said they hadn't seen or heard of any. After several hours of searching, we decided to knock on a few cabin doors to see if anyone in the area was aware of the caves. Still, no luck.

Just before dark we discovered a huge metal barn that was situated right above where the mouth of the caves should have been located. We walked over to it but it was locked up tight and there was nobody around. There were no signs on the barn or other indication as to what business was conducted there, but there was a small corral that suggested horses were trained or stabled there in the summer.

We continued to search for several more hours but finally gave up. Anticipating that this might happen and not wanting the trip to be a total bust, I had arranged for a guide on Sunday morning to take us striper fishing. Peter loved to fish and I wanted him to have some fun before we went home. That night we rented a room at the Armadillo Motel that overlooked the lake. It wasn't a place Rebekah would have stayed in, but it was good enough for a fishing trip. We ate catfish and blackberry pie at the diner near Camp Comfort where Steven had been taken after his accident, and then walked along the shore of the lake awhile. A half moon in the western sky gave us a good view of Cactus Island.

"I'm sorry we didn't find the caves," I said. "For a time there I was starting to believe there were aliens landing on Cactus Island."

"There still might be," Peter replied. "They're not going to make it easy for us to find them."

"That's the spirit. Never give up."

"We can look some more tomorrow."

"Nah. It was a bad idea. I can't believe I actually thought we'd find something. Let's just catch our limit of striper tomorrow and head on home."

"Okay. Maybe the fishing guide will know about the caves."

Suddenly there was a fluttering sound out in the lake that drew our attention. In the moonlight we could see hundreds of fish thrashing in the water. It wasn't unusual to see a fish frenzy of this sort. It often happened when a school of stripers cornered a school of shads. The shad, in a desperate attempt to escape, would go ballistic and jump right out of the water. The odd thing was that striper usually didn't feed at night and usually a fish frenzy would quickly subside as the shads were disbursed, but this one intensified. Another oddity was the size of the fish that were frantically jumping and thrashing about. They were much bigger than shads. As we watched the commotion in amazement a big green tail shot out of the water and then plunged back into the lake causing a huge splash. We both jumped.

"What the hell was that?"I said. "An alligator?"

"I don't know, but it was a big momma," Peter said excitedly.

We kept our eyes fixed on the spot where we'd seen the giant tail emerge, hoping we'd get another look at the creature who was causing all the commotion. Nothing happened for quite awhile, so I suggested we should head back for the motel. . . .

When my eyes opened, I was lying on my stomach on the beach. I was disoriented, wet, and cold. My side hurt, apparently from lying on a large jagged rock for God knows how long. I looked around and saw Peter lying beside me. What had happened to us? I checked Peter's pulse and made sure he was breathing. Then I gently woke him up.

"Is it time to get up?" Peter asked, rubbing his eyes. He looked around warily, then abruptly sat up. "Where are we?"

"I don't know. We must have fallen asleep on the beach, I guess. Come on. Let's get back to the motel."

When we got back to our room it was 11:59 p.m. We had left our motel room around 10:30 and now suddenly it was nearly midnight. Over an hour had gone by but it seemed like only a few minutes. I racked my brains trying to remember what had happened during the missing time but my mind was a blank.

We got out of our wet clothes and went to bed, but I couldn't sleep. I kept thinking of what Paula had said about the memory eraser. Did someone have a machine that could actually erase your memory at will? Was that possible? I had to find out what had happened to us. There had to be a way to reach back into the recesses of our minds and recover our memories. Then I remembered Martin Windsor's warning to Cheryl about hypnosis. Was it possible that there was a flaw in the memory-erasing machine? Hypnosis had helped Steven regain some of his memory, so why not us? Anyway, we could find out easily enough.

The next morning we met the guide at the bait shop anxious for our round of fishing. He apologized and said there wasn't any use going out because the fish hadn't been biting the last few days. For some reason they were scattered and difficult to find. The previous day he'd caught only one fish rather than his usual limit of twenty. Something was obviously wrong with the lake. Peter was disappointed so I suggested we rent a couple of jet skis for a couple hours before we headed home. He thought that was a great idea.

On the way home I took a detour to Plano where we stopped at Dr. Gerhardt's house with a dozen doughnuts. He seemed shocked and dismayed to see us, but invited us in anyway.

"What's going on? I don't usually see patients at home nor do I work on Sunday."

"I understand that, but this is an emergency. Something happened to Peter and me last night and we have to find out what it was."

"I don't understand. How do you know something happened

if you can't remember it?"

I explained to the doctor how we'd woken up on the beach. He seemed skeptical and asked, "You mean neither of you can remember lying down on the beach? It was late and you might have fallen asleep, don't you think?"

"No."

"Were you drinking?"

"No. Peter doesn't drink and I wouldn't have had a drink when I was alone with him. We had just left our motel room and the next thing we knew we're lying on the beach."

"So your memory lapse was over an hour?"

"Yes."

"Hmm. Interesting. So, how can I help?"

"I need you to hypnotize me so maybe I can remember what happened."

"Can't this wait until Monday? Why do you have to know right this minute what happened?"

"It's important. I think what happened to us last night might have a connection to the murder trial I'm involved in. It could be the key to proving our client's innocence."

"Well this is crazy, but I suppose you won't leave until I do it."

I smiled. "Right."

He shrugged. "Okay, then. Let's get on with it."

"Thanks, Doc. I appreciate it."

"Let's go into my study."

Dr. Gerhardt led us into his study and told us to make ourselves comfortable. We both sat and waited as Dr. Gerhardt got ready for the procedure. A few minutes later he looked at Peter. "You better wait in the living room. Sometimes these sessions can be quite intense."

"No," Peter said. "I want to know what happened."

I said, "He's right, Peter. It's probably better you don't know."

"Dad!" Peter protested.

"Peter! Go in the living room and read a magazine or something."

Peter threw up his hands and stomped off. When he was gone, Dr. Gerhardt took a small pen light and shone it in my eyes. He told me to watch it as he slowly turned it in small circles.

"You will start to fall asleep as I count to ten. When I am done counting, you will be in a deep sleep but you will be able to talk to me and tell me what happened to you and Peter last night. When I snap my fingers, you will wake up and remember everything that you told me about last night."

Dr. Gerhardt counted to ten as my mind began to drift. "Okay, you are very, very sleepy. It's Saturday night and you are with Peter at Possum Kingdom Lake. You are in your motel room. . . ."

"Snap!"

I woke up in a fog feeling disoriented. Where was I?

"Stan," Dr. Gerhardt said. "Are you with us?"

"Huh."

"Do you remember what happened now?"

"Remember what?" I said as Dr. Gerhardt's face came into focus."

"Your experience last night. I put you under hypnosis."

I strained to comprehend what he was saying but there was nothing but darkness. Then I saw a glow, the darkness began to fade, and the memories returned like the rays from the rising sun. "Yes, I think so. . . . Now I see it. We decided to take a walk on the beach. It was a beautiful night and the stars were very bright. We reached the beach and were starting to walk along the shore when we heard something out in the lake. We looked over and saw a huge lizard-like creature surface not fifty feet away. It was like nothing I'd ever seen before."

"Was it an alligator?" Dr. Gerhardt asked. "You don't usually see them this far north, but it's not unheard of."

"No. It was standing up like a man and was at least six feet tall."

"What?"

"It was greyish green and was watching us with its orange penetrating eyes. It had what must be an eight-pound striper in its mouth struggling to get free. Its arms seemed as functional as my own and looked to be incredibly strong. Peter was scared and started to scream. I put my hand over his mouth and told him to shut up.

"We slowly retreated from the beast, Peter trembling and breathing hard. The creature watched us closely as it chewed but didn't seem to care that we'd seen him. Once we were out of his sight, we turned and ran like hell back to the motel. With the door closed and the deadbolt latched, we both took a breath. Peter was pale and still trembling. I took him in my arms and held him tightly. We were both in shock and had little to say. As I held Peter, I thought back to his testimony in court about the frogmen who were supposedly the slaves of the aliens and provided the labor for operating the spaceship. As I recalled from the story, the spaceship landed at Cactus Island so the frogmen could feed off the fish in the lake. Could the story be true?

"Excited by the possibility that aliens might actually be visiting Cactus Island at that moment, I told Peter to stay in the motel room and I'd be right back. I rushed outside and looked out at the lake. There was a faint glow above the island. I ran toward the shore to get a better look, my heart pounding, not from running but from the thought that alien life might actually exist.

"A strong wind suddenly whipped up making the trees sway and the leaves rustle. There was a thin layer of clouds in the sky and the moonlight created an eerie ambience over the lake. Suddenly there was a flash of blue lightning from the island that stopped me dead in my tracks. Something hit me from behind startling me—scaring the shit out of me. I turned and was relieved to see it was only was Peter.

"I put my arm around him and we both gazed out at the island in amazement. There was one hell of a light show going on out there. By now the wind was blowing fiercely and we could hardly keep our footing. The glow from the island kept getting brighter and brighter. Then a giant object shot out of the island. It fired bursts of blue lightning as it came right at us. There was a terrible piercing noise that forced us to grab our ears or lose our eardrums."

"What sort of object is it?" Dr. Gerhardt asked.

"It was like nothing I'd ever seen before. It was a huge grey object, a spaceship of some sort."

"A spaceship. Are you sure?"

"Absolutely! Believe me. There is no doubt. I wish you could have seen it. It was incredible!"

"It could just be some kind of a delusion—stress from your trial," Dr. Gerhardt said. "The mind plays strange tricks on us sometime. You sure you weren't drinking or perhaps you took a Valium?"

"No, doc. It really happened. Apparently these aliens can erase your memory somehow. I think it's the blue lightning. Somehow it causes you to forget that they were there. It's pretty amazing, isn't it?"

"Yes, but if it's true, the ramifications of something like that would be quite astounding."

"Yes, so I'm going to have to ask you to keep this matter secret until I can figure out what to do."

"I won't tell a soul—Doctor-patient privilege—but Stan, you may not have seen a spaceship."

I smiled. "Yes, I did. When you see something that incredible you don't forget it. It will be imprinted in my mind forever. I can't believe it! There are alien beings after all. . . . Jesus, mother of God! I never thought I'd hear myself say that. . . . Thanks for your help, Doctor. Sorry I intruded on your weekend."

On the way home I had a serious talk with Peter and told him he couldn't tell anyone, under any circumstance, what had happened—not even his mother. He said he still didn't know what happened since I wouldn't let him go under hypnosis. I apologized for that but told him it was for his own protection. I made him promise he would keep his mouth shut about waking up on the beach and going to see Dr. Gerhardt. He was a good kid, so I was pretty confident he'd honor his pledge even though it would be difficult. I would probably eventually tell Rebekah, since she would sense that I was holding something inside, but I needed to wait for the right moment. She might not take the news so well. In the meantime I needed to sort everything out and decide what to do about this incredible discovery, that alien life existed and that somehow Martin Windsor was involved with them—maybe was one of them. It was a delicate situation that required much thought and consideration before moving forward with a plan to deal with it. If I went public with this information prematurely, it might be the end of my career. On the other hand, if I didn't use this information to help prove Cheryl's innocence, she might be convicted and never see her children again. And then there was the whole issue as to whether the public had a right to know that aliens were visiting Cactus Island and probably were landing at other locations as well. Why were they here and what were they up to? These were all questions that weighed heavily on my mind.

Chapter 44

Stubborn Client

On Monday morning I woke up at six and couldn't go back to sleep. Cheryl's trial was on my mind. There was so much yet to do. I got up, took a shower, put on my makeup, and picked out an outfit to wear. Bart was still asleep when I stepped out of the bathroom, so I went into the kitchen and put on a pot of coffee. Bart finally got up at seven and joined me.

"You're up early," he mumbled.

"Yes, I've got a lot of work to do to get Stan ready for Cheryl's trial. I still can't believe I won't be trying the case myself. It's so unfair to pull me off it at the last minute."

"I'm sorry, honey. I know how disappointed you are, but at least you can be there at Stan's side."

"I sure hope Paul comes up with something useful. Right now we don't have much of a defense. We have to find some evidence that Martin Windsor is alive or we're sunk."

"Paul will find something. He's a good detective and he knows how important it is to find a connection between Johansen and Martin Windsor. If it's there, he'll find it."

"I'm sure it's there. There's no other explanation for all of this."

Bart was being the perfect supportive husband who was doing his best to cheer me up. I kissed him goodbye and headed for the office. An unusually dense fog slowed traffic and made for a long tedious drive to work. As I drove into the parking garage I was surprised to see Stan's 300 ZX. It was unusual to see him there before 8:30, so I was anxious to talk to him to make sure everything was okay. He looked up when I walked into his office. I could tell something was wrong.

"Paula. How are you feeling?"

"Okay. You're here bright and early."

"Right. I couldn't sleep. Peter and I had quite a weekend."

Stan told me about his encounter with the frogman, the missing hour, and his visit to Dr. Gerhardt. It all seemed surreal. Aliens? Frogmen? Was this some kind of joke? I looked at the calendar—no, it wasn't April Fool's day. He must have sensed my skepticism as he went immediately on the defensive.

"Listen, you can talk to Dr. Gerhardt. I'm not making this up. I wouldn't have told you any of this if we weren't partners and agreed to be honest with each other. Maybe it was a mistake."

"No. No. But you've got to admit it's a little hard to swallow."

"Yeah. I know that. That's why we can't tell anyone else about this. I just wanted you to know so you'd understand my trial strategy."

"Which is?"

"Well, Jodie and I have been going through your notes and the evidence, and right now Cheryl's going to be convicted, absent some kind of miracle."

I nodded. "That's probably a fair analysis of the situation."

"Right. So, we have to convince Cheryl to let us hypnotize her so she can remember what happened on the day Martin disappeared. Then we'll put her on the stand and she can tell the jury."

"Do *you* know what happened?"

"Not yet, but I'm guessing it had something to do with our alien invaders."

"Oh, geez. Alien invaders. Come on. This is all too weird."

"Paula. I'm not joking! I saw a frogman and the alien ship take off from Cactus Island. The blue lightning from the ship must somehow cause a short term memory loss in the people in the path of the ship. There must be a portable version of the device that the aliens use for smaller jobs, like eliminating the memory of witnesses at a crime scene."

"It's just so hard to believe," Cheryl said.

"I know. I'm sorry, but remember the first thing they taught us in law school—you can't change the facts."

"Right. Facts are facts. I know. But do you think anyone will believe Cheryl? Won't they just think it's all an act?"

"Maybe. But we have other witnesses who can corroborate her story."

"Like who?"

"Like Barbara Falk and Steven Caldwell. We can even call Doc Verner and the fishermen who saw the spaceship."

"You're going to stir up all the science fiction and UFO fanatics again. It's going to get nasty."

"I can't worry about that. Can you think of a better strategy?"

I took a deep breath. As outlandish as the whole alien business was, if it was the truth, we had no choice but to use it to save Cheryl. I gave Stan a hard look. Was he telling the truth? I still couldn't believe he'd seen a spaceship, but I didn't think he'd lie to me either. Were he and Peter smoking pot out at the lake? I laughed to myself. I knew that hadn't happened. According to Rebekah, Stan hadn't smoked even a cigarette since he was 19.

"All right," I said. "I'm not 100 percent sold on your theory, but I'll support you if you're sure that's the path you want to follow. Just tell me what you want me to do."

Stan sighed. "Well, for starters you need to talk to Cheryl and start softening up her resistence to hypnosis. You've got to explain to her that Martin didn't want her to be hypnotized because he knew that her memory could be restored. He obviously doesn't want her to remember what actually happened."

"I'll try, but I know she's scared. She'll be worried about Martin hurting her or the kids."

"That's another reason to talk to her about hypnosis. If Martin is somehow monitoring her conversations, this might draw him out. I'm going to have Paul put her under 24–hour surveillance until the trial. If anyone makes a move to hurt her, we'll be all over them."

"You're going to use her as bait?"

"More or less, but we don't have any choice. If we do nothing, she goes to jail and she'll never see her children again."

"All right. I'll go see her this afternoon. Keep your fingers crossed."

"I will."

I was dreading talking to Cheryl because I couldn't really tell her Stan's theory without totally freaking her out. Her mental state was delicate, there'd been no progress made in locating her children and she was facing a murder trial in just a few weeks.

She opened the door and smiled faintly. Her pale face accentuated the dark circles under her eyes.

"Hey, girl. How are you?"

She shrugged. "As well as can be expected." She showed me in and we sat at the kitchen table.

"Sorry about the short notice, but there's been some new developments that we need to discuss."

"Sure. What is it?"

"Did you follow the Steven Caldwell murder trial that my partner handled?"

"Uh huh. It was all over the news."

"Well, did you know the victim, Jimmy Falk, was Martin's son?"

She looked away and didn't respond.

"Did you?" I pressed.

She nodded. "Yes, of course."

"Well, why didn't you mention it to me? It could have been important."

"How? Jimmy died in a car wreck a hundred miles away from here."

"Doesn't it seem a little odd that father and son died on the same day?"

"Martin isn't dead, is he?" Cheryl asked.

"I don't know—died or disappeared—either way it's a hell of a coincidence, don't you think?"

Cheryl swallowed hard and looked away again. "I never thought about it that way."

"I can't believe you didn't mention it to me. There must be some reason you didn't tell me."

Cheryl sighed. "Martin told me never to tell anyone about his relationship with Barbara Falk. He was very clear on that subject."

"So are you going to follow Martin's rules even if he's dead?"

She looked down. "He's not dead and I'll never see the children if I betray him."

"Have you heard from him? Is that why you're still scared of him?"

"No! I don't need to hear from him. I know him. He doesn't make idle threats."

Cheryl's complete stubbornness was starting to annoy me. How was I going to convince her to let herself be hypnotized when she was so scared of her husband? I finally decided I'd have to tell her about Stan's alien landing theory to get her to cooperate.

"Cheryl. Do you remember telling me about not remembering your delivery?"

"Yes."

"Well, there might be a connection between that and the memory losses you suffered the day Martin went missing and the day your children were kidnapped."

"How so?"

"We think your husband, or someone associated with him, has a device that can cause a person to lose a portion of their memory. Apparently your husband used that device to erase your memory of certain events."

Cheryl squinted. "I didn't know that was possible."

"I don't know how it works, but they used it on me in Tortola too, when I inquired about your offshore account. I ended up in jail."

"What? Are you okay?"

"Yes and no. I won't be your attorney at trial. Stan will have to defend you."

I told Cheryl about what had happened in Tortola.

"Why would Martin want to erase my memory?" Cheryl asked.

"I don't know yet, but there is obviously something that he's hiding."

"Like what?"

"Like maybe, well . . . you know . . . he might not be from this world. I'm not totally convinced of this, but Stan believes it."

Cheryl turned a shade paler. She looked away.

"Has that possibility ever crossed your mind?"

She shook her head. "No, of course not. That's absurd," she said tentatively.

"Are you sure?" I pressed.

"Well . . . I mean . . . the thought may have crossed my mind. . . . You know, one of those crazy notions you get, but I never seriously believed it."

"What made you consider it?"

She shrugged. "Well, lots of things. His paranoia about doctors for starters. He was always worried about getting into an accident or getting sick and being taken to a doctor without his knowledge and consent. He said it was because he thought most doctors were quacks and he didn't trust them, but I really think his fear was that he might be physically examined by a strange doctor. I often wondered what he was afraid a doctor would find."

"Right. So that's why you always went to the same clinic for medical treatment including your pregnancies?"

"Yes, the doctors there were the only ones Martin said he could trust."

"What about the convenient memory losses?" I asked. "It must have upset you that you couldn't remember your deliveries."

"I always thought it was just me. There were so many of times I couldn't remember things. I finally just accepted it as my own poor memory."

"But now that it seems to be a regular occurrence and happens to others, what do you think?"

"It is odd and kind of scary."

"Wouldn't you like to know what happened during those missing hours? Doesn't it bother you that part of your life went by without you knowing it?"

"Yes, of course."

"Well, Stan has been experimenting with this phenomenon with Dr. Gerhardt and they've been able to fill in some of those missing periods for several people."

Her body became rigid. "Through hypnosis?" she asked.

"Yes."

She shook her head emphatically. "Martin said no hypnosis!"

"I know, but Martin also took your children and stole all your money. You've got to help us out here, Cheryl."

She shook her head and looked away. I could tell I'd hit another brick wall. Why wouldn't she help us? It defied logic. She wasn't the same woman who had strolled into my office ready to file for divorce and take her husband to the cleaners. She was terrified of Martin and I could only imagine what he had done to her to make her that way.

When I told Stan that Cheryl was still refusing to consider hypnosis, he said we'd just have to find someone else to hypnotize. Alex came to mind, since he and I had witnessed the children's kidnapping, but I didn't figure he'd be too eager to help us out. I could have been hypnotized myself, but then I'd be a witness and couldn't help Stan with the trial. We had to find someone else, but who? It seemed we'd reached a dead end and Cheryl's defense seemed hopeless.

Chapter 45

Trial Strategy

Doubt crept into my mind almost immediately after telling Paula about seeing the spaceship. Was it possible my mind just conjured up the vision because, deep down, I wanted to see it? Was all this simply a figment of my imagination? Paula had believed me, or had she? Maybe she was humoring me because she didn't know what else to do. How could I possibly go into a court of law and with a straight face and allege Cheryl Windsor was innocent because her husband was abducted by aliens or, better yet, was an alien himself? I laughed as I pictured the spectacle in my mind.

If we were going down this road, we needed some hard evidence, but so far we had nothing but speculation. I needed a photograph of a frogman or one of the aliens. I thought of the big barn at the north end of Possum Kingdom Lake where the cave that supposedly led to Cactus Island should have been. Could the mouth of the cave be inside the big barn? That would explain why nobody had seen the caves. I pondered that for a moment and then decided to send a photographer out to stake out the barn for a few days and see if anyone showed up. If they did, I wanted pictures that I could introduce into evidence.

Paul returned from Tortola that afternoon and called from the airport to say he'd drop by our offices on his way home. An hour later he made good on his promise and Maria showed him in.

"So, I hope you've got good news about Walter Johansen," I said.

"Actually, I do. It seems Mr. Johansen has a lot of enemies and we were able to get some good information from a couple of them."

"What kind of information?"

"Well, Paula probably told you she met a couple of bankers at the Sugar Mill Resort."

"Yes, she mentioned that."

"They gave us the names of some clients Johansen screwed over pretty good. They were very cooperative in pointing out some of Johansen's skeletons."

"Impeachment evidence?"

"Right. He was convicted of money laundering, bribery, and conspiracy in Alabama, but only served one year. The SEC had him under investigation for securities fraud, but no charges were ever filed. He's on their bad boy list. That's probably why he moved to the British Virgin Islands."

"But nothing directly related to our case?"

"Well, not specifically. We do know Johansen legally controls a vast network of IBCs, but it's impossible to figure out who all the equitable owners are due to the bank secrecy laws."

"So, we don't have anything that's going to help Cheryl?"

"Not a lot, but we haven't stopped looking. We may find something yet."

"Okay, in the meantime I need you to get someone up to the Possum Kingdom Lake to do some surveillance work."

I explained to Paul what I wanted and he said he'd take care of it. I tried to think if there were any avenues of investigation we hadn't considered. Thinking of none, I decided it was time to put together my witness list and work on some voir dire questions. The judge had advised us that he wanted us to exchange witness lists seven days before trial, which was only a few days off.

The final ten days before the trial went quickly. We spent most of our time working on direct examination questions, cross examination points, evidence lists, and our opening and closing statements. Paula made me promise not to bring up the alien invaders unless we had no other choice. Although there was mounting evidence that they were somehow involved in the death of Jimmy Falk and his father's disappearance, the potential loss of credibility that we might suffer was too great to risk.

We decided our best chance was simply to create reasonable doubt by suggesting and producing evidence that Martin Windsor was still alive and his disappearance was just a cleaver ploy to protect his considerable wealth and gain sole custody of his children. Since Cheryl wouldn't allow herself to be hypnotized and had no recollection of what happened on the day of Martin's disappearance, we also decided it wouldn't hurt to put her on the stand. She would deny liquidating any assets and could genuinely express her anger and heartache over her children's kidnapping. This would be important to the success of her defense.

Chapter 46

The Trap

Depression set in with a vengeance the weekend before Cheryl's trial. I couldn't believe I'd be sitting mute next to Stan for the duration of the trial. It was the second time I'd been working on a high profile murder case only to be pulled off because of bogus allegations brought against me. The first time I was set up on hit and run charges. Eventually the truth came out and I was cleared, but only after I'd suffered immeasurable emotional distress and was forced to be a spectator at the trial. Now here I was again having to worry about another criminal indictment while my client was on trial. Practicing law wasn't supposed to be this way. I was supposed to be the defense counsel, not the accused.

A late norther blew through Dallas on Saturday, March 2, 1991 and left behind a thin blanket of snow. The clouds had gone by Sunday night, so the thermometer plummeted to the low 20s by Monday morning. I didn't much like cold weather and the freezing temperatures just exacerbated my depression and general bitterness over my bad fortune. Only with a lot of prodding from Bart did I manage to get up, shake off my general malaise, and get out the door by 8:00 a.m.

Fortunately the press hadn't taken nearly the interest in the Martin Windsor case as they had in Steven Caldwell's. It was nice to be able to enter the courthouse without being barraged by questions from a bunch of reporters. Only two reporters approached me when I walked in the basement of the courthouse, and one of them was my friend Jane Witherspoon.

"Paula," Jane said. "How are you feeling today?"

"Frozen," I replied. "It's not supposed to be this cold in Texas."

"Tell me about it. I've already complained to our weather people. . . . How is your client feeling this morning?"

"I haven't seen her yet. She's probably upstairs with Stan right now. She was really nervous last night, which is understandable, but she's confident in our judicial system."

"Are you disappointed that you won't be handling Cheryl's defense?"

"Yes. Extremely disappointed, but I know my partner will do a good job, so that's what's important."

"Do you still believe Martin Windsor is alive?" the other reporter asked.

I looked at him, wondering if I should respond. We generally didn't discuss our defense strategy with the press, but it might be a good idea to get people thinking about the possibility that Martin might be alive, and Wilkerson already knew that would be our strategy, so it wasn't like I was revealing a deep dark secret. I decided to answer the question. "Yes. We're quite sure he's alive. My client didn't kidnap her own children and liquidate assets she didn't even know existed. Only Martin Windsor could have done that."

With the seed planted, I thanked both of them, stepped into the elevator and pushed the button for the sixth floor. I anticipated the elevator stopping on the first floor to pick up more passengers and when it opened, I looked out onto a herd of eager faces anxious to get wherever they were going. Amongst the throng I saw a face that sent a chill down my spine. It was the Vanishing Man. There were several bodies between us and we didn't make eye contact. The door opened on the fourth floor and several people got out and several stepped in. When we got to the sixth floor he was closer to the door, so he exited before me. Since he knew me, I hesitated so he wouldn't see me, then stepped out and looked around for him. I wanted to know where he was going, so I could call Paul Thayer and get someone down here to follow him and find out who he was and how to contact him. We needed to subpoena him as a witness since he would know where we could find Martin Windsor, if he were alive. I looked both ways but he was nowhere to be found. I searched the halls, the stairwells, and checked every courtroom on the floor but he was gone.

"Disappeared again! Damn," I mumbled.

Even so, I thought. The fact that he was here was good news. If I spotted him again, I'd be prepared. I'd have a blank subpoena ready at the clerk's office downstairs and have the bailiff hold him until I could go down there and have his name inserted on the blank line. After taking one last look up and down the busy hallway, I went into the courtroom. Stan and Cheryl were at the defense table talking. Wilkerson and his new assistant were standing by the court reporter getting some exhibits labeled. The room was filling up fast.

At 9:01 a.m. Judge Abbott walked through the back door to the courtroom. The bailiff stood up and said, "All rise!"

The judge took the bench and surveyed the courtroom. He was a slight man no taller than 5' 2" and appeared to be in his mid-fifties. His greying hair and rugged face gave him a look of distinction. I'd read an article about him in the *Texas Lawyer* which claimed he was known for his uncompromising adherence to proper procedure and protocol but also for his compassion for those counsel on the short end of one of his rulings. He would never berate or belittle an attorney in front of his client, the article claimed, even if they deserved it. Consequently, he was well respected and always got the highest ratings in the bar association poll each year, according to the article.

For some reason though, Judge Abbott didn't like Rob Wilkerson. I had witnessed that myself. Perhaps it was because Rob Wilkerson was the antithesis of Judge Abbott. Wilkerson got off on berating and humiliating others whether it is defendants, judges, or witnesses and that's one thing Judge Abbott wouldn't tolerate. So, that was one point Stan would have in his favor and hopefully would give him an advantage.

The judge had the jury brought in and the voir dire began. Wilkerson gave his synopsis of the case and then began to question the jurors. At 12:30 p.m. the judge called a recess for lunch. He told everyone to be back at 2:00 p.m. Stan, Jodie, and I walked across Kennedy Square to the West End. We decided on a barbeque café and ordered sandwiches.

"You won't believe this, but I saw the Vanishing Man."

"Where?" Stan asked.

"In the elevator at the courthouse?"

"Really? That's pretty brash of him to show up at Cheryl's trial since he works for Martin Windsor and was one of the men who kidnapped her children. He must not realize we're onto him."

"Apparently not, or he thinks he's untouchable."

"Maybe he is," Stan suggested. "I think I know how he vanishes."

"How's that?" I asked.

"He uses one of those alien memory erasing machines. When he wants to get away, he just turns it on and it erases a minute or two of memory of the people around him. It seems like he just disappears because he's moved on during those lost moments."

"Whoa! That's freaky," Jodie said. "You mean he freezes time?"

"That's what it seems like, but actually time moves on. Everyone near that machine just doesn't have any recollection of those erased moments. So when they start remembering again there's a blank space which accounts for things suddenly disappearing or moving from one place to another."

"That makes sense," I said. "I think we can attribute the memory losses we keep coming across to this machine."

"So how are we going to collar this guy so we can slap a subpoena on him?" Jodie asked.

"We're going to have to take him by surprise, and a subpoena won't to be good enough," Stan said."We have to get him arrested—get some cuffs on him so he can't use his memory machine to get away."

Jodie wrapped her arms in front of her. I could see she was quivering. "You okay?" I asked.

"This is just too weird for me," Jodie replied.

"I know," Stan said, "but we're going to need you to distract our man long enough for the FBI to arrest him."

"The FBI?" I asked.

"Yeah, we'll call the agent in charge of the kidnapping case and tell him that you have spotted one of the kidnappers. They'll send over a couple men to arrest him but they won't realize how difficult that's going to be because they don't know about the memory device. We can't warn them about it either since they'd never believe us and it would compromise our defense. So, we'll need to engage him in conversation and distract him so the FBI agents can take him by surprise and prevent him from using the memory device."

"I'm confused," Jodie said. "How will the memory device

keep the FBI from arresting him?"

"Well, because if they approach him to make an arrest and identify themselves, he'll simply use the device, and they'll suddenly forget what they were doing and become so disoriented that he'll likely get away."

I shook my head. "Okay, I think I understand. I'll call Agent Barnes and tell him to get over here right away. Jodie, we'll scour the courthouse for our man, and if we find him, you'll have to charm him for a few minutes until Agent Barnes can sneak up on him."

"What if we can't find him?"

"I'm sure he's here to report to Martin Windsor what's going on. If that's the case, he'll have to show up in the courtroom. He probably figures if anything goes wrong he can simply use his machine to make a quick escape."

As predicted, when I called Agent Barnes and told him I'd seen one of the kidnappers, he said they'd be right over. We met them in the corridor running from the underground parking lot into the courthouse. I explained that he was armed and that they'd have to catch him off guard. We agreed they'd follow us as we searched for him and, if we got lucky, Jodie would distract him so they could get the jump on him.

Jodie and I went straight to the elevators. We got in and hit the sixth floor button. When we got out on the sixth floor we lingered briefly until the next elevator came up with Agent Barnes and his partner. Our man was nowhere in sight so we started walking down the noisy hallway filled with jurors, defendants, witnesses, spectators, and reporters all waiting for their cases to resume. When we reached the end of the hallway and hadn't seen our man, I looked at Jodie and shrugged. Then my attention was drawn to the swinging doors that led to the stairwell. Through a small glass window I saw our man smoking a cigarette. I nodded to Jodie and she looked through the window. She looked back at me. "Wish me luck."

I motioned to Agent Barnes. He and his partner came quickly and stationed themselves on either side of the doorway. Jodie reached into her purse and pulled out a pack of cigarettes. She pulled one out, stuck it between her lips, and then went through the swinging doors.

Our man stiffened when he saw her. She went over to him and asked, "Got a light?"

He looked at her suspiciously at first, but then a broad smile came over his face. Jodie's charm and good looks were hard to resist. He produced a lighter and lit her cigarette. Agent Barnes's partner took off down the corridor toward the stairwell at the opposite side of the building. I surmised that he was going down a floor, back to this stairwell, and then sneak up on the suspect from his rear. Agent Barnes gave him long enough to get into position and then walked in with a cigarette between his lips. While the suspect studied Agent Barnes, his partner snuck up from behind with his gun drawn.

"Freeze! Put your hands up," he said.

The startled suspect reached for his pocket, but before he got close to it, Jodie jammed her cigarette into his neck and pushed him into the railing. He screamed and grabbed his burning neck. This gave Agent Barnes time to wrestle him down to the ground where his partner cuffed him. I rushed in to be sure Jodie was okay. She said she felt sick and ran to the ladies' room. I followed her in.

The room was deserted and Jodie was hanging over the sink. I went over to her. "Are you okay?"

She turned and there was a big smile on her face. She said, "Was that cool or what?"

I laughed. "Well, I guess. You really like this shit, huh?"

"Yeah," she said with a gleam in her eye.

"Why are you so happy? You could have gotten hurt."

She lifted her hand and showed me a strange looking gun-like object. It was aluminum colored with black hand grips and shaped like a baton sprinters would use in a relay race.

"Oh, my God! The memory gun?"

"Yeah, I figured we better not let the FBI find this."

"Good thinking. Let's go show it to Stan."

Jodie put the gun in her purse and we went back to the stairwell where sheriffs' deputies were sealing off the area where the arrest had taken place. The witness had been taken away but Agent Barnes was still there talking to the bailiff as we approached. He looked up and said, "You okay, Jodie?"

She nodded, "Yeah, I'm fine."

"Nice job. You're one cool lady."

"Thanks."

"Listen," I said to agent Barnes. "We're in the middle of trial so we've got to get back. We're going to need to call Mr., what's his name— "

"Weldon Thomas Everett, according to his driver's license," Barnes said.

"Yes, we're going to need to call Mr. Everett as a witness. Will you keep him close by?"

"Well, that's the least we can do since you so expertly helped us collar him."

"Good. I'll call you when we need him."

"No problem. We'll take good care of him for you."

When we got back to the courtroom the trial had resumed. Wilkerson was still questioning witnesses, so I joined Stan and Cheryl at the defense table. I was dying to tell Stan what had happened but I couldn't talk while court was in session, so I wrote him a note on a yellow pad and passed it over to him. He read it and then looked up at me with shocked eyes. I shrugged and smiled. The judge saw us trading looks and frowned. I straightened up and tried to concentrate on Wilkerson's questions but could only think of the object Jodie had safely in her purse—a device of unimaginable usefulness to thieves, scoundrels and crooked politicians. One that no man on earth had ever owned but one that many would kill to possess.

At 3:30 p.m. Wilkerson asked his last question and Stan began his interrogation of the jury panel. At 5:30 the judge recessed the trial until 9:30 a.m. Tuesday morning. Then we'd make our strikes, the jury would be seated, and Wilkerson would begin the morning session with his opening statement. In the afternoon the prosecution would start calling witnesses. That gave us one night to deal with the memory gun and figure out how we were going to get our unexpected witness to talk. We all agreed to go home, have dinner, and then meet back at the office at 7:30. Jodie said she was afraid to keep the memory device herself, so Stan took it. He said he'd find a safe place for it.

On my way home a sudden fear came over me. If Mr. Everett was associated with Martin Windsor and had a memory device, he probably was an alien. If he were to get word to his friends that Stan had one of their memory guns, they might come looking for it. The thought also occurred to me that a device as sophisticated as that one might have a built-in tracking device. Either way, Stan's life could be in danger. I picked up my car phone and dialed Stan's number. There was no answer. "Damn you, Stan! Why don't you ever turn on your cell phone?"

Chapter 47

Memory Gun

From the moment Jodie showed me the memory device I couldn't wait to take it somewhere private to inspect it. Although I should have been listening attentively to Wilkerson's questioning of the jury, I barely heard a word he said. My mind was whirling over the ramifications of what had just happened. Had we just orchestrated the arrest of one of the aliens? Could it be true, or was this Everett guy just a hired gun for Martin Windsor? Either way somebody was going to be mightily pissed off when they found out we had their fancy weapon.

On the flip side, we had just stolen evidence in a federal kidnapping case. Granted, we had good reason to do it; nevertheless, we could all go to jail for a very long time for that impropriety. My stomach should have been in knots from this realization, but nothing could dampen my exhilaration over our find. This was one of those transcendent events in a person's life that dictated extraordinary action and the assumption of abnormal risks.

After I left the courthouse, I drove aimlessly for a few minutes. Where could I stash the memory gun where nobody could find it? I couldn't take it home. That would endanger my family. The office was too obvious and the security there wasn't that good. Then I remembered I had a safety deposit box at North American National Bank that only Rebekah and I knew about. That seemed like my best option at the moment, so I changed my course and headed in that direction watching my rear view mirror to make sure I wasn't being followed. On the way I stopped at Eckerd Drugs and bought a disposable camera. I figured I might need some pictures of the device to show Everett if I got him on the stand.

I got to the bank ten minutes before it closed, so I didn't have much time. I wanted to inspect the device before I put it in the safety deposit box, so I told the customer service representative I needed to inspect the contents of my box. She looked at her watch. I assured her it would just take a minute, so she took me into the vault where I got my box and then followed her back to a cubicle.

The device was about ten inches long, four inches wide, and an inch and a half thick. It was silver and looked like a stretched-out ping pong paddle. The top surface was rippled and the bottom was smooth. The light that the device apparently projected came out from the sides through a transparent blue plastic-like substance. Beneath the handle was a trigger mechanism that I was tempted to pull, but restrained myself out of fear of the consequences of such action. There was some kind of writing on the bottom of the device but it was in a language I had never seen.

There was a knock on the door. "Sir, the bank is closing," a female voice said.

I quickly put the device in the box, opened the door, and followed the lady back into the vault to put the box away. The front door to the bank was locked when I tried to leave, so I had to track down an employee to let me out. As I walked to my car, I felt uneasy. I scanned the parking lot to see if someone was watching me, but I didn't see anyone. As I pulled out of the parking lot to go home, I checked my rear view mirror to make sure I wasn't being followed. No cars pulled out of the parking lot after me, so I breathed a sigh of relief.

When I got home, Rebekah was standing over the stove stirring something. She looked up. "Hi, Honey. Paula called. She said it's important." I nodded and went over to the phone and dialed her number.

"Oh, it's you. Thank God," Paula said. "I was worried someone would come looking for the memory gun."

"I'm fine. Nobody followed me. It's safe and sound in my safety deposit box. They'd have to rob the bank to get it now," I chuckled.

"Good. We need that gun. It's the only proof we have that the aliens exist."

I told Paula to relax and then hung up. Rebekah was staring at me when looked up. "What was that all about?" she asked.

I took a deep breath and then began telling her about the day's events leaving out any word about aliens or the memory device.

It was much too dangerous for her or anyone else to know the truth at this point. Before I went to bed, I called Paul Thayer and told him Paula and I would need security at our homes for the duration of the trial. He said he'd take care of it.

That night I couldn't sleep. My mind felt like an over saturated sponge. I had taken three aspirins, but they hadn't helped. All I could think about was Weldon Everett and how I was going to get him to talk. By morning he was sure to have a lawyer and he'd instruct him not to say a word. I worried about that for a moment, but then decided it didn't matter. If he took the Fifth Amendment the jury would assume Martin Windsor was alive and that was the most I could hope for.

The last time I looked at the clock radio it was 12:30 a.m. What seemed like just moments later, the telephone rang. I glanced at the clock. It read 3:31 a.m. I fumbled for the phone.

"Mr. Turner?"

"Uh huh."

"This is Agent Lot, FBI. There's a situation I need to talk to you about."

I sat up and rolled my feet onto the floor. "A situation? What's wrong?"

"Sorry to bother you, but there's been a bank robbery."

"A bank robbery? Really?" I said, shaking my head, trying to get the cobwebs out. "Okay, so why are you calling me about it?"

"Well, it's a pretty bizarre case."

I took a deep breath and rubbed my temples. My mind was still foggy. "What do you mean?"

"Well, the robbers broke into the bank and managed to get the vault open. I don't know how exactly, since there was no evidence of a forced entry. There were more than three million dollars inside."

"Hmm. That's quite a heist. . . . So, what's my connection?"

"The funny thing is they didn't take the money."

"Huh? I don't understand. Wha—"

"The only thing they took was the contents of your safety deposit box."

"What? My safety—" I stood up abruptly knocking the phone onto the floor. "Oh, my God!"

"We'd like to know what you had in there."

I knelt down, picked up the phone, and set it back on the night stand. My mind began to clear. I scrambled for a response to Agent Lot's dangerous question. I couldn't tell him the truth, but if my answer wasn't convincing he'd suspect something. I took a deep breath and replied, "Damn it! The prototype. Shit!"

"What prototype?"

"Oh, of an invention that one of my clients gave me for safekeeping. Oh, God. He's going to be so pissed when he finds out. A lot of people have been trying to steal it from him. That's why he gave it to me."

"What kind of invention?"

My mind whirled again trying to think of something plausible. Any hesitation would give me away. "Ah. I don't know exactly. I'm not the scientific type, I'm afraid. I really didn't understand much of it. It has something to do with . . . with . . . air cleaning. It's kind of a device that shoots out a light that cleans and purifies the air instantaneously. It's pretty amazing."

"It must be very valuable to risk breaking into a bank to steal it. Do you think someone can reverse engineer it?"

"I don't know. There were important papers and a gun in there too—a .38. I carry it occasionally for protection."

"They took everything. I'm sorry."

There was silence. Relief swept over me as I believed Agent Barnes had accepted my story, at least for now. He told me he was sorry about the loss and that the FBI would do everything in their power to find the perps and get the invention and the rest of my property back. I bit my lip, knowing that would never happen. Before he hung up, I asked him about Everett.

"How's Everett?"

"He's resting comfortably in the county jail."

"Did he make a telephone call?"

"Yes, he demanded we let him call his lawyer."

"Damn, that was fast. Did he tell you anything before he made the call?"

"No, he wouldn't even acknowledge his name."

"Hmm. Let me know who his attorney is when you find out, would you?"

"Sure. . . . Listen, I know you're in trial, but I'll need to spend some more time with you on this robbery."

"No problem. Maybe on Saturday."

I hung up and fell back into bed.

Rebekah sat up. "What happened?"

"Our safety deposit box—everything's been stolen."

"At the bank?" she asked frowning. "How could that happen?"

"I don't know."

"There wasn't anything of value in there was there?"

"Just our wills, birth certificates, life insurance policies, and that old .38 revolver."

She looked at me. "What are we going to do?"

"It's all replaceable. Don't worry. Call our agent tomorrow and request a duplicate insurance policy. I'll drop by the county records building and get us new birth certificates. We'll have to reexecute our wills, but that's no big deal."

I knew Rebekah wasn't totally satisfied with my explanation. But she knew from experience she'd gotten all the information she was going to get. Finally she went back to sleep and my mind went back into high gear. Either I had been followed after all or, perhaps Paula was right, the memory gun could be tracked. I couldn't believe I'd lost the gun, but at least I had the photographs. God, I was glad I had bought that camera. After awhile I finally fell asleep, but it was a troubled slumber and I awoke at the crack of dawn.

At 6:30 I met Paula to work on our jury strikes. We met at Denny's on Coit Road near our office. I told her about the bank robbery.

"At least you didn't get hurt," she reasoned.

I showed her the pictures.

'These are good, but they're nothing like the real thing."

"I know. Damn it! I can't believe we lost it. I thought surely it would be safe at the bank."

"Well, there's nothing we can do now. We've just got to make sure we pick a good jury."

I nodded and we buckled down to our task of picking a jury.

Chapter 48

Lies

Over breakfast I explained to Stan my impressions about the jury panel. Stan indicated he was going to take my jury suggestions seriously this time, although I wasn't convinced of that after Palo Pinto. As I drove up to the courthouse, I noticed several more media trucks than had been there the day before. I guessed the arrest of one of the kidnappers had sparked a little interest in the case.

I quickly checked my makeup in the visor mirror and noticed black circles under my eyes. "Damn!" I moaned. I took a minute to dab on some makeup to cover the dark circles and then got out of my car and headed for the garage elevator. As I came out of the underground parking garage into the basement of the courthouse, a group of reporters rushed over.

"Ms. Waters," the first one said. "Will the arrest yesterday have any impact on your defense of Cheryl Windsor?"

"It might," I said. "But I can't really comment on it now."

Another reporter asked, "Was the bank robbery of North American National Bank last night related in some way to this case?"

I didn't want to step into that mud hole. "I don't know. What bank robbery?"

Luckily the elevator door opened allowing me to escape the reporters. I took a deep breath and tried to relax. What if I'd told them the truth? Talk about a media frenzy. The elevator opened and I stepped into the packed corridor outside the courtroom and nearly collided with Rob Wilkerson.

"What's the hurry, darling?" he asked. "As I recall, you're just a spectator today."

I glared at him. "Yeah, well . . . lucky for you."

He laughed. "Well, actually I am kinda disappointed. I was looking forward to burying your cute little ass."

I noticed Jodie approaching. "Good morning," Jodie said.

Wilkerson nodded at Jodie. "Excuse me ladies. I've got an

opening statement to give," he said and walked away.

"What was that all about?" Jodie asked.

"Oh, Wilkerson was just gloating over the fact that I wouldn't be trying the case."

"What an asshole."

"Tell me about it."

We made our way into the courtroom. It was already filled to capacity. Stan and Cheryl were seated at the counsel table talking, so we went over and joined them. Cheryl looked stunning in a red crepe suit with gold buttons and tan sandals. I wondered why Martin Windsor had abandoned her. In addition to being gorgeous, she seemed to be a devoted mother and a pleasant person to be around.

"I like your outfit, Cheryl," I said. "The men on the jury won't be able to keep their eyes off of you."

"Thanks," she said.

I took my seat next to Stan and started to unpack my briefcase. Stan was studying the jury list one last time and making notations by some of the names on the list.

"All rise," the bailiff yelled.

The judge took the bench and had the bailiff collect our jury lists with our strikes. A few minutes later the bailiff started calling off the juror's names who'd been selected and they took their seats. After the judge had given the jurors their instructions, he told Wilkerson to read the indictment and give his opening statement.

Wilkerson stood and faced the jury. "Your Honor, ladies and gentlemen of the jury, before you today is the defendant, Cheryl Windsor. Mrs. Windsor married Martin Windsor in 1982 and together they had three young children, Matt, Tony, and Kim. They lived together in a north Dallas home until in the spring of 1990 when they became estranged on account of an affair Mr. Windsor was having with another woman. Mrs. Windsor filed for divorce in early September claiming adultery and mental cruelty.

"Now we will show that Cheryl Windsor was not your typical betrayed housewife. When she found out about the affair she went to a shop specializing in electronic surveillance equipment and bought everything under the sun. She then surreptitiously placed the equipment throughout their home, hoping to catch Mr. Windsor in the act. You see, there was a lot at stake here. We will show that

Martin Windsor has business interests around the world worth millions of dollars. Mrs. Windsor wanted those assets for herself, so she set out to find the evidence she needed to prove her husband's adultery and to find out where his assets were located.

"We don't know what was going through her mind, but we can surmise that she wasn't finding the kind of evidence she needed to warrant the court awarding her the lion's share of the community estate, so she came up with another plan—an ingenious one that only an intelligent and cunning woman could pull off. Ladies and gentlemen, we will show that the defendant, Cheryl Windsor, is indeed a brilliant and ingenious woman who is confident she can get away with murder.

"On Monday afternoon, September 10, 1990 Martin Windsor didn't return to work after going to lunch. It had been his habit for more than ten years to keep in close contact with his staff, so his absence was immediately noted. When the police were called in, they discovered that the last person to see Martin Windsor was his wife. When questioned by police Mrs. Windsor, however, claimed to have no knowledge of Mr. Windsor's whereabouts. In fact, she claimed she hadn't seen him on Monday at all.

"Her story, however, doesn't hold water. We will show through the testimony of various witnesses that several persons saw Mrs. Windsor come and go from his home on Monday, but nobody saw Mr. Windsor leave. So, unless he's a magician and simply vanished into thin air, Cheryl Windsor must have killed him.

"How she did it we'll probably never know, but weeks later his charred body was found in his car not thirty minutes from his home. Although, the fire gutted the vehicle and incinerated the body so it couldn't be identified, there is no doubt it was Martin Windsor. The coroner will testify that the size, weight, and general build of the skeletal remains were consistent with that of Martin Windsor.

"But this is not the end of the story. Now that her husband was out of the way, Cheryl Windsor had to escape the sure hands of justice. She had to convince the world that she was a victim and not the perpetrator of this heinous crime. How did she do it? She staged the kidnapping of her own children and claimed that her husband was alive and had taken them from her.

"The final chapter of this ingenious plot was the systematic liquidation of the community assets into cash accounts which then quickly disappeared. Again she claimed her dead husband was responsible for this but the facts will show that the money all ended up in a bank account in the name of an international business corporation named Zorcor, Inc. which she controlled through a banker named Walter Johansen.

"Mr. Johansen will testify that Cheryl Windsor set up the offshore company through him and then had millions of dollars transferred into the corporation's bank account. This could only have been done with Mr. Windsor out of the way and possibly with the help of some of Mr. Windsor's partners and associates, all of whom have conveniently disappeared and will not be testifying in this trial.

"During the course of this trial you will hear much conflicting testimony, but I know you will carefully consider the evidence and the testimony and make a sound determination of the facts, which we will prove beyond any reasonable doubt. And those facts are that Cheryl Windsor intentionally caused the violent death of her husband, Martin Windsor, and then torched the car he was in to make it impossible to identify the body. She did it for money and to keep from losing her children who were the subject of a bitter custody battle.

"Ladies and gentlemen, you have an opportunity to thwart this ingenious plot and bring Cheryl Windsor to justice, and I'm confident you will do so."

The judge nodded. "Mr. Turner. Do you wish to make an opening statement?"

"No, Your Honor. We'll wait until we put on our case in chief."

"Very well, then. Mr. Wilkerson, you may call your first witness."

Wilkerson stood up. "The state calls Detective John Perkins."

Perkins walked to the witness stand, the judge administered the oath, and Wilkerson began questioning him. "Detective, were you told to visit the home of Martin Windsor in early September of last year?"

"Yes, there had been a missing person's report issued on Mr. Windsor by his secretary, Gloria Fellows. She stated that he didn't

322   William Manchee

report to work that morning and when she called his home there was no answer. We were ordered to go to Mr. Windsor's house and see if he was okay."

"So when you went to the house, what did you find?"

"Mr. Windsor was not there so we talked to two neighbors," Perkins replied as he looked at his notes," Ah . . . Monica Koontz and Herman Baxter. They both told us they had seen Mr. Windsor go out to get the mail at about 3:00 p.m. and less than an hour later saw Mrs. Windsor park in front of the house and go inside. Neither of them saw Mr. Windsor leave but Baxter saw Mrs. Windsor leave with two men later that evening at about 6:30."

"So, after talking to the neighbors what did you do?"

"We knocked on the door, looked around the exterior of the home, and peeked in the windows. Then Mr. Baxter let us in the house with a key that Mrs. Windsor had given him to use in case of an emergency."

"What did you find in the house?"

"Nothing. Mr. Windsor was not there."

"Did you have an occasion to talk to Mrs. Windsor about the disappearance of her husband?"

"Yes, we brought her in for questioning and she denied knowledge of his whereabouts. She claimed the last time she had seen him was at six o'clock on Sunday when he returned the children."

"Did you confront her with the fact that two neighbors had seen her at the house on Monday?"

"Yes, but she stuck to her story."

"Did you have an occasion to search the defendant's apartment?"

"Yes."

Wilkerson turned and looked at Cheryl, a smug look on his face. "Did you find anything of interest?"

"Yes, we found a gun—a 9-millimeter Smith & Wesson pistol."

"Had it been fired recently?"

"Yes."

"To whom did the gun belong?"

"It was registered to the defendant."

Wilkerson picked up the gun which was in a plastic bag on the prosecution table. "Is this the gun?"

Perkins took the bag and inspected it. Then he nodded. "It is."

Wilkerson brought the gun over to Stan and gleefully handed it to him. Stan snatched it away, gave it a cursory examination, and then handed it back to him. Addressing the judge, Wilkerson said, "Your Honor. We'd like People's Exhibit 13 admitted into evidence."

Stan replied, "No objection."

Wilkerson smiled broadly at Cheryl and then turned his attention back to Perkins."Anything else of interest found in the apartment?"

"We also found some surveillance equipment—bugs, small video cameras, and things like that."

"Do you have any idea what the defendant was using the surveillance equipment for?"

"Yes, when we searched Mr. Windsor's home we found some identical equipment. It was all purchased by Mrs. Windsor at a store in Plano called The Spy Shop. I can only assume she put it there to keep tabs on her husband and gather evidence against him."

Wilkerson nodded. "Thank you. Pass the witness."

The judge nodded. "Your witness, Mr. Turner."

Stan stood up and asked, "Detective, what was the condition of the interior of the house when you went inside?"

"There was no evidence of foul play, if that's what you're asking. "

"Did you send in a crime scene unit to inspect the premises?"
"Yes, we did."

"What was the result of that inspection?"

"They didn't find any evidence of third parties in the house."

"Was there any evidence of anyone having been in the house—Mr. Windsor, Cheryl, the children?"

"No."

"No fingerprints at all?"

"Not a single one."

"Isn't that rather strange?"

"Yes, it appeared the place had been thoroughly cleaned. There were no prints or fibers or other evidence of who might have been there."

"What do you make of that?"

"I don't know. All I know is that someone went to a lot of trouble to clean up that house."

"Thank you, Detective. Pass the witness."

Wilkerson took Detective Perkins on redirect as did Stan. Next Wilkerson called the two neighbors, Koontz and Baxter, to the stand to corroborate Perkin's testimony. On cross Stan asked Baxter about the two men he saw leave with Cheryl on Monday, September 10, 1990.

"They were wearing blue uniforms," said Baxter. The truck they were driving was from an air-conditioning company—Parr Heating and Air."

"Did the uniforms have a yellow triangle on the front?"

"Yes."

"Did you get a good look at the two men?"

"Yes, " Baxter said. "They were quite distinctive characters. I think I'd remember them."

Stan turned around and looked out into the gallery. He leaned over the table and whispered to me, "Go get me today's newspaper."

I frowned and started to protest but Stan gave me a look so I jumped up and headed for the law library on the second floor, borrowed a newspaper from the librarian and returned. The witness was describing one of the men when I walked in. I rushed up and handed the newspaper to Stan. He turned and looked at the judge. "May I approach the witness?"

The judge nodded. "You may."

Stan walked up to Baxter and showed him the picture of Weldon Everett on the front page of the *Dallas Morning News*. He asked, "Is this one of the men you saw at Martin Windsor's house?"

He looked carefully at the picture. "Yes, it is. That's the tall guy."

There was a murmur in the crowd, but the judge didn't seem to notice. He was looking down from the bench at the photograph. Stan asked that the newspaper photograph be admitted into evidence. Wilkerson objected, claiming it was hearsay, but the judge overruled the objection when Stan advised him Mr. Everett would be called as a witness and could be cross examined by the prosecution. Stan passed the witness, but Wilkerson had no questions, so Baxter was excused. Koontz testified next and backed up Baxter's testimony. After a short recess, the medical examiner, Winston Drysdale, was called to the stand. He was a tall, thin man in his late forties. He testified about being called to the scene where Mr. Windsor's car was found, examining the body, and performing an autopsy. Wilkerson asked him if he was sure this was the body of Martin Windsor.

"Well, like I said, the body was so charred that we couldn't get any DNA off it and apparently Mr. Windsor had no dental history, but judging from his skeletal size, projected weight, general build, and the fact that the body was found in Mr. Windsor's car, I would say it would be safe to assume that it was the body of Martin Windsor."

"What was the cause of death?"

"Two gunshot wounds to the heart and lungs. It was not possible to pinpoint the cause of death exactly since the body had been incinerated, but we were able to interpolate the points of entry of the bullets from damage we found to the victim's ribs. Based on the trajectory of the bullets either of the shots could have caused the victim's death."

"Did you find either of the bullets?"

"Yes, one 38-caliber bullet was found in the ashes of the body in the car."

"Were you able to determine the source of that bullet?"

"Yes, it came from the gun registered to the defendant."

The crowd erupted into chatter. The judge banged his gavel and admonished the crowd for their unruliness. Wilkerson got the bullet admitted into evidence, continued to question the medical examiner for some time, and when he was done, he passed the witness.

"Any questions, Mr. Turner?"

Stan stood up. "Yes, Your Honor. Mr. Drysdale, I believe you testified it would be safe to assume that this was the body of Martin Windsor."

"Yes, that's correct."

"But you don't know for certain whose body was in Mr. Windsor's car, do you?"

"No, like I said, the body was incinerated."

"So, is it possible that someone else put a body of similar size and stature in the car along with the shell from Cheryl's .38 Smith & Wesson and then torched the car?"

"Yes, without a positive ID, anything is possible, but not likely."

"Not likely? Have you done some kind of study of probabilities in this case?"

Drysdale smiled. "No. I'm just saying it's not easy to obtain dead bodies, particularly when you have to have a particular height, weight, and stature."

"But if someone were trying to frame Cheryl Windsor for the murder of her husband, that's quite likely how it would have been done, don't you think? Assuming they could get a body."

"I suppose."

"Do you know how the car got to the location where it was found?"

"No, I do not."

"Do you have any evidence that Cheryl Windsor drove it there?"

"No, not specifically."

"Thank you. Pass the witness."

The judge looked at the clock. "It's time for lunch. We'll recess until 1:30 p.m." He left the bench and the courtroom suddenly came alive with conversation as spectators began filing out into the hallway. As we were reorganizing our papers, Agent Lot came up to us.

"Hi, I'm Agent Lot. We talked last night by telephone."

"Oh, right. Any new developments on the bank robbery?" I asked.

"No, not really. Like I told you, everyone is pretty baffled by the manner in which it was done."

I shook my head. "It is pretty scary to think someone can walk right into a bank vault and steal from a safety deposit bank."

"Have you told your client his prototype was stolen?"

"Ah. . . . No, I'm trying to get in contact with him, but no luck yet."

He nodded. "Listen. I'm going to need to talk to you some

more about what happened as soon as possible."

Stan shrugged. "Okay, you can buy us lunch."

Agent Lot smiled and replied, "That's fair enough. What do you feel like?"

"Well, since the government's buying, let's go to the Palm," I said. "I feel like lobster."

Twenty minutes later Agent Lot, Jodie, Stan and I were in a booth at the Palm Restaurant in the West End. Jodie and I ordered Lobster Bisque off the starter menu and the guys ordered Shrimp Bruno. While we were waiting, Agent Lot began to question us.

"The Bureau is very concerned about the bank robbery last night."

"Why's that?" I asked.

"Well, it was the ease with which the bank's security was breached and the vault compromised. The robbery seems to have happened right in front of their noses but nobody can remember anything. Whoever did this managed to erase all the surveillance tapes as well. We've never seen anything like this before."

"Huh. I wonder how they did it?" Stan said.

"The thing is, they didn't leave a shred of evidence. In fact, they left the vault as clean as a hound's tooth."

"You know," I said. "I doubt a hound's tooth is all that clean."

Jodie and I giggled. I couldn't believe how cool Stan was. If I was being interrogated by an FBI agent and was hiding something, I'd be a nervous wreck.

Agent Lot frowned. "Well, you know what I mean. The place was wiped down and vacuumed. It was so clean we couldn't find a single print or even a speck of dust inside the vault."

I looked at Stan. He looked at me. Jodie said, "They probably wore gloves and ski masks."

"Yeah, I suppose, but now did they hack the combination and override the alarm?"

"Well, I wish I could help you," Stan said, "but I never was very good at safe cracking."

"The thing is, Stan. You're the only lead we have. We want to know why they hit your box."

"I told you why."

"Right, your client's invention. I remember, but that's not good enough. A federal banking institution was robbed and we have to figure out how and why. You realize, don't you, if you're hiding something you could be charged with obstruction of justice."

Stan glared at Agent Lot. "Listen. I'm a little tied up right now with this murder trial. Should I ask the judge for a recess so I can go track down my client for you? Is that what you want?"

"No, calm down. I'm not threatening you. I just need something more than what you've given me so far. I'm getting a lot of heat from upstairs."

Stan thought for a moment. "I'll tell you what. I'll have Paul Thayer try to track down my client. Maybe he'll be able to find him and then I can put you two together so you can figure out why somebody wanted his invention so badly."

Agent Lot smiled. "Great. I appreciate that, Stan. I'm sorry I came down on you so hard."

"Forget it. You're just doing your job like I'm doing my job. No hard feelings."

Stan had bought us a little time, but I was worried about him getting in deeper and deeper with the lie about his client's invention. Eventually he'd have to produce the client and some evidence the invention existed or he'd be in serious trouble. Stan didn't seem worried, so I assumed he had a plan for extricating himself from the lie at a later date. At least I hoped so.

Chapter 49

Witness Tampering

On Friday afternoon Wilkerson finally got to the end of his long list of witnesses. The final witness was perhaps the most important—Walter Johansen, the VP Banker from Tortola. Since we knew his entire testimony was going to be fabricated, we'd spent most of our preparation time working on ways to impeach it. Unfortunately, the more we prepared, the more we realized how difficult it was going to be to discredit him. The problem was the British Virgin Islands' secrecy laws which made it impossible for us to research bank or corporate records. So, we had no way of contradicting Walter Johansen's testimony.

Johansen looked like a banker in his charcoal gray suit as he walked to the witness stand. Paula had told me he was smart and a smooth talker, so he wouldn't be easy to impeach. At 1:31 p.m. Wilkerson began his direct examination. He asked Johansen about his background, education, and employment. Then he asked him if he knew Cheryl Windsor.

"Yes, she contacted me in late August of this year."

"How did she make contact?"

"By telephone at first. She called and said she'd heard about international business corporations and wanted to set one up. I explained how they worked and she said she wanted to move forward immediately as she was expecting to receive a large sum of money."

"Did you agree to do it?"

"Sure. That's our business."

"Did she set up a bank account as well?"

"Yes. Zorcor, Inc. did. That's what she called her IBC. Then she wired money into it."

Cheryl shook her head and whispered to me, "He's a lying sack of shit! I can't believe this guy. I've never seen him before in my life."

I nodded. "Yeah, this is what we expected."

"When was the first wire?" Wilkerson asked Johansen.

"Shortly after the account was set up—early September, I believe."

"And how much was transferred into the account?"

"About $3.7 million."

There was a gasp from the gallery and some of the spectators began talking. The judge frowned and banged his gavel demanding order.

Wilkerson continued. "Is the money still in the account?"

"I don't know."

"Why is that?"

"After Ms. Waters was arrested, my superiors took the account away from me, but even if I did know, the law prohibits me from disclosing such information."

"Thank you. Pass the witness."

The judge said, "Your witness, Mr. Turner."

"Thank you, Your Honor. Mr. Johansen, can you set up an IBC by telephone?"

"Uh huh. We just FedEx'd an agreement to the customer and they sign it and send it back. I sign all the corporate papers on their behalf."

"Does a customer have to come to the bank to set up the account?"

"No, I can send them the signature cards and account agreements, and they can sign them and return them to me."

"Is that what happened here?"

"No. She came to the bank. I personally met with her and we completed all the paperwork while she was here."

Johansen was a good actor. He spit out his lies like they were the gospel. The jury looked mesmerized.

"But it is possible for someone to do this entirely by telephone and through the mail?"

"Yes, but that didn't happen in this case," Johansen stressed

"How do you know it was Cheryl Windsor who set up the account? You didn't know her, did you?"

"No. She faxed me a copy of her driver's license and passport."

"Well, is it possible the documents she gave you were forged, particularly if they were faxed copies? That's pretty common in this day and age, isn't it?"

"I wouldn't know. They looked genuine."

"Couldn't Martin Windsor have enlisted the help of any woman to pretend to be Mrs. Windsor?"

Wilkerson jumped up. "Objection, Your Honor—calls for speculation!"

"Sustained," the judge ruled.

"Did you take any steps to verify Mrs. Windsor's identity?" I asked.

"Well, a few days later I called information in Dallas and got her telephone number. When I called the number, she answered."

Cheryl leaned over and whispered, "That's impossible. My number is unlisted."

"Why would you have to call and get the number from information? Wouldn't she have given you her number when she set up the IBC and the account?"

"She did, but when I called the number it wasn't in service. I figured she had transposed two numbers so I called information."

"What if I told you Mrs. Windsor's telephone is unlisted?"

"Well, I wouldn't believe you, because I did call information and they gave me the number and she answered the call."

"Now, Mr. Johansen. You realize you're under oath, don't you?"

"Yes."

"Have you ever lied in court before?"

Johansen stiffened. "Excuse me?" he said indignantly.

"Objection!" Wilkerson exclaimed. "That's argumentative, lacks foundation, and inflammatory."

"It's a legitimate question, Your Honor," I said.

"I'll allow it," the judge said.

"Did you not hear the question?" Wilkerson asked, "Should I ask the court reporter to repeat it?"

Johansen glared at me. "No, I heard it. . . . No. I've never lied in court before."

"What about when you were on trial for money laundering, bribery, and conspiracy in Alabama?"

Johansen swallowed hard. "I didn't lie then, and I'm not lying now."

"But you were convicted, were you not?"

"Yes, but I didn't lie. I was innocent."

"Did you testify at your trial?"

"Yes, I did."

"So, you testified you were innocent, yet you were convicted."

"A lot of innocent men are convicted."

"Right. But you will admit the jury thought you were a liar."

Johansen didn't respond, but just glared at me."So," I continued, "if you lied then, how do we know you're not lying now?"

"Objection!" Wilkerson spat. "Argumentative!"

"I'll allow it, but move on, Mr. Turner. You made your point."

"Have you ever met Martin Windsor?"

"No. I don't know him."

He was lying again. I could see it in his eyes, but I had no way of challenging him. I listed the names of all of Martin Windsor's various enterprises but Johansen denied ever hearing of any of them. Then I went through the names of several of Windsor's friends and associates to see if Johansen recognized any of them. He said he did not. Finally, I asked him one final question.

"Do you have any knowledge as to the whereabouts of Martin Windsor or his children?"

Johansen shook his head. "No idea whatsoever. I wouldn't know them if I saw them."

"Thank you," I said. "Pass the witness."

Wilkerson and I went one more round with Johansen but neither of us extracted any new information of value. After Johansen was excused, Wilkerson rested. The judge looked at his watch and said, "Mr. Turner, you can begin your case in chief on Monday morning at 9:30. We're in recess until then."

As we were packing up, I said to Cheryl, "Well, I doubt Johansen will have much credibility with the jury now."

She turned and I saw a worried look in her eyes. "I hope not," she said softly.

On Saturday morning Jodie, Paula, and I met to discuss our

witness list. The most difficult of our witnesses was going to be Weldon Everett, the disappearing man, who we felt was the key to our case. He obviously wouldn't testify candidly, if he testified at all. He could assert his Fifth Amendment right against self-incrimination. If he did take the stand, we either had to trip him up or somehow induce him to tell the truth.

Paula asked, "How do we get him to tell the truth?"

"We can't. We don't have anything to offer in exchange. If he testifies truthfully, he'll go to prison, not to mention piss off some very powerful people who might make sure he ends up dead."

"Too bad we can't inject him with some truth serum," Jodie said.

I thought for a moment. "Truth serum, huh?" I said. "That's not a bad idea."

"Sodium Pentothal doesn't necessarily make you tell the truth," Paula said. "We studied it at the DA's office when I was working there. It's just a mild sedative that makes you relax and feel talkative."

"I bet the CIA has some more advanced drugs that may be more effective. If we could get a dose of a drug like that and inject him with it, he might actually end up telling the truth."

"The judge wouldn't let us do it. It's unconstitutional," Paula cautioned.

"Obviously, we'd have to do it surreptitiously," I said. "I think it can be administered in liquid form. If not, Rebekah could teach us how to inject it since she's a RN."

"How are you going to administer it without Everett knowing about it?" Paula asked.

"I don't know. That's a problem we can tackle once we have the drug and decide to use it. I'll call Mo and see if he can get us something suitable."

"If we give him the drug and he finds out, he'll sue us or file a grievance," Paula complained. "We may end up disbarred."

"I doubt it. The last thing he's going to want is more publicity. He's more likely to kill us."

"Wonderful!" Paula replied. "I feel so much better."

"You don't want to end up in jail for the next twenty years for withholding evidence, do you?" I asked.

Paula sighed. "No. Not really."

"Then we're going to have to do something extraordinary—take some risks. We don't have any other choice."

We all agreed I'd call Mo to see if we could even obtain the drug before we decided what to do. When I got home, I put a call into Mo and he called me back an hour later. I told him what I needed. He said he'd look into it and see if he could help out. I thanked him and hung up the phone.

On Monday morning he called and told me to go to the men's room in the basement of the Records Building and I'd find what I needed. I thanked him and then stopped by the Records Building on my way to the courthouse. I took the stairs to the basement. Nobody was inside so I went in and looked around.

Now where would he hide the drug? In all the gangster movies I'd seen, the gun was always taped inside the toilet tank. Unfortunately these toilets didn't have tanks. I searched behind the toilets, under the sinks, and along the window sills but found nothing. Then I noticed the towel dispenser.

Its lock looked really flimsy. On my key ring I had a small luggage key, so I stuck it in the hole and twisted it around. Sure enough the cover fell open and inside was a small brown bag. I stuck my hand in the bag and pulled out a cinnamon brown bottle with no label. I stuck it in my pocket and closed the dispenser door.

A wave of fear suddenly washed over me. Aside from the obvious personal peril we faced, what if we were successful and Everett admitted he was an alien or was working for aliens who had infiltrated our society? What would be the repercussions of that?

When I got to the courtroom I took Paula and Jodie aside and told them I had the drug.

"What's it called?" Paula asked.

"I don't know. It's just a bottle with no label."

Paula gave me a horrified look. "Do you think we should be giving someone a drug we know nothing about?"

"I trust Mo," I said. "I'm sure it's the most advanced truth serum the CIA has."

"The problem now is how to administer it to our man."

"Someone could hand him a soft drink during the break," Jodie suggested.

"But the bailiff will see that," Paula said.

"He'd have to be distracted somehow and while he was busy someone could hand Everett a soft drink. If he's thirsty, he'd take it and start drinking. I don't think he'd suspect anything."

"Okay, I'll create a distraction," Paula said. "Jodie, you give him the drink."

Paula gave me a hard look. A chill darted through me as we put our plan into play. We were about to embark on an illegal and unethical course of action—witness tampering—the worst crime a lawyer could commit. Even though our goal was to discover the truth, it was still illegal and Paula and I would surely be disbarred and go to jail if we were found out. My heart pounded as I contemplated our fate if our scheme backfired. I just prayed it wouldn't.

Chapter 50

The Escape

Stan looked a little frazzled when the judge asked him to make his opening statement. It was understandable for many reasons. Aside from the trauma of the whole matter of the truth serum, we stood at a turning point, a fork in the road where an important decision would have to be made. Which way would it be? Whichever way we went there would be no turning back. Would it be simply that Martin Windsor had faked his death and framed his wife in order to deprive her of her property and her children, or was this something larger, darker, and more sinister—an alien plot to infiltrate our world for some unimaginable purpose?

Stan stood and faced the jury. He swallowed hard. "Your Honor, ladies and gentlemen of the jury, it is with great trepidation that I address you this morning. The defense we are about to present to you will seem strange if not bizarre, but I ask you not to pass judgement until the final witnesses are called and their testimony recorded. For it is our contention that Cheryl Windsor has been the victim of a complicated plot to take her money and steal her children and it is your duty to give our allegations fair consideration.

"It has not been easy to uncover and make sense of this conspiracy, nor will it be easy to explain to you such an intricate plot, but I believe we will be able to do so, and in the end you'll recognize it to be the truth. So I ask you to pay close attention and think hard and long about everything you hear and see. Don't jump to conclusions or let your prejudices cloud your judgment. There is much more here than meets the eye.

"Now, as the judge has instructed you, the state has the burden of proof. They must prove, beyond all reasonable doubt, that Cheryl Windsor intentionally or knowingly caused the death of Martin Windsor. To do that they must prove beyond all reasonable doubt that Martin Windsor is dead. This is where their case fails.

They have a body they claim is that of Martin Windsor, yet they acknowledge that it can't be positively identified. We will show through the testimony of many witnesses and the introduction of certain tangible evidence that Martin Windsor is probably alive. Unlike the prosecution, we do not have to prove he *is* alive, but only that there is a reasonable chance that he is.

"I know the next few days will be a trying experience. But we are confident you will persevere and in the end render a fair and just verdict. Thank you."

"Thank you, Mr. Turner. You may call your first witness."

Stan glanced down at his notes. "The defense calls Agent Doug Barnes."

Agent Barnes walked deliberately to the witness stand and was sworn in. Stan asked him about his occupation, background, and education. Then he said, "Do you know the defendant, Cheryl Windsor?"

"Yes, I do,"Barnes replied.

"How did you meet her?"

"Well, we were called when her children were kidnapped, and we've spent a lot of time together since then."

"How did she take the kidnapping?"

"She was, and is still, very distraught over it."

"Do you believe her emotions are genuine?"

"Yes."

"Did you at any time consider Mrs. Windsor a suspect in this abduction?"

"Yes, parents are always considered, particularly when there is a pending divorce."

"So, in the course of investigating Mrs. Windsor as a possible suspect, did you find any evidence supporting that theory?"

"No. We did not."

"So, you've eliminated her as a suspect?"

"Not entirely, but she's not at the top of our list."

"You said parents are always prime suspects. So, did you ever consider Martin Windsor as a suspect?"

"Yes, if he were alive, he'd certainly be a prime suspect."

"Why is that?"

"Because fathers, particularly busy fathers like Mr. Windsor, often have an uphill battle when it comes to getting custody of their children. The divorce courts tend to favor the mother, as you know. So, a father who is seeking custody of a child, and knows he isn't likely to get it, might resort to kidnapping."

"Now in the course of your investigation, did you look into the Windsor's finances?"

"Yes, we did?"

"Was there anything unusual about them?"

"Well, someone liquidated all of their holdings about the time of the kidnapping. We assumed it must have been Mrs. Windsor, but we were unable to confirm that."

"So, if Mrs. Windsor didn't liquidate the assets, who did?"

He shrugged. "We don't know for sure that she didn't cause them to be liquidated. Ultimately the money ended up in an account that she apparently controlled, but she denied liquidating the community assets and denied having anything to do with Zorcor, Inc. and its accounts. Now, of course, the money is gone and we don't know where it went."

"How do you know it's gone?"

"We acquired the account number and passwords from Ms. Windsor's attorney and checked on it. The account had only a few hundred dollars in it."

"Isn't it true that Mr. Windsor managed the community investments prior to the date he went missing?"

"Yes."

"So, do you think Mrs. Windsor would have had the knowledge, skill, and access necessary to liquidate the several millions of dollars in assets and then channel them into a bank account at VP Bank in Tortola, British Virgin Islands?"

Agent Barnes shook his head. "No, not really. She wasn't an officer in any of Mr. Windsor's companies nor was she active in the management of any of the various enterprises."

"In the course of your investigation of the kidnapping of the Windsor children, have you run across anything else that might be relevant to the prosecution's case against the defendant?"

"Well, there is one thing."

"What's that?"

"Mr. Windsor owned an interest in the Cocos Bay Resort in

Trinidad, and about the same time that he disappeared the manager of the Cocos Bay Resort also was reported missing."

"Really?"

"Objection, Your Honor," Wilkerson interjected. "The kidnapping of Mr. Quinlin from the Cocos Bay Resort is not relevant to this proceeding."

"It is relevant, Your Honor, since Mr. Windsor was a major stockholder in the resort."

"I'll allow it," the Judge ruled. "You may answer, Agent Barnes."

"Okay. What is even more coincidental is that Mr. Quinlin's children were kidnapped as well."

"Were these separate abductions?"

"Yes, the father and the children were kidnapped at different times."

"Any other similarities between these cases?"

"Yes, the crime scenes were both remarkably well cleaned."

"What do you mean?"

"Well, normally a kidnapper would not hang around a crime scene long enough to thoroughly clean it, but in each instance the crime scene was so meticulously cleaned that there was absolutely no evidence left behind."

"So, in your opinion, were these cases connected?"

"I think they were. Leaving a crime scene without dust, dirt, fingerprints, fibers, or residue of any sort is odd—so odd it links the cases."

"Thank you, Agent Barnes. Pass the witness."

The judge said, "Mr. Wilkerson, your witness."

"Thank you, Your Honor," Wilkerson replied. "Agent Barnes, did you search for Martin Windsor?"

"Yes, we did."

"Did you find him?"

"No."

"Did you interview anyone who saw him after the date of his disappearance?"

"No."

"Did you quit looking for Mr. Windsor when his body was found?"

"Yes, we did."

"Do you believe he's dead?"

"I don't know. I was instructed by my superiors to quit looking for him."

"But you don't know that he is alive?"

"No, I don't."

"Now, you said you didn't think Mrs. Windsor had the savvy to liquidate her husband's assets and funnel them into an offshore bank account."

"Right, I don't think she would."

"Did you know that she set up an elaborate array of electronic surveillance equipment throughout Mr. Windsor's home so she could monitor his every move?"

"Yes, I heard about that."

"That took a lot of savvy didn't it?"

Agent Barnes nodded. "True."

"So, is it possible that you've misjudged her financial savvy?"

"It's possible. It was just an impression I had from being around her for a while."

"Could it be that she's an attractive woman and it is only natural to be attracted to her?"

"No, I don't think that's it. And I didn't say she was attractive."

"Well, she is though, right?" Wilkerson snorted. "I bet you liked spending time with her. In fact, isn't it true you've developed a romantic interest in her?"

"Objection, Your Honor," Stan exclaimed. "Argumentative."

"Sustained. Settle down, Mr. Wilkerson."

Wilkerson shrugged. "Sorry, Your Honor."

"Now, Agent Barnes, you're telling this jury that each of the four kidnappings that you mentioned was linked just because there was no physical evidence left behind by the kidnappers?"

"Yes, the crime scenes were abnormally clean. Every surface must have been vacuumed or scrubbed down and, of course, there was the memory loss too."

"The memory loss?"

"Yes, in all four kidnappings all of the persons who were in a position to have witnessed the abductions suffered from a short-term memory loss."

"Is that really so unusual? People don't like to get involved when a crime takes place, so they conveniently lose their memory. . . . Thank you, Agent Barnes. No further questions."

After Stan and Wilkerson were done questioning Agent Barnes, the judge called a short recess. Stan said he was pleased with Agent Barnes's testimony and I agreed. A lot of questions had been raised that had to give the jury pause. On my way to the ladies room, I was intercepted by TV reporter Amy Tan.

"Paula, what was all that about scrubbing down the crime scene and memory losses? I didn't get it."

I shrugged. "Amy, we believe Martin Windsor is alive and he commands some kind of team or organization that can abduct people at will, sterilize the crime scene, and somehow cause witnesses to have a short-term memory loss. That's why they are able to come and go without anyone realizing they were there."

"And you think you can prove this?"

"We don't have to prove it. All we have to do is prove reasonable doubt."

"I know, but this is some really bizarre stuff. Do you think the jury will buy it?"

I laughed. "You haven't heard the half of it, girl. Just wait. The best is yet to come."

I left a puzzled Amy Tan and continued on to the ladies' room. I was sure she'd be on the phone soon and my quote would be all over the news. But it really didn't matter because, as they say, the train had left the station and there was no turning back.

On my way back to the courtroom I saw Agent Barnes and a bailiff escorting Mr. Everett to the jury room where he would be kept until we called him as a witness. I started to think about how I was going lure Barnes and the bailiff out of the witness room so Jodie could deliver the truth serum. I went over to them.

"Agent Barnes. I see you have our witness."

He nodded. "Yes, I promised you'd I'd bring him by to testify. So, here he is."

"Great. I think Stan has just one more witness and then Mr. Everett will be up. I'll tell Stan you're here."

"Okay, but I'm not sure he's going to have much to say."

I smiled. "Oh, don't worry about that. Stan has a way of relaxing a witness and getting him to open up."

Barnes shook his head and replied, "Okay, whatever you say."

When I got back into the courtroom, Barbara Falk was being sworn in. She took her seat and Stan began by asking, "What is your relationship with Martin Windsor?"

"He's my ex-husband."

There was a buzz in the courtroom. The judge looked disapprovingly at the gallery. They quickly quieted down. Stan continued.

"Now everyone knows you recently lost your son, Jimmy Falk."

"Yes."

"Jimmy was Martin's son, right?"

"Yes."

"And coincidentally, he died the same day that Martin Windsor disappeared."

"That's correct."

"How would you characterize the relationship between Jimmy and his father?"

"They were very close. Martin loved Jimmy very much."

"Why did Martin and you get divorced?"

"Infidelity. He started seeing Cheryl and they fell in love, I guess."

"Cheryl? The defendant?"

"Yes, Cheryl Windsor."

"Do you and Cheryl get along?"

"Yes. I'm over the bitterness. Cheryl and I are friends now."

"So have you and Cheryl compared notes about life with Martin?"

"Sure. Martin is an unusual man so we've had lots to talk about."

"Can you explain some of those peculiarities?" Stan asked.

"Sure. Let me see. I guess one thing that was odd was Martin's distrust of doctors. He made us go to a special clinic for all our medical care. All our children were born there too."

"You didn't go to a hospital?"

"No."

"Huh? What was the name of the clinic?"

"Ah, The Ujhazi Institute."

"Did you and Cheryl discover anything similar about your deliveries at these clinics?"

"Objection, Your Honor," Wilkerson said. "Where's the relevance of all this?"

Stan replied, "If you'll indulge me, Your Honor. The relevance will soon be apparent."

"Very well, objection overruled. The witness may answer the question."

Barbara laughed. "Well, the one thing in common is neither of us have any memory of them."

Chatter erupted in the gallery. The judge frowned and the bailiff stood up.

"Excuse me? Would you repeat that?"

"Neither of us can remember anything that went on while we were at the clinic. I couldn't even tell you what it looked like inside."

"That *is* strange. Do you have any explanation for that?"

"No, but our visits to the clinic weren't the only times we couldn't remember things. It was actually a fairly frequent occurrence. For a long time I thought it was just me, then I started talking to Cheryl and realized it was something that Martin had done to us."

"But you don't know how he did it?"

"Not exactly, but at night sometimes I'd dream of bright flashing lights and a loud piercing noise that was slowly driving me insane. I'm not sure if that has anything to do with any of this, but I feel like it does."

Stan continued questioning Barbara Falk in great depth about Martin Windsor while Wilkerson fidgeted impatiently in his chair. He obviously didn't like our defense much, but he was powerless to do anything about it. I couldn't wait to see his face when Mr. Everett got on the stand full of truth serum and started spilling his guts. That would be interesting.

By noon Stan and Wilkerson were done with Barbara Falk and the judge recessed for lunch. Stan advised the bailiff that

Weldon Everett would be our next witness when we returned. He said he was taking him down to the cafeteria for lunch, but he'd have him back in plenty of time.

After everyone had left the courtroom, Stan, Jodie, and I moved to the stairwell where we huddled to make last minute preparations to give Everett the truth serum. The jury room had two doors. One led to the hallway and the other one into the courtroom. I had decided I would simply knock on the jury room door and ask to speak to Agent Barnes. Jodie had been flirting with the bailiff all week so he wouldn't suspect anything when she dropped by offering a few extra cans of root beer. Her plan was to hand the can laced with truth serum to Everett, give one to the bailiff, and leave one for Agent Barnes.

"That's fine," Stan said. "The simpler the better."

Stan handed Jodie the bottle of truth serum and a syringe. "I think if you just pull the tab a little you can inject the serum without any trouble."

Jodie nodded and took the bottle. Her hands were shaking. I said, "You don't have to do this if you don't want to."

She turned and forced a smile. "No. I'm okay. This is just a little scary, but I can handle it. Don't worry."

Stan smiled and said, "Okay, let's make this canary sing."

Stan left and Jodie and I went into the ladies' room to inject the truth serum in the can of root beer. Jodie went into a stall while I kept watch outside. When she was done, I took the bottle of truth serum to my car and Jodie took a seat in the hall where she could be on the lookout for the bailiff and Mr. Everett. When I returned from the parking garage Jodie told me the bailiff and Mr. Everett had returned and they were in the jury room with Agent Barnes. It was curtain time.

The clock on the courtroom wall read 1:15 p.m. and we were due back at 1:30. There was no time to delay. I took a deep breath, walked across the courtroom to the jury room door and knocked.

"Who is it?" the bailiff asked.

"Is Agent Barnes in there?"

Agent Barnes opened the door and stuck his head out. "Paula, what can I do for you?"

"Ah. . . . Can I talk to you a minute?"

"Sure," he said.

While I was thanking Agent Barnes for his testimony on behalf of Cheryl, Jodie was knocking on the jury room door from the hallway.

"You know. It's not true. I never had any romantic interest in Cheryl Windsor," Agent Barnes said.

"Oh, I know. Wilkerson is just a prick. He'll say anything to discredit a witness whether it's true or not."

We continued to talk. When I was sure Jodie was finished delivering her root beer, I let Agent Barnes go back into the jury room. Then I went quickly to the stairwell where Jodie had agreed to meet me. She was standing just inside the door smoking a cigarette.

"How did it go?"

"Piece of cake. Now I just hope the truth serum works."

"You don't think the bailiff suspected anything?"

"No, he and Mr. Everett scoffed down the root beer like they hadn't drunk anything in a week."

Our conversation was interrupted by excited conversation in the hallway. We pushed open the doors and saw a crowd of people around the door to the jury room. I could hear Agent Barnes yelling at the bailiff. "Call 911. He's having a seizure. We need an ambulance fast."

We squeezed through the crowd so we could see what was happening. Everett was on the ground convulsing badly. Agent Barnes was struggling to keep something in his mouth so he wouldn't swallow his tongue. I rushed over.

"Is there anything I can do?"

"Just help me hold him down. He's a strong son of a bitch."

"What's wrong with him?"

"I don't know. He's having a seizure or something."

A jolt of fear shot through me like a bullet. Was he allergic to the truth serum or was there something else in that bottle? Had Mo given us a deadly poison by mistake? If Weldon Everett died and they did an autopsy, they'd discover he'd been drugged and eventually our plan would be discovered. My stomach was in knots.

The elevator door opened and two paramedics rushed out rolling a gurney. Agent Barnes and I got out of their way as they took his vitals and gave him oxygen. They called in his symptoms on the radio, put him on the gurney, and took him away. Agent Barnes followed them. I noticed Rob Wilkerson and his assistant watching from a distance. Wilkerson had a gleeful look on his face.

Jodie whispered, "You think I gave him too large a dose?"

I shrugged, "I don't know. He may have been allergic to whatever drug it was that Mo gave us. I'm sure he'll be okay."

I went back to the courtroom to get ready for the afternoon session feeling very depressed and scared. Our plan to get Mr. Everett to tell the truth had not only been a complete and utter failure, but if Weldon Everett died from the truth serum, Stan, Jodie, and I could all be charged with murder! As we were reeling from this latest development, Stan rushed in, a frustrated look on his face.

"You heard what happened, I guess?" I said.

"Weldon Everett, just escaped!"

"What? He escaped?"

"Yeah, apparently he faked an illness and somewhere between the basement and the parking garage he disappeared."

"Someone used the memory gun again. That so unfair!" I moaned. "Is Agent Barnes okay?"

"Yeah, he's the one who told me what happened. He's very upset that he lost his prisoner, but physically he's fine."

"Jesus! I can't believe this," I said. "Jodie and I thought we had poisoned him. I'm relieved we didn't, but now we don't have a witness."

Stan sighed. "Well, we don't know if the truth serum would have worked anyway. Who knows? We'll just have to do without Everett."

The disappointment in Stan's eyes was clear. He had been counting on Weldon Everett opening up under the influence of the truth serum and breaking the case wide open. Now he would be forced to continue chipping away at the prosecution's case, hoping that when the day was done he had cast enough doubt into at least one juror's mind to hang the jury.

Chapter 51

The Photograph

When the afternoon session started, I asked Judge Abbott for a 48-hour continuance so that I could find a replacement witness for Weldon Everett. Although the judge said he was sympathetic due to Everett's untimely escape, nevertheless he couldn't grant it in deference to the jury. It wasn't fair, he said, to keep them from their work and families any longer than absolutely necessary.

Since the memory gun had apparently just been used to free Weldon Everett, I thought it would be a good time to call some witnesses who had experienced a memory loss. First on my list was Steven Caldwell. He testified about his accident at Possum Kingdom Lake, the death of Jimmy Falk, and how he had no memory of what had happened to him until he underwent hypnosis weeks later.

"So, when you woke up on the side of the road," I asked, "you had no idea how you had gotten there or how you had escaped from your Jeep when it went over the cliff?"

"That's right. The last thing I remember was coming around the corner, hearing a loud noise, and seeing something overhead."

Wilkerson jumped up. "Objection, Your Honor. This is totally irrelevant to this case and highly prejudicial."

"Mr. Turner, what's the relevance of this testimony?" the Judge asked.

"Your Honor, our prime witness just escaped, yet no one can remember how it happened. We've heard testimony from Barbara Falk and Agent Barnes about frequent memory losses by a number of people associated with Martin Windsor. I believe that I can show that Steven Caldwell experienced this same phenomenon."

The judge gave me a hard look and then asked, "Unless you are prepared to enlighten us as to what exactly is causing these memory losses and who is behind it, I don't think it matters whether Mr. Caldwell suffered the same type of memory loss or not. If you can't do that, I'll have to sustain the objection."

348 William Manchee

Wilkerson smiled and sat down. I briefly considered enlightening the judge as requested, but I didn't have the memory gun anymore and I couldn't even bring it up without admitting to having wrongfully taken it in the first place. I had a picture of it, but the picture wouldn't necessarily prove anything. To convince the judge and jury that the memory gun existed, they'd want a demonstration. And even if I had the gun and dared to use it, I didn't know where it came from, who controlled it, or why it was being used the way was. I gave the judge an exasperated look."Pass the witness."

Wilkerson jumped up gleefully. "No questions."

Since the judge made it clear he wasn't going to allow me to stray from the narrow path, I returned to my original game plan and called George Gabbert, my forensic expert. He testified that he had inspected the body which the prosecution alleged to be that of Martin Windsor, reviewed the autopsy report, and the crime scene. "Based on my investigation," he said, "I do not believe the body is that of Martin Windsor." Unfortunately, on cross examination Wilkerson got him to admit that the body might be that of Martin Windsor, so I wasn't sure we had accomplished anything by the time George left the witness stand.

Fortunately, it was nearly five o'clock when George Gabbert left the stand, so the judge called a recess until the following morning. I was relieved because the only witness left, if we wanted to call her, was Cheryl Windsor. It was always dangerous to let the defendant testify, but we had come to the conclusion that we really had nothing to lose. Since Cheryl didn't remember what had happened the night Martin disappeared, she really couldn't incriminate herself. If she did testify, she could deny liquidating the community assets, setting up Zorcor, Inc. and the offshore bank account.

When I got home that night Rebekah said she had heard about our witness escaping on the afternoon news and wanted to know what happened. I told her I didn't know much more than what she had probably heard. She wanted to know how Everett's escape was going to affect our case. I told her I didn't know, since we weren't sure if Weldon Everett would have talked or not.

"I thought you weren't supposed to call a witness unless you knew what they were going to say," Rebekah said.

She was right. That was one of the first things they taught you in law school. "True, but he showed up unexpectedly and we were a little desperate."

Rebekah raised her eyebrows. Later, while I was eating dinner, the evening news came on and Amy Tan was covering the lead story.

"A memory-erasing device may have been used today to aid in the escape of a suspect in the Windsor kidnapping case. In a bizarre turn of events Weldon Everett, being held on federal kidnapping charges, escaped shortly after 12:30 p.m. today from the Dallas County Courthouse. Witnesses claim that Everett disappeared while being rushed to the hospital from apparent food poisoning. FBI Agent Doug Barnes and sheriff's deputies had just returned him to the courtroom where he was scheduled to testify as a witness in the Cheryl Windsor murder trial. When Everett became ill and started to convulse, he was rushed from the building to a waiting ambulance. The FBI refused to comment on how Everett escaped, but this reporter talked to defense consultant, Paula Waters, and was told that a memory-erasing device may have been used."

Paula hadn't told me she'd talked to the press about the memory-erasing device, but I was glad she had. It was just a matter of time before they found out anyway. I wondered what Wilkerson would make of Tan's report. I wished I was a fly on the wall at his home so I could see his reaction.

"We don't have specific details as to how this device works, or who might have used it, but there has been a lot of testimony in this trial about witnesses suffering memory losses of several minutes to several hours. The defense seems to be intimating that Martin Windsor is alive and is utilizing this device to manipulate the trial and torpedo Cheryl Windsor's defense.

"Tomorrow, the defense is expected to call defendant Cheryl Windsor to the stand but since she claims to have no memory of what happened on the evening Martin Windsor disappeared (perhaps due to the memory-erasing-device)it's unclear whether her testimony will be enough to shift the momentum of the trial that has clearly been in favor of the prosecution thus far. This is Amy Tan reporting from the Dallas County Courthouse."

After the depressing news report, I went into my study to

work on the questions I was going to ask Cheryl Windsor when I put her on the stand. As I was working, Paul Thayer called.

"Stan, I just heard from Lonnie Morrow, my photographer out at Possum Kingdom Lake. There's been a lot of activity at the barn that he's been watching."

Hope swept over me. I sat up. "Like what?"

"People coming to the barn, lots of vehicle traffic. It started about noon. Lonnie has taken dozens of photos. He says most people who went into the barn have stayed inside. Only a handful has come out. He wants to know what he should do."

"Tell him to get the photographs developed and bring them to us at the courthouse tomorrow. Maybe we'll get lucky and find somebody's mug that we recognize. If so, we'll need him to testify that he took the pictures. Get someone else out there to keep an eye on the barn and take more pictures, okay?"

"Consider it done," Paul said and hung up.

I was elated by the news of activity at the barn. If the aliens were using Cactus Island as a landing strip they'd have to get to it through the caves. That meant the entry to the caves was inside the big barn. That would also explain why people went into the barn but never came out. Somehow we had to get inside that barn. Unfortunately we couldn't go there until the weekend—and that might be too late.

The following morning, before I'd left the house, Paula called me to ask if I'd meet her and Cheryl before the trial was set to resume to discuss an idea she had. I tried to get her to tell me what it was over the telephone, but she said she was afraid someone might be listening. I told her I'd meet them in the courthouse cafeteria at 8:15 a.m.

The cafeteria was deserted except for two lawyers in the corner eating breakfast. Cheryl and Paula were already sitting at a booth when I got there. I got a cup of coffee and went over to them. Paula seemed upbeat but Cheryl had a grim look on her face.

"So, what's up?" I asked.

"I've been thinking about Cheryl's reluctance to be hypnotized," Paula said, "so, I've been wondering if there's any other way to make her remember."

I shrugged. "Any ideas?"

"Well, what about the truth serum?" Paula replied.

"The truth serum?"

"Don't you think it might help her remember?"

"I don't know. It might. " I said looking at Cheryl. "That's a very interesting idea, though. Would you consent to that, Cheryl?"

Cheryl thought a moment. "Martin didn't say anything about truth serum."

I laughed to myself at Cheryl's logic, but kept a straight face so as not to discourage her. I began thinking about using the serum. It would be dangerous to let her testify under the influence of the truth serum. What if she *had* killed Martin Windsor? But if she was innocent this might be the only way to prove it or at least create reasonable doubt. We discussed the matter for some time and finally agreed it was worth the risk. Fortunately, I still had the truth serum in my briefcase, so I gave it to Paula and she took Cheryl to the ladies' room to give her a dose. At 9:15 the judge took the bench and asked me to call my next witness.

"The defense calls Cheryl Windsor."

Cheryl stood up and walked casually to the stand. I looked at Paula's worried face and saw her do the sign of the cross. Cheryl looked out over the gallery and smiled. I got up and began by asking her general questions about how she and Martin had met, their children, and their life together. Then I asked her what went wrong with the marriage. She explained how she had discovered her husband's affair and had gone to The Spy Shop to buy surveillance equipment. She responded fully to all my questions without hesitation. I could tell the truth serum was working. Finally we got to the weekend prior to Martin's disappearance.

"Mrs. Windsor. What happened when you took your children to be with their father on Friday, September 7, 1990?"

"Martin wasn't home yet, so I had the house to myself just long enough to install the bugs and cameras I'd bought at The Spy Shop. I was expecting a difficult custody battle, so I needed dirt on my husband to use as leverage. When Martin finally got home, I left immediately. I didn't particularly want to talk to him since I was about to have him served with divorce papers including a TRO that would freeze all his assets."

"So did you see him anymore that weekend?"

"Not until Sunday night when I picked up the children."

"Did you talk to him when you picked up the kids?"

"No, he seemed anxious for us to leave so I just took the kids and left."

"Anxious?"

"Yes, he seemed nervous. When I asked him what he and kids had done over the weekend he seemed distant and preoccupied."

"Did you see Martin on Monday?"

This was the moment of truth. Previously Cheryl had claimed not to have seen Martin on Monday, the day he disappeared. I wondered if the truth serum would work. It didn't work exactly like hypnosis so there were no guarantees. Cheryl looked through me like she was watching a television screen that was behind me.

"Do you remember anything on Monday?"

She blinked and shook her head slightly. "There was a telephone call. It was Martin. He'd just been served with the TRO. I was expecting him to be livid, to threaten me, and promise I'd never see the children again, but he never raised his voice. He said he wanted to talk."

I glanced at Paula. She shot back a worried look. Wilkerson glared at me. I'm sure he thought we'd been stonewalling him. I shrugged. All eyes focused on Cheryl as she began to recount the events of that fateful day when Martin Windsor disappeared.

"Talk about what?"

She squinted. "He said there was no reason for us to get the courts involved. He wanted to sit down and work out a settlement that was fair to both of us."

"Did you believe him?"

She shrugged. "I wanted to, but I wasn't sure, so I brought my gun."

"For protection?"

She nodded. "Just in case he lost his temper and got violent."

"So did you meet him?"

"Yes. I told him I'd stop by that afternoon. I had an appointment with my hairdresser and some errands to run. When I was done, I went to the house."

"Did you go inside?"

"Of course. He asked me to come by to talk, but I almost immediately regretted coming."

"How's that?"

"He had found my surveillance equipment and thrown it in a box. He pulled out one of the video cameras I'd installed and asked me if it was mine. There was no use denying it, so I freely admitted it and told him I'd gotten all the evidence I needed to rake him over the coals in court. He began yelling and screaming—"

A flash of blue light flooded the courtroom. Dizziness overcame me and I collapsed. I heard footsteps running and then nothing. . . .

When I woke up, I was on the floor. My nose was killing me. I must have fainted and fallen flat on my face. My right wrist ached. Paula was slumped over in her chair. I heard moaning in the gallery. The judge and the bailiff were out cold. I struggled to my feet and rushed over to Paula.

"Paula! Are you all right?"

"Huh? What happened?" She asked as she sat up and began rubbing her eyes.

"I don't know. I think we've been unconscious."

The judge awoke and looked around his courtroom in shock. "What the hell happened? . . . Bailiff!"

The bailiff, who was pulling himself up off the floor, stumbled over.

"Yes, Your Honor."

"What the hell happened?" he repeated.

"I'm not sure. There must have been some kind of electrical short or something."

"Call maintenance," the judge ordered. "Is everyone okay?"

I looked out over the gallery. People were coughing and moaning. Everyone seemed to be in a daze. Wilkerson was shaking the cobwebs out of his head. The judge looked over at me then back to the witness stand. He frowned, came to his feet, and screamed, "Where's the defendant? . . . Bailiff! . . . Where the hell is the defendant?"

I quickly scanned the courtroom. Where was Cheryl? It was clear someone had used the memory gun to stop her from testifying and now they had kidnapped her as well. Where had they taken her? The door to the courtroom opened and a man rushed over to me. He handed me a package. I took it, glanced inside, and then asked the man to wait outside the courtroom. He nodded and left.

"What's that?" Paula asked.

"My pictures from Possum Kingdom."

I started looking through them one by one. "Oh, my God!"

"What?" Paula asked.

The Bailiff said, "The defendant is gone, Your Honor. She seems to have disappeared."

The judge glared at me. "Where is your client, Mr. Turner?" he yelled.

"I don't know, Your Honor. I think she may have been kidnapped."

"Kidnapped! Did you see someone take her?"

"No, Your Honor. I was passed out just like everyone else."

"Well, I'm going to give you fifteen minutes to find her or I'm forfeiting her bond and issuing a warrant for her arrest," the judge snarled.

"Yes, Your Honor."

I took Paula's arm and we rushed out of the courtroom and into the stairwell where we could talk. "Either Martin Windsor or the aliens must have taken Cheryl," I said.

"What are we going to do?"

"We've got to find her. We should have never let her take the truth serum. I'll die if something happens to her."

"Where do you think they've taken her?"

"I've got an idea, but first we have to wrap up this murder trial."

"How the hell you gonna do that?" Paula asked.

We went back into the courtroom. Precisely fifteen minutes after he'd left, the judge returned. He looked over at me and asked, "Well, Mr. Turner. Did you find your client?"

"No, Your Honor. Like I said, I think she's been kidnapped." The judge took a deep breath and shook his head. "But I don't think there is any need to revoke her bond or issue an arrest warrant," I quickly added.

The judge frowned. "And why is that?"

"Your Honor, if you'll let me put on two quick witnesses, I'm confident I can prove that Cheryl Windsor is innocent."

The judge frowned, studied me for a moment, and then asked, "These witnesses are here now?"

"Yes."

"Objection," Wilkerson protested. "I don't think we should proceed until we find out what just happened."

The judge looked at Wilkerson and then back at me without responding. Finally, he said, "It may be some time before we know what happened here today. The FBI and the sheriff are already looking into the whereabouts of our missing defendant. In the meantime, we've got a jury waiting, witnesses apparently ready to testify, and I'm anxious to see if Mr. Turner can make good on his promise. So, let's just get on with the case. Objection overruled. Call your next witness, Mr. Turner."

"The defense calls Lonnie Morrow."

The bailiff went out in the hall and brought in Lonnie Morrow. He took the stand and the judge swore him in. I took out the photographs that he had taken and asked the judge if I could approach the witness.

"Please state your name for the court."

"Lonnie Morrow."

"What do you do for a living?"

"I'm a photographer."

"For whom are you employed?"

"I work freelance. Right now I'm doing a job for Paul Thayer Investigations. I believe you asked Mr. Thayer to find a photographer."

"Yes, I did. And what were you hired to do?"

"To watch a barn out at Possum Kingdom Lake and to take pictures of anyone coming and going."

"And did you do that?"

"Yes."

"And are these the photographs that you have taken?"

"Yes, sir."

"When were these photographs taken?"

"In the last ten days since the trial began."

"Thank you, Mr. Morrow. . . . Your Honor, I request that

these photographs which are identified as defense exhibits 23 to 48 be admitted into evidence."

The judge looked at Wilkerson and asked, "Any objection?"

I took the photographs over to Wilkerson and let him examine them. When he was done, he shrugged and said, "Objection, Your Honor. I don't see the relevance of these photographs."

"Oh, but Your Honor," I replied. "These photographs are quite relevant. If you'll just let me call my next witness, the relevance will become quite apparent."

"I'll withhold my ruling on the introduction of these photographs until after your witness testifies. Mr. Wilkerson, do you want to cross examine this witness about these photographs?"

"Not at this time, Your Honor, but I reserve the right to do so later, if need be."

"Very well. The witness may stand down."

Morrow left the witness stand and went back out into the hall. The judge said, "Call your next witness."

"The defense recalls Barbara Falk."

Barbara Falk stood up, a confused look on her face and walked slowly up to the witness stand. The judge said, "You've already been sworn in, Mrs. Falk. Do you understand you're still under oath?"

"Yes, Your Honor."

"Very well, Mr. Turner. Your witness."

I picked up the photographs and shuffled through them. When I found the one I wanted, I took it and approached the witness. "Mrs. Falk. You testified earlier that you were once married to Martin Windsor, is that right?"

"Yes. We were married for seven years."

"And when was the last time you saw Mr. Windsor?"

"About a week before he disappeared."

"Mrs. Falk. I want you to brace yourself and then take a look at this photograph that was taken less than 10 days ago."

Barbara gingerly took the photograph from me and studied it. Her eyes suddenly widened and she exclaimed, "Oh, my God! Oh, My God! It's Martin. He's alive! Martin is alive." She pointed to a man in the photograph. "It's Martin! He's alive!"

There were gasps and screams in the gallery. Reporters got

up and rushed out of the courtroom. The judge banged his gavel trying to quell the bedlam but to no avail. Finally he gave up and recessed the trial for fifteen minutes.

When the trial resumed Wilkerson took Barbara on cross and tried to get her to recant her identification, but she insisted the photograph was that of Martin Windsor. Wilkerson then called the photographer and quizzed him for more than thirty minutes about his taking of the photo, how it was developed, could it have been doctored. He went on and on until the judge finally sustained one of my objections for badgering the witness and told him to wrap it up.

Finally the judge recessed the case until the following morning. He said he needed time to digest what had happened and consider how to proceed. When he left the bench, Barbara Falk came over. We embraced. She said, "I'm glad Martin's alive. I still love him, you know."

"I know. I could tell by your reaction to the photograph."

We talked a minute and then I said to Paula, "I've got to go see Dr. Gerhardt."

Paula gave me a hard look. She shook her head. "Are you sure you want to know?"

"Yes, I have to know. I can't pretend this didn't happen. Are you going to come?"

Paula took a deep breath. "Oh, God. I don't know. Part of me would like to know, but I'm afraid."

"I don't plan to tell anyone what I find out. It would just be nice to have someone to talk to about it."

"You could still talk to me about it, even if I don't remember it."

"I know. But you'll never truly believe this happened unless you can remember it yourself. Let Dr. Gerhardt hypnotize you. Don't you think it's better to know the truth?"

Paula took a deep breath. "I'm sorry, Stan. I don't want to know what happened. I'm afraid everything will change if I know for sure aliens exist and are living amongst us. I'm happy with the world the way it is. You go. I know you must."

I rushed out of the courthouse and almost ran to my car. It was only thirty minutes to Dr. Gerhardt's office. I just hoped he wasn't busy and could see me immediately. When I got there, I found a parking spot and then rushed into the building. His secretary met me with a disapproving look.

"Mr. Turner. Do you have an appointment?"

"No, it's an emergency. Can the doctor see me?"

"He's with a patient, but he should be through in five or ten minutes."

"Good. I'll wait."

As I sat down in the reception room, I immediately started to worry about Paula. In my rush to leave, I hadn't given any thought to how scared she must be with yet another kidnapping. She had grown fond of Cheryl and must be sick with worry. I wished she had come with me so I could comfort her, but I understood that she had finally got what she wanted in life and didn't want to jeopardize it. I wondered why I wasn't like her. Why was I was always driven to go on, even when I didn't know where I was going nor what I might find when I got there? Despite the obvious danger in knowing the truth, I could barely contain the anticipation of being hypnotized. I had to find out what had occurred back at the courthouse. I had an idea what had happened, but I wanted to see it, or remember it, for myself. Although the aliens could easily kill me, I didn't feel threatened for some reason. They could have killed a lot of people but they hadn't. Their purpose on Earth wasn't conquest, but something else. I was almost sure of it.

The door that led back to Dr. Gerhardt's office opened and a man walked out. He gave me a quick glance and then went out the front door. Dr. Gerhardt stepped out behind him.

"So, it's you again. Don't you make your clients make appointments?"

"I'm sorry, but this is an emergency. If you can squeeze me in, I would really appreciate it."

"Well, I had a cancellation so you're in luck. Come on back. Did you have another encounter?"

"Yes." I explained briefly what happened, then I got up and followed Dr. Gerhardt to his office. He waited until I was inside and closed the door.

"So, you want me to hypnotize you again, huh?"

"Yes."

He nodded and took a deep breath. "Some truths are better

not known."

"That's what Paula said, but our client is missing and I can't just abandon her. The aliens must have taken her, so I have to learn as much as I can if I'm going to have a chance of saving her."

"Do you think you can stop them?"

I shrugged. "I don't know. Probably not. I don't know who they are or what they want. That's why I need your help."

"Tell the FBI what you know and let them find her."

"They'll never believe me. I'm Cheryl's only hope."

"Very well, take a seat."

I lay down on the sofa. Dr. Gerhardt got out his pen light and pulled up a chair in front of me. "Okay, you know how this goes. Relax, watch the light, and do what I tell you."

I let my muscles relax and sank deeper into the blue leather sofa. Dr. Gerhardt shone the light, I focused on it and began to drift off.

"Follow the light," Dr. Gerhardt said. "You're feeling sleepy now. Your mind is clearing. You're very relaxed. . . . Now I'm going to count to ten and when I finish you will be back in the courtroom at the moment Cheryl Windsor disappeared. You will see all that happened and remember everything. Then when I clap my hands, you will wake up. Here we go. . . . One . . . two . . . three . . . four . . . five . . . six . . . seven . . . eight . . . nine . . . and ten. . . ."

Clap! Clap!

My eyes opened. I blinked a few times and then looked around. Where was I?

"Stan, are you all right?" Dr. Gerhardt asked.

I struggled to a sitting position and tried to focus on the voice I was hearing. "Yeah, I think so. What happened?" I asked, rubbing my eyes.

"I hypnotized you."

"Hypnotized. . . . Oh, right."

"Do you remember?"

I closed my eyes and tried to bring back the memory but—"

"Courtroom," Dr. Gerhardt said. "Cheryl is on the stand. She's talking about what a mistake it was to meet with Martin."

"Oh, right. Now it's coming back. She says he yelled and

screamed at her and said she couldn't have his children for it was the time of the returning. She asked him what that meant and he said he was taking his children to another world—a place far better that this one. She said she'd see him in hell first and pulled out her revolver. His eyes widened in surprise. She heard footsteps outside and feared they'd break in at any moment, so she pulled the trigger. He didn't fall at once, but just looked at his chest where the bullet had struck. The door suddenly crashed open and men rushed toward her. She shot him again and this time he fell hard to the ground. There were flashes of light, one of the men grabbed her, and then everything went blank.

"She awoke on the floor in Martin's kitchen. It was quiet. Everyone was gone. She got up and looked around. There was no sign of Martin, no blood where he had fallen, nothing. She wondered if it had all been a dream. She took one last look around, grabbed the box of surveillance equipment and rushed to her car. She saw a neighbor looking at her as she fled but she was too scared and confused to care."

"What about the abduction. Do you remember what happened to Cheryl?"

"Right. The soldiers in blue rushed into the courtroom. The bailiff and deputy tried to stop them but they were easily disabled by some kind of device the men carry. The judge yelled, protesting the intrusion, but they seized the courtroom anyway. Two of them escorted Cheryl away. There were flashes of blue light. They were so bright, they nearly blinded me. I couldn't see a thing. I heard Cheryl screaming and the judge demanding they stop, but I couldn't see a damn thing."

"Very good, Stan. Now you know what happened."

My head was throbbing and my heart was racing like I'd been running. "Jesus, who were those men?"

"Soldiers from another world, it seems," Dr. Gerhardt said. "I warned you about this. Now you may never sleep soundly again, knowing that they are lurking out there. Frankly, I'm a little shaken myself."

"So it seems, " I said.

Dr. Gerhardt looked into my eyes for a moment and then said, "How do you feel?"

"I'm okay, but they have Cheryl. I've got to do something."

"What could you possibly do but get yourself killed? Forget about them. Let them go."

"No, I can't do that. I can't let Martin Windsor get away with this."

"But he must be one of them," Dr. Gerhardt exclaimed. "How else could he be alive and why would he be at Possum Kingdom Lake if he wasn't getting ready to board the spaceship?"

"I need to go there and stop them."

"That is foolish!" Dr. Gerhardt exclaimed. "They travel in space, for godsakes. Do you think your .38 is any match for them?"

"No, obviously not, but I can't sit idly by and do nothing. Call Paula and tell her I need a security team sent to the barn at Possum Kingdom Lake. She'll understand. I just want Cheryl back. That's all."

Before Dr. Gerhardt could try to further dissuade me, I ran out the front door and rushed to my car. Dr. Gerhardt followed me out and said, "Stan, don't do this!"

I turned, shrugged, and then got in my car and cranked the engine. I hesitated a moment, wondering if I was doing the right thing. I knew it was probably foolish to go after Cheryl, but I felt I had no choice. For some inexplicable reason I was being drawn to Possum Kingdom Lake and I was helpless to resist the force that drew me there. Yet even though I knew my life would be in danger, I felt no fear. I still felt the alien beings, who had for some reason settled in our world, were not an evil people, but had a good reason for their visit. How I knew that I didn't know, but I was sure they meant us no harm.

As I pushed the accelerator, I heard a screech from across the street. A van was approaching quickly. On the side of the van it read: Parr Heating & Air. That was Martin Windsor's company so I was sure now he was one of the aliens. Before I knew it, the van had cut me off, the side doors were flying open, and men dressed in blue uniforms with black helmets had me surrounded. They each had a memory gun along with other assorted weaponry that I didn't relish them using on me. I raised my hands. One of them opened my door and pulled me out of my car. Two of the men went into Dr. Gerhardt's office and emerged with him at their side a minute later.

They tied our hands, blindfolded us, and made us sit on the floor in the back of the van. They were firm but didn't use excessive force.

The fact that we were alive led me to believe they needed us for some reason. As I felt the van accelerate, I was pretty sure where we were going. The first stop would be Possum Kingdom Lake. From there, well, I just hoped it was some place on mother earth and not a distant planet.

Chapter 52

Pursuit

When Stan left to go to see Dr. Gerhardt, I was filled with trepidation. What were they going to do with Cheryl? What would they do to Stan if they knew he was on to them? Why were aliens living in Texas? What was their purpose?

On my way out of the courthouse I was intercepted by a mob of reporters asking me what had happened. I shrugged and said I didn't know. They weren't happy with my response, but that was the truth. I didn't understand any of this.

Bart was at the condo when I arrived. I ran into his arms and all the pent-up fear and anxiety exploded in tears. Bart hugged me tightly and said, "I was so worried about you when I heard what happened. How could anyone get through all the courthouse security and pluck a defendant right of the stand? That's so unbelievable."

I couldn't tell anyone about the memory gun, not even Bart. If I mentioned anything about it, there would inevitably be more questions and eventually I'd have to tell them everything I knew. "I don't know how they did it," I said. "I must have been unconscious or something. I don't remember a thing."

"They must have used a gas or something to knock everyone out. Do you remember a gas cannister exploding?"

"No, maybe they introduced it through the heating system."

"Maybe. How are you feeling? Should I take you to the doctor and have you checked out?"

"No, I'm all right—just a little shaken. I could use a drink."

Bart poured us a drink and we went into the living room and got comfortable. A little while later the telephone rang. It was Maria. She said Rebekah had been calling looking for Stan. She'd heard the news and was worried about him. I told her he went to see Dr. Gerhardt and she should try there. She said she would. Another wave of fear came over me. What if they had followed Stan to Dr. Gerhardt's office? I called the office to see if Maria had gotten through to Stan.

"There's no answer at Dr. Gerhardt's office. He must be on his way home."

Tears began to well in my eyes. I said, "Bart. We have to go to Dr. Gerhardt's office. Something is wrong. I can feel it."

"What is it, honey?" Bart asked.

"I don't know. Stan's missing and I've got a bad feeling."

As I was hanging up the telephone, I noticed there was a message on the recorder. I hit the play button.

"Ms. Waters. This is Dr. Gerhardt. Stan told me to call you and tell you to get a security team out to Possum Kingdom Lake right away. He said you'd understand. . . . Hey! Who are you? What are you doing in my office? Take your hands off of me."

"Oh, my God!" I screamed. "They've taken Stan."

"Why would they take—"

There was a knock at the door and Bart went over and looked in the peep hole."It's Agent Barnes," he said and opened the door to let him in.

Barnes stepped inside. "I need to talk to your wife. I didn't get to talk to her before she left the courthouse."

"Agent Barnes," Paula said. "I'm so glad you're here. I think Stan is in trouble. I was just listening to a message from Dr. Gerhardt when someone apparently broke into his office and took him away. Stan was with him."

"Do you know where Gerhardt's office is?"

"Yes," I said.

"Then let's go. I'll call for backup."

As we drove, I told Agent Barnes that Stan had gone to Dr. Gerhardt's office to be hypnotized in hopes he'd remember something about the persons who kidnapped Cheryl Windsor. Agent Barnes thought that was a very imaginative idea and was amazed Stan had acted on it so quickly. As we rounded the corner and pulled up to Dr. Gerhardt's office building my heart sank. Stan's car was sticking out into the street with the driver's side door wide open. We pulled up next to the car and we all jumped out. The engine was still running and Stan's briefcase was in the backseat.

"Oh, God! They have him," I said.

"Don't touch anything," Barnes said and ran inside. Dr. Gerhardt's secretary was lying on the floor in the reception area.

"Is she dead?" I asked.

Agent Barnes knelt down, felt her pulse, and then tried to revive her. I watched a moment and then slipped into Dr. Gerhardt's office to use the telephone. I picked it up with a tissue so I wouldn't disturb any fingerprints and called Paul Thayer.

"Paul," I whispered. "You've got to get some men out to Possum Kingdom Lake. They've kidnapped Stan and Dr. Gerhardt, and I'm sure they're taking them there."

"I've got two men out there already," he replied. "I'll alert them and get some more on the way."

"Hurry, Paul. You've got to stop them. You've got to save Stan."

I hung up the telephone and went back into the reception area where Agent Barnes was still working on Dr. Gerhardt's secretary. She suddenly woke up with a lurch. She blinked her eyes and frowned at Agent Barnes. "What are you doing?" she said, scrambling to her feet.

"Be careful," Agent Barnes said. "Are you all right?"

She brushed herself off. "Yes. But you didn't answer my question. What are you doing here?"

"I'm Agent Barnes of the FBI," he said and showed her his identification. "What happened?"

"I don't know," she replied.

"You don't remember anything?" I asked.

"Remember what? Where is Dr. Gerhardt? Does he know you're here?"

"No. I'm afraid he's been kidnapped."

"What? That's impossible. He was just here."

I put my hand on Agent Barnes's shoulder. "I think they are taking him to Possum Kingdom Lake."

"Who is *they*?" Agent Barnes asked.

"The kidnappers, of course."

He turned to look at me and frowned. "How do you know that?"

"Stan mentioned he thought that's where they were taking

Cheryl."

"Where on Possum Kingdom Lake?"

I told Agent Barnes the location of the barn where Paul Thayer's men had been posted the last few days. He called in the location to his office and told them to get someone out there immediately. By the time we got back outside, backup had arrived and they were cordoning off the crime scene. Then I thought about Rebekah. How was I going to tell her that Stan had been kidnapped?

After summoning my courage, I went inside and made the call. Peter answered and said his mother was at the grocery store. I didn't know whether to tell him that his father and Dr. Gerhardt had been kidnapped or not, but finally I decided I had no choice. He'd find out soon enough anyway.

"Who took them?" Peter asked.

"I don't know, but the FBI and one of Paul Thayer's security details are on their way to Possum Kingdom Lake."

"Oh, Jesus! The aliens have them!"

I wondered how Peter had found out about the aliens. Surely Stan hadn't told him. "Don't worry, Paul's men will intercept them and the FBI will be there soon."

"What if they don't? I've got to do something!"

"No. Just wait for your mother."

"I can't wait. I'll leave her a note."

The phone went dead. "Peter!" I screamed into the telephone.

When I returned to the reception area, Bart gave me a hard look. "You okay?" he asked.

"Peter's on his way to Possum Kingdom Lake. He's very upset. I guess I shouldn't have told him what happened. Damn it!"

Bart shrugged. "He's an hour behind Stan. It may be all over by the time he gets there."

"I know, but if anything happens to him, it will be all my fault."

Bart put his arm around me to comfort me. Eventually he called us a cab and we went home. When I got there, I called Paul to see if there was any news. He said his two men were monitoring the barn and five others were on their way and should be there well before Stan and his kidnappers. I couldn't tell Paul about the caves and the possible spaceship waiting on Cactus Island to take off, but I knew if they got Stan into the barn he'd be lost forever.

"Paul. Tell your men they can't let them take Stan and Dr. Gerhardt into the barn. They have to rescue him outside. Do you understand?"

"Yes," Paul replied. "But why?"

I couldn't tell him about the spaceship so I cut him off. "I don't have time to explain. Just keep them out of the barn."

"I got it. I'll tell them."

"Oh, and keep and eye out for Peter Turner. He may be on his way out there too. He's very upset about his father being kidnapped."

"Sure. I'll pass the word to keep an eye out for him."

Bart handed me another drink as I hung up the telephone. I thanked him and sat down at the kitchen table. He began rubbing my shoulders. My muscles were in such hard knots that even his expert fingers couldn't loosen them. I closed my eyes and wished I could awaken from this nightmare. Would Paul's men have even a chance of saving Stan and Dr. Gerhardt? They'd probably be no match for the soldiers in blue. I took a deep breath and said a silent prayer for God's intervention.

Chapter 53

The Recruitment

The sounds of police sirens awoke me. I was lying in a field surrounded by a half dozen men. One of the men sat up and looked at me curiously. The others were stirring as well—moaning and groaning like they'd just been through a fierce battle. Beyond the men was a smoldering building and beyond the building was a lake—Possum Kingdom Lake, I was sure. The siren was getting closer and finally a sheriff's car pulled up by the smoldering building. As I stood up, I noticed I had a bottle in my hand. It had no label but I recognized it to be the truth serum that Mo had given me.

A sheriff's deputy got out of the car and came toward me. "Stan Turner?" he asked.

"Yes. What happened here?" I asked as I slipped the truth serum in my pocket.

"You were kidnapped and they apparently brought you here. We got a call that there was gunfire and an explosion."

The deputy looked over at one of the men who had finally struggled to his feet and said to him, "I guess these men rescued you?"

The security man frowned and then said, "Yeah. I guess so. It was some battle, let me tell you."

"Did you recognize the kidnappers?" the deputy asked him.

The security man scratched his head. "No. Never saw them before. When they blew the place up, we must have been knocked out by the blast. When we woke up, they were gone."

As the deputy drove me back to the sheriff's office, I tried to remember what had happened. Then I remembered the truth serum. It had allowed Cheryl to remember what had happened to her, why not me? I unscrewed the cap. Just a couple drops will do, I thought, and carefully poured two drops into the cap. I threw my head back and let the two drops drip onto my tongue. After a moment I began to relax, I closed my eyes. . . .

When I woke up, I was very groggy, but as my mind cleared I remembered sitting Indian style in the back of the van driven by the soldiers in blue. Having made so many trips to Possum Kingdom Lake in the past few months, I could almost tell where we were at any given moment even though I was blindfolded. I felt the sharp left turn on the ramp onto I-30W and then the acceleration as we eased into the freeway traffic.

When we got to Fort Worth I felt us slow down through the downtown traffic. The hum of the road changed as we left Ft. Worth on our way to Weatherford. We slowed as we exited off the freeway onto Highway 180 and blended into the flow of the Weatherford traffic through town. Our pace picked up again as we left town. We made good time for about an hour until we slowed as it began to rain hard near Mineral Wells. The car swayed in the heavy winds and I heard thunder in the distance. Now it was less than thirty minutes to Possum Kingdom Lake and I feared the end of the road for Dr. Gerhardt and me.

Throughout the long drive I worried about Rebekah and the kids. What would they do without me? Of all my children Marcia would be devastated the most. She was so young and definitely a daddy's girl. Tears welled in my eyes. Would I ever see her again? The van leaned as it went around the first big bend where the road turns south along the lakeshore. We were almost there. I prayed that Paula had been able to get through to Paul and that a rescue team would be there to save us.

The van slowed and I felt the crunch of the tires crossing the gravel road that led to the big barn that Peter and I had discovered. We'd had a good time together and an experience neither would ever forget. Now I was in for a special treat—a guided tour of the caves that lay under the lake connecting the north shore to Cactus Island. For the first time, fear began to well up in me, choking me as the van came to a halt and the doors flew open. I felt a hand on my shoulder urging me to get up. These soldiers in blue didn't talk much. I hadn't heard a peep out them for nearly three hours. But then again, maybe they didn't need to speak. Perhaps they were telepathic.

Dr. Gerhardt was breathing heavily. I felt bad that he'd been dragged into this mess because of me. The poor man had just been minding his own business until I'd shown up demanding his help. It had never occurred to me that I might be endangering his life. I wondered if he had a wife and family. I'd never even bothered asking him.

The hand pressed me forward. I heard a door open and felt the warmth of the indoors. The hand guided me through another doorway, and then I was stopped. I stood there a moment wondering why I'd been isolated. Was this my cell? I listened hard for even the faintest of sounds, but I heard nothing but dripping water. Was I in the caves already?

It was quite awhile before the door opened again. Someone walked in wearing heavy shoes with hard soles. Fear gripped me again as I felt I was about to be confronted by one of the soldiers in blue or worse yet, one of the frogmen. My blindfold was suddenly ripped off. I blinked and then saw, with great bewilderment, the man who stood before me.

"Mo?"

Mo smiled. "Hey, Stan. How ya doing?"

I shook my head thinking I might be hallucinating, but the image of my old CIA client didn't change. It was him all right. "Ah. Well, I've been better actually, but you're a sight for sore eyes."

Mo laughed. "Yeah, I bet. I'm sorry about the blindfold and bindings. It was for show."

"For show?"

"Yeah. It's a little complicated. Let me explain."

Mo pulled over a couple chairs and motioned for me to sit down. He removed the bindings on my hands. As I rubbed my wrists, he began his explanation. "About five years ago I was assigned the task of overseeing the Agency's secret Tarizon Repopulation Project."

"Tarizon? Where is that?"

"Tarizon is a planet out there in the galaxy somewhere. Don't ask me where."

I shook my head trying to make sense of what Mo was saying. "Another planet? You've been in contact with aliens from another planet?"

"Yes."

"For five years?"

"Actually longer than that. I think it dates back to the sixties. It's not a matter of public record, obviously. Only a few people in the government even know about it."

"Does the President know about the project?"

"Yes, but only that it exists. He doesn't know the details except that we are helping them in exchange for technical information."

This was blowing my mind. I was just getting used to the idea that there was intelligent life in space and now I was finding out that, not only had the government known about it for thirty years, it was engaged in a joint operation with them. I shook my head in shock and amazement.

Mo continued, "Anyway, the human population of Tarizon has been shrinking due to atmospheric contamination caused by a series of earthquakes and super volcanos. Unfortunately the contamination has made most of the women of Tarizon sterile. In the first ten years after the seismic events the population of Tarizon has dropped nearly 11 percent.

"Their scientists have been making great strides in cleaning up the atmosphere, but completion of the task is still decades away. So, they sent emissaries here in the 60s asking for our help, and the CIA was given the task of handling it. The Tarizonians wanted to bring their men here to find mates, have children, and then take the children back to Tarizon."

"And the government agreed to this?" I asked, incredulous.

"Yes and no. The agency agreed but it has kept the details of the operation a secret for obvious reasons. I don't think the President or Congress wants to know. They just want the technology we're getting in exchange for allowing the cultivation and harvesting of children."

"Oh, my God."

"Why do you think the United States is so much more advanced than the rest of the world?"

"I can't believe this. We're trading children for technology?"

"Yes, I'm afraid so. I know it sounds horrible but the technology saves a lot of lives too."

"So, let me guess, Martin Windsor was one of the men from Tarizon?"

"Yes, he was. He staged his son's death so that he could take him back to Tarizon with him. Jimmy Falk isn't dead. He's on the ship that's about to take off. So are Cheryl and the children."

"Does Cheryl want this?"

"She has no choice. She knows too much. Thanks to you and the Spy Shop."

"They'd kill her if she stayed?"

"No. One of the conditions of our cooperation is that no Americans are to be injured or killed. If Cheryl elected to stay, which she could, they would strip her memory. The problem with that is that she would likely be left mentally impaired, if they did that. Exposure to one or two of the blue flashes strips about fifteen to thirty minutes of memory, but in the process it turns off thousands of brain cells. To strip several hours of memory would cause noticeable brain damage."

"So, she can go to Tarizon with her family or stay here and risk becoming a vegetable?" I asked.

"Probably not a vegetable, but not the woman she was when she woke up this morning."

I shook my head in disgust. "This is horrible. I can't believe the government is allowing this."

Mo shrugged. "It was hard for me to accept too, but the stakes are high."

"So, why were you setting up Cheryl to take the fall for Martin Windsor's death? Why didn't you just take the kids and leave her alone?"

"That was my idea," Mo said.

"What?"

"As you can probably imagine, this kind of operation isn't easy to keep secret. When a child goes missing a lot of people get upset. Each extraction of a child has to be carefully planned to make it appear there is a natural explanation for the disappearance. It can be a staged death, a parent kidnapping, a simple runaway, or whatever. Anyway, sometimes these extractions go wrong. That's where you come in."

"I don't understand."

"We set up Cheryl as an extraction that went wrong. We wanted to see how you would handle her defense. That's why we had to take your partner off the case."

"We?"

"I work with a local commander named Kulchz. He and I set up the test. We were looking for an attorney to represent Tarizonians who get in trouble while they are here on Earth. I got the idea when I heard you were defending Steven Caldwell. I told Kulchz you may be our man. He wouldn't just take my word for it though, so we set up the test. We wanted to see how you handled it. You probably noticed you were being followed."

My head felt like it was about to implode and the sick feeling I had in my stomach was intensifying geometrically. I didn't like the way this conversation was going at all. It seemed Mo and his friend Kulchz were about to make me one of those Mafia-type offers that I couldn't refuse.

"So, was your friend disappointed?" I asked.

"No, to the contrary, you were the first one in thirty years to figure out what was going on."

"So Kulchz can't be happy about that?"

"No, but what impressed him is that you kept it to yourself and didn't go to the police or the media. I told him we could trust you and now he believes me."

"So what are you saying? You want me to represent these Tarizonians?"

"Exactly. We need someone who understands what's going on and can deal with any legal problems that arise."

"What about your soldiers in blue? They seem to be doing a pretty good job of dealing with any problems that arise."

"Yes, but those SWAT type operations are dangerous. They can lead to injury or death to Americans, and thus endanger the whole project."

"Listen, I'm flattered that you thought so highly of me to recommend me to your friend Kulchz, but what if I can't stomach any of this? It sounds like a really sick business."

"Well, it's your choice. If you don't want to play ball, there are other options: we can strip your memory and you'll never know you were given this opportunity, or you can get on the ship and live the rest of your life on Tarizon. I hear it's beautiful this time of year and they'd love to have you."

A cold chill washed over me. It seemed the only acceptable option was to take the job. I didn't want to return to Rebekah as a halfwit. Nor did I relish the idea of spending the rest of my life on another planet without Rebekah and the kids. Suddenly a bell began to chime. Mo stood up.

"The ship's about to leave. You've got to make a decision quickly."

I got up and rubbed my temples. "Okay," I said. "I'll do it."

Mo smiled. "Good. I didn't want you to get hurt, Stan. I'm sorry to put you through all of this, but we're doing some good work with this project—saving a planet and ensuring the security of the United States. This is a very patriotic thing you're doing."

I shrugged. I couldn't feel good about any of this despite Mo's pep talk. "So, now what?"

"Your rescue party is outside. We've kept them at bay, but in a minute we'll let them through so they can rescue you. Just pretend they got to you just in the nick of time. Tell them the whole place is rigged to blow up in two minutes."

"Okay," I said.

"One last thing. You know the truth serum I gave you?"

"Yeah."

"Keep it and use it whenever someone is less than candid with you. It only takes a drop or two and the truth will come pouring out."

"Wow."

Mo stuck his hand in his pocket and pulled out a small device that looked like a pager but without any buttons or dials. "Also, here's a telepathic modulator. If you're ever in trouble simply hold it tightly in your hand, close your eyes, and your thoughts will be sent to your support team."

"You've got to be kidding."

"It's no big deal. They'll always be nearby anyway. Keep that in mind, if you know what I mean," Mo said. He left the room locking the door behind him. His last words seemed like a warning. What did he mean they'd always be close by? Surely they weren't going to have me followed 24/7.

After a few moments I heard gunfire, loud voices, and the sound of men running around. Suddenly the door flew open and a security man came rushing in. I raised my hands.

"Turner?" he asked.

"Yes," I replied.

"Thank God. We thought you were a goner."

"Listen," I said moving toward the door. "We've got to get out of here now! This place is about to blow. I heard them talking about it."

"All right, let's go," he said, following me out the door. I hesitated. He pointed left so I rushed down the corridor and out the front door. He yelled to the others to get out immediately as the place was about to blow. After clearing the entrance I ran a hundred yards away from the barn and then turned and looked back. The security team was right behind me and coming fast.

As they all gathered around me, the building exploded into a fiery inferno. We all hit the ground and covered our heads to protect ourselves from flying debris. When the dust had settled, I sat up and looked at what was left of the building. Then the wind began to swirl, the sky became dark, and there were flashes of blue light coming out of Cactus Island. Suddenly from the depths of the island a huge spaceship emerged and came straight at us. The men in the security detail looked up in amazement. Then there were more blue flashes. . . .

The car stopped in front of the sheriff's station. I blinked and looked around. Paul Thayer came rushing out of the building. I got out and embraced him. He said the sheriff needed to talk to me for a few minutes and then he'd drive me home. I waited on a bench outside the sheriff's office. Had this night actually happened, or was it just an incredible dream? Then I remembered the telepathic modulator Mo had given me. I stuck my hand in my pocket and pulled it out. This was no dream. The modulator was the size of a cigarette lighter and very light. It had some writing on it similar to what I'd seen on the memory gun. I shook my head and put it back in my pocket. I was confused and tormented by the dark and troubling secret that had been cast upon me by Mo and the CIA—a secret that I knew would torment me for the rest of my life. I felt alone and helpless. Would God approve of my new role or was I now in the service of Satan himself? I didn't know. I needed time to think and adjust to this new reality. I felt like Jimmy Falk must have felt—helpless as my Jeep skidded out of control—about to plunge into the abyss. Then my cell phone rang and I felt the actual horror of going over the edge. It was Rebekah and she was frantic. "Stan! . . . Have you seen Peter? Is he with you?"

"No," I replied.

"Oh, my God! Peter is missing! . . . My boy is missing!"

Chapter 54

The Unthinkable

The trial of Cheryl Windsor continued the following morning without the defendant, who had pulled off the ultimate escape—to another planet. The judge called us into chambers and told us that in addition to losing the defendant the court reporter had gaping holes in her transcriptions and all the backup tape recordings had somehow been erased. In light of this he said he had no choice but to declare a mistrial. He further commented that if Martin Windsor was alive, as the evidence seemed to suggest, the whole matter was moot anyway. After he had informed the jury of the mistrial, the case of the State of Texas vs. Cheryl Windsor came to an end and Wilkerson indicated it was not likely to be reopened. He also said the DA was dropping any plans to prosecute Paula as well, since Cheryl Windsor had been vindicated.

When I got home, Rebekah was talking on the telephone to a police detective. Her eyes were red and she looked pale. Marcia, Mark, and Reggie were crowded around her. When Marcia saw me, she got up and came running over to me. "Daddy. Have you found Peter?"

I scooped her into my arms and replied, "No, honey. I'm sorry. I was at the courthouse."

Reggie said, "They found his car somewhere near Palo Pinto. They've got a search party out looking for him. They think he might have been swept away in a flash flood."

My heart sank. He couldn't be dead. It just wasn't possible. Tears welled in my eyes.

"I just wish I'd have been home," Reggie said. "I'd have gone with him."

I couldn't believe Peter had drowned? So many times I had lectured the kids about staying away from high water. They knew not to drive when there was flash flooding. As a child I had been nearly swept into a creek in a flash flood in the Mojave Desert. I had told them that story many times and warned them of the danger of rushing water. I sat down next to Rebekah and put my arms around her. "Maybe's he's okay," I said.

"If he were alive, he'd have called by now," she replied.

"He may be in a hospital or—" I didn't know how to finish the sentence. It had been nearly 18 hours since he left the house. If he were alive, he'd have called or someone would have called to tell us where he was. Rebekah began to cry hard. I held her tightly fighting off my own tears. The door bell rang. It was Paul Thayer.

"I've sent some men out to help the police look for Peter," Paul said. "They'll sweep the whole area. If he's out there, they'll find him. "

"Thanks, Paul. I really appreciate your help."

"Agent Barnes is also out there. The FBI is helping in the search as well."

"Do they think it's a kidnapping?" I asked.

He shrugged. "Well, with people disappearing left and right, until they find him, they have to consider the possibility of an abduction."

"Oh, my God!" Rebekah exclaimed. "Why would someone take Peter?"

A chill suddenly shot through me. Had the aliens taken Peter? No. That couldn't have happened. He hadn't seen anything. At least nothing that hadn't been erased. I thought back frantically to everything he'd done with me that day at Possum Kingdom Lake. When I was being hypnotized by Dr. Gerhardt we had made him leave the room, but what if he hadn't left? What if he had been just outside the door listening. Could he have overheard my recollection as to what had happened? Did he know about our encounter with the frogmen and seeing the spaceship take off? The only way I could find out would be to contact Mo. I slipped away and put in a call to him. He didn't answer, of course, so I left a message on his recorder.

That night neither Rebekah nor I slept. We stayed up all night talking about Peter, reminiscing about what a wonderful son he'd been, and waiting by the telephone for news of the search to find him. When the sun began to rise in the east, I decided to drive out to where they'd found Peter's car. I was hoping to find one of the FBI agents so I could quiz them. I was curious as to whether they had any evidence of an abduction—particularly an *alien* abduction. Mo hadn't returned my call which was odd. Nearly eight hours had passed since I called him. In the past he'd always called me back within a few hours. Maybe that meant Mo didn't know what had happened to Peter and was doing his own investigation. It was just going to be a waiting game, I could see that.

When I got to the staging area for the search, I ran into Detective Perkins. "Sorry about Peter," he said. "What a weird thing to happen."

"Thanks. Any news?"

"Nothing so far. No body yet. That's good."

"Yes. Is there anybody out here from the FBI?"

"Agent Barnes was here. I think he and his partner went to Denny's for breakfast. You probably passed it on your way here."

"Yes, I did. I'm going to look at Peter's car and then, I guess, I'll go join them."

"Good idea."

Peter's car was a wreck. The exterior was scratched and battered like it had been in a war zone. All but the rear window had been busted out, one headlight was smashed, and two tires were flat. It made me sick to think Peter had been trapped inside it in the raging flood. It would be a miracle if he were alive. Dejected, I headed back to Denny's to see Agent Barnes and his partner. When I got there the waitress advised me that I'd just missed them. Since I had no idea where they'd gone and I hadn't eaten breakfast, I decided to stay and eat. While I was drinking a cup of coffee and searching the newspaper for news about what had happened the previous night, I looked up and saw Mo standing over me. He looked distressed. He said, "I got your call. I decided I'd better meet you in person."

"You did," I said in shock. I knew a personal visit was bad news—like the military vehicle pulling up in front of your house and two uniformed officers stepping out. It meant my worst fears were reality—either Peter was dead or—

Mo sat down and began. "I'm sorry, Stan. I just found this out. I guess Peter was with you when you saw Dr. Gerhardt and you were hypnotized."

"Yes, but we made him stay in the other room," I said.

Mo looked away and continued, "Apparently, his curiosity got the best of him. He left the door cracked and listened. He heard everything and there was no opportunity to erase his memory."

"He wouldn't have said anything. He wasn't a threat," I said frantically.

"They can't take any chances, Stan. There's too much at stake. He knew too much. . . . They'll treat him well."

Tears welled in my eyes. "How do you know that?"

Mo shrugged and replied. "The Tarizonians are an honorable people."

"Honorable? How can you say that when they're seducing women into fraudulent marriages and then stealing their children?"

"Because they could just randomly take any child they wanted and we would be powerless to stop them. Hell, they could kill us all and move their entire population here and there's not a damn thing we could do about it. Trust me, Stan. I've seen how powerful they are. What you've seen so far are just parlor tricks."

I closed my eyes, fighting off an urge to scream and wail in agony. Finally, I asked, "Will I ever see him again?"

Mo swallowed hard. "I don't know. They might let you communicate with him somehow, once they're sure they can trust you."

"God, I hope so. He must be so scared. Can you imagine waking up and finding yourself on another planet? Oh, Jesus!"

"He'll be okay, Stan. They've promised not to harm him. . . . I've heard Tarizon is a very nice planet—a lot like Earth."

"Rebekah will never see him again. That will kill her."

"It's better she thinks he's dead. She'll get over that. People get over death."

"But how can I live with that secret—knowing that he's alive and not being able to tell Rebekah?"

"You'll have to. You have no other choice."

I just looked at Mo in disbelief. I'd lost my son and there was nothing I could do about it. Mo left without further conversation. He said they'd be in touch with my first assignment. I couldn't imagine what it would be. Finally, I paid my bill and drove home.

Rebekah was in bed fast asleep. I looked at her and wished I could wake her up and tell her everything. Having to keep such a dark secret was going to be a daunting task, yet the aliens seemed to have eyes and ears everywhere, and according to Mo were omnipotent. I didn't seem to have any choice but to do their bidding. I remembered Dr. Gerhardt's words: *fear is a great motivator.*

As I drove home, depression engulfed me. I'd become nothing more than a lowly slave to these alien intruders. I wondered if it might be better just to expose this diabolic alliance even at my own personal peril—put and end to it now! . . . But was that even possible and what would be the consequence if we didn't cooperate with them? I didn't know enough to answer these questions now, but I'd keep my eyes and ears open hoping to learn enough to some day know what to do. And if exposing the Tarizon Repopulation Project was what needed to be done, then I'd do it no matter what the consequence. In the meantime, I'd do my job as best I could and pray to God these Tarzonians *were* honorable people as Mo had assured me they were.

About the Author

William Manchee lives in Plano, Texas with his wife, Janet. They have four grown children and three grandchildren. Bill practices law with his son Jim and in his spare time writes novels. Cactus Island is his twelve book since he started writing in 1995. His novels are inspired by actual cases from the past and some of his greatest inspirations come while he sleeps. Above he and Brandy, A Jack Russell Terrier, are hard at work.